SAVANNAH

Tim Johnson

An Old Line Publishing Book

Hampstead ◊ Maryland ◊ USA

Printed in the United States of America

ISBN-13: 9781937004910
ISBN-10: 1937004910

This book is a work of fiction. Any references to real people, events, establishments, organizations, or locales are intended solely to provide a sense of authenticity and are used fictitiously. All other characters, incidents, and dialogue are drawn from the author's imagination and are not to be construed as real.

Cover design by Christopher Saghy

EXPRESS YOURSELF

Old Line Publishing, LLC
P.O. Box 624
Hampstead, MD 21074
Toll-Free Phone: 1-877-866-8820
Toll-Free Fax: 1-877-778-3756
Email: info@oldlinepublishing.com
Website: www.oldlinepublishing.com

To "Mom",

Thank you so much for the support and for coming tonight. And goodness, thank you so much for everything you did for me when we worked together.

Jim

>25

SAVANNAH

DEDICATION

To my Grandma, Dorothea, who is my biggest fan.

5

ACKNOWLEDGEMENTS

I would be remiss if I didn't thank a few people for their contributions to the creation of this novel.

First and foremost, I need to thank Andrew. Without your help Savannah would not have been worth reading. I can thank you a million times, and still feel like I should thank you again. I can't wait to read your book, so start already.

Secondly, I need to thank Sarah who was there for me throughout this entire process. I will always be indebted to you for your help and support. Thank you.

Next, I feel compelled to thank Russ Fairly of RF Productions for all his work with the video production and editing of Savannah's book trailer. The time and effort you put into that project, without seeing a dime, is something only a true friend would do. Thank you so very much.

Lastly, my parents, Gary and Mary. What a great way for me to thank you for everything you've done for me throughout my life. Your love and support has always been all a son could ask for…and then some. Without you, I wouldn't have succeeded in life. Thanks for the slight nudge, the gentle push, and heavy-footed kick to get going.

CONTENTS

SAVANNAH

SAVANNAH

CHAPTER 1
THE LETTER

Sitting down at her computer, she stared at the photo of her dead brother and tried to understand how it all went wrong. Susie Taylor had been in hiding for seven weeks from the same men who murdered her brother, Michael. He was the reason she needed hiding, and the reason she was still alive.

For longer than she cared to recall, Susie lived in fear for her life.

Her living quarters, although adequate, weren't hers. More than once she longed for the day when she could relax in her own space. Her own home. Looking out a window, no more than two feet wide, her lungs ached for the kind of air that didn't come through a dirty screen first. The basement apartment was small. There was a small bathroom, with a stand-up shower, a cramped kitchenette with a clean sink, and a livable separate bedroom with no windows. It was bigger than most apartments Susie had lived in. But unlike her former residences, she knew leaving wasn't an option.

~~~~~~~~~~

On a rather gloomy, overcast day in late May, Susie returned home from her summer job as assistant to the head pharmacist; not exactly rocket science, but it was okay. Tired and barely able to muster up the energy to climb the six steps up to her rented home, her eyes noticed something out of place. The mailbox lid was open. Odd, Susie had mastered the habit of ignoring the mail. Overdue bills and junk advertisements didn't interest her enough to expend what precious energy she had left after a twelve hour shift. For whatever reason, she felt compelled to finally gather the mailbox's offerings and bring them into the house.

Emptying the mailbox had been an exercise in filling her recycling bin for months. This time was different. A thin envelope corner jabbed in between Susie's finger tip and nail, making her wince from the pain. She pulled her hand out, sucking on the small trickle of blood. She peered in. There sat the back of a small, crisp envelope. Unusual mail for her to receive. The rear flap looked to have been opened, then hastily resealed. She grabbed it. Instinct took over.

She flipped the envelope over, checking the sender's information. Purple ink from a stamp made a rectangle that was crookedly angled. It read, *INMATE MAIL* in bold purple letters. It didn't make sense. Her eyes searched for an explanation. The return address held her brother's name, *Michael Taylor*. But the words below didn't make sense. *KINGSTON PENITENTIARY.*

She hadn't spoken to Michael in months. She dug back into her memory, searching for her last conversation they had. She recalled a rushed phone call. During the conversation, he was quick to change the subject and redirected her questions whenever she inquired about him. Her reassurances to him, that she was doing well at the University and that she was happy, ended the phone call. She had been busy studying that day. Long hours at the pharmacy pushed the strained conversation from her forethought.

Stunned, Susie fumbled with the key and stumbled through the door. She began to feel a bit foolish for staring at the envelope while standing outside on the porch of her rented townhouse. She hated dramatic people. Now she was one of them. She dropped all of her belongings at the front door. Her heart raced. She scaled the stairs to the privacy of her bedroom. She wanted to be alone. She wasn't sure if her housemate was around. Maybe she would be curious. She always was a little too nosey.

Her fall semester demanded a massive course load if she was to achieve her goal of graduating pre-med in three years. Six courses, coupled with part-time work at the pharmacy, left little time to think about anything else. It was Easter before she realized it had been months since last speaking with Michael.

Her school semester melted away with Spring. Replacing it was her concern for Michael. It began to overwhelm her. She called his cell phone daily. It only offered a recording, indicating that the number she dialed was no longer in service.

She had no idea what he had done to be incarcerated or that he was even serving time in prison. The envelope made her stomach turn summersaults. In the privacy of her bare bedroom, Susie tore open the letter. Tears began to stream down her face. Small stains were left on the front of her shirt as she began to read. She hoped the letter from Michael would explain all the questions that ran through her mind.

She read the letter. This time, more tears fell onto the paper instead of her shirt.

14

Her eyes burned. Fear rose inside her, causing her breathing to become quick and shallow. She lowered the paper after she finished reading. Her face was temporarily frozen. Susie was stunned, unable to move. Had she read that right?

She snapped her head, listening hard for movement inside the empty house. The trance was broken. She rushed down the stairs and fastened the deadbolt on the door. She spun around and sprinted to the rear sliding glass door. She needed reassurance that the door was fastened shut. After closing the shades and drawing the curtains throughout the lower level of the house, Susie returned to her bedroom and frantically threw handfuls of clothes onto her bed.

Trust between Michael and Susie was never an issue. Growing up, they formed an unbreakable bond. His life was filled with criticism and disappointment, not from her, but from *him*. Their father. Being the older brother, he took a lot of the flack for Susie. If she had forgotten to finish a chore, Michael took the beating from *his* leather belt in her place. He was that way. Always protecting her. Always looking out for her first.

Susie idolized Michael and never forgot the times he protected her. She never questioned his judgment. She listened and carried out every task he asked of her. If he told her to quit school and become a circus performer, she would have. "Go to school and study hard," he told her, "get out of this life and be something."

She did. That was the kind of relationship she had with her brother. Rock solid. Never faltering.

Grabbing her largest duffle bag, she rapidly tossed in only the most essential items. The pile on her bed was a good start, but she needed more. She frantically combed her dresser and closet. Once satisfied, her toiletries were thrown in last, before she sealed the zipper on the bag.

Moving in a near panic, she almost lost her footing on the carpeted steps. Her feet moved too quickly. The heavy duffle bag slung around her shoulder, altered her balance. She made it to the bottom landing safely. Her feet carried her into the kitchen. The few remaining parts of her duffle bag were stuffed with as much food as she could manage. Her pants pockets became storage containers for granola bars and small bags of M&M's. Essential items.

The half eaten bag of pretzels, she had been nibbling away at, was hastily thrown into the duffle bag's smaller side pocket. She quickly scanned the rest of the kitchen's contents. No items grabbed her attention.

Pausing and whirling around, she reconsidered one last item to add. Her eyes locked onto the butcher block. There, in the side pocket where the pretzels sat, she laid a razor sharp butcher knife. Tip down, handle up. Just in case.

She never questioned whether or not she believed Michael's warning. His letter was clear. She only hesitated on her next step, unsure what to do. She left her townhouse permanently.

Her roommate wasn't home. Susie figured she was away with her boyfriend for the evening again. She made a mental note to call Lisa on her cell, after she figured out where she was going.

From the time she read Michael's letter, to the time she walked out the front door, Susie was packed and driving in less than ten minutes. Her duffle bag was roughly thrown onto the back seat of her '95 Nissan Sentra. It ran well enough and was efficient enough on gas to allow her to overlook its decrepit appearance. She had nicknamed it the Marshmallow, a mixture of white paint and rust; the same color as a fire toasted marshmallow. The growing grocery list of repairs it needed was extensive, if it was to survive another Canadian winter. Tender loving care from a mechanic would have to wait another day. She stomped hard on the accelerator, away from the danger of her townhouse.

Driving aimlessly was a sickening feeling. Her stomach burned. Fear, coupled with the realization she had not eaten since the morning, caused her to stop at a McDonald's. She nervously ate a hamburger and fries. She drank a coke, even though every guilty sip gnawed at her conscience. Looking over her shoulder with every mouthful, Susie wondered if she was safe there. She moved to the parking lot. The strangers in the seating area caused the room to close in on her. The open air seemed, somehow, safer.

The noise from the passing cars helped her think. Their constant rumbling cleared her head, the way silence worked for others. Scenarios played over and over in her mind. Each time it always ended with her spending a sleepless night in her car.

She needed help. She ran through the contacts in her cell phone while she finished sipping her coke. Susie finally came across a name. Her eyebrows rose up ever so slightly. A glimmer of hope. Not much, but something. She spoke the name "Emmett" as it appeared on her phone.

Emmett met Susie at a party their mutual friends had thrown over a year ago. He was interested. She wasn't. She didn't have the time or energy to pursue a relationship. Susie wasn't bothered the way being single troubled her girlfriends. She always focused on the big picture. The picture Michael told her to focus on. She wanted a better life than she had growing up. School was her only ticket.

He is a stranger. Sure we met, but it's been months since we spoke last. How do I ask him for help? C'mon Susie, get it together. It's not exactly like you have a ton of options here. Put your pride aside and call him.

Susie gripped her cell phone. She dialed. The hand that held the phone was damp. Nervous sweat. She was unsure how he would react or even if he would answer the call at all. The last time they spoke, she had shot down his advances. Pride is frail in some men. She hoped Emmett wasn't one of them.

He answered the phone on the third ring. He seemed delighted that Susie had

16

called. She explained that she needed to talk to him and could really use his help. Suggesting that they meet at a restaurant to talk business, Susie bashfully mentioned she had just eaten a hamburger and wasn't hungry. She suggested meeting in a coffee shop near Emmett's house. Within fifteen minutes, the pair sat across from each other with steaming coffees as their only barrier.

"Susie, holy crap, wow. I'm shocked you called. I thought I would never hear from you again after the last time we talked," he started.

She smirked, trying to cover up the true meaning of this meeting. She replied, "Emmett, c'mon. You know it was never you. I was just super busy with school and work, and I still am. I just couldn't find the time to date. It was nothing against you, I promise. The timing was just all wrong."

"Yeah, I understand. So, what's up? Why the call now?" he said, switching to his most professional tone.

Emmett was a twenty-seven year old private detective. In his childhood, he watched every black and white gumshoe movie he could get his hands on. He only wanted to follow one career path his entire life. After high school, he went to community college and graduated with a two year degree in criminology. At twenty, he studied for months on end before taking his private investigator's exam, which he passed the first time. Ever since then, Emmett's life was dedicated to practicing and honing his private detective skills.

Securing gigs to fill his self-employed schedule proved difficult for the young private detective. Most people didn't want to hire him. Potential clients hesitated handing their money over to an unproven twenty-something. People assumed he was unreliable. Most twenty year olds are. Emmett worked harder and more professionally than most private detectives. He had to. Once given an opportunity, every client was thoroughly satisfied with the quality of his work. Every single one. Every time. Word spread about the discreet, professional manner. A career was born.

"Listen Emmett, I need to hire you," Susie said, before quickly sipping her black coffee. After setting the cup back down, "I got something I could really use some help with."

Emmett pulled out a digital tape recorder. "If it is okay with you, I would like to record this conversation, for professional reasons." It was his way of showing how serious he always took his clients. He carried the thing with him everywhere.

She nodded. The little gesture reassured her that Emmett was able to separate his personal life from business. She liked that.

"Susie. Before you elaborate on *the something* you need help with, I feel obligated to ask you if you're alright." His skillful eye detected a subtle shake in her hand as she placed her coffee cup onto the table.

Looking toward her feet, Susie muttered, "I'm not really sure how to answer that. I mean, I'm not injured or anything, but I definitely don't feel safe." Her eyes rose, meeting his. "I got this letter from my brother in the mail today. I am super freaked out. I want to hire you to find out some answers. I need to know what is going on."

Susie retrieved the folded, crumpled envelope from her black leather purse. She hesitated.

Emmett saw the hesitation, "Whatever the letter says I can handle it. I'm a professional." He nodded before continuing, "I've done this before. I want to help you. I need to see the letter to know just what we're dealing with." His tone was a mix of reassurance and confidence, as though he had meetings in coffee shops like this every day.

She handed the letter to Emmett. Her hands were strangely cold. *Odd in May*, he thought. Susie warmed her hands on her still full coffee cup, a small piece of comfort.

Emmett opened the letter and began to read. He seemed to read and reread every sentence. He took a very methodical approach, which took longer than Susie expected. Before Emmett finished reading the letter, she had emptied her coffee.

Emmett not only read it, but tried to memorize every detail. He had trained himself by reading countless love letters from unfaithful spouses, focusing in on each word of every sentence. The process was time consuming, but with practice, he had trained himself to memorize the pertinent facts in just a single reading.

Susie,

I know it's been a long time since we've spoken, so I want to start off by apologizing. Please don't be angry with me. It wasn't you. It was me. I've been wrapped up in my own affairs and trying like hell to get out of the hole I've dug for myself.

Where to start with the mess I've made? I'll start from the beginning and try to help you understand. A few years ago, I started playing a lot of poker. It was harmless enough and we played for relatively low stakes. Remember when Uncle Jerry taught us how to play? Well, I'm not sure if you ever knew, but he taught me some shuffling cheats. I used what he taught me and improved it, a lot. I got really good at it and took it to a poker room that was run by the Russian mob. Initially, I didn't know that. I guess that doesn't matter now because they caught me cheating.

Before they caught me, I was making so much money there that I didn't know what to do with it. The fact of the matter is, they did catch me and it wasn't pretty. I couldn't contact you after that because of what they did to me and what they told me. They knew more about me than I ever

18

imagined. They knew where Mom and Dad lived and knew that I hated them. They even know your name and address. And that's why I'm writing you this letter.

When I got caught, they didn't just consider it cheating, more like stealing from them. And they demanded repayment of their money. Every month I pay them $10,000. Before I could even dispute the amount, they read off your name and address and even what you're studying at University. They said that if I missed a payment, even by one day, they would pay you a visit. That's all they said. I don't know what that means, but these guys aren't the kind of guys who bluff.

I wish I could say that was the end of my problems, but it isn't. I know by now you saw the return address on the envelope and noticed that I'm writing you from prison. I was arrested and sentenced to prison 58 days ago. You see, I was in a really tough spot when the Russians said they required $10,000 a month. I tried like hell to use my poker skills to make some cash, but without my cheating ability, poker was just not working. I played with a guy who was connected with a biker gang called the Outlaws. I delivered packages across the border for them. The jobs were simple enough and paid a lot, keeping the Russians at bay and earning some money for myself. The bikers called me a "mover," and people like me, who deliver high risk packages with a specific time and place. I was moving large quantities of these packages for the bikers and never broke their trust once. Until I was arrested.

To add to my problems, when I was busted, I had a lot of the Outlaws' packages hidden away in my car. It was a huge delivery for me and would have paid me potentially enough to satisfy the Russians for awhile. Now the bikers want their packages back that were seized. I think I've managed an arrangement that will keep them from hurting me while I'm in prison. But they know about the Russians and the monthly payments.

As I'm writing this I can't believe that this is my life. I can't believe I did all this. The Russians and the bikers have guys inside prison who still expect me to make my promised payments to them. I had enough for one payment. The problem is, the next payment is due on the first of the month, and there isn't any money left to pay the Russians.

Susie, you've got no other options at this point. I know this is all very hard to read and understand, but I need you to get what I'm saying here. You need to leave everything behind and just go. I am fairly certain that I'll be dead by the time you read this letter, but at least you'll have a head start.

God, I'm so sorry. I'm sorry for everything. I never meant to put you in harm's way. I love you more than anyone or anything in this world.

Michael

P.S. *I've sent Melanie Cooper a similar letter explaining everything because she and I were dating before I was arrested. We were in love. When she visited me last, I gave her a copy of everything I've written since I was in here. It details everything from my poker playing, to the Outlaws and jail. I asked her to read it and get it to you, but she's going into hiding as well. You might need to find her because she's not as strong as you. My journal explains everything much better than this letter can. I'm so sorry.*

CHAPTER 2
CHILDHOOD

Susie's auburn hair, highlighted with streaks of blonde, sat flat against her head. Running her right hand through her shoulder length hair, she tousled her bangs back to life before they fell limply to their original place. Her usually striking green eyes continued to look tired and red. Her pale lips quivered on the edge of hysteria as she pursed them together. It was the only way they stopped their shaking.

While Emmett thoroughly read through Michael's letter, Susie's eyes stared off into space, rewinding time and replaying her past for the thousandth time. Each time was difficult to revisit these often abhorrent, long repressed memories. Some things didn't get easier.

Their family didn't have money. Not ever. They were provided with the necessities of life, but Michael and Susie always yearned for more. Susie, unlike Michael, was vocal about wanting more out of life than constantly toeing the poverty line. She dreamed of going to college and becoming a professional. When Michael would ask what she wanted to study, Susie always responded, "Anything that will get my ass away from here."

Living in an apartment above a tool and die workshop, their father was a painter at the local mental institution. That was his day job. At night, he was a heavy drinker. An abusive drunk. He wanted nothing to do with either of his two kids when he got home from work. They quickly learned to stay out of his way and slowly learned to expect little from him.

By the time Susie was seven years old, Michael, who was three years older, had taken so many beatings for her that his teacher called home concerned. He used the excuse that he had been playing tackle football with some older boys. Their mother soothed the teacher's worries, similarly explaining his bruises. After hanging up the phone, his mother never mentioned it again.

The fourth grade teacher believed Michael's claim. She didn't pursue it any further. That's the way Michael was. He was so believable whenever he spoke. People just believed him.

Their mother was an obese deli clerk in the only grocery store in town. She worked behind the counter, alongside high school students, earning minimum wage. She told anyone who would listen that she hated her job, whenever the conversation allowed. The spicy salami selections she brought home were *his* favorite and her way of pleasing him. It was the only way she could make up for her laughable pay checks. Working for minimum wage in your thirties and forties was one thing, but never receiving a raise over the course of fifteen years illustrated the kind of worker Michael and Susie's mother was.

Their mother's continuous bragging of how she stole the cold cuts infuriated Susie. It left little doubt to what she didn't want to become. Most little girls she went to school with idolized their mother. Not Susie. In fact, the opposite. She knew one day she would leave her parent's apartment, never to return. She knew that. Other than Michael, no one would care.

When Michael was old enough and smart enough to be able to take care of himself, he finally left. There wasn't a going away party for him. No token handshake from their father. No long embrace from their mother. Nothing. Not even a mention of where he was going. One day he didn't come out of his bedroom for breakfast. Susie called him to come and eat the runny eggs and toast she had made for the both of them that Saturday morning. Michael's bed was made and half his clothes were gone.

Realizing he had left, Susie smiled. She sat on the edge of his bed and ate both of their breakfasts, grinning the entire time. She knew he was going to make it. More than anything, she was happy that he wouldn't have to endure *him* any longer.

It was three days before her father even asked about Michael. He didn't care. He had only asked because the garbage hadn't been placed at the curb the night before. Susie responded that she didn't know where Michael had gone. Not wanting to lie, she quickly added that most of his clothes were gone.

Her father grunted at her. He walked toward his bedroom. Same pattern every day after work. Home. Beer. Bedroom with TV. Before his customary door slam, indicating that he wasn't to be disturbed, he said loud enough for her to hear, "Then it'll be your job to take care of his chores around here."

Not only did she have to do the cleaning, the laundry, and keep her bedroom tidy, now she was expected to find the time, and energy, to finish his list of chores too. The garbage was the easiest. It was once a week and not too taxing. The chore he spent the most time scrutinizing was keeping the kitchen clean and the dishes washed. Her father's obsessive hatred of dirty dishes and their inability to afford a dishwasher left Susie's hands dry and scaly from the soap. Dish pan hands at fourteen.

The kitchen had one wall of chipped cabinets, which never closed properly even when slammed. Before he left, Michael and Susie used to joke that their father's job was to paint for other people, but their home had the worst looking kitchen cabinets they had ever seen. Half the cabinets were designated for the kitchen ware and utensils. The other half was a pantry for boxed and canned food. They were never full. Never. Rarely did they have anything in them that anyone would want to eat. The pantry's only items were packages of Ramen noodles, boxes of macaroni and cheese, and the occasional can of Campbell's soup. Those never lasted long. *He* would take those to work and eat them for his lunch before anyone else had a chance. By the time Susie was eight, she had memorized the ingredients of Kraft Mac 'n' Cheese better than she knew her times tables. While waiting the six minutes for the noodles to soften, she repeatedly studied the label on the box and its nutritional facts.

Their corroded sink seemed to always contain dirty dishes. Susie was expected to make sure that it wasn't. It was a never ending cycle of washing, drying, and putting away dishes. Right before her sixteenth birthday, when she had a particularly heavy load of homework over the weekend, her father silently crept behind her. She could feel his boozy breath warming her neck. Without warning, he slapped the back of her head while she read her history textbook. He pointed toward the sink and shouted, "Why, after I work so hard for this family, do you think it so fucking hard to wash a few goddamn dishes?"

She knew better than to answer. Anything she said would have been considered talking back, and met with more violence. Her best course of action, which she had learned the slow, hard way, was to quickly walk over and complete the chore, silently. Learning not to cry when he hit her took years, but it helped defuse his anger and shorten the beatings.

Washing dishes once a day was easy. Washing them three times a day, even though she hadn't dirtied them, was the tough part. Before school, after school, and after dinner was enough to drive a sane person mad. Susie developed a nervous habit of checking the sink's contents every time she came into their apartment. And before she left. And every time she used the bathroom.

If she found even one utensil sitting inside the basin, she immediately washed, dried, and put it away. Her father's jokes fueled a fire that slowly grew inside her. Over and over he told the joke of how he didn't need to spend money on a fancy new dishwasher because *he* had a fifteen year old dishwasher that never broke.

She would close her eyes tight. In her head, she would scream at him, "Shut up! You're the reason Michael ran away, just like I will one day! You're an abusive drunk. You loser."

Opening her eyes, she could feel the fire die down, but she knew it would never go out.

Family gatherings were especially difficult for Susie to endure. At any time her father's family came over, she was expected to not only have the kitchen spotless, but also to wait on them hand and foot as if she were their personal servant. When Michael had lived at home, both of them were expected to serve everyone beers from the fridge, refill the snack bowls with chips or pretzels or whatever their mother stole from work, and then clean up everything afterward. The sole duty fell onto her after Michael bolted. Being forced to serve those drunks and other losers filled her with rage.

Those family gatherings only ever consisted of three things: drinking, gambling, and one-upping one another's stories of stealing and thievery. Her mother's side rarely visited. Her father wouldn't allow it. She came from a soft, quiet family that was always proper and polite. He claimed they made him feel like a loser when they asked about his job. When gifts were given to his children, he felt emasculated. When they spoke about politics, he assumed they were mocking his lack of education. He made it clear that they weren't allowed in his home.

Susie's mother was trapped. He would never allow her to leave him. She did the only thing she could. She adapted. Over the years, his torment and controlling behavior turned her into a different, darker person. She became a thief and quickly became able to bury any guilt.

Once, during a family gathering that had gone late into the night, Michael came into their shared bedroom after Susie had already fallen asleep. Whispering in her ear through the darkness, Michael recounted, "You have got to hear this. Mom said that she's been stealing more than cold cuts at work."

"Are you sure?" asked Susie skeptically. Her eyes squinted to see Michael's face through the darkness.

"Just listen. I'll tell you what she's doing and how she gets away with it," he said as the excitement grew inside him. He inadvertently raised his voice from a whisper to a hushed tone.

Not wanting to alarm anyone that they were awake and talking, Susie placed her index finger gently to his lips, silently demanding Michael to lower his voice. He nodded in agreement.

"When I finished brushing my teeth, the bathroom door wasn't shut all the way. I could hear what they were talking about at the kitchen table. Between the poker chips and the belching, I overheard Mom gloat about how she's been ripping off the grocery store for months. She said that she and Joanne from work devised some scheme together to make more money than those cheapskates were paying them. She called it getting her rightful pay raise," Michael whispered barely loud enough for Susie to hear.

Susie sat up on the edge of her bed. She hung on his every word, shocked that her mother would dare do such a thing.

"She said that whenever a customer wanted to cash out at the deli, with their purchase of cold cuts or the deli salads in the flimsy plastic containers, Mom weighs the purchase, slaps the sticker receipt on the container or bag and then hands it to the customer. Then she goes to the cash register and rings in that same amount. She never actually hits the final CASH OUT button to record the actual price into the register's memory. The screen on the register displays the correct amount, so the customers think everything is on the up and up. All Mom has to do is remember the cost of the product and then pocket the cash. It only works if the customer wants to buy a single product because Mom said she can't add more than one cost together in her head," said Michael. His matter of fact tone made the statement sound so obvious, as if both of them already knew that.

Susie sat speechless.

Michael continued, "After she gets the cash from the customer, she goes to the register, appears to put the cash into the register, but really she slips it into the front pocket of her apron. The security camera that faces the register sees her, what looks like, putting the money into the register, but in reality she's actually canceling out the cost of the purchase that she entered into it in the first place." He took a deep breath. His voice rose again. Susie waved her hand in the air. He nodded and continued in a whisper, "I heard her telling Uncle Jerry that the rest of the registers in the store use some barcode system to make sure that the cashiers input the correct price, but not in the deli. Apparently the cheapskate owner won't replace the deli counter register because it doesn't get used often enough to offset the cost of switching them to the newer, more expensive ones. So every now and then, Mom and Joanne pocket some money and split whatever they take at the end of their shift."

After inhaling deeply again, he continued, "Uncle Jerry said that Mom's scam was a decent one and that it would be much better if she could actually add a couple of items together in her head. He said doing that once or twice a shift would be more profitable and less risky for her."

Susie's eyes bulged out of her head. She couldn't believe what she was hearing. She whispered her response, "Mom steals? Is she going to go to jail if she is caught?"

Smiling and nodding, Michael responded, "Yes, Mom steals. And from the sound of it, she's been doing it for a long time. So, no, she's probably not going to jail. It sounds like she's got a good system."

It was no wonder Michael left at seventeen years old, never to return. And no wonder Susie followed him not long after.

25

CHAPTER 3

CONFIRMATION

Emmett read the letter. He slowly slipped it back into the envelope, careful not to put any new folds into Susie's sacred paper. He slid the envelope across the table.

Before he spoke, he closed his eyes and searched for the words. Then calmly he asked, "I need to ask you some questions that might not be very pleasant. Are you okay with that?"

Susie nodded, not trusting herself to speak. Tears were on the brink. Talking might make them fall, and never let up. She cupped her empty, yet still warm coffee cup for comfort.

Emmett bounced a clenched fist gently off of his pursed lips, trying to find the words he needed. Pulling it quickly away, he suddenly found the courage to blurt out, "Before you got this letter from your brother, had he ever misled you?"

She quickly and emphatically answered, "No." Her face scrunched up. The question stung.

Her answer assured Emmett of their unwavering trust. He didn't know Michael. He instinctually questioned the motives of Susie's jailbird brother. He continued his line of questioning that felt more like an interrogation rather than a coffee shop conversation. "You're sure that Michael wouldn't deceive you to try to get some money or get out of a jam?"

Blinking back tears, Susie said, "Emmett, let me try to make you understand something. Michael was the only person I've ever trusted in my entire life. He wouldn't ever put me in harm's way. My whole life he protected me from everything. So no, he isn't trying to scam me or whatever you're thinking."

"I'm not trying to upset you Susie, I'm just asking the hard questions that need to be asked," said Emmett raising both of his hands in surrender. "Have you ever heard of this Melanie Cooper person that Michael mentioned?"

"No. Not ever. But like I told you, I haven't heard from my brother in six months. And even then he was reluctant to talk about his private life." She wiped the dampness off of her hands onto her jeans before continuing, "The last time we talked, I asked him if he was seeing anyone and his response was that he wasn't seeing anyone special."

"So we are going to trust the validity of this letter," commented Emmett. He meant it more as a statement of fact than a cynical comment. He hoped Susie took it that way because suddenly she started crying.

Emmett felt awful, thinking he may have pushed too hard, too fast. *Way to go, hotshot. Real smooth.*

Shaking her head slowly, with tears pouring down her face, she found her words through silent sobs. "Emmett, I am more scared than any other time in my whole life. My brother would never lie to me. Never. OKAY?" She used a cheap paper napkin to dab her eyes. "If Michael says my life is in danger, then it is. I don't know who Melanie Cooper is or her connection to Michael aside from what he wrote in the letter. I can honestly say that I didn't even know Michael was a serious gambler or a mover or whatever that is. He being in jail is a major shock to me."

Susie took another napkin from the dispenser for her runny nose. Emmett sat, listening with his hands folded. He couldn't have felt worse. Now he was certain he pushed too hard.

Wiping her moist eyes with the cuff of her sleeve, she continued, "What I do know is that my brother protected me his whole life and is a good man. I don't know where to go or what to do next. What I do know is that I need help. I need to know what has happened to Michael. And I need to find Melanie Cooper. Will you help me, because I…"

Emmett raised his hand to stop her from going any farther. He used his most reassuring voice to say, "I'll help you. You need somewhere safe to stay and my house has a renovated basement apartment that no one lives in. I think you should stay there. It would be best for now."

Susie wiped her eyes once again. Then her nose. When she finished, she whispered, "Thank you Emmett. I'll pay you for everything when I can. I have some money and I think…"

Interrupting her again, with a gentle pat on her hand, Emmett motioned towards the parking lot, "I suggest we get everything out of your car and leave it here. We'll take mine. C'mon."

Emmett's car was the opposite of what Susie had envisioned. He had already been seated at the corner table when Susie arrived, so she wasn't able to see which car was his. She expected him to drive the typical car the private detectives drove on TV. A big older model sedan filled with takeout wrappers and empty coffee cups. Instead, Emmett drove a black Ford Escape with tinted windows. The SUV was in exceptional condition. The outside sparkled. No scratches. No dirt. No grime. The interior seemed as though it had just been vacuumed. Susie felt as though wearing her shoes inside the car was somehow like wearing her shoes inside someone's house.

Susie swam in the spacious passenger seat. Emmett looked at her. In his Escape, she seemed so small and delicate. Her slender frame was toned and muscular. She took care of herself. Yet as she slumped in the seat, Susie looked frail.

The car ride only took a few minutes. Emmett lived in the nearby community. They drove directly into his garage. He shut the large door with his remote opener as soon as his SUV was in far enough that it could safely close behind them. The inside of the garage was meticulously organized into specific sections. Susie looked out through the passenger window. She noticed the far wall. It housed his tools, perfectly arranged on a peg boarded wall. Each tool had an outlined stencil on the peg board. Any missing tools were easily identifiable. Two tools were missing. Their lonely outlines gave it away. A screw driver. A pair of pliers. They must have recently been used and not returned.

In front of Emmett's SUV were several racks of shelves that housed all the cleaning products, recycling bins, and odds and ends that a garage generally stores. The intriguing part of the garage was the raised loft. Susie was immediately impressed. The wooden frame looked like a patio deck that was attached to the walls of the garage and raised up enough to snuggly fit the front end of Emmett's SUV perfectly below. A wooden baluster railing crossed the full length of the loft's exposed side. On top of the loft was a home office. Susie marveled at the beauty.

"I do most of my work at the desk here. It's a place where I can concentrate and get work accomplished. It's like I'm not at home there. You know what I mean?" he asked, motioning toward his area.

As she climbed the five steps to the top of the loft, Susie noticed the pristine area, the size of a decent walk-in closet. His dark walnut desk was beautiful. The desktop was nearly empty except for a small lamp, a couple file folders, and a pen. Filing cabinets book-ended the desk. They were made out of the same wood, but finished in a more ornate manner. The intricate detail on each filing cabinet face showed expert craftsmanship.

The inside of the house, like the garage and SUV, looked like it was staged and ready for sale. The countless hours Emmett spent cleaning each week was evident to Susie. No item was out of place. There wasn't any dust anywhere. Everything was polished, swept, or recently vacuumed. He took special care that his basement apartment was the same.

Without showing her the rest of the house, Emmett carried Susie's bags down the winding stairs to the fully furnished apartment. Beige carpet wrapped over each step and had vacuum lines that couldn't have been more than two days old. The walls were a warm taupe that calmed frayed nerves. For being a basement with few windows, the apartment was surprisingly bright and welcoming.

He showed her every inch, doing his best to radiate the most welcoming feeling he could. Emmett expressed how he wanted to get to work right away. He had some contacts he needed to call.

Susie didn't know exactly what that meant, but she took it as a good sign that he intended to get to work. His passion reassured her further. *I made the right decision to trust him.* She felt a sort of peace knowing there was someone who was going to be investigating her brother's whereabouts.

Gently shutting the door behind him, Emmett left. Susie sat on the couch. She began crying for her brother again. Then it hit her. For the first time, she knew that he was in serious trouble.

She sobbed uncontrollably until eventually falling asleep. She woke up in near pitch black. Day had turned to night while she slept. She managed to find a wall switch. The corner lamp flicked on.

The warmth of the apartment was welcoming. Too often in her life she had been cold and without warmth. Growing up in her family's apartment, Michael and Susie were forced to bundle up for comfort throughout the winter. They frequently fought off colds and runny noses because of the frigid temperature. The crappy radiator in their bedroom rarely worked. *He* didn't care enough to try and fix it. Their bedroom window was drafty. *He* didn't care, it wasn't his bedroom.

Being in the warm basement, with its lush carpeting, she felt her body ache for more sleep. She undressed and slid underneath the comforter on top of the bed. Before the thought of her brother could creep back into her thoughts, Susie fell in a deep, restful sleep.

~~~~~~~~~~

She woke to the gentle rapping of knuckles on the basement door. The bedroom where she slept was dark. Minimal light seeped through the door frame. She figured Emmett was coming to check on her. She called, "Emmett?"

He walked slowly through the bedroom door. He was hunched over, looking exhausted. He plopped onto the corner of the bed. Holding two coffees and a white paper bag stuffed with donuts, it was evident that he hadn't found his bed that night. "Did you sleep well?" he asked.

"I did, thank you. You have a wonderful home. I don't know how I'm ever going to repay you for helping me," Susie answered as he handed her a large cup of hot coffee and the bag of donuts.

"I didn't know what kind you liked, so I got a few different ones. And don't thank me just yet. I've got some news to report," Emmett uttered in a somber tone.

Susie's body sank further into the mattress. She already knew what he was going to tell her. She braced herself for the worst. She held onto the hot coffee cup with both hands, the same as she did in the coffee shop.

"I called a few contacts I have around the city. I have some bad news. Terrible news, really. I hate to tell you this, but a buddy of mine, who is a police officer, confirmed that Michael was killed yesterday in the Kingston Penitentiary. The prison report stated that he was found dead in the laundry room. He had been stabbed repeatedly and bled out. The report stated there was a shank lying next to him. The apparent murder weapon was a piece of scrap metal that was sharpened and wrapped with some electrical tape as its handle. I'm very sorry to have to tell you all of this," muttered Emmett. His eyes fell from Susie's gaze as her tears began to well up. He lowered his head out of respect for Susie's dead brother.

~~~~~~~~~~

A fog came over Susie. Her head began to spin. Her ears felt plugged. The room began to close in on her. She caught herself before spilling the hot coffee. She shook her head back and forth, trying to clear the fogginess. She set the cup of coffee onto the night table. Her eyes slowly blinked, trying to focus on what Emmett was saying. Suddenly, her body went limp.

The reaction from the smelling salts Emmett broke under her nose cleared her head like a shotgun. Susie, alert, sat up. Emmett dabbed her forehead with a cool, wet washcloth. Her feet were elevated on the cushy throw pillows she had noticed on the couch. The thought of Michael rushed back to her. She buried her face into her hands, crying more tears of grief.

Emmett held her shaking body. His arms were strong and his embrace tight. Exactly what she needed. She had hoped Michael would be alright. This hope kept her emotions in check. Hope now dashed, everything poured out.

"Susie, I'm so sorry for your loss," whispered Emmett into her ear as she cried on his shoulder. He held her for what seemed like hours before adding, "I have more news too. It won't be easy to hear, but it'll be better than what I've already told you."

"Go ahead Emmett," she managed through the tears.

"I've confirmed a few things that needed firming up. The first is that there is definitely chatter on the street about your name. I have a contact who has assured me that the Russian mob has been inquiring about the name Susanne Taylor. This confirms that what Michael wrote in his letter is indeed correct. This also is some good news."

She frowned, unsure what he meant.

"It means they don't know where you are. The Russians wouldn't ask questions if they already knew the answer. It appears that your departure from your townhouse was perfectly timed. My contact also told me that the Russians have put the word out that they are willing to pay for information. That's another thing they wouldn't do unless they're absolutely clueless," said Emmett. His voice was upbeat, trying to highlight the only positive news he had.

Susie sat in shock. She couldn't fathom how yesterday she had fretted over filling prescription orders and today her brother was dead. Not to mention that there was a hit put out on her life. Emmett patted her knee gently. "I want you to stay here in my apartment for awhile. I think it's a good idea for me to try and find Melanie Cooper. If she has this journal your brother wrote in, then the Russians may very well be looking for her too. His journal might shed some light on the questions you have about your brother."

Again the tears fell, dropping untended onto her lap. Susie sat slumped over and began to sob uncontrollably. It was all too much to process. Emmett stood up, placed a gentle hand on her shoulder and whispered a few words of condolence. She nodded her head when he asked, "Would you like me to give you some time alone?"

Once again Susie was alone, crying tears for her dead brother.

Chapter 4
Padded Handshakes

Without Susie noticing, two days passed. She stayed in the apartment, doing little in bed, crying until she slept. When hungry enough, she ate the meals Emmett left on a tray table. Every time she checked, there was a new plate with different food for her. She never heard him bring the new food or leave with the old. Aside from the sound of running water, when the toilet flushed or shower ran, Susie didn't know whether he was home or not.

On the third evening, Susie grew restless. Sitting in the basement watching TV was a waste. She wanted to talk to Emmett about the case and thank him for the meals. She also wanted to tell him that he could stop with the deliveries. She intended on cooking meals for him in return.

She noticed it was night outside as she climbed the stairs to the main level of the house. The hardwood floor on the main level was the reason why she never heard Emmett walking around. The rich, solid floor was well insulated. Tongue and groove. Very solid.

Susie called out, "Emmett?"

No one answered.

She wandered into a kitchen, which appeared to be cut out of a homemaking magazine. The first thing to grab Susie's attention was the pristine cabinetry. Her mind was instantly brought back to the filing cabinets in the garage loft. The same ornate craftsmanship was on display with each cabinet and drawer face. The backsplash tiles appeared to be hand selected from multiple designs. Countless hours of organizing and planning had surely been needed to make them flow seamlessly together. The countertop was dark, black granite with white ripples coursing throughout. The sunken sink was empty and dish free, "Just the way *he* would have wanted," she muttered to herself. The table appeared to be set for dinner, although no one was in the kitchen nor was any food being prepared. The hand rolled cloth napkins rested in shiny silver napkin rings. The pairs were laid on top of ivory flatware. Spotless wine glasses sparkled in the overhead light.

Susie called out again, louder than before, "Emmett?" She felt as though she was intruding on his home, even though she had been invited.

More silence.

She decided to check to see if his SUV was in the garage. She felt silly. He might not have been at home. Opening the door and walking out onto his garage loft, her ears caught faint classical music playing in the background.

There, seated at his desk reading the newspaper and resting his feet atop the polished surface, was Emmett. He appeared much older than his age. He reminded her of an old husband looking for peace and quiet from a nagging wife.

She smiled and said, "Hi. I just wanted to…"

Emmett sprang to life. He flung his feet to the ground and shot out of his seat. Interrupting her mid-sentence, he shouted, "Quickly, go back down to the basement. I'll explain everything in a second."

The tone in his voice was harsh. Susie knew she shouldn't hesitate. As quick as she could manage, she turned and walked back down the stairs. She was puzzled, slightly hurt. She replayed his frantic words in her head and sat on the couch. *What was it? Why had he reacted that way?* She waited for him to come down and explain himself. The feeling that her situation had somehow grown worse slithered its way in.

Emmett walked down the stairs carrying a file folder with a name written in large black letters across the front.

"Emmett, what's going on? And who's the *Roxanne Cooke* on your file folder?" Susie asked him before he could start the conversation.

"You are. But slow down and let me explain," said Emmett. He sat next to Susie on the couch and said, "What I mean is, the name *Roxanne Cooke* is going to be your name for the time being. Some things have changed. I'm sorry if I scared you by yelling at you. I realize it may have been kind of abrupt."

"What's changed? What do you mean? Whatever it is, just give it to me straight. I can handle anything after the news of Michael's murder was dumped on me," Susie fired back at Emmett in a tone much tougher than she felt.

Emmett angled his body to face Susie, while taking both of her hands in his. He said, "Yesterday I got a call from my buddy Mason. He was the guy who got me the prison report. He told me that there had been another murder. Apparently, it was gruesome." He hesitated, waiting for Susie.

33

She nodded.

He continued, "The details are sketchy right now, but he said that someone went out of their way to make a point. They used an innocent woman as the messenger. Does the name Lisa Cappolla mean anything to you?"

Closing her eyes and lowering her head, Susie felt warm tears racing down her cheeks again. Whispering, she said, "Yes."

"I thought it might. I wasn't sure."

"She was my roommate. We went to school together. Oh God Emmett, what happened to her?"

"She's dead Susie," Emmett said straight away. "Mason told me that the crime scene and method of killing points to torture."

"Oh Lisa! No! God, no! This is all my fault. What have I done? How could I have forgotten to warn her?" Susie screamed on the brink of hysteria. She buried her hands in her face. Her sobs, forcing their way out through cupped palms, shook her body.

Emmett placed his hands on Susie's hunched shoulders, trying to comfort her. "No. Susie, this isn't your fault. You didn't kill her. You didn't even provoke the people who did. You did everything you could have." He squeezed her shoulders with his strong hands.

"What did they do to her?" she asked. Susie couldn't bring herself to look Emmett directly in the eye.

He took a deep breath. "It appears that they were looking for information. When they weren't getting anything, they tortured her until she died. That's the reason I reacted the way I did in the garage when I told you to come back down here. After hearing about Lisa, I'm certain the Russians are desperate to find you. This is way beyond payback for your brother cheating them. They have a reputation to uphold. They can't look weak. Ever. Not being able to find you makes them appear soft to their competitors. This is about sending a message to anyone who might think that they can steal from the Russian mob and get away with it."

"But Lisa had nothing to do with this. Why was she murdered?" Susie asked, even though she already knew the answer.

"Because Susie, the Russians didn't know if she knew something about your whereabouts or not. The only way that they would be able to know for sure was to torture her and get the information they needed. When she couldn't give them any, they had crossed the line of no-return. They had to kill her as a message. There's another thing too," he paused, searching for the right words. "I put out a couple of feelers, about Melanie Cooper. It appears she's in the wind like you. There haven't been any other killings similar to Lisa's, so it is likely that Melanie is still alive and hiding somewhere," remarked Emmett.

His cell phone, which was holstered to his hip carrying case, rang out just as he finished. His eyes bulged in excitement as he listened to the caller's voice. Susie noticed how his body language had turned from sorrowful to energetic in a matter of a few words. She listened in on the conversation.

"You're kidding. Really? That's great. You got an address for me? Hang on let me write this down. Oh man, thanks Mason, I owe you one." Emmett bounded up the stairs in search of a pen to write down the information.

Mason had run Melanie Cooper's credit card statements. He looked for any recent transactions on hotels or motels. Emmett explained to Susie that there was a transaction for the Travel Lodge, which showed up on her credit card from the night before.

"Odds are, if she stayed there last night, she's probably still there. I really want to talk to her and see what she knows without spooking her. If she knows I'm coming, she might make a run for it. We could lose any chance of retrieving Michael's journal," said Emmett. He put his hand to his chest, "If it were me, I'd already be gone from Toronto, for good."

"Let's hope she's still there. How do you do that? I mean, how are you going to make sure she's there?" Her concern for Emmett's safety was genuine, but her tone came across more questioning than she intended.

Raising his eyebrows and slightly cocking his head, Emmett replied, "Listen, Susie, I know I'm younger than most private detectives, but I know what I'm doing. I'll use the front desk clerk to verify Melanie's still checked in. If she's there, I'll gently knock on the door." He stopped himself before continuing. "Trust me on this one, I can handle it."

Susie did trust him. He had an air of confidence about him. It soothed her nervousness. Emmett explained his plan to her, down to how he was going to execute it, leaving no details to the imagination. Susie felt as though she could relax. She returned to the basement apartment, waiting for him to return.

He was going to run a scam on the front desk clerk that didn't require much more than the element of trust. If the clerk trusted Emmett, then the information would be given. He knew he needed to appear trustworthy and credible.

Emmett dressed in his suit that had cost him a month's earnings and a pair of wire-rimmed glasses. His shoes were polished black wing tips which looked as though this were their first steps outside of the original shoebox. He combed his hair with a side part. Finally, he carried an expensive looking briefcase, which ultimately was an empty prop.

Adding to his persona, Emmett needed to make three stops on his way; first and foremost, he needed money. He figured Melanie simply wouldn't hand over Michael's book to a stranger in a nice suit. More than likely, she would ask for money, and probably a lot of it. She would need it. He would do the same thing if the roles were reversed.

SAVANNAH

Luckily for Emmett, his ATM card had a $1,000 maximum amount he could withdraw in a twenty-four hour period. Typically, banks set a much lower maximum for their clients in case of theft. However, Emmett, having previously required large amounts of cash during non-banking hours, had set up an increase in his maximum limit. He would only need to find an ATM to satisfy Melanie's financial requirements for compensation.

The second and third stops were to add to his hoax. Showing up at the front desk of a motel late at night and asking for a guest's room number, even if you are wearing a $3,000 suit, definitely would alarm the desk clerk. Suspicions would be raised. A rock solid story to go along with the inquiry was a must. He called ahead to an expensive Italian restaurant that he knew would have their name plastered across the outside of the takeout bag.

The other stop was to the liquor store. He arrived just in time before the store clerk was about to lock up for the night. Emmett bought a decent bottle of pinot noir to complete his facade.

In his left hand, Emmett was armed with an expensive looking briefcase. In his right, the bottle of wine and takeout food. Expensive suit, nice briefcase, a bottle of red wine, and a decent takeout dinner. If that wasn't non-threatening and trustworthy, he didn't know what was.

In the past, Emmett had paid hotel clerks for information. Those cases were usually all the same. Some big shot husband was bored with his marriage and decided to find excitement elsewhere. When the wife, usually some stay-at-home mother with too much time on her hands, grew suspicious enough, Emmett was hired.

Those cases were easy. All Emmett had to do was get the room number and run surveillance on the husband walking out of the room. Simple. A few snapshots of the husband and his female mistress walking out together were more than enough evidence. To get that type of room number, Emmett always resorted to paying. A hundred dollar bill Emmett concealed in a handshake was the standard bribe. Occasionally, an honest desk clerk would balk at the initial bribe, but eventually would come around to a few extra bills in the handshake. The most Emmett ever paid for a room number was $400. One time. To a woman desk clerk. A real stickler.

This time was a little more complex. Waiting in his car and snapping some photos was the minor leagues. This was his big call up to the majors. He needed more than the room number. He needed an access card, if Melanie was uncooperative. A detailed story, convincing props, and a padded handshake were hopefully enough for the desk clerk. *Just not a woman. Not again. Please, not again.*

SAVANNAH

The Travel Lodge was located in a part of Toronto that was perfect for Emmett's back story. It was an older part of town that had slowly given way to crime and poverty. It was littered with cheque cashing stores offering payday loans for a nominal interest rate. Legal loan sharking. These stores were hard to find in the part of town Emmett lived. They were a good indicator of where the imaginary line was drawn between the good and bad parts of town.

The motel's storefront featured simple décor. A few small house plants gave a homely feel. Their strategic placement covered up the spots on the walls where the paint had chipped off. The orange-peach color that filled the room offered the feeling of relaxation and quality to its guests. At least twenty years ago it did.

What a dump, thought Emmett. The stone floor hadn't been waxed or polished in years. Stale cigarette stink filled the air. His anxiety of having to deal with a woman calmed from a rolling boil to a simmer as he walked through the front double-door. He spied a male front desk clerk. *Perfect.*

He knew half the battle was to present with confidence and stick to his story. The other half was the padded handshake. A winning combination.

Entering the lobby, he sauntered to the front desk with his shoulders pushed as far back as they would go and head held high. He made direct eye contact with the clerk. Emmett smiled. "I am meeting a friend here this evening and require a key to her room," said Emmett. He spoke confidently. His voice echoed in the empty lobby.

The clerk was caught off guard with the directness of Emmett's request. He replied, "Good evening sir. I'm sorry, but our policy is that our guest's information is private. We don't give out room information. We value the privacy of our guests."

Emmett could tell from the speed of his reply and the dropping eye contact, the employee was new to the job and not very confident in his abilities. He eyed the kid who couldn't have been more than twenty-one years old, smiling subtly. The clerk seemed as though he may have been working his way through college and taking the night manager's position for the raise. An extra few bucks an hour for the graveyard shift.

Emmett continued, "Very well. What's your name son?" He regretted it immediately. *Crap. I'm probably six years older than this kid, and I called him son?*

"Jim Kennedy. I'm the night manager here tonight sir," came the quick nasally response of the young manager.

Good, he hadn't caught on. Emmett bent down, placing his briefcase on the dirty marble floor. He dipped his hand into his jacket pocket. His fingers wrapped around and palmed the folded hundred dollar bills.

SAVANNAH

He extended his padded hand to the night manager. "Nice to meet you Jim, my name is John Smith. I'm meeting a friend of mine here tonight and would like to bring her some dinner and have a couple glasses of wine." He tilted his head and widened his eyes a little. *Play along dummy.* "You seem like a reasonable man. I'm not looking to get anyone in trouble here, just trying to have a relaxing evening after a stressful week. You understand what I mean, don't you Jim?"

Following social norms, Jim took the hand that was offered to him. He felt the bills within the shake and quickly gazed into his palm to satisfy his curiosity. He hadn't expected that.

Jim looked around the empty lobby, checking to see who may have seen the transaction. No one was around. He nodded his head and muttered, "Yes sir. I understand. You meant to say that you misplaced your room card and need a replacement."

"That's precisely what I meant Jim. Thank you," said Emmett as he beamed inside. He held together his poised, confident persona.

Jim turned to his computer screen, clicking a few buttons. He asked, "Since you have forgotten which room number you were staying in and your wife checked in, may I have her name please?"

"Melanie Cooper." Emmett smiled to himself.

"Just one moment, while I find the room and make up a copy of the key for you sir," said Jim. He pocketed the wad of money. It doubled what he would have made in a week of working the graveyard shift. He entered in the name and almost instantly the room number 209 appeared on his screen. He punched the numerical code into the card swiping machine. He swiped a new key card. Within thirty seconds, Emmett had the card he needed to get Michael's journal for Susie.

Emmett gave a half nod to the clerk as he handed him the card. "I appreciate your discretion Jim. Have a good evening."

"Thank you sir, I will," responded Jim. He thumbed the wad of cash in his pants pocket, proud of himself.

CHAPTER 5
STAY-A-NIGHT

Room 209 was on the second floor of the two-story complex. Taking the outdoor concrete stairs up to the covered hallway, Emmett plopped down his briefcase next to a pop machine. It was stationed in the corner of the second floor landing. The word *COKE* was diagonally smeared along the side, as if the single word could entice the thought of refreshment.

Emmett no longer needed unnecessary props. They could get in his way. What if Melanie became violent? That was how his brain worked, always asking "what if." He didn't, however, throw out the wine or food. Those could come in handy. He figured Melanie wouldn't have eaten in a few days. Paranoid people don't tend to venture out when they're being hunted. Emmett assumed she wouldn't have risked leaving the rented sanctuary.

Emmett hadn't pre-planned his approach once he was granted access to Melanie's room. His entire plan involved getting the key card. "Relax Susie, I've done this before." Isn't that what he had said? He felt foolish, amateurish. He knew he should have planned further.

He stood next to the pop machine. He pulled the card out of his right pants pocket and thought about different approaches. Shaking his head, he muttered to himself, "Rookie mistake. How could I make such a careless error?"

He was certain Melanie would be surprised by his visit. He was almost positive she would be violent. She probably was armed.

He thought about waiting until it was late enough that she'd be in bed, under a heavy, unwashed comforter and a thin, cheap sheet. The usual dirty crap associated

39

with cheap motels. It was less likely that she'd be armed.

He played the scenario out in his head. He winced. A pistol could easily be under her pillow or on the bed side table next to her. If Emmett went with that approach, he would have to rush in, locate the weapon, and disarm Melanie. *Bad idea. Think harder. Too much risk.* He decided on rationally discussing things, rather than showing unnecessary aggression.

Emmett talked himself into believing that Melanie wouldn't shoot someone for knocking on her door. If he used the key card and barged in, all bets were off. The relationship would get off on the wrong foot. Maybe he wouldn't leave with the journal. Maybe Melanie shoots him. Maybe someone overhears her shouts and calls the police. All bad things he didn't want to happen.

He needed Melanie to trust him. He needed her to see that he was who he said he was. A friend, not a threat. Once he was inside, he could show her the key card he already had, as proof that he approached with more grace than he needed to.

He nodded to himself. His newfound plan would work. It had to. *Nice and easy. Don't provoke her, she's already on edge.*

Emmett walked up to room 209 and tapped on the door with three soft knocks. He tried to be as gentle as possible. Accompanying the three light taps, Emmett said, "I'm a friend Miss Cooper. I assure you I'm not here to harm you." He tried to ease the words out as calmly as possible, removing all the threatening bass from his baritone voice.

He stood there, waiting. He spun around and looked out past the rusted railing onto the parking lot. Nothing moved. He refaced the door.

No response.

He waited. After what felt like a minute, Emmett tapped on the door a second time, repeating his initial statement, "I'm a friend Miss Cooper. I'm not here to hurt you."

This time the curtain covering the window to the right of the door moved ever so slightly. It alerted Emmett that Melanie was inside and had seen him standing there. He held the bag of dinner and bottle of wine up next to his shoulders. His peace offerings. He hoped she was peering through the peep hole.

Rustling came from inside the motel room. He tried to appear as calm and unintimidating as he could. His heart pounded as the time passed. After waiting another thirty seconds, he heard a faint voice. "I have a gun. Keep your hands where I can see them and I'll open the door."

His adrenaline spiked. His heart raced faster. His palms began to sweat. "Yes ma'am, Miss Cooper. As I said, I'm not here to hurt you. I've come on behalf of Susie Taylor, Michael's sister. May I come in and speak with you?"

As he waited for the next move, he imagined the anguish on Melanie's face. She had a big dilemma on her hands. She had to be scared out of her mind. Naming

Michael's sister, whom she was supposed to deliver his journal to, probably helped, Emmett hoped. If she thought it through, she would recognize that as a sign he could be trusted and was truthful.

Emmett didn't like dealing with people who were armed, especially when he was unarmed. He needed to convince her to let him in. "I know you're not sure what to do, but honestly Melanie, I'm a friend. What hit man would bring you dinner and a bottle of wine?" he asked.

He heard the deadbolt on the door disengage. The heavy motel door opened. He stepped through the threshold and froze in his tracks. From behind the door, he was greeted with the cold tip of a gun barrel pressed against his temple.

"How do I know you're not going to kill me once I close this door and drop my guard?" Melanie whispered in Emmett's ear. She pressed her gun harder into the flesh of his head.

Emmett stood in Melanie's dark motel room. Only the faint light that came from the bathroom lit the room. He fumbled to find the words to ease Melanie's anxiety.

"Listen Miss Cooper, let me explain. My name is Emmett Smith," he lied. He never used his real last name when working. "I am a private detective who was hired by Susie Taylor. She received a letter from her brother a few days ago stating that he thought he was going to be killed. In the p.s. section of the letter, he indicated that you would be receiving a similar letter. That should be evidence enough that I am who I say I am. There is no way anyone else would know that information."

Melanie lowered the barrel of the gun and muttered softly, "So, the letter is true then? Is Michael dead? Is Susie safe?"

"Unfortunately, yes the letter is true. I'm sorry to say, but Michael was killed in prison just days ago. Susie is safe. The people who are searching for her won't find her. May I come in and sit down please? We have some things to discuss," Emmett replied. He lowered his hands to his waist, which still held the bag of dinner and bottle of red wine.

Melanie gestured with her left hand to the small circular table in the corner of the room. Two chairs adjoined it. Nothing special, more cheap crap to fill an otherwise empty area of the room.

She sat in the chair tucked in the corner, setting her black semi-automatic gun on her lap. "I'm sorry I had to point this at you, but I don't need to explain why, do I?" she asked.

"No. You don't. I understand," answered Emmett, trying to win Melanie over by remaining calm and moving slowly.

"What's in the bag? Is it really something from Antonio's?" inquired Melanie, eyeing the white paper bag Emmett had placed on the table.

Smiling, Emmett opened the bag. He slowly pulled out a circular silver takeout tin. The edges of the white top were crusted with marinara stains. Cheese oozed out of the edges, nearly falling down the sides. He opened the lid. A plastic folk and knife exited the bag. Everything was slid across the table. "Consider this my goodwill gesture. I figured you may be hungry. While you eat, I'll fill you in on what I know. Would that be ok with you?" he said, sitting down opposite of her.

Melanie nodded. She pounced on the takeout dish. "Thank you. I've only had the lousy garbage from the vending machine downstairs. I've been too frightened to go farther than that. I'm starving," she managed to spit out between mouthfuls of spaghetti. An enormous meatball had been stabbed by her fork. She lifted and bit it like a child would eat a candied apple. As she chewed, she said, "Fill me in on what you know Emmett."

"Ok, first off Melanie, I'm here on Susie's behalf to retrieve Michael's journal. Do you have it with you?" he asked, getting down to business. His relaxed posture and crossed legs indicated to Melanie that she could let her guard down.

"Yes I have it. I've been reading it, and it's more than a journal."

"What do you mean exactly?"

"It's more like a book. I've read it twice. I don't know Susie, but some of the content will probably shock her. I know Michael fairly well. I mean, I knew him. I hate saying it like that. We were in love. You know? Like really in love. He hid things from me. Even I was shocked at the things I read," she said, her voice trailed off.

"I need that journal Miss Cooper. It is rightfully Susie Taylor's property and I would like to bring it to her, if you don't mind," replied Emmett.

She shook her head as she chewed what remained of the meatball. After swallowing she said, "No! That book is all I have. I'm not just going to hand it over because you say so. I've got the gun here. Remember?" Her left hand slid down on top of the pistol and came to a rest, driving the point home.

Inside, Emmett's adrenaline spiked again when her hand touched the pistol. He hated guns. He especially hated guns that were pointed at him in the hands of mentally unstable people. *Stay calm. Act relaxed and unthreatened. Don't push so hard.*

"Miss Cooper, I assure you that I am not looking for trouble. I merely want to retrieve Michael's journal or book or whatever it is and bring it back to Susie. What would it take for me to get it from you?" Emmett asked calmly. He sensed Melanie was more on edge than she was letting on.

Looking up from the pile of food in front of her, Melanie's eyes drilled holes through Emmett. "Two thousand dollars in cash and it's yours."

Emmett held Melanie's stare. A hint of fear shot across her eyes. He had the upper hand in the negotiation. He knew it. He calmly said, "I'm going to slowly reach into my pocket and pull out all the money I have on me. I thought you might want to be reimbursed for your trouble, and under the circumstances, I don't blame you. I think you're entitled to every dime. All I have right now is seven hundred dollars. I was only able to withdraw one thousand from my account from the ATM and needed three hundred of it to bribe the night manager. I will gladly give you this money and the remaining amount tomorrow if you'll agree to let me bring Michael's journal to Susie tonight."

She nodded.

"Good. Miss Taylor will be very appreciative and surely will want to see you're fully compensated for your efforts."

As promised, he slowly lowered his hand into his pocket. He pulled out the cash.

She said, "I'll take the seven hundred you have now, but I want to know everything you've found out about Michael." Before she even finished speaking, Melanie reached for the stack of hundred dollar bills laid across the table.

"Absolutely Miss Cooper, but first I must insist on seeing the journal. You may keep it in your lap, but I need assurances that I haven't just flushed all that money down the toilet," remarked Emmett as he re-crossed his legs in the opposite direction.

He returned to a relaxed, calm position in the cheap motel furniture. His eyes followed her as she stood up, still carrying the gun with the safety engaged and walked to the opposite end of the motel room. Her hand didn't wrap around the grip. She held it more like a hammer, with her hand around the barrel. A normal person, who was unfamiliar with guns, would only ever carry a gun that way. Trusting the safety to prevent a discharge was gun handling 101. Never do it. Mechanisms fail. It made Emmett even more nervous. He resisted the urge to squirm in his seat.

She stopped at the TV stand, reaching behind it. There pinned between the wall and the back of the TV was a small paperback book. It appeared to be the size of a thin novel.

Melanie returned to her chair; she flashed him the blank cover and thumbed the pages for him to see. Page after page held penciled words written on cheap newsprint paper. He had no idea if the book was really Michael's or a convenient knockoff that Melanie had fashioned together. Everything about her told him he could trust her. Then again, desperate people do desperate things. He didn't like it, but he knew that he was going to have to trust a complete stranger, just as she had to.

"Here it is. When you've answered my questions, I'll give it to you and you can leave," said Melanie in cold, harsh words. Emmett was reminded of just moments before when she had pressed the gun hard into his head.

43

"Ok, that's fine. I appreciate you being fair with me Miss Cooper. You ask the questions you have, and I'll do my best to tell you what I know," Emmett agreed.

Melanie then asked in a much softer, more delicate, feminine voice, "Do you know what happened to Michael?"

"Unfortunately, I do. He was killed in prison. The prison report states he was stabbed repeatedly. I don't know who did it or which people are responsible," answered Emmett in an equally soft voice.

"And Susie? Where's she?" continued Melanie, fighting to hold back tears.

Shaking his head as he began to answer, Emmett said, "I'm sorry, no. I can't tell you that. It is a matter of safety and trust. She has hired me and I abide to a strict code of conduct with my current and former clients. That way, they know they can trust me with their private dealings. What I can tell you is that she's safe."

Emmett continued and lied to Melanie convincingly, "No one knows where she is. I contact her through a prepaid cell phone. She said she is some place safe, somewhere out of the city."

Melanie stared Emmett down, questioning the honesty of his last statement. She seemed to find what she was looking for. "Okay Emmett. In the letter I got, Michael wrote that he owed some nasty people a lot of money and if his payment wasn't received on time, they might come after me. Is that the same thing Susie's letter said?"

"Essentially, yes," he nodded as he answered.

"And?" Melanie blurted out, looking for more answers than Emmett offered.

"And what?" Emmett fired back, feeling the tension suddenly rise in the room.

Melanie took a deep breath as she closed her eyes. She searched for the patience the stress seemed to have stolen from her. Realizing she may have come across as a basket case, she whispered, "I'm sorry. I am just so on edge and I haven't eaten or slept in three days. I can't think straight when I'm this tired. Can you just tell me what you know? Please Emmett, can you do that?"

Emmett saw the true Melanie. The scared one. The one who, as a little girl, was too scared to jump off a moving swing. The one who, as a swimmer, nervously stood on the diving board trying to fight back tears. For the first time, he saw her. He replied, "Alright. But after this, I get the journal, agreed?"

"Yes," nodded Melanie, too tired to barter anymore.

"Here's what I know. Michael was killed in prison. By whom is uncertain at this point. The police are looking into the murder, but prison killings are almost always unsolved. Inmates rarely come forward." He took a deep breath, the adrenaline was coming down. "Susie is safe. I've been told there are definitely people who are inquiring about her name and whereabouts. When I spoke with my contact, I didn't know about your status, so I wasn't able to ask if anyone had inquired about you. I think it's safe to assume that if these people are asking about Susie, then they're also looking for you too," explained Emmett.

"Tell me this isn't for real. This will just blow over, right?" Melanie asked.

"At this point, I have reason to believe that they are connected to the Russian mob. I will have a much clearer picture of who these people are once I have a chance to read Michael's journal. For now, I have to answer with a firm no. This isn't going to blow over."

"Why are *you* looking into Michael's murder? I mean, why not the police? No offense, but it seems like the police should be doing this job," asked Melanie in a matter-of-fact tone.

Emmett nodded his head. "I agree with you. But the police don't have any solid evidence to go on. Right now they have a prison murder of an inmate and nothing else. Like I already said, most prison murders go unsolved due to the lack of eyewitnesses. According to the police, there isn't even a," he made quote marks with his hands, "real threat on your life or Susie's. What I need to do is gather some evidence for the police on Susie's behalf, and convince the police to start an investigation into Michael's death."

He stood up, as though he was about to leave. "There is another thing I left out. Susie's roommate was tortured and killed in her townhouse. Susie had already fled, and wasn't able to contact her about the danger in time. Even if she had, there wasn't much she could have done. These people are monsters. They won't stop."

Tears silently ran down Melanie's tired face. Her fears morphed into reality. She tried to hold back the flood of emotions. She was too tired. She broke. Her body began to shake and tremble.

He had seen this type of response before. Susie had cried like this. His heart ached for Melanie and the pain she had to endure.

Between sobs she asked, "What am I going to do? I can't stay here in this motel forever like some hermit. Help me Emmett! Tell me what to do."

He reached out and patted her hand gently. Same as he had done with Susie. He knew he was already committed to helping Melanie get through this horrendous mess. Walking away wasn't an option. That ship had sailed long ago.

"Melanie, I want to help. It's going to take me a few days, but I think I have some friends that may be able to figure something out for you, long term. I need to make a few calls and touch base with them," he said, comforting her.

His words gave Melanie enough hope to raise her head and say, "Really? You would help me? Why?"

He stared at her gray blue, but bloodshot, eyes. He could see that on a normal day, her eyes were probably quite attractive. He lowered his voice. "You need help. I can't turn my back on you now. I mean, there's a threat to your safety. Let's just call it professional obligation on my part."

The last line came out with a slight smile. He felt corny saying it, but it was the truth. He couldn't live with himself if something actually happened to Melanie. He was involved.

It made Melanie feel as though trusting Emmett was the right move. He had a sense of dignity and honor. Like old fashioned chivalry. In reality, she had no other options. She forced a weak smile and asked, "Who are these friends of yours? I don't mean to be forward, but I'm curious who these people are that help complete strangers."

"It's no problem. I don't want to promise you anything before I have a chance to contact them. But, since you're asking, they are an underground network that help abused women. Typically, they get women and their children away from abusive husbands and fathers. They set them up with a new life and all the credentials they need. They are kind of like a private witness relocation program, but without the witness part," Emmett explained to Melanie. As he explained, he slid his hand away from his new client. He had a very strict policy on relationships with clients. *It has never happened and it never will.*

Continuing, he added, "You are now my client. We can discuss the obligations and details later. But for now, I think it prudent to deal with the most pressing matters. First, we need to move you to a new location. Tonight. Right now. If I found you, then your location isn't exactly secure."

Emmett's last sentence forced Melanie back to the gravity of the situation. She was being hunted. She twisted her face and asked, "How did you find me anyways? I haven't left my room more than three times."

"Your credit card. You used it to pay for the room. I have a guy who did me a favor. He ran your credit card information for the past seventy-two hours. If I can do that, then whoever else is looking for you can too," explained Emmett.

"How will the Russians, or whoever is looking for me, be able to run my credit card information? Are these people that advanced?" The fear was back in her voice. This time, she made no attempt to hide it.

Emmett put both hands up in the air, palms forward. He tried to calm Melanie's growing anxiety. "If they could, then you'd already be dead. That or they are a little slower than I give them credit for. In cases such as this one, I do not like to underestimate my opponent. I always assume they are more sophisticated than I am, so I like to think a few moves ahead. For tonight, I think we should err on the side of caution and move you to a new location. This way, you can check in under an alias and pay in cash."

Melanie's voice softened. The fear seemed to evaporate as she said, "I don't know where to start thanking you. I never thought that I could be tracked like that. I just…"

Emmett stood up and cut her off, "I really don't think we should waste anymore time. We can talk more in the car and in your new location. Pack your clothes. I'll wrap up this pasta to take with us. Let's get a move on." His words came across with a perfect blend of leadership and assertiveness, without the growing anxiety he began to feel.

Melanie left the table but returned to Emmett's side before he had finished sealing the container lid on the pasta. In one hand, she held a very expensive looking purse, something perfect for a wealthier woman in her early thirties. Emmett didn't know for sure, but it looked haute couture. In the other hand was a small gym bag.

"I'm ready to go. I didn't bring much," she said with a forced smile which showed her perfect set of teeth. She had a beautiful smile, something that most men liked. Emmett was no different from most men. He hastily threw the food back into the paper bag. He stuck his hand out like a snooty waiter, waiting for a tip. He cocked his head to one side and smiled.

"What?" asked Melanie.

"The gun. C'mon, give it to me," replied Emmett assertively.

Without hesitation, Melanie reached into her white Chanel purse. The flawless exterior appeared brand new. A pair of white C's interlocked by creative stitching, displaying the company's logo. *Expensive taste. Whatever, as long as I have the gun from now on.*

She pulled out the lightweight Sig 9mm pistol. The black gun was smaller than it looked when it was pointed at him. Emmett took the gun out of her hand and removed the clip. He pointed the gun toward the ground and pulled on the chamber until it slid all the way back. He flipped the pistol upside down, removed the bullet, and slipped it into the breast pocket of his jacket. The clip went into his pants pocket, along with the loose round.

He remarked, "No offense, but I'm not much of a risk taker when it comes to guns. If the situation calls for it, I'm certain that the gun is better off being in my hands. Like I said, no offense, but I shoot regularly."

"It's fine. I just want to get going so I can feel safe. I'm so tired. I need a good night's sleep," nodded Melanie in reply.

The night air was cooler than when Emmett had first arrived. The parking lot was still relatively deserted, except for the same smatter of parked cars. They stepped through the threshold. Emmett pointed to his car. He lowered his voice barely above a whisper, "Mine is the Ford Escape. Walk to the passenger side quickly and silently. Stay close to the building. Move in straight lines when you walk. Don't run. Don't appear panicked. That will draw attention. Stay calm and cool. I'll be right next to you the entire way."

With a reassuring tap on her shoulder, Emmett whispered, "Go." It started Melanie off on the walk. On the way, he stopped to retrieve the briefcase next to the side of the pop machine.

SAVANNAH

Getting to the car was easier than Melanie had expected. The way Emmett had coached her left her feeling as though she was walking into an ambush. A weight lifted off of her shoulders as they drove away from the Travel Lodge. She turned to Emmett. "Thank you so much. You're a good person and I'm so glad I didn't shoot you when you came to the door."

Emmett snickered. He turned his head and replied, "Me too. I kind of like my head the way it is." He smiled, changing the subject, "I know a crappy little hole-in-the-wall. A real no-tell-motel. No questions asked. I'll pay in cash for a couple of nights, which will buy me some time to get in contact with my people. I'm going to swing by a gas station and pick up a prepaid cell. This way, we can stay in contact."

"Emmett, I don't know what to say. God, thank you. I don't know what I would have done if it wasn't for you," said Melanie.

Waving his hand as if to brush off her comment, Emmett continued, "The game plan is simple. I'm going to get you into a room that is safe and sound, and then get Michael's journal back to Susie. From there, I'm going to make some phone calls tomorrow morning and see what we can do about your situation. It may require a few days to organize all the details, so I'll need you to be patient." He softened his voice. "You'll be safer now. I'm sure of it. When I'm getting the prepaid cell, I'll also grab you a whole bunch of food and some drinks to hold you over for a couple of days. Tomorrow I'll grab some groceries. You ok with all of this?"

Melanie grinned and nodded. "I sure am. I can do a few days, no problem."

Emmett stopped at a gas station along a busy intersection. He put the gun inside his center console. The fifteen round clip stayed in his pants pocket. Melanie reclined in the passenger seat and closed her eyes. With most of the fear gone, the adrenaline stopped pumping. She was crashing, hard. She curled up and tried to get comfortable.

Emmett returned to find Melanie in a deep sleep. Even in her sleep she looked hot. He could see why Michael fell for her. Her hair was like silk in the way it hung over her face. Emmett looked further, examining her hands. It was something he always did, though unsure why. If a woman had manicured hands with polished nails, that was it for him. He was intrigued. He was attracted to women who took care of themselves, sometimes even pampering themselves.

Melanie did. A slight pinkish hue colored each nail as though she had just come from a salon. He shook his head. *Maybe in another life.*

He opened and closed his car door gently. Not a sound. It was a nice feature of his Ford Escape. It was an SUV, sure, but it was quiet if you wanted it to be. She didn't stir.

The check-in process was always easier when Emmett paid with cash. Many motels and hotels required a credit card for deposit purposes. This particular style of motel offered leniency toward the check-in process. Such privacy was vital for the survival of the seedy Stay-A-Night motel.

Their business came from people seeking solitude for affairs, drug deals, or prostitution. The Stay-A-Night's policy was, as the sign in the motel's office stated, *"If we don't see it. It ain't our business."* True to form, the motel's staff, which consisted of a manager who worked the front desk, and a daytime cleaning maid, often overlooked many of their visitor's various indiscretions.

After checking in and getting the room key, which was attached to a foot long length of cut-up hockey stick, Emmett knocked on the window of his Ford Escape. Melanie bolted awake as if she was a jack-in-the-box that had reached its last note. Emmett waved for her to come out, putting his index finger to his lips. The universal motion to be quiet.

He accompanied her into room number four. The small room was dingy. It appeared to have been forgotten since the 1970s. Emmett flicked the switch, turning on the light. A florescent bulb above the headboard illuminated the room's shortcomings. The Travel Lodge seemed like a stay at a four star Hilton in comparison. The carpet and bedspread were covered in stains and burn marks from forgotten cigarettes. The TV appeared to be nearly thirty years old. The controller was attached by a cord. The smell was a mix of old ash trays and stale beer. Vomit may have also been detectable. Both Emmett and Melanie pushed that thought away.

Melanie walked into the room, setting down the paper bag of pasta and bottle of wine on the bed. She headed toward the bathroom, hoping for something manageable. She cringed when she flicked on the fluorescent bathroom light. Gold colored tiles. Green paint. A mustard colored sink, chipped from years of use. It was the original sink installed when the motel had been constructed. The toilet featured a mismatched seat, ocean blue on the mustard ceramic.

The mirror above the sink had more cracks in it than Melanie could count. She wondered if the cracks were caused by fists or heads or both being slammed into the reflection. The bathtub was concealed by a shower curtain covered in a thick layer of soap scum and mildew. She couldn't bring herself to look behind the curtain. No way would she step foot into the shower.

After explaining how to use the prepaid cell phone and going over the details again, Emmett left. Before shutting the door, he said, "You're safe now. Just sit tight and let me figure things out. I'll call you tomorrow and bring by some groceries. Until then, just try to stay calm and relax."

CHAPTER 6
RAGE

Susie held Michael's book in her hands, tears already fell onto its cover. It was all she had left of her beloved brother. She could feel him through it.

Emmett handed over the book and explained everything in vivid detail. The desk clerk. The gun to his head. Melanie. His plan to help her.

Susie listened intently. She said, "Thank you Emmett. You took a huge risk to get me this. Thank you. And it sounds like Melanie really needs your help too."

Emmett sank into his basement couch, relaxing for the first time in front of Susie. The rush of the adrenaline was wearing off, like Melanie had done in the passenger seat, he allowed it to overtake him. He exhaustedly whispered, "You're welcome Susie. I need a shower and some sleep." He slowly rose. Before he climbed the first stair he said, "Oh, I almost forgot, I talked with Mason again."

"Oh?"

"Yeah, he called with some more information about the investigation. It's not good," answered Emmett.

"Whatever it is, just hit me with it. I'm stronger than I look Emmett," pleaded Susie, anxious to hear the information.

"Alright. The investigation into your brother's death is officially closed. When I asked why it had been closed so quickly, he offered a quick apology to you. A few details are making it impossible for Michael's case to stay active," explained Emmett. He fidgeted with his hands. He hated being the bearer of bad news.

Emmett continued, "The security cameras were covered up by the killer or killers. That fact illustrates that Michael's murder was planned. The cameras

50

located in that part of the prison are on an older network and haven't been updated in fifteen years, so there wasn't any audio evidence that the police could use. They also don't have each other on screens. What I mean is, on the newer networks, the ones that have been installed in the past five to ten years, the cameras are required to include at least one other camera in their view. It's a backup feature to always have a set of eyes on whoever might think of messing with the security cameras," explained Emmett.

"Wait a second Emmett. Are you telling me that Michael was in the wrong place and that's why his case is being closed?" Susie inquired with a sad puzzled look on her face.

"No. What I'm telling you is that whoever killed Michael knew which camera they needed to obstruct in the laundry room, making the guards blind to what was going on. A towel or a rag was used, effectively eliminating every piece of evidence aside from the murder weapon."

Susie began silently sobbing. She reached for the box of tissues stationed on the end table. She grabbed one and wiped her moist eyes. "Oh Michael," she said to herself. "He didn't stand a chance. What about the weapon used? Can the police get any fingerprints off of that?"

Emmett shook his head. "Sorry Susie, but the shank was wiped clean and left at the scene. Whoever killed Michael knew what they were doing. They didn't leave any usable evidence. My guess is that it was a contracted hit. This killing sounds professional." He lowered his head before adding, "I'm so sorry Susie. I feel awful telling you all of this. It must be very hard to hear."

Susie closed her eyes and held them shut. She squeezed them tight. She responded quietly, "It's ok Emmett. I appreciate you sharing what you learned. I would much rather know than be kept in the dark. I need some time to process all of this. Do you mind? I don't mean to be rude. I just need to be alone right now."

"Not at all. I'm off to bed. Good night Susie," replied Emmett.

He dragged his tired body up the basement stairs. She watched him walk away before turning her attention to Michael's journal, which rested on her lap. She had no intention of sleeping. Not until she read everything.

Curling up on the couch, Susie opened the cover. She recognized Michael's handwriting and was overcome with emotion. She cried until the tears couldn't come out any more. She tried pulling herself together. She wiped her face. She blew into a tissue. Then she started.

The hours sped by. She read every word methodically. Her brother's writing captivated her. She felt his pain. She imagined his life. The more she read the clearer it all became. She understood why Michael hadn't contacted her. He couldn't have. He was in too deep.

Seven hours after opening the cover, she finished the entire journal. No tears left. Raw and blood-shot, she rubbed her fatigued eyes. She had a plan. Sleeping wasn't a part of it.

Susie walked over to the computer nook. She sat down in Emmett's black leather chair and began copying down every word from the journal. She was determined to copy it all. The words needed to be saved. She needed to do it. Needed to. Compulsion overtook her.

Typing was therapeutic. The second time reading each sentence was easier. With each passing minute, it became more and more clear to her what she needed to do.

Her brother was murdered. That much was clear. According to the police, there was no chance that anyone would be punished. There would be no justice. None for Michael. None for Lisa. Nothing. She couldn't accept that.

Susie's sorrow transformed into rage, just as it did all those years ago with *him*. The more she typed, the more it swelled inside her. She felt more energized than she had in a long time. Vengeance fueled her.

Enraged, she swore aloud. To herself. To her dead brother. To her tortured roommate. "I will do everything I can to avenge your deaths. I won't be denied by a legal system that doesn't give a shit. I'm taking matters into my own hands. They'll pay for what they did to you. All of them. I don't care how many there are. I promise you, there will be justice."

CHAPTER 7
MY BIBLE

Excerpt from Michael's Journal

Susie,

Let me first start off by saying how embarrassed I am. The content of this journal is saddening, really. It's going to change your perception of me. For that, I'm sorry. I'm still your brother and I'm still the same person you've always known. I just got caught up, you know? I got greedy, plain and simple. Too often in my life, I started off doing just fine and then got greedy. In fact, as I sit here in the corner of my prison cell, I realize that, in every situation, that's exactly what happened. Greed really is the root of all evil, especially for me.

A lot of the details in this are going to be hard to read. Sorry Sis. Trust me, it's hard for me to write them too. I'm not proud of the things I've done or that I've ended up in prison. Just the opposite, I'm embarrassed. At least now, I have the chance to reflect upon the choices I've made, and try to clean up this mess. Or make amends. Or whatever.

I figure I better tell my story, while I still have the time. God, I'm so incredibly sorry for everything.

*I honestly am sitting here not knowing where to begin. I guess I'll just start. I entitled this journal **Savannah**. I think you will understand why I named it that once you're finished reading about it.*

SAVANNAH

Savannah

I had probably spent more hours at a poker table than any other kid I've ever met. Every family gathering involved cards, no matter what the occasion. My Uncle Jerry taught me how to play Texas Hold 'Em at five years old. At six, he was tired of having to shuffle and deal every hand. He was that way, a lazy bum. If he could get me or my sister to do something for him, he would. No matter what it was, including running to the store to buy him cigarettes.

He coached me on shuffling a full deck. Around my ninth birthday, when he was drunk, he explained to me why he always won whenever we played. My uncle opened my eyes on the fine art of cheating. *What a guy. Thanks a lot Jerry.*

More specifically, he showed me how to cheat while shuffling the cards. It wasn't that difficult a skill to learn. It took me only a few months to get good at it. The difficulty had been in being able to shuffle, see the cards as they were flipped into place, and remembering their order. Deal them out, remember the cards.

I practiced by myself in my bedroom relentlessly. I mastered my shuffling craft in no time flat. I had it perfected, or so I thought at the time. I was nine and I had already trained myself to be able to see the first six cards in the pile.

In the poker game Texas Hold 'Em, each player is dealt two cards to start the game. Each player has to decide whether to play their two cards or to fold them. Typically, players will fold their cards if they aren't very good. On the contrary, if a player has two cards that they favor, they bet against other players.

Players try to make the best possible poker hand they can using the five community cards that are flipped in the middle of the table and their two cards. The community cards are available for every player to use. In all, there are four rounds of betting on each hand dealt.

Each time I dealt the cards, I had a distinct advantage. I knew one of the cards each of the other players had. This type of cheating wasn't a sure fire guarantee of winning, but it gave me an advantage over everyone else. And the best part was no one else knew. And I just turned ten years old.

The larger my hands grew, the easier it became to shuffle. Learning to shuffle at six made shuffling at ten a breeze. The older I got, the more comfortable I became shuffling a full deck of cards. As my hands grew to their adult size, they became finely crafted tools of shuffling.

By the time junior high ended, I had won a closet full of other kid's collectible toys. By my sophomore year of high school, my sock drawer was overflowing with other student's lunch money. I still remember the Crown Royal purple sack of coins I hid away from everyone in my bedroom vent. I used to sneak away late at night onto my apartment porch to count my winnings in secrecy. If my mother or father ever found out about the money, I was convinced they would take it away. They'd come up with some accusation of me stealing from them. That's just the way my parents were. Pathetic.

Let me make myself completely clear. I am not blaming my parents for what happened to me. I'm not one of those guys who blame other people. I made my own choices and I have to live with them. That being said, they certainly didn't help me growing up.

I was behind the eight ball from the beginning. A betting man would have been wise to wager that I would have ended up in jail. And, low and behold, he would have won.

I dropped out of school before the beginning of my junior year. Instead of studying, I organized poker games out of my garage every night. My parents didn't even notice. They couldn't have cared less about what I was doing, as long as I was out of their hair and finished my household chores.

The apartment we lived in had a garage below. The simple setup had none of the frills of a casino or poker room. The floor was a mess of odds and ends that my father hoarded throughout the years. It took me three hours to clear an area large enough for my flimsy card table to fold open. After borrowing some folding chairs from the next door neighbor's house, I finally had set up my first poker game. The oil stained concrete floor and stale cigarette odor completed the ambiance of my garage. Even with the garage door open, the fresh air never seemed to blow away the foul stench.

For more than three years, I played on that rickety old table with the same guys from high school. We played for pocket change. A good night could bring in as much as $35. That brings a smile to my face. $35. That was a big deal to me, once upon a time.

I had become very talented with a deck of cards. By my seventeenth birthday, I was able to shuffle, sneak a peek at the cards being laid, and remember the first eight.

Typically, five of us sat at the table. Me and four others. Seeing the first eight cards was crazy. The advantage was much greater for me than before. I knew both cards of the first three players and one card from the fourth.

I mean, c'mon, that's an unbelievable advantage to have. When the first three community cards, called *the flop*, were turned over, I was able to tell if the other players had made a pair or completely missed. It was like seeing the future. *I was a Poker God.*

If the players missed the flop, then I would bet. They would fold. If their cards were better than mine, I would fold and save myself from losing any money. My cards didn't even matter. I was unbeatable, and still no one knew.

Of course, I had to learn to hide my advantage. I did not win every time I dealt. That was a bad idea. I would have alerted the other players of my skill. Good poker players recognize patterns. Betting patterns. Winning patterns. How players react to good cards. I didn't give them the chance to catch on.

I had to become a serious actor. I had to fold winning hands. I had to let inferior players win smaller pots so I could steal the larger ones. And best of all, I began acting upset when I was actually pleased, nervous when I was confident, and disappointed when I let my opponents win. Acting at the poker table became my passion. I loved having the other players not know the truth about how I was actually feeling.

Spending untold hours playing poker, night in and night out, sharpened my sense of awareness. We played every night, sometimes until 3 a.m. Other times, it would be earlier, depending if I took the other players' money too quickly. Some guys stopped coming around. I messed up and had to learn. They left because they never won. At first, I would say to the other guys, "Who cares. We got their money. Let them leave."

The more I thought about it, the more I realized I was wrong. Dead wrong. If those same guys kept coming back, then I could slowly, methodically take their money. If they stopped coming altogether, the money would eventually dry up. I slowly realized the need to keep those guys coming. I learned to "take the temperature of the players" at the poker table.

- A player who constantly loses hand after hand tends to get a little hot under the collar. They become suspicious and pay closer attention to small details. Eventually, these were the players who stopped coming altogether.

- A player who isn't getting good cards becomes a cold player. They start to complain, creating an anxious poker table. That atmosphere lends itself to players inspecting the dealer's every move. Clearly, that was not what I wanted.

- A player who just won is busy stacking his chips into neat piles. They relax. They don't watch the dealer shuffling the cards. They feel good. They proudly sort and count their winnings.

By "taking the temperature" of the poker table, I knew which players needed to have a winning hand to loosen up the table. Timing became my greatest skill when I won, when other players needed a win, and when to bet big.

Players continued to return and continued to pad my winnings, all due to timing. Each night, I could predict, within $50, the amount of cash I would add to my growing bank roll.

I wasn't satisfied with my skill set, yet. I still took hefty losses on nights that I played with especially keen players. I was left with a helpless feeling, which I hated. I wanted more control. I wanted more winnings.

When I turned twenty years old, I began studying professional players on TV. Poker on television became popular. I was able to witness their betting habits, the traps they laid, and most importantly, their table presence.

SAVANNAH

Poker is a fickle game of uncertainty. I was growing tired of losing hands to unpredictable turns of fate. A lucky card for another player occasionally left me with a huge loss. Professionals rarely lost that way. I wanted what they had. After a particularly awful night, when I lost over $500 on two different hands, I had enough.

Surfing the Internet brought me to a website on counting cards at blackjack tables. Further searching delivered me to my Bible. It was a website that took me hours to find because of its relative obscurity. It was as if the website didn't want to be found. I entered my credit card number and paid the $49.99 annual membership fee and found the con of a lifetime. I named it "Savannah." It would make me hundreds of thousands of dollars and change my life forever.

Savannah was a shuffling maneuver like no other I had ever seen. It was a blackjack shuffling scam that allowed the dealer to order the cards on top of the deck while appearing to shuffle them. I had already mastered shuffling. I was damn good at spying the top cards of the deck. But my skills were small time in comparison to what Savannah gave me.

It expanded on just seeing the cards. Savannah taught me to order the cards for each player. That's the greatest advantage I can think of in poker. If I was a god at a poker table before, now I was the king of gods. I deemed which cards everyone got, all while shuffling.

The website showed a video of a group of friends playing a blackjack game. The dealer needed to shuffle the cards many times, over and over again. The video slowed down to slow motion to explain what he was doing with each shuffle. The more times the dealer shuffled, the more cards he would be able to use to deal out.

One specific reason for shuffling multiple times was to throw the other players off. If a player consistently shuffled ten times, for example, the other players at the table were less likely to watch the dealer every time.

I chose to shuffle exactly nine times each deal. Every deal. No matter what. It felt like I was conditioning the other players to be less suspicious of me. Same routine. Same consistency.

Savannah was about keeping the top cards on top of the deck, and not shuffling them back in. I was able to see those cards, remember them, and then reorder them. The skilled part was adding only one card on top of the deck, thus keeping the same order with one added card. Nine shuffles gave me ample time to find some good combinations to deal out.

Think about it. I could give player number one a good hand. Maybe he gets a pair of 8s. Then player number two gets a pair of Jacks. Both players would like their hands. Both would bet. The pot would increase. The winner wins more money, has a bigger payday.

Making small talk became important. When I continued chatting, while shuffling, it appeared that I was meticulously shuffling, as usual. A quick glance at the right time and Savannah was on. I trained myself to look down quickly, and then bring my eyes back up.

Making eye contact was important. I tried to give the impression that I was a thorough shuffler. In reality, I was actually ordering the cards for each player, creating the scenario I wanted.

I was able to give the other players the cards I wanted them to have. I could give a cold player two good cards, flipping his fortune and relaxing the table's atmosphere. If a particular player was winning too often, I could give him decent cards and another player a better opening hand. No one was safe when I shuffled.

By this time, we had stopped playing with spare change and lunch money. Only five, ten, and twenty dollar bills made their way onto the table. Three years ago, a good night's winnings used to be $35. Now the stakes were higher.

The top winner each night usually won in the neighborhood of $300. I commonly took more than $100 a night, but tried to make sure it wasn't more than $200.

I made sure the other players won frequently enough that they kept coming back. I developed the strategy to never allow myself to be the top winner. If the same person is the biggest winner every night, then other players would start to take notice. No one really notices the guy who happened to be the second place winner. Even if it was every time we played.

This kept the suspicions off me. By rotating the biggest winner amongst the other players, the other players' watchful eyes never stayed on the same person too long. That kept every one returning to the poker games in my garage. And, most importantly of all, kept my bank roll steadily increasing.

Savannah changed my life. I found the control I was looking for.

Over the course of the next nine months, I made $26,000. And no one ever suspected that I was cheating.

CHAPTER 8
THE RIVER

Excerpt from Michael's Journal

Savannah was enough for me to guarantee that I would win every time I played. After awhile, in classic Michael Taylor fashion, I wanted more. The excitement of winning eventually died off. Adding a hundred here and a hundred there lost its magic.

I wanted more. I got greedy. I went in search of something bigger than my garage games.

I began at the casinos. They offered me a chance to go after bigger winnings than the garage games. The problem was that casinos are tight, and the players there are good. It took me $900 to realize the harsh reality that, without Savannah, I was a regular old nobody.

Casinos weren't the answer. They wouldn't let me deal.

There were other options. Arch was a semi-regular player at my garage games. His three hundred pounds were evenly distributed amongst his numerous tattoos. Even his bald head featured tattoos of eagle's wings from the edge of his forehead to the base of his neck. He was the happiest guy when he was winning. When he wasn't, his attitude quickly turned ugly toward the winner.

He had slipped up one time and spoke about a poker room he played in. Once a week he said he went to this place to play poker for big money. He described it as a simple casino where most of the guys there weren't very good. He bragged about how on some nights he walked out of there with $1000. My eyes lit up.

SAVANNAH

One particular night, I made a habit of dealing Arch good cards to keep him in a good mood. His huge stack of chips softened his attitude. After some begging, Arch agreed to take me along with him to his poker room. He warned me that I was to never speak of it, especially of its location. I can still hear his words, "Crossing these guys is a very bad idea Michael. Don't. No matter what, just don't."

Toronto's underground poker rooms are run by organized crime. No matter where you are in the city, you can be certain that there is a poker room nearby with direct ties back to the organized crime family who maintains that area.

I wanted to play somewhere that didn't provide their own dealers. I couldn't use Savannah if I couldn't deal the cards. I needed a place where Savannah could come and play with me.

Scarborough, on Toronto's east end, had the exact kind of poker room I was looking for. It was located in the back room of a carpet distributor. It was an invitation-only place. The security was heavy. The amenities were light, nearly absent altogether. The poker room required me to get formally introduced before I was allowed to play.

When we arrived, Arch told me to stay at the door while he spoke with the floor manager. He mentioned he had a friend who wanted to play. He was required to vouch for me. His name and mine. Attached. Permanently. In order for new members to join, a current member has to use their name as collateral for the person, becoming their sponsor, so to speak. If there were problems with the new member, the sponsor was responsible for their actions. I never asked what that meant, but I was pretty sure I didn't want to find out. The entire time I stood at the entrance waiting for Arch, I could feel the hair on the back of my neck standing at attention.

A week after paying my $500 membership fee, I received a text message that read, "Tuesday night. $1/$2 no-limit. Tell no one. 8 p.m."

Being one of their slower nights of the week, new members were permitted to come and play on Tuesdays. The rules were clear. The sign hanging above the cashier table listed the items in bold print.

1.) Money must be paid up front, no I.O.U.'s.
2.) No cell phones.
3.) If there is a problem, raise your hand. A pit boss will resolve your concern.

Having only ever played poker in my garage, at other people's houses, and a brief stop in a casino, my initial experience inside the poker room was very intimidating. It felt like the pit bosses were watching my every move. Each player I was seated with seemed to study the dealer, determined to catch them cheating.

SAVANNAH

When my turn to deal came, I shuffled nine times as usual, but didn't make any attempt to look at the deck or use Savannah. I wanted to learn the layout and feel my way around this place before attempting anything. Truth of the matter was, I was scared shitless. My heart raced each time the deck was passed to me.

After four hours of playing, I was up a little more than $300. I hadn't cheated once and wasn't involved in too many hands. I played ultra-conservatively. I was seated with a table full of gamblers. Experience told me I was whipping up a recipe for success.

I was right. I walked away, the first night, with $360 more than I came with. On my way out, the pit boss who oversaw my table and another adjacent table, motioned me over. He invited me to come on Thursday night.

Those nights were when higher stakes games were played. Apparently I made an impression. Poker skill? Respectfulness? Or something else? To this day, I still don't know. But the pit boss told me, "Thursdays we play $3/$6 no-limit. Bring more money. You'll win more."

I felt incredibly proud. I won a fair amount of money, without cheating, and was invited back on a more exclusive night. I didn't need to be worried or nervous when I was in the poker room. I figured that I was like everyone else who goes there, except I had an ace up my sleeve. Savannah.

I left with tons of confidence. The invitation helped the initial intimidation wear off completely. What remained was the itch of greed. Driving home, my mind raced through scenario after scenario of how Savannah was going to win me a lot more money on Thursday night.

The next two days melted into one long practice session with Savannah. I wore out four new decks. The cards at the poker room were always new and crisp. Practicing on old, flimsy cards didn't make any sense to me. I had to practice the way I was going to perform.

I rented half of a duplex. In my lease, I arranged to have exclusive rights to the garage, in order to maintain my poker nights. It was similar to the old one, except mine was fresher smelling. It was still messy, as rented garages usually are, but it was mine and I liked the freedom. My apartment also had an adequate sized kitchen, where I spent most of my practice time. I used the beat-up, old table to simulate the feel of the poker room.

On the following morning, I went out and purchased the most basic video camera I could afford. I spent my entire winnings from the night before and then some. The camera was attached to a small tripod and stood on the corner of my kitchen table. I angled it directly at me, pretending it was the eyes of my opponents.

I shuffled and dealt out the cards to a standard six person table. In the poker room, there were only ever six chairs at a table. I didn't have to worry about eight or ten person tables like at casinos.

61

SAVANNAH

I used the zoom feature and brought it in on my hands and eyes. They worked together with Savannah. I recorded ten imaginary hands, and then watched myself on the camera's playback.

The camera's screen was too small to catch any of Savannah's subtle nuances. I hooked the camera directly to my TV. It was then that I noticed how tense and ridiculous I looked. My shoulders were positioned wide. My back looked as though I was wearing a back brace. My posture was that of a soldier standing at attention. Savannah might have worked in my garage games, but if I wanted to make some money in the poker room, I needed to create a persona.

For the next day and a half, I practiced Savannah in front of the camera, and nothing else. I recreated the posture I would use at the poker table. I wanted to look like I was slouching, like I was leaning onto the table for support. I wanted the other players to think they intimidated me. If nothing else, I wanted my body language to scream *amateur* and *unconfident*. By carrying my head low and never meeting the eyes of the other players, I tried to capture the most non-threatening appearance I could manage.

The video camera raised my confidence with Savannah more than ever before. I dissected every one of my weaknesses and turned them into strengths.

~~~~~~~~~~

The room was packed that night and more tables had been added since Tuesday. I was seated at a high stakes poker table. The players at this table looked as regular as the people you might see on the bus or in a restaurant. Two of them were middle aged men who didn't take particular care of themselves. They were overweight and looked like they had fallen on hard times. Neither player had shaven in weeks. Their fingernails were uncut and yellow. Their eyes were hidden behind reflective sunglasses. I suspected that their eyelids drooped halfway down in front of bloodshot eyes.

The three other players were men in their mid to late thirties. These men carried on as though they were the top players in the world. On every hand, they simultaneously leaned forward, resting their elbows on the padded edge of the table. They quickly looked at their cards and never looked again. They spoke very little and concentrated on every other player's movement. When they won, they calmly pulled the chips from the middle towards their chest as if the chips had only been out on loan. Rarely did they show any excitement.

It was clear to me that these players were either excellent actors or they had spent a lifetime seated at a poker table. I was reminded of the saying Arch told me before I sat down at my first table, "Act as though you've won before."

Playing slow and methodically resulted in a steady decrease to my chip stack.

SAVANNAH

In the first ninety minutes, I had already lost half of the $5000 I had brought. I was in over my head. The other players at the table were much more skilled than I was. I needed help.

When my turn to deal came, I eyed the other players and pit boss. The time had come to unleash Savannah. The pit boss turned his attention toward the other table he was responsible for as I began to shuffle. I arched my back and rolled my shoulders forward. My elbows leaned heavily onto the table. I distributed the cards.

The player directly on my left had amassed a small fortune. I dealt him a pair of nines. A good starting hand. He bet, big. The pot grew.

I had given the player next to him a pair of tens. *Lucky for him.* Each player raised their bets. Everyone else folded. When the dust settled, Savannah had turned the fortune of the player with the pair of tens. In that one hand alone, he had won $14,000.

Savannah worked like a thing of beauty. Inside, I beamed with pride. I felt like God and no one suspected a thing. No eyebrows curled. No shouts of "cheater" erupted. No pit boss put their hands on me. My goal that night was to test Savannah and see if it could work in a real poker setting. Mission accomplished. It passed with flying colors. I wanted to try it again the following visit.

Being greedy is the downfall of most cheaters; that, and making a mistake from being too nervous. I had officially mastered Savannah. With the deck in my hands, everyone's chips were mine for the taking. Controlling my nerves was the next obstacle. I had proved that in the poker room I could perform Savannah without getting caught. I gave the man with the pocket tens a small fortune that night. Now I needed to perform Savannah for my benefit.

When the dealer wins, other players tend to notice. No one suspects the dealer of cheating for another player. I knew using Savannah more than once a night was asking for trouble, so I had to wisely pick my spot.

~~~~~~~~~~~~~~~~~

The following Thursday was similar to the previous week. I walked in and was grouped at a table with five players that had deep pockets, and plenty of experience. Just as the prior week had started, I quickly found myself down a few hundred dollars in the first hour. *Patience. Wait for the opportune moment to strike.*

Three hours later, it finally felt right. Savannah needed to come out. The pit boss was occupied by some loud mouth at my neighboring table. The players at my table were letting their attention dwindle.

I dealt the Asian guy, three spots to my left, an Ace and a King. Typically, this hand is raised by the bettor. It's a strong hand. I got a pair of Kings. Pocket Kings. Cowboys. To say I felt confident with this hand is an understatement. I called and raised his bet of $1000 by putting an additional $3000 in the pot.

SAVANNAH

After he called my raise, I turned over the flop. A Queen, a three, and a nine were shown. He bet another $1000. I matched his bet, raising him another $1000. The Asian gentleman called. The turn card was an eight. He showed little emotion as he slid yet another $1000 of chips into the growing pot.

I had a pair of Kings and felt like I was slowly taking all of his money. It was great. I knew his cards. I was beating him. He hadn't paired either of his cards, nor was there a chance for a straight to be made.

I announced, "I'm all in."

Every chip I had in front of me was slid into the middle.

He carefully deliberated over his decision. He called. The middle of the table held $19,500. He closed his eyes in agony after I showed him my Kings. He flung his Ace and King. He stood stoically behind his chair, subtly showing defeat.

He was beaten. I had him. I had two Kings. He didn't have anything. In my mind, I was already raking in nearly $20,000. That was, right up to the point where I flipped the river.

The river card is the final community card. Sometimes it's the card that makes or breaks a player's night. There were three remaining Aces in the deck. Any one of them could beat me. The odds were extremely low of one of them coming, about an eight percent chance.

An Ace appeared. It gave him a pair of Aces, defeating my pair of Kings. The players at the table erupted in shock. The Asian man threw his arms up, cheering for his good fortune. He quickly grabbed the mountain of chips. He spoke quickly in Chinese to another man at another table. I couldn't understand what he was saying, but I got the gist. He was excited.

I found the flaw in Savannah, the only one, and it cost me a lot of money to find it. Savannah could be defeated by long shot odds.

I graciously congratulated my opponent and left. I wanted to draw as little attention to myself as possible. Even though I had lost, I had still cheated. I still could make more money winning large pots in the future, but not if I drew attention to the fact that when I dealt, there were big pots. Either way, it didn't matter. I left with empty pockets.

~~~~~~~~~~

The next few months were productive for me using Savannah. I continued hosting the garage poker games four times a week and meticulously practiced with Savannah. I continued to increase my bankroll, but only by a few hundred dollars a night. A winning night in the garage bored me. Last year, if I had made that much money a night, I would have felt as if I was the greatest poker player alive. But now that Savannah had come into my life, I wanted more and knew where to get it.

SAVANNAH

On Thursday nights, I took Savannah to work in the back room of the carpet distributor. It was a large enough room to hold about twelve poker tables and accompanying chairs. The walls were lined with wood paneling, straight out of the 1970s. The carpet was the running joke between the players. Being housed in a warehouse, where tens of thousands of dollars of carpet was stored, I cringed every time I stepped on what was laid in the poker room. The cigarette burns and stains from unintended spills made the room feel and smell dirty. The spots where gum had stuck, and then been stepped on, dotted the carpet. The room was dim and dirty, but the action couldn't be matched.

The suits the pit bosses wore stood out. Each one was large. Very large. Huge barrel chests were gripped by broad shoulders. Their attire was identical every week: black shoes, black pants, and a black three button jacket that was custom tailored to disguise the firearm they concealed in their shoulder holster. I spotted their hidden guns the first night. Casinos didn't have those.

The bulge on the left side of each pit boss's lower chest was well concealed. Still, I saw them. I recognized the need to be in the good books with these men. And I paid handsomely to stay there.

Each time I arrived, I made a special trip to thank the pit boss working my area. I often had to walk out of my way to be in the pit boss's line of sight and shake his hand with a $100 bill hidden in the hand shake. As I left, I always kept an extra $100 to thank the pit boss for hosting the game and keeping the games friendly. I never knew why I tipped so well. Maybe it was a guilt thing for using Savannah and a subtle way of thanking the pit bosses for not catching me. Whatever the reason, I tipped them, always before I played. Others tipped after, but I was the only one to ever tip before. And that's why I think I received an invitation to play in Friday night's action.

Friday night at the poker room wasn't different from Thursday night. Everything was the same, except that the amount of each pot was about twice the size of a Thursday night pot. The largest pot I ever saw on a Thursday night was the $19,500 one I lost to the Asian guy. Within the first hour, on my first Friday night, I saw six pots over that amount at my table alone.

The room was the same size with the same amount of tables and chairs, but it seemed smaller. Adding as many people as they could to every table made my anxiety flare up. There were more eyes on me than ever before. Each table went from six to eight players. And the amount of pit bosses increased from one for every two tables, to two for every three tables.

There were more obstacles than ever before to make Savannah work. More players watching me shuffle, more money on the table, and now more pit bosses. I lost my nerve the first Friday night. Just like I had done on my first visit to the poker room, I sat back and learned everything I could.

65

SAVANNAH

I noticed the other players. They were much more serious than on Tuesdays and Thursdays. These guys had to have been professional. They carried themselves with a confidence I had never seen. They dressed differently than I did. I wore jeans, a golf shirt, and casual slip-on shoes. Not these guys.

Some wore hooded sweatshirts, sunglasses, and baseball caps that were pulled low over their eyes. The strings on their hoodies were pulled so tight, a face couldn't be seen inside. Others wore reflective sun glasses to conceal their eyes.

There were other players. They wore very expensive suits, showcasing their success. One particular player dressed so well, he wouldn't allow his elbow to touch the edge of the table out of fear that grime would transfer onto his jacket. In all the time I saw him seated, he never had less than $50,000 in chips in front of him.

That first Friday night, I saw that the pit bosses were the same guys as on Thursday night. This meant they worked two nights in a row into the early hours of the morning. The poker room closed at 5 a.m. each morning to allow a cleanup crew enough time to put everything away before the carpet distributor opened its doors for business. On Thursday night, the pit bosses were attentive. I found myself timing Savannah's use to when they weren't looking. I was initially concerned. With more pit bosses on duty Fridays it appeared it would be more difficult to perfectly time Savannah's use.

Around 1 a.m., as the electricity in the air began to fade from the heavy action, the pit bosses showed their weariness of two night shifts in a row. No one can stay focused all the time.

They stood in their normal spots, faking attentiveness. The more I watched them, the more I noticed how tired their eyes really were. They turned their heads and watched each table as before, but I caught them watching the clocks that hung high on the walls, when they should have been watching the tables. At 2 a.m., their scheduled breaks started. They would spell each other off, going down to one pit boss per two tables.

I smiled to myself. It was the opening I needed.

The following Friday night, I had to wait until 2 a.m. And then I unleashed Savannah.

CHAPTER 9

FRIDAY NIGHT

Excerpt from Michael's Journal

Friday night consumed my thoughts for the following week. I practiced Savannah relentlessly. I wore out more decks of cards than the previous practice week, and still, I felt nervous. As far as I could tell, there wasn't a larger stage for me to use Savannah than that poker room on Friday night. There was so much money to be won. And I wanted it. All of it.

The men that ran the poker room were Russian, I think. I'm still not entirely sure. The tattoos on the pit bosses' hands and neck gave it away. I watched movies. I saw documentaries on Russian mobsters. They were portrayed as tattooed thugs, each one with a meaning. Each one earned. Their accent reminded me of the one I heard in the movie *Rocky IV*. The Russian boxer named Drago spoke with nearly the same accent.

Amongst themselves, I frequently overheard them talking in their native tongue. Not knowing Russian, or any other language for that matter, I wasn't sure what to make of it. Not that it mattered because if I was caught cheating, they would have considered that the same as stealing.

Some players at my table talked one night. A guy's wife went missing, just days after he was caught cheating. No one knew anything. Apparently, even the police were clueless. They claimed the guy knew. He was the only one that knew. His face said it all. Someone made her go missing. All because he cheated. All because he was caught.

SAVANNAH

Needless to say, hearing these stories made me even more nervous. Nervous isn't the right word. Scared shitless is more like it. For a few hours, I contemplated not returning the next week. Every time I told myself I wasn't going back, the mountain of cash in the middle of the poker table pushed the doubt aside.

As Friday evening approached, I looked myself in the mirror and gathered my courage. I battled within myself for the entire car ride to the poker room. One part of me wanted to turn around and go home. I knew I wasn't strong enough to actually do that. Savannah was too powerful. The greed was in control now.

My bank roll had grown to $40,000 and I knew, on a good night, could double, maybe even triple. My garage games were comical at this point. Winning $60 pots by using Savannah left me feeling hollow. I knew the poker room could fill that void. Larger pots excited me, and I chased that feeling. I wanted it. Needed it. I now know how drug addicts feel.

Savannah made me greedy. But, to be honest, I was always greedy. Savannah just made my chances of actually achieving wealth much greater. It changed me from a nervous small time gambler to a big league cheater. I tried to stay smart about when I could use Savannah and setting myself up by shuffling exactly nine times when it was my turn to deal. I used the same routine I had practiced countless times before. The only change was the location. I set up the move for hours before I actually saw the opening to use it.

I made two small adaptations for Friday night.

The first was that I started to wear sunglasses whenever I played poker. They were the large reflective aviator type. For $25, I bought myself a shield from the other player's eyes. My quick glances toward the deck were hidden as long as I didn't angle my head down when I snuck a peek. That was the hardest habit to break. It took me hours in front of the camera to finally train my head to be still.

The second change was the amount of money I brought to gamble. My usual amount was no more than twenty percent of my bank roll. But since I was in the big leagues, I had to bring my entire bank roll. My $40,000 of life savings and earnings were changed into four unimpressive stacks of poker chips that fit neatly into one carrying tray. In one hand, I held everything I had worked for. The white, blue, green, and red chips made me feel more nervous than ever. My mind raced through "what if..." questions. Everything was on the line, including the lives of my loved ones.

As Friday night wore on, the pit bosses became tired, less attentive overseers. When they took their scheduled breaks at 2 a.m., I decided the time was right. I was the next to deal and our pit boss was facing our table. That was perfect because as the deal finally came to me, he turned his attention toward the other table.

I knew Savannah would work. It had to. I had practiced it obsessively. The previous hand at my table was a big one. The player across from me just won over

$10,000 in chips and was very talkative about how he "just knew" his cards were winners. Meticulously stacking his chips, he continued to discuss his clairvoyance with the losing player and grabbed the table's attention. *Thanks buddy. Keep talking.*

He jabbered on about how he had never had this much money in his life. The loudmouth even went as far as to count out his $60,000 in chips to everyone. *Perfect. Thanks for becoming my target.*

My hands moved effortlessly as I shuffled the cards nine times. I stroked the ego of the winning player and congratulated him on his good fortune. *Poor guy.* He didn't have a clue what was coming.

The table was tired of his nonstop bragging. Who could blame them? The guy was an idiot to boast like that. I shuffled for the seventh time and noticed that with two more shuffles, I could give him a pocket pair of Queens and myself a pocket pair of Aces. He had enough chips. I didn't feel bad about taking his. He could afford to lose the peak of his mountain of chips. Savannah has no feelings. Greed knows no emotion.

On Friday nights, the Texas Hold 'Em game had a $200 minimum bet. The small blind puts in $100. The large blind puts in $200. There was already $300 in the pot as I dealt out the cards.

The braggart received his cards, took a glance, and put his hood up, indicating he was going to play his cards. This reaction was met by a groan from the rest of the table. He pulled the strings on his gray hooded sweatshirt. He buried his forearms into the padded edge of the table and stroked his nearest stack of hundred dollar chips. Ignoring the heckling from the players at the table, he raised $900 into the pot.

A player at the table said loud enough for the entire table to hear, "He's bluffing."

He figured the braggart was exaggerating on his good fortune and trying to steal the $300 in the pot. The other players must have agreed with him. The two players seated next to him quickly called his $900 bet. As it often happens at poker tables, the egos of players took over. Either the two players wanted to exact some revenge upon the braggart or they had become bored while he won hand after hand.

Scanning back into my memory, I pictured the cards I had given the other two players. The first had a King-seven. The second had a Jack-ten. Those hands are slightly above average. To call a $900 raise, which is three times the size of the pot, with those cards didn't make much sense. The player representing the large blind also called the braggart's "bluff" by putting his additional $600 in. I was happy to jump on the band wagon of players who called. It appeared that I was just another player who was betting on the bluffing braggart. In total, there were five players at this table who called the braggart's raise. A $4,600 pot before the flop had even been turned over.

SAVANNAH

Maximizing my profits, on the sole hand where I used Savannah, was my main goal the entire week leading up to Friday night. I had planned on targeting the player with the largest chip stack, but never had dreamed that other players would dump their money in too. The poker gods were smiling on me. On the inside, I was smiling back.

The flop came three-nine-seven of all different suits. The guy next to the braggart had hit a pair of sevens, making three of us likely to stay in. The man that represented the large blind hesitatingly checked his bet to the braggart. It was pretty clear that the large blind didn't pair the flop and didn't want to waste away more of his chips on this hand. That or he wanted to see what the braggart was going to do.

Without moving an inch of his body when the flop was shown, the braggart threw out $1800, doubling his previous bet. He swiftly pounded the stack of chips in the center of the table, showing confidence in his bet.

The man with the Jack-ten folded. The man with the King-seven called, leaving me to decide what to do next.

The big blind was certain to fold his Queen-ten, so I thought about maximizing my profit. All week I was going to use the strategy of sitting back, waiting until the final bet to raise and lay down a large bet. However, now that I had another fish on the hook, I decided that stringing these fish along might not be the best strategy. I didn't want to lose Savannah's hand two weeks in a row to another long shot bad beat. *Bet it big and take the win. If they fold, you still get a decent pot.*

There were two cards left to be flipped over. If one of them was a king, then the King-seven would have two pair, beating my aces. I couldn't risk that. The pot was up to $8,100 and I was happy to win that amount. I called the braggart's bet and threw in an additional $20,000 in red chips.

When you make a $20,000 raise, it doesn't go unnoticed. You can't hide. Mountains of chips in the center of the table demand attention. Pit bosses focus their attention solely on the action. Other players quickly perk up. They study the reactions of the other players involved. Adrenaline starts to pump. Heart rates spike. The players in the hand have to ask many questions. Do I fold this hand? Or should I man up?

The braggart didn't hesitate for more than a few seconds. His eyes were fixed on me from inside his hood. He started counting out $1,000 chips. With one hand, he pulled the pair of strings attached to the sweatshirt even tighter, making the opening no bigger than the size of a golf ball. With the other, he slid a stack of twenty red chips next to the growing mountain on the table.

The player next to him, who had paired the sevens, thought long and hard about his decision. He ran his fingers through his greasy black hair and rested his forehead in his palms. He appeared to have fallen asleep. He didn't move for what seemed an eternity. As he closed his eyes and bit the tip of his tongue, he pushed his cards away, indicating that he was folding. He slowly stood and stared at the multi-colored mountain that he had given up. For the remainder of the hand, he held his breath from behind his chair.

Me. The braggart. No one else was left. My hands slid to the deck. I flipped a Jack of Spades, showing the turn.

My eyes weren't privy to the secrecy inside his hood. I couldn't read his thoughts, but I sensed that he was smiling at the Jack. His pair of Queens was still better than any pair anyone could make using the community cards. He had no reason to worry. There wasn't a straight possibility nor was there a flush chance. Being the first to act, the braggart deliberated on his next move. His hands rested on the edge of the padded table in a calm, relaxed, folded position. He slowly lifted his hand and lightly tapped the felt on the table twice with his middle finger. He checked his bet.

The chips left in front of me totaled exactly $19,500. My stomach was a churning whirlpool. Everyone in the entire poker room was watching me. I couldn't help but smile. I pushed my entire bankroll into the middle.

I said whispering, "I'm all-in."

That was it. Those were all my chips, all my money. I didn't have any more. Not with me at the poker room or in my house. I had just pushed two years of savings into the middle of a game. A game of chance, nonetheless. It was, albeit, a game that I had rigged to give me a huge advantage, but still, there was one Queen loose in the deck. For all I knew, she was going to come and show her face on the river card.

The braggart had more than enough money to call my "all-in" bet. He reached for his tightened hoodie and pulled apart the opening to reveal a smiling face. A huge, arrogant smile. One that made you want to hate him even more than just for being a braggart.

He counted out his chips, tipping over the tall stack into the waiting mass. The move was a gesture of over-confidence. Splashing the pot, as it's called, doesn't make friends. Just the opposite. It shows up the other players, which is a bad idea in a group of alpha males all vying for the top spot.

He took hold of his Queens, turned them over, and slammed them down. He lifted his sunglasses. His brown, smug eyes shattered when I turned over both of my Aces. I gingerly flicked them on top of his two cards. On the outside, I was stoic. I wasn't going to be like him. *Stay humble.* Inside, my stomach was doing somersaults. One remaining Queen was still out there.

All of my worries were extinguished when another Jack came on the river. The braggart collapsed into his seat, sulking over his massive loss. He still had more chips than when he arrived earlier that night, but I had stolen most of his money.

I didn't organize the chips into neat stacks. I didn't brag about how lucky I had been. I didn't make everyone at the table hate me. Instead, I held my emotions in check, showing respect to the braggart, to the game. I was beside myself with this feeling of confidence and pride. But I kept it all in check. I didn't react at all.

Savannah worked, and I planned on using it again. But pit bosses are renowned for having long memories.

I had to be cool.

I needed to stay calm.

Next week, Savannah might bring me another large payday. My mind fast-forwarded through a scenario. I envisioned a pit boss becoming suspicious after recalling me acting arrogant and loud. I needed to do my best to erase any memory of me winning. *No extra attention.*

I played the rest of the hands that night following my routines. I showed little emotion toward anything. I shuffled exactly nine times every deal. I kept my poor posture. I barely spoke. An hour and a half later, I cashed in my poker chips with the cashier.

When I arrived at the poker room, I carried one full tray of chips. As I walked to the cashier, I needed three.

That night, I left with $89,000 stuffed into every pocket. I shook hands with the pit bosses in my usual, respectful manner and made for the exit. Walking to my car, I couldn't help but smile. The weight of the cash was impressive. Even in hundred dollar bills, the cash felt as though I was carrying my old Crown Royal sack of loose change.

Chapter 10
Money Changes People

Excerpt from Michael's Journal

The next morning I woke up and for the first time in my life, I felt good. I mean really good. Not just happy or excited. I mean everything felt good. I was proud of myself.

I never once heard the words, "I'm proud of you." Never. There was never a teacher who told me I did a good job or that they liked my work. Not once. How could they? I was barely surviving at home, let alone thriving in a classroom. Most teachers were probably happy just to move me on to the next grade. Once I overheard my teacher on the classroom phone saying, "I'm just happy to start over with a new group of students next year." I remember the feeling I had when I heard that. That was the exact opposite of how I felt that morning.

Laying in perfectly leveled stacks, on my cheap wooden night side table, were eight hundred and ninety-one hundred-dollar bills. $89,000. I made four stacks of two hundred bills, then another of ninety.

When I woke up, I recounted all of them. I never took so much pleasure from recounting my money. Holding each bill in my hand and feeling the coarseness, a tidal wave of pride surged over me.

I don't ever recall sitting so straight or carrying my head as high as I did that day. But there, on my night table that I bought for $6 from a garage sale, laid more money than I had ever seen, let alone ever owned.

I was thinking clearly and strategically. The money hadn't gotten to me yet. The greed hadn't consumed me. Yet.

SAVANNAH

After I counted the money for the third time, I sat on my mattress, with its mismatched box spring underneath and thought about what I was going to do with it. Not necessarily what I was going to spend the money on, but really, what I was going to do with that amount of money.

I had never planned on having that kind of cash. Building up my bankroll for the poker room was one thing, because it had a purpose. I wanted to keep a solid bankroll of $50,000. The remaining $39,000 left me with a smile smeared across my face. In a single night, I had increased my bankroll by $10,000 and still had $39,000 to do whatever I wanted. I couldn't stop smiling. Life was perfect.

After a quick, hot shower, I sat down at my desktop computer. I wondered if I could simply put the cash in the bank. My Internet search brought me to a news article about banking deposit regulations. The police were alerted to low level drug dealers because they were depositing tens of thousands of dollars into their savings account every month. The article stated that banks in Canada were required to report all deposits made over $10,000. I also found another website that told me any patterns of large deposits were mandatory for banking officials to report.

That sparked a chain reaction of thoughts. There were thoughts popping up in my head that I had never even considered. Ideas came to me about taxes and banking abnormalities. If I suddenly started showing a pattern of spending large sums of money, was a police agency going to start asking questions? Could I go to jail for winning? What was I going to do with my cash? How was I going to take care of it?

I knew the poker room was technically illegal. In my eyes it was the same as a casino. I never considered what to do with Savannah's winnings.

Another Internet search into the *Canadian Revenue Agency* showed me that, like the American version of the IRS, the CRA takes tax fraud extremely seriously. Their website appeared user friendly and fairly non-threatening to the normal visitor. But to me, I was instantly terrified.

I didn't need, or want, the government asking me any questions. I figured that putting an odd figured deposit once into my account wouldn't raise too many suspicions. I thought that $7,894 was the amount I would deposit. I came up with that number off the top of my head and could always claim that I consolidated other savings accounts to one account, if asked. As I researched more about *banking protocols for reporting large deposits*, I learned that suspicious transactions are also reported. This concerned me.

My bank accounts were a mess, much like my life. I frequently was overdrawn in my checking account and never had more than a few hundred dollars to my name at any one time. Had some hyper-vigilant bank manager over-stepped their reporting duties, my banking history would have been a prime candidate for review. That would certainly lead to a phone call to the CRA with follow-up questions that

I couldn't possibly answer honestly. I wasn't about to take that chance. Banks were out of the question.

While sitting at my computer researching what to do, I rebooted and restarted four separate times. My frustration level peaked. It was time that I had a computer that was not someone else's hand-me-down. I grabbed six $100 bills from each stack and carefully folded the wad into my jeans pocket. It felt great. As I dressed for my shopping trip, I remember thinking that a new laptop was going to be the only treat I would buy for myself.

Smiling in the rearview mirror and puffing out my chest, I sat in the driver's seat of my cherry red 1986 Honda CRX. To be honest, the color wasn't exactly cherry red. It was more rust colored than anything else, but it did have some original paint left on the front paneling. It wasn't anything more than rusted metal held together by extensive amounts of duct tape and luck. As good as I felt, the car slammed me back to the reality of my shitty life.

The interior door paneling rattled loose every time I eased the door closed. Every time I had to shove it back into place. Unless I rested my left knee against it, holding it into place, it would constantly vibrate. The cracked exhaust pipe caused the car to roar down the road, making pedestrians and other drivers stare. A haze of blue smoke billowed out as I accelerated. To add to my car's unimpressiveness, the radio didn't work. A small boom box sat on top of the passenger seat, but only received nearby radio stations. To make matters even more embarrassing, the tape player was broken.

A new Best Buy store had opened near my house. It featured thousands of products to choose from, all of which used to be completely out of my price-range. Things had changed. I entered and found the large *COMPUTERS* sign written in bold letters hanging near the back of the store.

Starting when I was young, I always noticed things that other people overlooked. Things like the security cameras attached to the ceiling, the arrangement of workers in particular sections, and security stickers. I always paid special attention to those features. Every store; no matter which one. As I became more aware of each store's level of security and the intricacies of theft prevention, I created realistic scenarios of how I would steal different items. Never having the courage to bring my ideas into reality, I didn't do more than hypothesize.

Most stores do an effective job of hiding their security from their customer's attention. By concealing their cameras in the paneling on the ceiling, a more welcoming atmosphere for customers is created. Best Buy made no such attempt to hide their cameras. Rather, they chose an open concept feel to their new store with high ceilings and low cameras covered by dark brown globes.

Every purchase I ever made was a personal battle of want versus need. Before I ever bought anything, I often struggled whether spending the little cash I had was worth it. Usually I would forgo the purchase because I simply couldn't justify it. The practical side of me consistently won. For a short period before Savannah came along, every one of my credit cards had been maxed out. With almost no cash to my name, the dollar store's vast inventory of instant dry noodles saved me from starvation. Three packages for one dollar offered what I had called "dinner" on many evenings.

This time was different. This time I had money in my pocket. There was going to be a systematic approach for me to pay off those credit cards. *Nice and easy, Michael.* This time I wasn't going to struggle. This shopping experience was going to be fun and stress free. I was going to buy a new laptop without regard for the additional costs of extended battery life, a wireless mouse, or a warranty.

~~~~~~~~~

Sitting here with this journal in my lap and pencil in my hand, I realize something. That was it. That's the exact moment where I can honestly say, that was where everything went downhill. That was the beginning of the end for me. Money really does change a person. I never planned what I would do if I won a ton of money from the poker room.

I focused on how to get the money, not what I would do once I had it. This was the one oversight that would eventually lead to my downfall.

CHAPTER 11

MY RETURN TO THE POKER GAME

Excerpt from Michael's Journal

Using the braggart's money, I carried the laptop out of the store, adding to the euphoria. The cheap, yellow plastic bag held my receipt and wireless mouse. But in my other hand, I openly flaunted my new laptop to everyone. It felt like I was holding success.

My euphoria came to an abrupt end. My trusty Honda let me down in Best Buy's parking lot. A dead car battery. Or maybe an alternator. It didn't matter. I had to walk home. With the key in the ignition and my forehead on the steering wheel, I decided to never again deal with the embarrassment of that jalopy. Massive amounts of cash can help you forget about mundane worries such as car troubles. Before leaving the car, I took a deep breath. *Just buy another one.*

The walk home probably would have lasted me a solid half an hour, but stopping at a used car dealership delayed my return. There weren't waxed bodied cars parked on the curb with their hoods popped open. Nor were there balloons and promotion signs about *end of the month deals not to be missed*. No blow up gorillas. But there was something. It caught my eye and drew me across the six lane street.

Growing up, my favorite TV show was *The Dukes of Hazzard*. The main characters drove a Dodge Charger called the General Lee. It was beautiful. The car would jump off of ramps and spin around dirt corners. I used to lie in bed and envision myself sliding across the hood of my own General Lee, like they did in the TV show.

SAVANNAH

I saw it. An orange muscle car sat on the corner of the lot. Every childhood memory flooded back to me. I was ten years old again. As if in a trance, I walked across the major intersection, holding the laptop in one arm and the plastic bag in the other. Cars honked at me. They swerved out of the way. It didn't matter. I was in love.

My mouth never quite closed. The best I could do was to pull my tongue back into my mouth. I stalked in circles around the imitation model of the General Lee. The body work was exactly the same as the original, minus the racing numbers on the doors and the Confederate flag on the roof. Through the windows, the sunlight highlighted the spotless leather upholstery and polished dashboard. Every inch of my body wanted that car, needed that car.

I was an easy target for the salesman by the way I was gawking. He stood next to the rear fender of the car and allowed me to drink in its beauty. And I was thirsty. He was experienced. He stood in silence for awhile. Three minutes. Maybe more. He let me fall deeper and deeper in love.

He knew the car had me. After test driving it, I knew it too. *I'll pay asking price, no wait. I'll pay whatever you want.*

The small detail of actually purchasing the car was remedied by a quick pit stop home during the test drive. The salesman waited in the car. I depleted the size of my five towering stacks. I dumped out the wireless mouse and receipt onto my unmade bed. The shopping bag was empty. I filled it with $35,000, wrapped in several rubber bands.

I had found the car of my dreams. I cut through the haggling process by roughly slamming the bundle of cash on the salesman's cluttered desk.

"Paper trails make me nervous," I said.

He stared at the bundle of cash.

"I'm certain we can work something out to your liking," the salesman said.

With a handshake, I left the sales office carrying the keys to the car of my dreams.

~~~~~~~~~

Spending money was a rush. In a single morning, I spent nearly $37,000 and had never felt any sensation as glorious as spending someone else's hard earned cash. Buying the laptop was good. Buying my dream car was intoxicating. I wanted it again. And again.

When I returned home, I sat down on my bed, again, and counted my money. Steady sum of $50,000 for my bankroll, check. I wanted to make sure that if I had a hand where Savannah could give me a huge pot I would win more. The more money I brought, the more Savannah could win me, within reason. My goal was to go one-on-one with a big stack. Savannah gave me the best odds against one player.

78

If I only brought with me $25G's, then, conceivably, the most I could win was about the same amount. Winning $25G's sounds great, but bringing $50G's would win me twice as much.

I had a little over a thousand dollars left. Instead of spending it right away, I made a list of things I wanted to improve immediately. Money can't buy you happiness, they say. What do they know? It certainly made my life better.

Using my new laptop, I listed the things that I wanted to purchase with next Friday's winnings. I knew I couldn't save the money in the bank, so I might as well spend it.

Better furniture. Living with the furniture I had was fine when I didn't have any money, but now, I suddenly envisioned beautiful leather couches and end tables to go along. Looking around my under-furnished living room, it hit me that a visit to the furniture store was overdue. I also wanted a bedroom set. There was nothing worse for me than waking up next to mounds of cash and lacking a dresser for clean clothes. First things first, I needed to get rid of the plastic milk crates that housed my clean clothes.

A flat screen TV. A 27" box TV, with the remote that didn't work, was ridiculous and embarrassing and well, just plain awful. I picked it up at the same garage sale where I bought my bedroom night table and I think the former owner felt bad about selling it to me. He gave it to me for only $10. Carrying the TV was a challenge. It wasn't just heavy. It was bulky and awkward. I realized why the owner had given it to me so cheap, he didn't want to carry it back into the house. A new flat screen would fit my new lifestyle much better.

Nicer clothes. The clothes I had weren't bad. They were clean and without holes, but they certainly weren't nice by any stretch of the imagination. My typical outfit was a pair of jeans, a T-shirt, and running shoes. I was comfortable. As I drove home from the dealership the first day with the Charger, I saw the reaction of a gorgeous woman I pulled up to at a red light. She was driving a new sparkling silver Chevy Cobalt. She must have just come from the car wash because I can still recall the shine on the hood of her car.

As I pulled up, evening my window to her, her face changed from a sly smile to a slight grimace, as if she had smelled something bad. She stared forward for the remainder of the red light. I am not a very good looking man, but I am by no means ugly. My hair was cut and combed. My face was washed and shaven. I knew right there, if I was going to drive a nice car, then I had to start to dress the part.

Accessories. My watch was a simple Timex, one I had won in a garage poker game. It was the first time Savannah had won me a hand that didn't just include cash. The watch worked well and its digital display was accurate, but as I began wearing more expensive clothes, it stuck out. And not in that ironic, conversational way. I needed something more trendy and fashionable than the small plastic piece of crap.

SAVANNAH

I had already started assigning the money that Savannah was going to bring in. *Good future planning.*

The rest of the week was divided between practicing Savannah, driving my own General Lee, and researching the items I was going to buy. I wore out a couple more decks of cards practicing Savannah and honing my skills. I was better than I had ever been. The video camera revealed nothing when I dealt. My sunglasses hid my only movement, a quick glance at the deck.

Driving the General Lee into the carpet distributor's parking lot brought more attention than I was comfortable with. The previous week I arrived in a dilapidated old jalopy. Roaring into the parking lot, I inadvertently received a lot of sneers my way. Looks that scream, "You think you're better than me?" and "Look at Mr. Big Shot all of the sudden."

It was the exact opposite of what I needed. It wasn't one of my more thought out plans.

That night, the poker room was as busy as the previous week. The same pit bosses manned their stations. I cautiously made my way in with $25,000 in both front pockets. Turning them into chips and taking my seat, each player at the table was new to me. I hadn't seen them before, but I've seen their types a hundred times. Their eyes were filled with the hope of winning. Their bodies had spent too many hours at a poker table gambling away their life. I wondered which one would be my victim.

At 10 p.m., I knew I had to wait for about four more hours to use Savannah. Two in the morning was the sweet-spot. Until then, I wanted to find the target, establish my routine with the other players, and feel out the table.

The table had five other players. Three were talkative and friendly. One focused so much on his cell phone that I wasn't even sure how much attention he was paying to the game. The lone other player became my target.

He was a twenty-year-old white kid who was well dressed and was extremely serious. I believe the correct term is a "shark." His blue Lacoste dress shirt, with the little green alligator above his heart, screamed of success. In the four hours leading up to Savannah, he spoke exactly three words, mainly grunting responses. He wore ear buds, attached to a long white cord, connected to his iPhone. Over the dull roar of the poker room, I heard his endless playlist featuring blaring dance music.

I was envious of his upper-class upbringing. And he was a very skilled player whose chips steadily increased each hour. He went from about $20,000 in chips at 10 p.m., to double by midnight, and double again by 1 a.m. He and one of the talkative players at the table were engaged in a large pot around 1:30 a.m. in which "iPhone listener" turned over his cards and revealed three of a kind. The other player's two pair wasn't enough to beat him and ultimately ended his night. With about $55,000 in that pot, "iPhone listener" created huge, towering stacks of chips that dwarfed everyone else's at our table.

SAVANNAH

I estimated that he easily had over $100,000 in front of him and expected him to cash out sooner, rather than later. He seemed like that type of kid: once he got what he wanted, he'd take his ball and go home. He had a mountain in front of him and I impatiently waited for my turn to deal. As I organized the cards in my hands, "iPhone listener" stood up and acted as though he was leaving. He sat back down, calming my frayed nerves. He just stretched his legs and sat down and skipped forward to the next techno song.

Savannah came naturally. I ordered the cards exactly the way I wanted them. The previous Friday, I had given myself a higher pocket pair than my target. *Why fix what isn't broken?*, I thought to myself.

With well over $100,000 in chips, "iPhone listener" was sure to call a reasonable raise to the pot with the pair of Jacks I dealt him. He was in the big blind. He would be the last player to bet before the flop of cards was displayed.

The rest of the players received odd combinations of cards and folded. I wanted the "iPhone listener" all to myself. The week before, other players called the initial betting and raising, which added to my winnings. I didn't want more players in on Savannah's hand. The more players in on the hand, the better the chance of a fluke appearing. Not this time. This week, Savannah made sure there were only two players in the hand; "iPhone listener" with a pair of Jacks and me with a pocket pair of Aces. I had huge odds over him to win the hand.

His Jacks were good enough to call a raise of three times the large blind. I knew that, so I opened with a raise of $1500. The man who represented the small blind, on my immediate left, took his time before sliding his cards into the middle of the table, folding his hand. I knew he had a two-ten. His slow fold told me he wanted to appear as though he liked the hand, but made a tough, calculated decision. His $250 small blind and "iPhone listeners" $500 large blind were the only other chips on the table, before I added my raise.

As soon as the small blind's cards were past the yellow fold line, "iPhone listener" reached for a tower of chips and slid a re-raise of $7000 into the pot. I hadn't expected that. A re-raise never crossed my mind. I hoped for a call of my raise. The excitement grew inside me. Savannah had brought me another pot that was sure to be large.

After he had added his $8500, I slowly, cautiously reached toward my chips. A massive win was in my grasp. I had to be wise here. I knew I had my fish on the line. Too large of a bet could scare him off, I thought. Maximize your winnings, and stay in character.

My poor posture and grimacing facial expression were my tactics to show my lack of confidence. I wanted to keep the "iPhone listener" off balance. My betting and my body language were polar opposites. I came over the top with another $10,000, after calling his $7000 bet. I gently added $17,000 to the pot.

Savannah

He waited all of three seconds before he decided that he was just going to call my bet. He buried his right thumb into his curled fist and laid a gold chip there. With arrogance, only found in the extremely wealthy, he flicked his thumb and shot the coin, end over end, into the air, landing it in the middle of the table.

Gold chips were the largest chips the poker room used. At $10,000 each, they weren't common. In fact, I had only seen one once before at another table across the room. This was my first chance at holding and owning one. The "iPhone listener" was confident, just the way I liked it.

The flop came as a mess of nothing for either of us. An eight of Spades, a ten, and five of Hearts. Being first to act, "iPhone listener" felt even more confident that his pocket pair of Jacks was higher than any pair that could be made from the flop. The pot of chips was over $37,000 and he opened the next round of betting with another gold chip.

I felt something move inside me. First it started with my left foot twitching. Then my right leg trembled. A sensation of energy came over me, as if I had touched a live electrical wire. As the feeling made its way through my chest and arms, all my self-control disappeared. My eyes blinked behind my sunglasses. I moved them around, side to side. I still controlled them. My ears were hot. I couldn't hear anything. It felt like ear plugs were jammed into their openings.

My arms acted as though something else controlled them. My lips announced, "I'm all-in." Pushing all my chips into the middle of the pot was not part of my plan. I needed to string him along more. I needed more of his money.

"iPhone listener" eventually folded his hand, without entering more money. I had won $47,750. I had pushed too hard. I could have taken more, much more from him. The curious size of my raise scared him into thinking that I had something better than his pair of Jacks.

I walked out of the poker room shaking my head. Again, my pockets were stuffed with gobs of cash, but I had missed so much more. I laid my head on my pillow after I counted Savannah's winnings. $68,375.

I profited $18,375 that night and was very pleased. However, something worried me that prevented me from falling right to sleep. I had felt *IT*. I didn't know what to call *IT*. The sensation, the feeling, the warmth, the energy, whatever it was had lost me a lot of money and I couldn't explain why I had been so greedy.

Lying in bed, my eyes shot wide open and I sat up. The uncontrollable force, the "*IT*", was my greediness. Greed. Uncontrollable greed. It was a demon that took control of my body, my actions, and my mind. I had no idea such a force lurked inside me. I was worried. Though, I wasn't sure what exactly I was worried about.

That was the first, but not last, time I met *IT*.

CHAPTER 12
MELANIE

Excerpt from Michael's Journal

I didn't think or worry anymore about *IT* the next morning. I woke up excited to cross some items off of my shopping list. As I dressed, my full length mirror informed me that the first priority was to buy some nicer clothes. I wasn't going to be embarrassed at a red light over my clothes ever again.

Breakfast was a rushed bowl of generic cereal, supposedly imitating the delicious taste of frosted flakes. Wasn't buying them again. More changes needed to be made. The food I ate and my general diet needed a makeover. Eating like a college frat boy was fine for me when I had struggled to pay my bills. But with Savannah bringing in more cash, I started buying more nutritious food.

The mall had always been something of a mystery to me. I had been inside before, but never to actually buy anything. In my teenage years, my friends would hang around outside of the mall and skateboard. We used the curbs of the entrance ways, which irritated the security guards. They were constantly on the lookout for us and repeatedly had to chase us off.

They would drive their SUV security truck where we were hanging out. With fake police lights flashing on top of their trucks, two guards would park directly on top of the curb we were grinding on. They would open their door slowly, wearing fake police uniforms and bullet proof vests and shout at us about trespassing. We'd leave, every time. But we'd always return.

SAVANNAH

This time, I returned with $6000 in cash and a plan to transform my wardrobe. As I passed the next generation of skateboarders outside the mall, I smiled.

"Don't let those rent-a-cops scare you off. Stand up for yourself."

They stood, staring at me. It was advice I wish someone would have given to me.

The mall was extremely forgettable. I bought a lot of the trendy jeans, button down shirts, designer T-shirts with fancy graphics, and a few pairs of shoes.

Two parts stuck out about that day. The first was purchasing my first suit. The salesman, Ralph, carried a tape measure around his neck like a sash. His feet and hands moved like the wind as he measured me on a small, elevated podium. In forty-five minutes, he paid more attention to me than anyone I had ever met. Maybe it was the half dozen bags I carried into the store or the five percent commission. Either way, he made sure I looked good, right down to the cufflinks.

I bought two suits. Ralph suggested a dark gray traditional three button suit and after some discussion, I selected a more casual jacket, with matching pants. It was a natural linen blazer with notched lapels and a bright blue shirt to contrast underneath the jacket. Ralph demanded that I wore the shirt and blazer home that day.

Ralph said with a heavy lisp and English accent, "No, Michael. I insist you wear this outfit home. You look absolutely darling."

It sounds corny writing it, but I left like a new person. I felt confident and established. Most of all, I liked how I felt. I thought back to the woman at the red light who snarled at me. I would have loved to be able to go back and see her reaction, had I been wearing that outfit.

As I situated my shirt and jacket just right, I caught sight of the Timex watch I had on my left wrist. I slipped it off and pocketed it. The thick wad of money that previously bulged in my pocket had diminished to a measly $900, wrapped next to a $20 Timex.

Ralph, also, noticed my Timex. Looking down at my wrist, he shook his head.

Ralph said, "No self-respecting man shops for a watch in the mall. A man of your taste should drive eight minutes up the road to an elegant little jewelry store, called Marshall's Jewelers."

He waved his hand like he was swatting flies.

"You sure? It's kind of out of the way," I said.

"I'm telling you, their selection will provide you with something much more fitting," Ralph said.

Ralph wouldn't let me leave until he hugged me, and smoothed any wrinkles he may have made across my chest.

Marshall's Jewelers was the other part of the day that stuck out. The ornate design in the store's front added to its sense of opulence. The store's interior was ablaze with lighting that focused your eyes on their display cases. Their walls sparkled with mirrored art pieces that made the small display room feel much larger.

That's when I met Melanie. I was standing near the watch display case. The vast selection of high end time pieces captivated my attention. Rolex, Cartier, Panerai, Tag Heuer, and Omega. I was alone in my own fantasy world of watches. Owning one of these watches used to be one of my dreams.

I felt much more attractive than I had with any other woman before. My blazer and shirt lifted my confidence to a whole new level. She walked over.

"I'm Melanie. Are you looking for a watch today?" the saleswoman said with a soft, smooth voice.

The sexiness in her delivery sent shockwaves through me.

"I am. Nice to meet you Melanie." I stared directly into her eyes the entire time. "I'm Michael and yes, I'm looking for a watch for myself."

"Okay. May I ask how much are you looking to spend?" Melanie said.

"I'd like to get something nice. Something under a grand, I need to wear it every day."

My budget was actually $900. But my response elicited a smirk from her mouth.

"Great. Let's get started with some of these," Melanie said.

She motioned me away from the Rolex and Cartier watches. She opened and held out different watches for me to try on. As I passed my hand through the opening, her delicate fingers caressed my hands ever so slightly, every time. The air was electric. Her eyes told me she was interested. Her hands told me more.

She guided me toward a new brand of Russian watches that had just broken into the Canadian market.

"None of your friends will have a watch made by Soyuz. Their line of eight different watches featured similar characteristics of the other major competitors. Soyuz watches are made by the company that used to be involved in the Russian space program. When that wasn't profitable anymore, they branched out, creating exquisite time pieces," Melanie said.

Her elongation of "exquisite" held my attention. "I really like the look of the 'Great Spy' model."

I tried not to sound as though this was my first time watch shopping. The sapphire glass casing and alligator strap screamed expensive. Once on my wrist, I had to own it. "No need to look any further. This is the one."

Four hours, one shopping trip, and $6000 later I felt as transformed as anyone could in my situation. I had a car that fulfilled my childhood dream, clothes that made my confidence explode, and the nicest watch that has ever sat on my wrist. Not a bad day, but I wanted more.

SAVANNAH

I handed over the nine hundred dollars to Melanie and waited for my receipt while staring at my new purchase. I kept letting my arm relax at my side, hiding the "Great Spy" under my shirt sleeve. Then I would raise my wrist to tell the time. Each time I did this, its beauty stunned me, demanding I gaze into it again.

Melanie returned with my receipt and a seductive smile. She placed the receipt on the spotless glass top counter and slid it across toward me. Instead of letting go of the receipt with a pleasant "thank you," she held her hand there until our hands touched, again.

She didn't pull back her hand. Her eyes gave me the sexiest look I had ever seen.

"It was very nice to meet you Michael. I hope to hear from you again, very soon," Melanie said.

Her eyes darted toward the receipt and back up to hold my gaze. I raised the receipt and found her hidden clue. Her phone number, with her name written in red pen across the top. *Holy crap, the suit really did work.*

"That's for you. In case you're wondering, the answer is no, I've never given my number away to a customer," Melanie whispered.

"Don't get me wrong, I'm flattered. But, why me?"

"There's something about you. I can tell. We have this sort of connection. Do you believe in fate?" she said.

"Ask me that question last week and I would have laughed. Today, well, I would at least entertain the possibility."

Before leaving, I smiled. *Think of something smooth to say.*

"Thank you, Melanie, for your help. You can be sure that you'll be hearing from me soon."

Did that just happen? Since when do I get attention from hot chicks? I had no idea what I was doing. I hadn't dated in a long time. I focused all of my time and energy on poker and Savannah. I saw some women socially, but I didn't date any of them. I wasn't even sure what to actually do with Melanie's phone number. She was good looking and obviously was interested in me, but when I got home I stared at the watch receipt for the better part of an hour trying to decide what to do.

I had no idea how to proceed. Do I call her right away? Do I wait, like they do in the movies, a couple of days before calling? I Google searched for advice. I typed "appropriate dating practices" and learned that I should wait at least a day before calling her, maybe even two. The webpage went on to say that I should act "uninterested" when I called her because that would make her even more interested in me.

This confused me. A lot. *How long have I been out of the game that I can't act like myself? Is my personality that bad that I need to act different in order for Melanie to like me?*

I clicked on a different webpage, which was clearly written by a woman. Her picture was at the top of the webpage. Her writing was angled toward men who were recently divorced and starting to date again. A lot of her tips made sense to me and were well written.

The best tip I found was number three. I remember this one because as soon as I read the tip, I picked up my phone and dialed the number Melanie had written in red ink.

Tip #3: Women hate when men play games. Be yourself and act respectful and women will be more interested in you.

The phone rang only once before going to voice mail. Shaking my head, I realized she was probably still at work, with her phone turned off. I listened to her soft, delicate voice asking to leave a message. I suddenly became very nervous because I hadn't thought out what I was going to say. If she had answered, I was simply going to ask her out for a drink that night. No playing games, right? That's what the website said to do.

As her message ended, I scrambled for words. What came out was something direct and to the point.

"Hey Melanie. This is Michael from earlier today. I was wondering if you would be interested in going out for a drink when your shift ends? Call me back when you're free and we'll go from there."

Quick. Neat. To the point. *Just like the website instructed.*

As I hung up the phone, I smiled at how ridiculous I had sounded. I tossed the phone onto my torn-up, old couch. *You're an idiot, Michael. But that just might work for her.*

I organized my new clothes in my closet, throwing away most of my less fashionable wardrobe. I had my very own fashion show in front of my full length mirror. My dark boot cut Gap jeans, lime green Polo golf shirt, and casual dark brown Steve Madden loafers were perfect for a first date, if she called back. Then the phone rang.

I hadn't reconnected the caller ID on my account. About a year ago, I noticed I was paying $12 a month for a feature I couldn't afford. How could I justify eating $.33 instant noodles for dinner, but paying $12 a month for a phone feature? It didn't make a whole lot of sense.

"Hello?"

"Michael. Oh hey, it's Melanie."

"Hey, how's it going?"

"Good. I only have a couple minutes to talk because I'm on a short break, but yeah, I'd love to go for a drink with you. I get off at nine."

"Okay, sounds great. You okay with Rizzo's? I've never been there, but I heard it's nice."

"Perfect. I'll see you there around quarter after nine," Melanie said.

Her voice was so silky and confident. I was mesmerized by every word.

My perfect first date outfit and new Soyuz watch had me feeling like a millionaire as I walked into Rizzo's restaurant. It was dimly lit, featuring a massive mahogany bar wrapped around half of the seating area. I headed to the bar and pulled out a giant cushioned bar stool that left my feet dangling. A female bartender asked me what she could get me, while wiping a large wine glass with a white cloth.

As promised, Melanie arrived at 9:15, wearing the same outfit from earlier. She smiled and waved as she made her way over. After settling on the giant stool, she spun toward me and continued flirting with me as she had in Marshall's Jewelers.

She wore a black sundress hidden underneath a sky blue cardigan. Her auburn hair, with blonde highlights, was pulled into a simple ponytail. A few wispy bangs dangled around the outside of her eyes. After a few minutes, she removed her cardigan, showing perfectly tanned shoulders.

She wore only one piece of jewelry, an expensive watch I hadn't recognized. Our conversation came to an awkward moment of silence; I broke it.

"Your watch…it's nice. Who makes it?"

"Thanks. A few of my girlfriends bought it for me as a gift for my twenty-fifth birthday last year. Michael Kors makes this watch. I cherish it because it's the nicest gift I've ever received. The girls put a lot of thought into getting it for me."

It was dazzlingly white all over with a solid gold rim around the face. The golden hands on the face of the watch sparkled in the bar's light.

Our first date ended with a gentle kiss in the parking lot. My new watch, outfit, and the way Melanie was into me, made it easy for me to be confident enough to kiss her. The kiss was brief, but electric. We drove our separate ways after I kissed her soft lips. She went back to her place, and I returned home to Savannah, which was constantly on my mind.

An interesting thought popped into my mind as I left Rizzo's. If I hadn't gone clothes shopping that day, taken Ralph's advice and gone to Marshall's Jewelers, worn my new shirt and blazer, and purchased an expensive watch, would Melanie have still given me her phone number?

I laugh at the irony. I'm sitting in a jail cell writing my life story. I can't believe that I actually worried about something as mundane as whether Melanie was only interested in me for my money.

CHAPTER 13

SAVANNAH 2.0

Excerpt from Michael's Journal

After our first date, I wanted to continue to impress Melanie. My place was a dump. The furniture was old and beat up. It was dirty and embarrassing. A new TV, some new furniture, and a thorough cleaning were needed before Melanie could come over. If things progressed and she came over to my place, she would have had a lot of questions. With Savannah's winnings, I started to see everything in a whole new light.

I went out that morning and bought a new TV, a living room set, and called the phone company to reinstall my caller ID. Shopping was fun. I didn't worry about spending like I used to. When I had finished with the salesperson he asked the time tested question of, "Will you be paying for your purchase by credit card today?"

His face dropped when I pulled out a huge wad of cash. Seeing his reaction will never get old.

The last item on my makeover list was getting the caller ID reconnected. The phone company said that it would only take a few minutes for the system to recognize the change. I needed someone to call my house in order to test whether it was working or not. Rarely did I get phone calls. The only times anyone called me was if a charity was looking for a clothing donation or a company was offering to replace my windows.

As soon as I had moved the couch into the optimal viewing position for my new fifty-two inch TV, the phone rang and the caller ID displayed "Melanie

SAVANNAH

Cooper." I was surprised. *Good to see the caller ID works. I must have made quite the impression.*

I pretended I didn't know who it was. *Playing it cool. Mr. Smooth. Nice, Michael.*

"Hello?"

"Michael. Hey, it's Melanie. How are you doing?"

Remembering advice from the website and being myself, "I'm good. I had a great time last night. It was fun."

"Yeah, me too. That's why I'm calling. I really liked how you didn't play any games and had the balls to call me right away, instead of the typical, childish two day waiting period."

"No, that's not me. I don't like to play games. If I like something, I go after it."

I shook my head. *What an idiot. Who says that?*

"I like that about you. Listen, let me return the favor. What are you doing tonight? Want to go out to dinner?"

"I know the perfect place."

I met Melanie at a restaurant called Hot Stones in the heart of downtown Toronto. It was featured in an article I read in the "Food" section of the newspaper. It said, "Hot Stones offers an interesting twist, on the age old method of cooking." I didn't read the entire article. *Never do.*

The restaurant was a swanky new place tucked in between two buildings on a busy downtown street. We sat at the bar enjoying overpriced cocktails while we waited for our table. The metallic bar stools were curvy and contoured to your butt. White painted brick lined the seating area. Behind the bar, massive windows held a breathtaking view of the CN Tower lit up. The waiters wore long, white aprons that nearly scraped the floor as they walked. I could tell Melanie was impressed.

I ordered a New York strip steak. Big mistake. I guess in the literal terms of things, I got a steak. In fact, I was brought a completely raw, cold steak, taken directly from the restaurant's refrigerator and slapped onto a dinner plate. The waiter brought a stainless-steel tray with a square cut, flat stone, which was hot. We were instructed, by the waiter, to cut the steak into strips. Then place the strips onto the hot stone and cook it to your liking. Hence the restaurant's name: Hot Stones.

The experience was unique. Together we cut raw pieces of meat and tried our best to cook it. The meat was rubbery and chewy. The stone was too hot for proper cooking. I paid the outlandishly high bill.

"You want to go somewhere else to eat, because I'm still hungry?" I said.

It was a full-fledged disaster. Laughing about the awful experience, we walked two blocks down the street to a restaurant that I knew would cook the food for me.

We ordered more drinks. While we waited for our second dinner of the evening, Melanie started to ask questions about me. The alcohol had me feeling

90

buzzed. My tongue was much looser than before and I felt connected to Melanie. I wanted to continue impressing her. But, I didn't have anything, aside from my newfound wealth.

"So, what do you do for a living?" Melanie said.

Taking a drink from my $14 glass of pinot noir I said, "Well, uh, I don't exactly have a traditional job."

"So, you're unemployed?"

"Not exactly. I just don't have a job that requires me to regularly go to work," I said shaking my head.

"Are you a drug dealer, Michael?"

"No. I'm not."

"Then how is it that you drive such a nice car and can afford expensive watches? Wait a second. Are you involved in something that is going to get me killed?"

"Look Melanie. I don't do anything that is going to get you killed. I'll tell you, but you have to promise not to laugh at me."

"Laugh at you? No, Michael, I'm not going to laugh at someone as successful as you are."

"Alright, here it goes. I guess you can call me a professional poker player."

"Really? Poker? That first day in Marshall's Jewelry, I had you pegged as a business owner or maybe even a money manager," Melanie said shocked.

"I guess you could call me a money manager of sorts. I just happen to be good at managing my money at a poker table."

"Are you serious Michael? How do you make so much money that you can afford all those things?"

"Well, that's the beauty of the whole thing. Poker is a fickle game of skill and timing and sometimes luck. When I win, I win big. And if I lose, I try to limit the amount of chips I give away. Lately, I've been pretty successful, so that's allowed me to purchase a fancy new watch and a great car."

"Are you that good? How do you win so frequently?"

"Oh yeah, did I forget to tell you? I actually scam all the other players I play by cheating when I shuffle. I give myself good cards and deal them good cards that are just a smidge worse than mine," I said sarcastically.

"Really?"

"No. God no. I'm just playing around. I can't lie to you anymore. I'm actually a small business owner, whose been fortunate." I realized how the alcohol had loosened my tongue.

"I knew it. I have a special sense when it comes to things like that. What kind of business is it?"

"I actually own a few self-serve car washes. You know, the coin operated ones where you wash the car yourself. A few of those."

SAVANNAH

"Wow. Really? That sounds interesting. How do you work it all? And where are they located?"

"I have one in town and a couple more scattered around the outskirts of Toronto. They're not that difficult to run, they just require me to be handy with the equipment and generally maintain them in a working order. Other than that, I sit back and rake in the big dough. One quarter at a time."

"Oh, I'd love to see one of your car washes. That sounds pretty interesting."

I changed the subject. I had to figure something out to keep the charade of owning a self-service car wash going. No way I could go back to the poker story after what I said. Otherwise, my relationship with Melanie would be over before it even got off the ground. I didn't want that. I liked her.

Our second date ended the same way the first had. A parking lot kiss less awkward than the first time. Even though we had to go to two restaurants to have a decent meal, I had a great time. Melanie was fun and interesting and most of all, she was interested in me. Each time I saw her, I wanted to see more of her.

Right before I got into my car to drive home, Melanie stopped me halfway into the car.

"Michael, on our next date, will you take me to see one of your car washes?"

"I'll show you the ropes of the self-service car wash industry."

~~~~~~~~~~

I woke up earlier than usual the next morning, motivated to find a solution to my "not owning a car wash" problem. With a cup of coffee in my left hand and the wireless computer mouse in my right, I trolled the Internet in search of a *self-service car wash* for sale. Searching Google for "car washes for sale," I wasted nearly half an hour. Two cups of coffee and an hour later, I crossed paths with a website that offered free postings to sellers to post their product. *What kind of an idiot shoots his mouth off and can't back it up? What am I, in high school?*

I entered Toronto as my location on Kijiji and my search became more specific. I entered *"car wash"* and a long list of items came up. Anything including the word "car" or "wash" in its description showed up. After looking at a long list of *"toy cars"* and *"power washers"*, I narrowed my search even more by only using the words "coin operated."

The first page was filled with old arcade game collector items, rebuilt for personal use. On the second page of the search, I hit the jackpot. Right under a "slot machine" posting was a listing for a "coin operated car wash" in the Greater Toronto Area. The listing didn't offer a price, instead asking any potential buyer to "please contact" the seller.

The Kijiji site didn't offer any more relevant listings. I continued searching and

92

found franchise opportunities on another company's website. They offer new owners "*help to break into the exciting market of small business ownership.*" The website's FAQ section said that the lag time in between buying the franchise and having it up and running was anywhere from six to eighteen months, depending on permits. That wasn't an option. I could maybe dodge showing Melanie for a date or two, but eventually she'd want to see something soon.

Taking a quick break, I mulled over my options. On one hand, I could confess to Melanie and explain that I didn't actually have the car wash up and running. Too many follow up questions. Won't work.

I regretted talking about poker at all. Not only did I put myself and my livelihood in jeopardy, but I might have put Melanie in harm by opening my mouth about the poker rooms' existence. I barely knew this girl and here I was, after having a few drinks, blabbing like a little school girl. I promised to myself, right then and there, to never speak about poker again, especially to Melanie.

The idea of investing money in a business solved the problem of laundering Savannah's winnings. "Stop thinking short term. Think long game," I said to myself, gently knocking my fist to my forehead. If the good times were going to keep coming, I couldn't keep paying for everything in cash and stockpiling thousands of dollars on my end table. Too many bad scenarios.

Owning a small business started to sound plausible, even a good idea. If Savannah kept the cash coming in, then there wasn't anything stopping me from being a *coin operated car wash entrepreneur*.

I picked up the phone and called the Kijiji listing. The details were limited. I had a lot of questions. The location, the condition of the facility, the reason why the owner was selling, and most importantly, how much the owner was asking for the car wash.

After two phone rings, a woman answered the phone.

A woman with a thick Indian accent answered, "Hello?"

"Hello. I read on Kijiji about a posting for a car wash…"

"No. No. No. You talk to my husband. You hold please."

A man out of breath with a thick Indian accent continued, "I apologize for the wait. My name is Akbar. You're interested in my car wash?"

"Yes, possibly. My name is Michael Cooper. I have some questions that I'm curious about."

"Yes, please. Ask as many as you like."

"What condition is the equipment in? How regularly do you maintain it? And why are you selling your business?"

"Yes, oh yes. No problem. The car wash is in perfect working condition and has always been well maintained. I am the original owner, so I can assure you, through my maintenance records the valves, stems, and nozzles have all been

93

properly flushed and replaced. My family and I are moving away from the area. I don't wish to commute the long distance necessary to properly run the business," Akbar said.

"Okay Akbar. That all sounds good. I am very interested, but need to ask one final question. What is your asking price?"

"Please Michael. Let's meet face to face at the car wash so I may take you through the entire process before we talk money. Agreed?"

Akbar was a middle-aged, bulging Indian man with a gentle disposition and a firm handshake. His quick smile flashed often as he went into great detail about the business. He carried with him a briefcase, containing the original sale of the property, all the costs of the hardware and equipment and its maintenance, and a file folder with the receipts for the property maintenance.

Two hours later I was inspecting hoses, nozzles, brickwork, drainage system, pavement, and the shingles on the roof, pretending to have some previous experience. For all Akbar knew, I was well acclimated in the car wash business, potentially looking to expand my business venture. That's what I hoped he thought.

The building was a five bay design, made completely of red brick. The sign on the front of the building read *Coin Operated Car Wash* in bold black letters against a white background. The pavement was in pristine condition and looked to be recent. The hardware looked to be in good condition and worked perfectly on every bay.

Akbar didn't try to deliver a "hard sell." He allowed me to walk the property at my own pace, only speaking when I asked questions. As he showed me the documents on the hood of his black Honda Accord, he slowly took me through the numbers of each piece of paper. Finally he gave me his asking price: $70,000.

I didn't have $70,000. I had close to that, but wasn't willing to dip into my $50K bankroll. That was untouchable. Some things have to be sacred.

A sudden thought flashed across my mind. The paperwork of the sale would be filed. Assuming Akbar was a "by the book kind of guy," the Canadian Revenue Agency would then be informed that I was the rightful owner. Then they would have good reason to open an investigation on me and my tax background. Not good.

For the past few years, I hadn't paid taxes. One year I didn't submit taxes, because, well, I forgot. The next year, seeing as I didn't receive any paperwork from the government looking for the back taxes, I figured I could skip that year as well. The third year, I was on a roll, why stop?

I had eluded any investigation so far and didn't want to do anything to draw extra attention to myself. Buying property and transferring ownership requires paperwork and payments to the proper government authority. If that had been done, my name would certainly be red flagged for investigation to make sure everything was correctly filed and the correct payment was received. I couldn't risk that exposure.

After thinking it all through, during a second walk around the building, I approached Akbar.

"Akbar, I'm interested in making you a counteroffer, but it comes with a condition."

"Please, go on, let me hear what you have to say."

"I can offer you $60,000, in cash," I said.

"But, what is the condition you speak of?"

"Here's the deal with my offer, I am not interested in paperwork or paying tax on our business transaction. We pay the government enough of our money through normal living expenses, so we shouldn't have to pay more because you're moving your family away. I can tell you work hard for your money. So do I. Which is why I refuse to pay any additional taxes that leech away our money."

After taking a moment to think it through, Akbar shook my hand firmly, accepting my offer. My short speech worked. We planned to meet back at the car wash on Saturday to exchange the money and the keys.

I didn't have $60,000. My bankroll was sacred, which left me with $4000 from the previous Friday. My new wardrobe, new watch, new furniture, new TV, and expensive dates had quickly ripped through my cash.

That was a Tuesday. I had one visit to the poker room in order to make at least $56,000 in order to pay Akbar. I had won close to that amount the first time I used Savannah. The circumstances behind the massive pot flashed back to me. There were multiple players in on that hand because they had thought the braggart was bluffing and had contributed to a very large pot.

I realized I needed to recreate similar situations. Having multiple players in on hands would grow the pot. Maybe even large enough to pay for the car wash. This car wash had suddenly shifted my brain into high gear.

~~~~~~~~~~

Necessity breeds invention.

I had to develop Savannah's capabilities to deliver multiple good hands during the same deal. I planned on having myself, and three other players, receive good opening cards. Getting good enough to create four good sets of cards wasn't an issue. I was already there. I was confident enough with Savannah. I wasn't even glancing at the shuffle every time. Every other shuffle was all I required to spot the cards and reorder them into the sequence that would best fit to my advantage.

The part that I needed to develop control over was the cards that represented the flop, the turn, and the river. These community cards were previously unnoticeable to me. They were just too deep into the deck for my eyes to catch a glimpse of them.

When it was just another player and I, the odds were so severely tilted the other player essentially had no chance at winning. That's not to say they couldn't win, just that I would win the vast majority of those head-to-head pots.

If four players were in a hand together, and I had the best pair of cards to start the hand, then I still had the best odds. With each additional player in a hand, my odds of winning the huge mountain of chips dropped. Using Savannah with four players was risky because I had a very real chance of losing the hand. I couldn't risk that type of loss. Savannah was supposed to guarantee that I won, not just help improve my odds of winning.

Savannah needed to morph. It had to become more powerful and more controlling. I needed to guarantee that I would win. The realization was right in front of my eyes. I needed to see the flop, the turn, and the river. Then I would know the outcome of the hand, before the other players were dealt their cards.

The rest of Tuesday, all of Wednesday and Thursday, and most of Friday were dedicated to Savannah's recreation. I entitled my new creation "Savannah 2.0" because she was bigger and better than the original Savannah.

Eight packs of cards, countless cups of coffee, three bottles of eye drops, and Savannah was reborn. I spent Friday afternoon napping and practicing. I rested just enough to stay alert at the poker table and make sure I was on top of my game. The more I practiced Savannah 2.0, the more confident in her capabilities I grew. *She was a beauty.*

She erased any chance of losing. Never before had I felt so powerful. I was a new man. I had never been so comfortable walking into the poker room and shaking hands with the pit bosses. Savannah 2.0 had been transformed and along with it, so had I. At 2 a.m., she was to be unleashed.

CHAPTER 14
"IT" RETURNS

Excerpt from Michael's Journal

I couldn't have written this down back then, even if I was keeping a journal. The whole thing would have sounded made up. I'm writing in the darkness of a jail cell, which I share with a man who snores louder than most people play their car radios. The only light comes from an exit sign. Its taunting four letters meant to tease the inmates. The guards call it fire safety protocol. Its glow is all I have to write with.

~~~~~~~~~~

The poker room was different that night. There were less people there than usual. I almost called the whole night off. The thought of disappointing Melanie and Akbar kept me from leaving.

I sat with a group of five players, instantly changing into my alternate personality. Poor posture. Sloppily dressed. Non-threatening. Arriving after the table had been seated. I was no match for the men at their mighty poker table. Little did they know about Savannah's rebirth.

Time dragged its lazy legs as I waited until Savannah 2.0 could make her grand entrance. At 2:09, the deck of cards came to me. The pit bosses had a glazed appearance, signaling a green light.

After my ninth shuffle, the cards were perfectly arranged. I saw everything.

97

SAVANNAH

There was only one player who was going to be spared. He was on my right and had the lowest chip count. I hadn't felt bad for him or pitied him. It was business. I targeted the four players with the most chips.

Savannah 2.0 had one hiccup. The four players that had their cards arranged had to be in a row. It was either the first four players or the last four players, it made no difference. Skipping a player in the middle was impossible for me to keep track of.

I glanced at my cards to make sure the two Kings were delivered as promised. They were. The other players at the table had, in order, pocket tens, pocket Jacks, Ace of Spades and Queen of Diamonds, pocket 8s, and the last guy had a six of Clubs and four of Hearts. No player had the same set of suits, thus eliminating any flush possibilities.

The flop was going to be three low cards, a black three, a red seven, and red two. That was all I needed.

All week I had planned on conservative betting, keeping all the players in and maximizing the chips I would win. The betting began just as I predicted it would. Each player liked their hand.

The player number one with the Ace – Queen acted first. He called the big blind of $500 and raised a modest $1000.

Player number two, the pocket pair of eights, must have liked his chances because he, not only called the raise of $1000, but raised another $1000. I wanted to let the others play it out and sit back and play the role of the sheep.

The six-four folded right on cue. I called the raise and slid in $2500.

Player number three, the small blind with the pocket pair of tens, called the previous raises. He was in for $2500.

Player number four, the pocket Jacks, called too.

Player number one, with the Ace – Queen, called the remaining $1000 and squared the pot.

The black three, red seven, and red two came up, causing the other players to smile in their own subtle way. Player number two shifted his weight in his seat. Player number four rubbed his nose. Player number three blinked rapidly at the cards.

Each player liked the cards. The players with pocket pairs had been shown a very weak flop. They believed their pair was the best hand.

Player number one, with the Ace – Queen, seemed satisfied. None of the three cards were high enough cards for other players to make a pair. Most players wouldn't call a bet of $2500 with a two, three, or seven in their hand. They were likely to fold, regardless of their other card. Big money will do that; weed out the chasers.

Player number three started the betting. He represented his pocket tens with a $1,000 bet.

98

SAVANNAH

Player number four, with pocket Jacks, called and raised another $1000.

Player number one, Ace – Queen, thought long and hard. Finally, after a lifetime, he tossed two black $1000 chips into the middle.

Player number two, with the pocket eights, wasn't scared off. He called the $2000 bet.

I was sheep-like, just following along. Calling bets. No threat to anyone.

Player number three, pocket tens, added his additional $1000. I revealed the turn, a nine of Clubs. Good for everyone, except player number two. His pocket eights would be beat by a nine in any hand.

A check was laid down by player number three, quickly tapping the table twice. Player number four, who was the raiser after the flop, continued alpha male betting. He laid a continuation bet of another $2000, which was called by player number one.

Player number two, who was figured to fold, made a bold call, even though the board had a higher card.

I slowly dropped two black chips into the pot and tried to act as unexcited about it as I possibly could. Inside I was like a little kid on Christmas morning.

Player number three also called, adding his $2000 into the middle.

The pot had grown to $32,500, with five players involved. The river card was the reason I knew to sit back and allow the other players to dictate the betting. A Queen of Spades crushed each player's honest hope of winning, except one.

Anyone who knows poker knows a pocket pair is worthless if a higher card appears on the table. Player number three (pocket tens), Player number four (pocket Jacks), and Player number two (pocket eights) all sneered at the Queen. They knew they were beat. *Cut your losses,* they all must have thought.

Player number one (Ace – Queen), on the contrary, was stone faced as ever. He paired the river, giving him the highest possible pair of all of the community cards. His Ace meant he had the highest possible kicker to go with his pair of Queens.

After checked bets, Player number one arrogantly flipped a $10,000 gold chip into the pot. End over end, it splashed the chips on the table, causing perfect stacks to collapse.

Through my darkened sunglasses, I glared at Player number one. I hadn't given him anything the entire hand. No hints. No tip-offs. No reason for him to think I had a superior hand. I called his bet and raised him $15,000. The second golden chip, with five black $1,000 escorts, drained the blood from his face. His face turned ghostly white.

The other players quickly flung their cards into the middle, folding their hands.

The ghost stared at me. His eyes scrutinized me hard. I held his gaze for what seemed like minutes. My heart pounded inside my chest. Keeping my hands steady required me to steeple my fingers, contradicting my previous table behavior.

Finally, he reached for his chips. He called the $15,000 bet and displayed his Ace – Queen to the crowd that had gathered. He leaned on the table, after standing, to see my cards. I flung my Kings to their intended landing pad. Right on top of $82,500.

Excitement exploded inside me. I had never seen, let alone had, that much money in my life. My best five years together, still couldn't match what I pulled towards my location on the table.

I said nothing, not even cracking a smile. Stoically leaning forward, I organized the chips in front of me. I acted as bored as I had in my garage games winning a measly $25.

In the past, my strategy was to play a little longer and commit as few chips to the pots that I could after I had won big. I planned on making a quiet exit between three-thirty and four. Savannah 2.0 was no different. I wanted to hit big, draw minimal attention, and slide out quietly.

I stayed in character and waited for departure time. The deck was passed around to me to deal again, five hands later. As I was shuffling the cards, exactly nine times as always when *IT* suddenly returned. *IT*. My greed.

It was as though I had blacked out, yet remained aware of everything around me. Someone else seemed to control my hands, my fingers, and the cards. It was the same feeling as the last time in the poker room. I couldn't do anything, except watch. All control was lost.

I saw myself arrange the cards according to Savannah 2.0 guidelines. My hands dealt out cards that were favorable to every player, me with a pair of Queens. Again. Two deals in a row. My fingers tossed chips into the growing pot, over and over again.

I was scared. No control. Lots of attention on another large pot, which I dealt. What if one of the players noticed?

Control came back, though not until I had won a second large pot of $39,750. Swallowing hard, I rose and made my way to the cashier's table before exiting. I could feel everyone's eyes on me. Everything I had done to keep attention off of me was ruined. The other gamblers heckled out, "Get lucky and leave quick, really classy." One overweight chain smoker shouted through cupped hands, "Fish!"

$122,750.

That was enough to buy the car wash from Akbar. Hell, it was enough money to buy two car washes.

I didn't sleep one minute that night. I was terrified that a group of thugs were going to knock down my door, burst through with their pistols drawn, and open fire on me.

I was more frightened by what I couldn't explain. I had done it. It was me. I was the one seated in the chair, shuffling the cards, stealing the chips. There wasn't a hidden puppeteer controlling me. Yet, I didn't control *IT*. I had never felt greediness like that. I never wanted to again.

When I was gripped by whatever commanded me, the urgency to get as many chips as possible was all encompassing. I needed bigger winnings. I needed more chips. Winning felt so good. So soothing.

IT had increased its grasp each time. The first time I felt it was at the end of the betting when the other player bet a $10,000 gold chip. It controlled me for only a few seconds. The second time was after I had won the largest pot I've ever seen, littered with gold chips. The second time was for more than a minute.

What would happen once I returned to the poker room? Would *IT* control me for multiple hands? Would someone spot me using Savannah 2.0 and put it together that when I dealt, there were larger pots that I won? What would happen if *IT* never let go?

I decided because it made detrimental choices for me, that it was a darkness that lived inside of me. I named it: *IT*.

CHAPTER 15

PURCHASE

Excerpt from Michael's Journal

I arrived at the car wash at our scheduled time on Saturday. As promised, Akbar was waiting in his black sedan. He exited, carrying his briefcase and shaking my hand vigorously. I apologized for the manner in which I brought his money.

Four envelopes contained $15,000. Embarrassingly unprofessional. With a wave from his right hand, he accepted them and began counting the money.

I basked in the day's glorious sunshine while laying against my windshield. I felt like a hippie. Free and happy to be in the fresh air. The nervousness caused by *IT* finally began to fade. As it left, exhaustion set in from the lack of sleep.

"I'm sorry Mr. Taylor. (Holding out the additional $5000 I had included in the last envelope) I counted the money three times. There has been a mistake," Akbar said.

"The additional cash is a gesture of my gratitude for not filing the paperwork. Look at that money as a gift from me to your family. I would much rather give it to you than lose it to the tax man."

"Oh no, I couldn't accept such an amount. It wouldn't be right. (Trying again to push the money back into my hand). I couldn't."

"Akbar here's the deal. I see it as payment for you keeping up your end of the deal. I don't have any way of knowing if you're going to keep your word. At least now, you have some compensation for keeping your end of the bargain."

CHAPTER 16

BRADLEY WEISNEWSKI

Outside Akbar Rahmin's Residence

Sticking to his word, Akbar didn't file any paperwork. He didn't claim any property transfer taxes. He didn't even declare his business income on his taxes. He kept his word.

He did make one fatal mistake. Akbar left the meeting not feeling comfortable carrying $65,000. He stopped at his local bank, which offered Saturday banking hours, and deposited the entire sum of the money.

Banking officers have a duty to report any transaction over $10,000. An automatic red flag is placed on any financial deposit above $9,999. It is put on hold until the government authorizes the transaction, two to three business days later. This is a safety measure the government put into effect so that businessmen, legal or illegal, cannot launder money through personal bank accounts, avoiding taxes on under the table funds. Government officials believe the $10,000 limit is set too high to catch tax dodging citizens.

Canada's version of the United States Internal Revenue Service (IRS) is known as the CRA (Canadian Revenue Agency). Just like the IRS, the CRA's main purpose is to ensure that every citizen is properly paying taxes. One division of the CRA is dedicated to banking regulations and investigating red flagged deposits. They dig around and ask questions about large deposits. Frequently, the investigations end up as dead ends. The people in this division are considered "the paper pushers" and "fact checkers." The real action, if you can call it "action," is in investigating fraudulent tax claims.

SAVANNAH

Bradley Weisnewski is a middle of the road investigator for the CRA. He examines red flagged accounts, with deposits over $10,000, for any fraudulent activity. He determines whether he should personally investigate deposit irregularities. More often than not, Bradley finds himself on the fifth floor of a downtown Ottawa office building, stuck between cubicle walls for days, if not weeks, at a time. Therefore, when an irregularity crosses Bradley's computer screen, similar to the one early that Tuesday morning, he quickly jumps at the chance to leave his desk.

NAME: Akbar Rahmin

STATUS: Permanent Resident

AMOUNT: $65,000

# of TRANSACTIONS ABOVE LIMIT: 0

With a click of his mouse, Bradley was looking at Akbar Rahmin's banking statements and transaction history. He wondered how a car wash owner, who made regular deposits of $1000 - $2000 a week, could suddenly make a deposit of $65,000 into an empty account. He back searched two years worth of banking statements and tax returns, finding nothing irregular. Akbar appeared to be an honest tax payer who owned his own small business, paying him a steady yearly profit of $28,000.

Bradley brought the red flagged account to his deputy commissioner, including all the taxes Akbar had filed over the previous two years of living in Canada. He explained how he believed Akbar had either withheld taxable income from the previous tax years, therefore committing tax fraud, or he was involved in some sort of illegal activity. With permission, Bradley was given the "go ahead" to launch a full investigation into Akbar Rahmin.

With more than six months in that cubicle, Bradley was anxious. He packed everything into his green Jeep Liberty. In a matter of five hours, Bradley Weisnewski, fraudulent tax investigator, arrived from Ottawa to the residential suburb of Ajax. The welcome sign to Ajax mentioned how it was situated *On the Lake,* with a population of 100,000.

Bradley's GPS, suctioned to his windshield, had brought him to Akbar Rahmin's home. In a file folder, he had all the information about Akbar. Address. Phone number. Wife's and children's names. Anything provided on a tax return.

He thumbed the papers, refreshing his memory. An informal visit to the suspect's home was much more conducive to the truth, Bradley learned. Acting respectful, non-threatening, and "just-fact-checking" elicited the truth before most people realized they were being investigated.

Bradley Weisnewski was just another forty year old man with dark brown hair cut short and conservative. His clean shaven face featured a pair of wireless rimmed glasses. He regularly wore a boring beige dress shirt tucked into olive green khakis. Nothing about Bradley screamed excitement. At first, and usually last glance, he was a boring pencil pusher who lived a boring, dull life.

SAVANNAH

Bradley opened his car door and walked to the front door of the home of Akbar Rahmin. The door was opened by a balding, middle-aged man with a gut that protruded over his belt buckle.

Under threat of legal fines and a possible jail sentence, Akbar admitted to receiving payment for his car wash without filing the appropriate paperwork.

Bradley got the name and number of the buyer who paid extra money to Akbar not to file the paperwork. Michael Taylor. Akbar was given two business days to file the appropriate forms as a professional courtesy in return for being honest and providing the contact information.

Thirteen years of experience told Bradley something was wrong. People who pay extra not to file the sale have something to hide. Everything screamed "illegal activity" on this investigation. Laundering money through small businesses is difficult for the CRA to identify if the accountant who is "cooking the books" is familiar with CRA protocols. Bradley always felt crooked tax evaders had the upper hand.

Checking into a cheap hotel, he mulled over how to approach the newly developed situation. He needed more information on Mr. Michael Taylor of 57 Broadview Avenue in Toronto. He headed to the house and began surveillance. In the morning, he would have all of the tax statements and banking records.

In the driveway he found the same car Akbar had described. His information seemed credible, but until he received the "Michael Taylor" file from his office, Bradley wasn't sure of anything yet.

~~~~~~~~~~

Sitting on his Super 8 hotel room bed, Bradley opened the attachment labeled Michael Thomas Taylor, DOB: 04/26/87. The secretary of his division emailed him all relevant available files. One click of a button, and he had everything. While sipping on his awful tasting hotel coffee, Bradley smiled.

At first, Bradley had his legs stretched out, resting his laptop on his lap. The more he read, the more his legs eased their way toward the floor. As he finished, both feet were already on the floor, ready for action. Three missing tax statements. His version of hitting a homerun.

In all of Bradley's years at the CRA, he had never had a case where he actually got to investigate a real criminal. He was excited for the hunt. He daydreamed about the future accolades that came along with a high profile bust. His American colleagues at the IRS regularly busted drug dealers and money launderers who failed to pay their taxes. Al Capone was even captured and put in jail by the IRS. Now it was his turn.

Dressing in another boring tan dress shirt and dark brown pair of cotton dress pants, Bradley readied himself for a day full of surveillance. He sat in his Jeep down the street from Michael's house.

CHAPTER 17

SURVEILLANCE

Excerpt from Michael's Journal

Melanie and I had been out late the night before. We had met up for a late dinner and drinks at our favorite restaurant, Rizzo's. We shared a couple bottles of good Chianti and picked at delicious appetizers. Melanie, being more flirtatious than usual, played with the back of my calf with her bare foot under the table. Such advances were new to me.

With two bottles of $47 wine drained, we walked outside into the night air. Our hands met, our fingers tangled themselves together. Her soft hands were cold, while mine were warm and sweaty.

"I don't want to end the night," Melanie said eyeing me playfully.

"Oh la la. What did you have in mind?"

"Maybe I'm feeling dirty. I want to see your car wash."

"Persistent, aren't you Miss Cooper? Alright, I'll take you. But be warned, the inner working of a coin operated car wash isn't that sexy."

"We'll see about that. I can make a lot of boring things very, very interesting."

We drove our cars to my car wash, speeding the entire way. My abandoned unit impressed her.

"Okay good looking. You own a car wash. What else do you do, aside from looking so scrumptious I could eat you?"

"Running five car washes is a full-time job you know."

"Five? Oh. That's impressive."

I lied. But Melanie was turned on like a light switch. She pounced and passionately pinned me against my car door. Her hot lips sucked mine into her mouth. Her tongue circled the underside of mine as our hands explored each other's bodies.

"My... House... Now."

Melanie's tongue licked my neck and ears, making the drive home a challenge. We paused long enough to unlock the door. I nervously prayed that the decks of cards that I had practicing with earlier in the day were cleaned up.

Through the door, Melanie continued her attack. Standing on the tips of her toes, she kicked off her high-heeled shoes and began unbuttoning my gray dress shirt. My front buttons undone, Melanie stepped back admiring my sculpted chest and rippled abdomen.

"Oh God, yes," she said.

I shrugged off the sleeves of my shirt and gave her what I knew she wanted.

"Oh," Melanie said.

I had never lifted weights. I did, however, frequently spend the odd hour working out while watching TV. I can't sit still and watch. I become fidgety and restless. Push-ups and sit-ups during the TV show's commercials managed that energy. I began challenging myself as the exercises became too easy. The more my chest and abs grew, the more I pushed myself to stay entertained.

Each commercial gave me two minutes and thirty seconds to perform as many push-ups as I could do without stopping. Once I reached my limit, I flipped onto my back and crunched my abs, counting down, from the push-up number, to zero.

My numbers began to take off and soar to new heights. The teenage days of doing nine push-ups were long forgotten. Exceeding forty-five push-ups was my current best. My abs were challenged to finish before the commercials ended.

Push-ups + crunches + little money for food = good muscle tone with little fat.

Running her fingers across my chest and down my stomach, Melanie's eyes filled with a hunger. Mouthing words of amazement, she stroked the curves of my pectoral muscles and ran the tips of her fingers over each abdominal muscle. She locked her arms around my neck, pulling her legs around my hips. Her body felt on fire.

With a renewed and amplified excitement, I effortlessly carried Melanie to the couch, easing her onto the cushions.

Her tanned curves gleamed in the bright moon light. She slipped off her black lace bra and matching panties. The moon caught my attention, hanging outside my window. The wine fueled our passion as we made love to each other. Our bodies pulsated rhythmically with each other on the firm couch. Over and over again, until we were both finally exhausted.

It wasn't until the sun peeked over the horizon, illuminating Melanie's back,

107

that I finally saw her exquisite body. I ran my hands along her flat stomach, circling her naval. Her smooth, flawless skin made my hands seem reptilian in comparison. The tickling woke her from her sleep, back to the reality that she needed sleep before she was due back at work.

With a smack of my naked buttocks, she winked at me and dressed in her scattered clothes.

Melanie kissed my forehead, "Sleep my little stallion. I'll call you later today."

"Yeah, okay. Are you alright to go?"

"Oh, I'm more than alright. You were amazing. Now, go get some sleep."

After she left, I dragged my weary body to my bed's cushioned embrace and collapsed. Sleep came easily. Melanie had given me the best night of my life.

CHAPTER 18

VISUAL CONFIRMATION

Outside Michael's Residence

Surveillance for Bradley had begun well after Melanie had left, leaving Michael to settle into a deep sleep. The part of surveillance that Bradley dreaded was providing visual evidence to his superiors. Instant emails were expected.

Through his windshield, Bradley watched the house. He sat and waited, becoming skeptical that anyone lived there. At 4:15 p.m., convinced no one was home, he set his mental countdown for fifteen minutes. Frustration had set in over the wasted day. No movement. No evidence to email. Questions would be asked. He would have to explain.

His body finally went rigid with excitement. His surveillance finally was coming through. He snapped pictures of his subject juggling car keys before entering his car.

Finally, visual confirmation. Target identified. He snapped more digital pictures using his SLR camera as the car passed. The camera's wire had been attached to the USB drive of his laptop. He previewed the pictures, deciding which one to send off. After selecting the best one, he quickly typed a short caption.

SUSPECT: Michael Taylor

DOB: 04/26/87

INTEREST: Suspect has definite connection to fraudulent activity. Gathering further evidence.

CRA Agent Bradley Weisnewski was never formally trained in surveillance techniques when he was promoted from the mailroom. His promotion came due to a recommendation from his mailroom supervisor to the deputy commissioner of fraudulent banking activity. Bradley had been a particularly keen employee in the mailroom and frequently went beyond his job description, which didn't go unnoticed.

Staying late to finish the day's work, if another mailroom clerk was on vacation or sick leave, was common for him. He took the delivery of the Agency's mail as serious business. Nothing else made him feel that sense of accomplishment. After four and a half years, Bradley was given an in-house promotion with little fan fare. His fellow colleagues in the mailroom had been extremely jealous.

Nine years later, Bradley was still in the same position. Stuck in the same cubicle. With limited outside experience. He frequently found fraudulent cases, but was forced to hand everything over to more experienced agents. He needed training. He needed a chance.

Regular visits to Ottawa's public libraries provided Bradley with material on how to survey a target. Photography books came later. They educated him on lighting and shade. His SLR camera was state-of-the-art. It had a dozen features for rapid photo taking, with crystal clear resolution.

He also studied Hollywood spy movies. Those were his favorite. He practiced his spy techniques on weekends. At a large park, he would target an individual and tail them. His practice made him feel creepy, but the training was necessary. He knew it would all pay off. He would receive recognition. His dedication would shine through.

~~~~~~~~~~~

Michael arrived at the car wash and parked in the far rear corner. Only one bay was in use, a middle-aged man washing caked-on mud off of his Ford F-150. Off-road trail. Had to be. Too much mud. The height of the mud on his window suggested fast driving through deep mud puddles. The man happily power sprayed the soapy foam off of his truck.

Bradley pulled up to the car wash and watched Michael unlock the storage locker that housed different colored bottles of fluid. He snapped pictures of him collecting coins and filling soap dispensers.

He had no desire to make contact. Instead, he emailed more information and pictures to his deputy commissioner. Questions still loomed. Where had Michael Taylor got the money to purchase such an expensive business? Why did he buy a car wash, of all things?

His plan was to wait and follow until he had answers. He was confident he was onto something. Had he brought Michael in then, with only the unfiled tax years and missing paperwork, he would have received nothing more than a slap on the hand.

Bradley knew something deeper lurked in the waters surrounding Michael. He just needed to find out what it was.

CHAPTER 19

MY THUMB

Excerpt from Michael's Journal

The rest of that week was filled with thoughts of Melanie and Savannah 2.0. *IT* worried the hell out of me, but I convinced myself that I would be able to control it this time. I knew it was there. I knew it wanted control and I was determined not to let it have what it wanted.

I thought about *IT* a lot. Twice in the same night, in back-to-back deals, it had exerted its control over me. I was scared of all the attention. I actually feared for my life. As time passed, and I wasn't brutally ambushed and killed, my thoughts turned to going back to the poker room and making more money.

Thursday night, I saw Melanie again. Dinner. Then a movie, typical date. We had a great time, but not until after the horror movie. She invited me back to her place.

"Can you just come in and make sure no one is waiting in my place?" Melanie said.

Excellent. A clear cut invitation. That night, from there on in, was identical to the previous date. The only difference was that I was the one who had to leave at 3 a.m. Very much worth the loss of sleep.

~~~~~~~

On Friday, I dedicated a pot of coffee, five new Hoyle decks of cards, and four hours to polishing Savannah 2.0. Control. I needed control. I was determined to control my betting and my actions. *IT* wasn't going to have any control over me.

This was not the week to attract more attention. I needed a cool down week. A week where I finished the night close to even would go a long way showing the pit bosses that last week was a fluke. *Look, see, I lose like everyone else.*

I dressed in my usual costume. Old jeans, a worn T-shirt, beat up old shoes and my gas station sunglasses. $50,000 was divided amongst my front pockets. My slouch was in full effect, even before I arrived.

Nervousness stung my stomach. I was usually nervous, particularly during the first visit, but it faded more every time. This time, the nervousness had grown more than ever. It consumed me. Driving to the poker room, it felt as though I was driving off of a cliff.

The carpet distributor's building appeared the same as every other time, with the exception of more cars. I parked, nearly vomiting from the nervousness. I walked casually through the front door and back toward the poker room. I was greeted by a few extra looks from the guards. Usually they didn't even grant me a glance. *You're just being paranoid, regular players get recognized.* I was sure that if the Russian crime family, who ran the poker room, knew I had cheated last week that I wouldn't have been permitted in. I would have been shot on sight, or worse.

Once inside, the glances stopped. I seemed to be just another poker player. I relaxed after a few hands. I even won $1000, honestly. I was in control and in character. That was, right up to when the player next to me went all-in, with $63,000. It wasn't unheard of. Rather, it was a nightly occurrence. The player next to him muttered a soft toned, "I call."

That was the last hand at the poker table when I felt in control. It was right before my third deal of the night, much too soon for Savannah 2.0. Slowly, like easing yourself into a hot tub one inch at a time, *IT* came upon me. It started with a tingle in my feet. I curled and uncurled my toes. No help. It rose over my knees. I knew what was happening. I tried to stand. Couldn't. It wouldn't let me. *IT* wanted the massive pot. *IT* needed it.

After the warm tingle reached my shoulders, I gave up all hope. I prayed to make it out unharmed. *I won't play again. I'll be a good person. I'll donate to charity.* The greed controlled me. I underestimated it. *IT* was powerful. I never stood a chance.

The player at my table who had pushed $63,000 in won. His mass of chips was well over $100,000. The player who lost had nothing left. He was busted and walked away hanging his head low. I imagined him having to explain to his wife how he had lost everything. Would she leave him? Was this just another loss in a life full of mountainous highs and ocean-bottom lows?

My curiosity ended as the deck scraped my right hand as it was passed. It was my deal. *IT* was in full control.

SAVANNAH

My body was gone, but my mind was still mine. Thoughts raced in and out. Hope of not getting caught. Excitement grew inside me. The cards fell into place with each shuffle. Behind my sunglasses, my eyes read the digital clock stationed next to the cashier's station, 11:24 p.m.

To the outside observer, I hoped I appeared the same player as always. Shuffling exactly nine times, keeping my back humped over, and moving my head and hands very little. But inside, I knew it was too early. The pit bosses are still alert at this hour. My thoughts toggled between the hand I was playing and the looks from the other players. Nervous doesn't begin to explain how I felt. Panic attack, that's close.

I looked down at my pair of aces. I felt control come back to me after I laid down my two black aces alongside the red ace on the flop. Three aces. Three of a kind. A set of aces. They won me an astonishing amount. I had wagered about half of my chips and beat out two other players.

As I reached for my winnings, I seemed to be floating. Out of my seat I rose. My feet no longer touched the floor. Under my arms, something lifted me out of my seat and away from my winnings. I flailed, trying to regain my footing. No use, I was being carried through midair. When I was slammed against the nearest wall, I finally saw what effortlessly had carried me. Two men. The same two men who guarded the entrance (and were eyeing me as I entered) had a hand under my arm with their other holding my nearest wrist out to the side. I made a giant "T" against their wall.

Time seemed to speed up. Not since I was a teenager had I been in a fight. It was the same sensation. The sudden spike of adrenaline caused me to panic. Their grasp crushed my arms. I screamed out, asking what was going on. I kicked my feet, trying to break their hold. I wasn't getting anywhere.

The man holding my left side said in a thick Russian accent, "Shut your mouth! Only speak when spoken to. Last warning."

I felt my right hand come free. I raised it in a fist. The futile nature of my thought became evident as more men rushed in.

A man I had never seen appeared in front of me. His dark blue suit and pale yellow shirt were accented by a purple pocket square coming out of his jacket's breast pocket. Tattoos crawled out from under his open shirt collar. He was clearly connected to the family. He looked Russian. His eyelids barely opened. When he spoke, his teeth remained clenched.

I looked into the man's eyes and saw evil. Pure evil. The kind that the movies can never get right. He didn't have red eyes or black orbs in his eye sockets. He looked rather normal, except for the dead look in his eyes. As we made eye contact, I saw something dark wash over his face. He liked the position he was in. He took pleasure in seeing me two feet off the ground, pinned against a wall. I was at his mercy.

SAVANNAH

When I looked into his eyes, terror washed over me. It consumed me. Every hair on my entire body stood on end. I was staring at death.

The men that flanked him wore jackets that bulged from their shoulder holstered weapons. They seemed to simultaneously unbutton their jackets. The black butt ends of their guns were exposed. Not good.

I kept my mouth shut. I knew it was my best option. My only option after my "Last Warning." My heart froze. No pulse. Nothing. Just frozen. Sweat beaded down my forehead.

The well dressed man spoke something in Russian and I was carried out through a back door I had never seen before. His look of disgust erased any hope wafting through the air. Two sets of very strong hands threw me in the back of a cube van. The carpet company logo was on its side. Falling onto the floor, my jaw dropped. Two sides had metallic benches anchored down. Similar to the seating used by soldiers riding into battle. No frills. Just benches. The rear of the cargo van had a single chair and stainless steel table. Heavy bolts held them in place. On the table, two leather scraps with notches in them were open, waiting for a wrist. Both men climbed in after me and roughly tossed me into the chair, closing the restraints.

I was scared. I had cheated and clearly the Russians had caught on. I had ignored all the signs.

The door to the cargo area was shut tight and the engine started. Seated with me were both of the gigantic monsters that carried me like a rag doll, one pit boss I had shaken hands with multiple times, and the well dressed man. Their eyes drove spikes of fear deep inside me. Every second the truck rumbled toward its unknown destination, my stomach inched up my throat. When the truck finally stopped, I was certain I was dead. My body never to be found.

The silence that followed the deadened engine was deafening. None of the men moved. The cargo door was raised and the driver jumped out. In unison, the men exited the truck. All the men, that is, except for one man dressed in an exceptional suit. The leader. He rose from his seat and eased closer to where I was strapped down.

A scar across his left cheek hid behind his beard. It started at the corner of his mouth and ended at the base of his ear. The stubble hid the scar, but there was nothing that could hide the glare from his eyes. The whites of his eyes were blood shot with rage. As he moved closer still, I smelled the scent of pine, reminding me of cheap air fresheners.

With only the leader in the truck, my fear began subsiding. *Maybe I have a chance.* Two more men entered. One carried a black case; the other slammed the door shut behind him. My anxiety peaked. I lost control. Tears ran down my face. I wasn't a hardened criminal. I wasn't accustomed to pain. Death scared me. I was an idiot card player who cheated at poker.

114

SAVANNAH

The hair on the back of my neck stood up. I was certain I was staring at my killer. I was terrified. Urine filled my pants. Vomit rose in my throat. I was barely able to hold it down. I had convinced myself that the leader was going to kill me for cheating. I looked up at him. Again those evil eyes stared back at me.

Three men and I sat in the back of the cargo van. The only light came from a small dome light. It barely made the photos that were gently spread across the table visible. In silence, the black case was unrolled revealing torture devises. Knives. Pliers. Scalpels. Small hammers with rounded edges. All stainless steel. All shining in the dim light.

My mouth was suddenly bound by a piece of fabric that smelled of mildew. It tasted metallic, like being gagged by a roll of pennies. Tears poured down my face, absorbed by the heavy cotton weave. They added a salty taste.

The leader spoke. His English was rough. He spoke in a whisper. His words were that of a man who was very calm and in control.

"My name is Evgenii Marchenko. The men you see are under my command. They are the most loyal men I have ever known."

Evgenii stood. He removed his jacket and rolled up his sleeves. His arms were covered in an impressive amount of tattoos. Russian writing, random pictures, and one item that stuck out: A large gray spider crawling over an ornate cross.

Evgenii positioned himself right in front of me, placing his hands atop mine. He curled a fist and punched me hard across the chin, nearly breaking my jaw. He waited for me to recover. My head throbbed. My jaw felt like it had detached and then roughly put back in place. Then he hit me again from the opposite direction.

"My men informed me all about you, Michael. I want you to listen very carefully. I am going to ask you some questions. The amount of pain and suffering you endure depends on your answers. As you can see (motioning toward the torture instruments), lying to me would be a poor choice. Do you understand Mr. Taylor?" Evgenii said.

I nodded quickly. I didn't want to get hit again.

"Good. My men tell me you have been coming to my poker room for about a month and a half. You have done very well for yourself. Is that true?"

I nodded once.

"Look at the photographs on the table Michael. Who is driving that vehicle?"

I shook my head. I wanted to speak. My gag prevented anything audible. Only a gargled muffle. This worried me. I had no idea who the man was.

"We have driven about thirty minutes north of the poker room to an area that is abandoned. We are in a thick forest of pine trees. My men are patrolling the area to make sure we are alone. So, let me make myself clear. You have one chance. I will remove your gag, but if you scream or shout, you will be punished. Am I clear?"

I nodded vigorously.

115

"Okay, remove it," Evgenii said. Then looking back at me. "If I think you are lying Mr. Taylor, you will not like the consequences."

With a mouth that felt like it was full of cotton, "I won't lie."

"Who is seated in the green Jeep Liberty?" Evgenii said.

"I don't know. I have never seen that truck before. Or that man."

"This photograph was taken by my men who patrol the parking lot. They informed me that the man driving that vehicle did not exit his car. He was taking many pictures of you as you walked into the poker room. Then he snapped a few more of your car. Currently, he is still parked in my lot, with his camera resting on his lap."

Evgenii's tattooed finger pointed directly toward a dark image of Agent Bradley Weisnewski.

"I swear. I have no idea who that is or why he was taking pictures. You got to believe me. I'm telling you the truth."

"Let me explain how this works. You're going to tell me what I want to know one way or another. If I believe you, then you live. If I don't, my men add your body to a grave next to the last person who lied to me."

"Evgenii, I assure you, I am not lying. I honestly do not know who that man is."

"After your car was followed in, my men watched you closely. They tell me you are a very skilled shuffler. They also tell me that you have won many large pots in the last few weeks. Was it good luck? Fortunate breaks? I found it interesting that each was won when you dealt."

My eyes sunk from his glare. He had me. I knew it. He knew it. Lying to him would be painful. My chest was heavy. Breathing became a chore.

Evgenii said, "How can that be Michael Taylor, of 57 Broadview Ave., brother to Susanne Taylor, currently living with a roommate in a rented townhouse at 34 Flagship Ave., and boyfriend to Melanie Cooper, employee of Marshall Jewelers?"

"I…how? How do you know all that?" I said.

"It is my job to ensure the players at my poker room are not associated with the police. My men perform thorough background checks of every player. We know everything about you Michael, right down to the car wash you recently purchased. Not really on the, how do they say, up-and-up, is it? Tisk, tisk, tisk Michael," shaking a finger at me. "Lying to me isn't an option. I'll be polite and ask you again. How is it that you have won so many large hands over the past month?"

"I have been playing poker for a long time and…"

Evgenii turned his head to his left, quickly nodding. My right wrist was yanked by the silent man who sat next to me. Before I could finish my sentence, he jerked my wrist, stretching the restraint. He grabbed a Ball-Peen hammer. He snapped the hammer down onto my middle finger, breaking it instantly. The pain shot through

116

me like lightning. I shouted out in pain. Tears dripped down my cheeks, staining my shirt. Every heartbeat brought a new bolt of pain. Gritting my teeth together to bite away the pain, I changed my answer to Evgenii.

"STOP! STOP! I'll talk. Just stop. I cheat. I win because I cheat when I shuffle."

"I already knew that Mr. Taylor. It is about time you showed respect and stopped lying. The surveillance system I have is as sophisticated as in any casino. State of the art, is that how it is said? Whatever, mine is better. Mine is completely hidden."

Evgenii nodded to his left. This time, my left hand was yanked. The man grabbed the same hammer and smashed it down into the end of my ring finger, missing his intended target. My last knuckle cracked. Pain took control. I screamed uncontrollably. I writhed in pain. I jerked against the restraints. A pair of hands from behind pinned my elbows to the table.

"How am I supposed to believe a man who has cheated me? You come into my poker room, cheat at my tables, and then lie to my face?" Evgenii said angrily.

"I'm sorry. I'll tell you everything I know. I'm sorry."

"I will ask you one more time Michael. The next time will not be *YOUR* hand that is broken. It will be that of your sister's."

"Anything you want. I'll talk! I'll tell you what you want."

"Explain how you cheat in my poker room."

"I have practiced countless times a shuffling maneuver that allows me to reorder the cards the way I want them. I give a player at the table a good set of cards and deal myself a better pair."

"Who do you work for? The man in the green Jeep? Is he your boss?"

"No, I swear Evgenii. I have no idea who that man is. I've never seen him before. I swear to God I'm telling you the truth."

Evgenii slammed both tattooed hands down onto my broken hands. "Then why is he taking pictures of you in my parking lot?"

The pain was even more intense than when my hands were first broken. A white flash blinded me for what seemed like a minute. I screamed louder than I can ever recall. I begged for mercy. I begged for Evgenii to believe me.

"I honestly don't know. I have no idea who he even is. You have to believe me. I'm telling you the truth!" I said sobbing.

Evgenii lifted his hands off of mine. "Maybe we need Melanie here to help your memory."

"Evgenii, please. I don't know who he is. I'm being honest. I admit that I was cheating the other players in your poker room, but I didn't lead that guy to the poker room. This is all a big mistake. There has to be something I can do to make this up to you."

Evgenii's cell phone rang, as if the governor had called in the last reprieve before my execution. He walked toward the back of the truck. Quick Russian bursts were whispered into the phone's receiver. He listened and then snapped his phone closed.

"It appears the man in the Jeep has left the parking lot. Maybe you're telling the truth. Then again, maybe it is a coincidence and you are continuing to lie to me," Evgenii said.

"No. No. Evgenii, I'm not lying to you. I am a poker player who cheats to win. That is all. I have never told anyone about the poker room. I didn't lead anyone there. Please! You have to believe me. I'm nothing more. Please don't hurt my sister or Melanie. They have nothing to do with this."

Evgenii stroked his bearded stubble and paced back and forth. "Let us say I do believe you Michael. Let us say that you aren't a police informant or snitch and just a man who is very good at shuffling cards, as you say. In our homeland, if a man steals from you, you have no choice but to kill him. Your honor and that of your family is at stake."

"Please! Evgenii, No! I'll do anything. Anything at all."

"Here, in Canada, we are not the same as in Russia. We do things a little differently. We have a reputation to uphold, a business to run. If a man steals from you or snitches on you, we don't kill him. You see, in a business, money must be made. If we kill you, we get nothing. Instead, we kill someone you love. For you, that means Melanie and your sister."

I shook my head wildly. "No Evgenii, please! PLEASE! I admit I cheated at your poker room, but I didn't steal from you."

"Cheating in my poker room is the same as stealing from me. As far as I'm concerned Mr. Taylor, you owe me a lot of money."

Hope rose inside of me. "I agree Evgenii. I do owe you. Let's work something out. No one has to get hurt."

"From what I am told, you have enough money. So, here's the deal. You pay me $2500 a month for the rest of your life…"

"…that sounds like a fair deal. I'll take it."

"I am not finished. You pay me $2500 each month and I'll let you choose which person we kill, as a reminder that we're serious about our deal."

Hope drained from my body. "Evgenii, please. Isn't there a way we can work something out where both women live and you still get your money?"

"I'm afraid not," Evgenii said.

"You run a business, right? Your goal is to make money. Let me help you. I'll pay double each month for both of their lives to be spared. That's $5000 a month. No one gets hurt."

"I like how you think Michael, except I cannot allow you to ever return to the poker room. Such an act would diminish our reputation around the city and give our competitors cause to think we have become weak..."

"...okay, sure. I can understand that," I said.

"Again you interrupt me before I finish, which is an annoying habit. Do it again and you lose a hand. Your offer of $5000 a month isn't high enough for both women to live. $10,000 and we have a deal. Both of their lives will be spared, for now."

I was willing to agree with any terms in order to secure both Susie's and Melanie's safety. "Okay. I agree. Thank you."

"One last thing, Michael Taylor. Money isn't enough to make sure you understand the gravity of the situation and our seriousness."

"What do you mean? We agreed that for $10,000 a month both women would be unharmed."

"Yes, both women will remain unharmed. However, a couple broken fingers isn't enough to show anyone else what happens if you steal from us."

"Please! Evgenii. No!"

Evgenii nodded his head to the men that surrounded me and walked out of the cargo van. I never saw Evgenii Marchenko again.

As the cargo door closed after him, both of my elbows were pinned to the table. A massive body slammed the side of my head down, folding me in half. I yelled out in fear. I didn't want the pain. Not again. Through a thick accent, the other man whispered in my ear.

"What hand do you write with?" One of Evgenii's men spoke.

"No. No!"

"Answer the question or I will take a guess," he continued.

"Right. I'm right handed. Please, no! You don't have to do this. I'm already going to pay $10,000 a month. That's reminder enough. No!"

My left wrist was grabbed. I struggled to make a fist and pull away from the powerful grasp. The pain was furious. The man's hands felt like a vice grip compared to my efforts. Each movement sent shockwaves of pain. I attempted to squirm away from his grip. There was no escaping him. Sweat poured down my forehead. The man behind me loosened his grip on my right elbow and reinserted the gag in my mouth.

Two men against a man half their size seated in restraints wasn't a fair fight. Not by a long shot. They had total control over me. I stopped struggling long enough to attempt to reason with them through my gag. I tried making sounds from my throat, indicating that I wanted to talk. Their grip lessened around my wrists and elbows. The weight on my head pulled up a bit. The less I struggled, the more they drew back.

I felt something metal around my left thumb, like a loose ring. I couldn't see it. I tried to angle my head around. Its cold feeling surprised me. Then darkness.

That was the last time I had two thumbs.

CHAPTER 20

THE HOSPITAL

Excerpt from Michael's Journal

Flashes. Not full memories. Just snapshots and pain. I remember waking up after being tossed out of the back of a moving van in front of the emergency room entrance. I was shirtless. Falling onto the pavement, I scraped my elbows and back. The next flash was a memory of confusion. And pain. The pain was deafening. It was blinding. All I could focus on was how much everything hurt. Being awake hurt. It was easier to slide back into the blackness.

My shirt was wrapped around my left hand. A nurse was unwrapping it. The bandage was soaked with blood. I saw it. Black.

I came to and heard fast talking people. They circled me. They all wore green scrubs. I couldn't focus. They spoke to me. I muttered something. Black.

A hand touched my right elbow. The hand squeezed the consciousness into me. It parted the fog. I feared the Russian men were back, having changed their minds. Some sick joke I thought. Torture me, send me to the hospital, and then kill me. Some Russian rite of passage or something.

A nurse had come to check my status.

"Sir, how is your pain?"

"Bad," I said.

"The doctor ran a blood test and screened for drug use. You're drug free. You've been installed with a morphine drip," the nurse said.

"Thank you."

SAVANNAH

The nurse handed me the single button device. "It's controlled by pressing the button. That will release drops into your IV. Do you know what has happened since you arrived?"

"No."

The nurse also informed me of the surgical procedures that had transpired. She explained that since there wasn't a thumb to reattach, the doctors had cauterized the skin where my thumb was previously attached. The thumb had been detached between the two knuckles. One knuckle remained. A stump.

"Eventually, you'll learn to use it," the nurse said.

I needed relief. With every heartbeat the pain grew. My whole body ached.

The memories from the previous night came crashing back to me. I looked down at my right hand. The middle finger was swollen and bruised. There wasn't a cast, just a simple splint. It was broken. Evgenii and his thugs.

My left hand was heavily wrapped with thick white gauze. Three finger tips stuck out of the club. My ring finger throbbed. Underneath the surface of gauze was my broken knuckle, swollen three times its normal size. I reached for the morphine drip button. A Velcro restraint restricted my movement.

It was the second time I was in restraints that day. When I politely inquired why I was restrained to the bed rails, the nurse explained that it was hospital protocol.

"All patients who are to be questioned by the police are temporarily restrained. Don't worry, the police will remove them. Usually it's the first thing they do," the nurse said.

In less time than it took me to shake away the cobwebs in my head, two uniformed police officers walked in and surrounded my bed. Their presence was intimidating. Their bullet proof vests enlarged their stature. Broader. Thicker. Their snarls showed shear annoyance, as if I had already started lying. They didn't remove the restraints. The bigger one nodded to the nurse. She left. The shorter one spoke.

"Name?" the short police officer said.

"My name is Michael Taylor. Do you think that you could..."

"We'll ask the questions. You answer them," the tall officer said.

"Sorry."

"We already know your name Mr. Taylor. We don't like being lied to, so don't even try it."--reviewing his pad of paper—"What do you do for a living?" the short officer said.

I knew telling the truth would mix as well as a lit match and a gas can. The Russians would definitely kill Melanie and Susie. I didn't have any proof to offer for the police to believe me, aside from the poker room. Divulging the poker room's whereabouts was suicide.

121

"Small business owner. I operate a car wash. Nothing fancy, just the coin-operated-self-service kind."

Already bored the short officer said, "Uh, huh. And can you explain to us what happened to you?"

"Wood working accident."

"Pardon me, sir?" the short officer said.

"Wood working accident. I was doing some do-it-yourself repairs around my home. I slipped and accidentally cut my thumb on the table saw."

The idea came to me from a movie I watched. The main character witnesses the mob torturing an innocent man by cutting off his fingers with a saw, one at a time. They figured he knew more than he was letting on. Actually, my truth wasn't too far from the movie scene.

"Can you explain the sudden arrival at the emergency room?" the short officer continued.

"I don't understand your question."

"Mr. Taylor, the nurses here report that you were found lying on the ground outside the emergency room entrance. How did you get there?" the short officer said.

"Taxi. I live alone. There wasn't anyone to drive me. I walked to the corner and hailed a cab. After that, I'm not sure. I blacked out and didn't come to until a few minutes before you guys walked in."

"Uh, huh. And if I call the cab company and inquire about this, your story will match up?"

"Yes. Can you remove my restraints now?"

"And your broken finger on your other hand? How did that happen?" the short officer said.

"Must have happened after I passed out. I have no clue how I did that."

"Do you use drugs Mr. Taylor?"

"Never."

"And you say there isn't anyone who can vouch for your story?"

"I suppose the cab driver could."

"Did you pay him?"

"Who?"

"The cab driver."

"I don't know. I can't recall."

I could see the apathy of a dead case glaze over their eyes. They must have assumed the cab driver had sped off in anger after not getting paid. Locating a single cab driver who drove to the hospital and didn't collect a fare would be a next to impossible task. Most cab drivers are reluctant to divulge when they get stiffed.

Before leaving, they removed the restraints. Their departure was a massive

122

relief that brought back the gravity of the past twelve hours. In the past seven weeks, I had gone from using Savannah occasionally, to engineering Savannah 2.0, making boat loads of cash, getting my dream car, buying a small business, buying all the things I have ever wanted, meeting an amazing woman, to having my left thumb severed. Not to mention my new monthly payment. $10,000 for the rest of my life, like some instant lottery game, except backwards.

I had some savings to hold off the Russians for a couple of months. Losing my bankroll was a huge blow. I had, sitting in neatly stacked chips, over $120,000. Most likely, it was in Evgenii's hands now.

The *IT* was uncontrollable. I hadn't even thought about that aspect. In order of relevance, it didn't hold too much weight compared to losing a thumb. Or having a Russian crime family break your fingers. Or owing them a ridiculous amount of money each month for the rest of my, potentially lessened, life.

Tears began to flow down my face, again. My body silently shook. Grief and despair set in further. *How could I have let this all go downhill so fast?* Wiping the tears away with the back of my right hand, I thought of Susie and Melanie and how close their lives had come to ending.

I found a box of Kleenex on the side table. Using one to absorb my tears, I squeezed the corners of both eyes and cursed myself. I let the rage flow.

"Idiot. Idiot! You're an idiot Michael. Goddamn it! How could you have been so stupid? You're no better than your moron father and his selfish ways."

I heard the hospital room door open.

"Nurse, can you give me a few minutes and come back later, please?"

"Michael Taylor?" a man responded.

Removing the tissue, I looked up. I instantly recognized the man standing at the foot of my bed. He dressed in a pair of drab olive slacks and a dark brown shirt. He was the man from the photographs. The man Evgenii forced me to look at and tortured me about. This was the man who caused me to lose everything. "Michael Taylor? Do I have the correct room?" the unknown man said.

I nodded, playing it as cool as I could manage. He knew who I was. Uneasiness crept over me. The safety of the hospital room seemed to be sucked out through the ventilation ducts. I was vulnerable. I had a broken finger on each hand and was missing a thumb. Any movement caused me great pain. A physical confrontation would have been bad. Very bad. I didn't stand a chance.

The man pulled up the only chair in my room and flashed his credentials. His Canada Revenue Agency identification looked to be as official as a dollar store sheriff's badge. The name on the badge said "Bradley Weisnewski." An awful photograph of him wearing a different pair of glasses and a fake smile was in the right corner.

Showing him I was clearly not in the mood for a discussion, I said, "Nice photograph."

Bradley Weisnewski opened his zipped file folder case, "Thank you Mr. Taylor. May I call you Michael?"

"Sure. What's this all about Bradley?"

"Agent Weisnewski."

"Pardon Brad?"

"Right. Well, Michael. First, I would like to express the CRA's deepest condolences on your accident. I'm told you lost your thumb in a home repair accident."

"Yeah. Thanks. This isn't a good time."

"Interesting how your car isn't at home. It's parked at some carpet warehouse and has been for some time."

"Is that what you're here about Brad, may I call you that? Parking fines? Since when is the CRA interested in parking fines?"

"Sorry if I misled you Mr. Taylor, but the CRA isn't interested in parking fines or where your car is parked. The CRA is interested in taxes. Specifically speaking, the taxes that the CRA is rightfully owed."

"I'm sure I don't know what you're talking about Brad."

"Mr. Taylor, let me be honest with you. I am an investigator for the CRA and my sole purpose is to make sure the agency receives the proper amount of money from all taxpayers."

"What does that have to do with me?"

Bradley Weisnewski looked down at his opened file folder on his lap and thumbed through some papers. "Well, Michael, I have been investigating you for almost a week now and I haven't found a tax receipt with your name on it for the purchase of your business, the vehicle you're currently driving, or any tax filings in the past three years. Do you care to explain how you failed to pay all those taxes?"

"Look Mr. Weisnewski, clearly you have thoroughly done your job. I suppose there isn't any chance you might give me an opportunity to thank the CRA, specifically you, for a job well done with a donation of sorts?"

"Are you attempting to bribe me Mr. Taylor?"

"Me? No. I was simply trying to find a resolution to this without going any further than this hospital room."

"Attempt at bribing a CRA agent is a serious offense Mr. Taylor. It's punishable by up to thirty days in jail and/or a $1000 fine."

"Well, good thing I wasn't trying to bribe you then. I wouldn't want anyone to think I was doing that," I said.

"The fact of the matter here sir, is that you still haven't explained to me the missing tax returns and the absent paperwork from the purchase of your vehicle and business property."

"How do you know for certain that the vehicle and property are mine?"

SAVANNAH

"For one, your vehicle is registered as a late model Honda Civic. And furthermore, Mr. Akbar Rahmin has confessed his fraudulent activities to me pertaining to the sale of his car wash. He identified you as the purchaser and initiator of the cash sale. Is that evidence enough?"

"I would like to contact a lawyer before I say anything else."

Bradley Weisnewski closed his folder and beginning to zip up its lining. "Fair enough Mr. Taylor. I will leave you with my card. Advise your attorney that you are facing tax fraud charges and will be charged the day after I return to Ottawa. You may contact me using the phone number on the card. I wish you well in your recovery."

With that, Bradley Weisnewski stood and walked out of my hospital room. I couldn't help but laugh at how awful my day had turned out.

CHAPTER 21
THE DAY AFTER

Excerpt from Michael's Journal

For Susie's sake, I'm going to intentionally skip the anguish I endured from losing my thumb. The phantom pain. The nightmares. Watch a war movie where a character loses an appendage. Take the pain that is shown and multiply it by ten and you will be right in the ballpark of what I felt. I'll just leave it at that, for Susie.

With a pat on the back and a pharmacy bag full of pain medication, I was released from the hospital. There were some pressing matters that I needed to take care of. I had to find a good tax lawyer. I also needed to figure out how long I could hold off Evgenii and his men. Every $10Gs bought me a month.

Getting home was a relief. Exhaustion and constant pain settled in. Scouring the yellow pages and Internet, I researched multiple attorneys. Their bold print advertisements claimed they could "ease my tax worries." I needed a lawyer. A lawyer who was good enough that he didn't need to advertise in the phone book. Slime ball ambulance chasers did that. The snakes who claimed they would "get you off the hook." Not much help. I knew the type of lawyer I wanted was expensive.

The yellow pages were useless. Searching the Internet proved rather helpful. I found the upscale and professional website of Goldstein, Bryant, and Dunn. They offered a team of lawyers to represent me. One lawyer was good. A team of lawyers would be better. I called them.

A legal secretary took down my name and phone number and assured me that a lawyer would call me back that day. Apparently, all of the lawyers in the entire firm were too busy to talk with me. Lawyers. So damn important.

My answering machine had a few messages on it. Nothing pressing, until the third one. It was Melanie. I had forgotten about our date. I had stood her up. She sounded both confused and concerned in her message. As fast as my fingers could dial her number, I called and explained what had happened. Not the truth. I decided she would get the same story the police received, with minor alterations. Tell one lie, stick with it.

I was helping a friend lay down some base board and was using a chop saw. She sucked in a breath in anticipation. *I had accidentally cut off my thumb and panicked from all the blood.* A little sound sneaked out. *I passed out from the sight of so much blood.* Her hand silently covering her mouth. *My friend panicked and didn't search for my thumb and rushed me to the hospital.*

"I'll be over in ten minutes," she blurted out, finally releasing her held breath.

Melanie's sympathy and compassion was overwhelming. She insisted she would wait on me hand and foot. Like a scene out of a sappy love story, she helped change my bandage. She didn't even flinch when she saw the remnants of my thumb, nicknamed "the stub." Once the new bandage had been applied, she kissed it and whispered, "Feel better."

I had to ask a huge favor. My car was still at the poker room from two nights ago. I assumed it would be safe for me to retrieve it. Explaining to Melanie why the car was in a carpet shop's parking lot was the difficult part. I hadn't given it any forethought to why my car would be parked in such a strange place. On the fly I lied through my teeth about how my buddy couldn't drive my car all the way back to my house.

"Can you believe that after I lost my thumb working for him, he couldn't even bring my car all the way back to my house?" I said.

"It's okay, we'll go get it," Melanie said.

"He told me something about not having enough time to drive the entire distance, so he dropped it off around the halfway mark of our houses."

She bought it.

The parking lot looked completely different in the daylight. Only a few cars dotted the black asphalt. The sinister carpet distributor looked normal, like nothing exciting ever dreamed of happening there. Identifying my bright orange car should have been easy, except, my car was nowhere to be found. I always parked in the same spot, part of my routine. Two nights prior it was there, right where I had left it. Now, it was gone.

Obviously, Evgenii knew it was my car from the security footage he had. The car was his for the taking because there was no way I could report the car missing or stolen. Police attention would force Evgenii to act drastically. Feeling more and more beat down, I walked back to Melanie's car, I couldn't hold back my emotions. My anger boiled over. The anger that I hadn't been able to let out when Agent Bradley Weisnewski walked in.

Sitting back down in the passenger seat, I exploded. I shouted at the top of my lungs. My roar ended and I sat there quietly. Melanie's eyes gazed at me. She started the car. We exchanged only two words the entire ride home.

"It's gone," I said.

She got the point. She didn't speak another word of it.

The next day I counted my remaining cash. Buying the car wash and losing my bankroll was a severe blow. $17,775 was all I had. Not even two months of safety for Susie. Or Melanie. Or both.

The law firm never returned my phone call. After leaving another message, insisting that I couldn't wait another day, I got a call back from an attorney.

Richard Brantley, a tax attorney at Goldstein, Bryant, and Dunn law firm specialized in the complex and technical field of tax law. Speaking over the phone wasn't a good option. After meeting Agent Bradley Weisnewski, paranoia set in. Had he tapped my phone? Was it legal to bug my house?

Richard preferred face-to-face meetings as well. We set an appointment later that afternoon. Before we met, he explained that his fee was $300 an hour with a $5000 retainer. If my case went to trial, the fee would raise to $400 an hour with an additional $5000 retainer. I agreed, without a second thought. I needed Mr. Brantley to represent me. He seemed experienced and knowledgeable. As we spoke, I felt better. The stress began to melt away. I actually felt relaxed just knowing there was someone helping me.

More pressing matters demanded my attention. Evgenii Marchenko. The moment I agreed to the terms with him, I knew life would never be the same. I was tied to a Russian crime family. I would never be allowed to break from their grasp. They had me for $10,000 a month. $120,000 a year in cold hard cash, assuming they didn't raise the price.

The car wash was a source of income, for the time being. Akbar estimated that he made $1500 a month, if business was slow. The fall and winter were the low seasons. No one washes their car then. In the spring and summer, $3000 a month. I low-balled the number to $2000 that would be used towards paying the Russians each month. That meant I needed an additional $8000 each month, to satisfy the terms of our agreement.

I sat on my new leather couch, resting my feet on the coffee table. I stared blankly at the wall. I pondered the possible ways I could make $8000. Poker would never again be a steady source of income. Without a left thumb, Savannah was dead in the water.

My mind wandered to gambling. The potential for large sums of money were there. Blackjack, craps, and high-end slots seemed like an option. The image of Susie's dead body flickered into my daydream. I couldn't gamble again. The stakes were too high. I needed a large stream of cash that was steady and reliable.

I didn't have an education. To make the kind of cash I needed, I had to land an upper management position. Those weren't filled by guys like me. I was street smart and savvy. No one was going to give me a high paying job in an office somewhere. The types of jobs that I could get employment in weren't going to pay enough money.

Coming up short one month wasn't an option. Leniency wasn't one of Evgenii's better qualities. If I failed to deliver, even one time, I knew what would happen. I would be tortured again. They wouldn't kill me. But Melanie or Susie's life would come to an abrupt end. I made this happen. I caused this. I swore to them both that as long as I was alive, the Russians would get their money.

The guy who originally introduced me to the poker room, Arch, was my answer. His real name was Lonnie Archibald, but no one dared to call him that to his face. Huge. That's the only word that described Arch. The only reason I was privy to his real name was his wallet fell out of his pocket one time on my garage floor, during my garage poker days. Picking it up for him, I dared a quick glance at his driver's license. He loved gambling, and was connected.

Aside from being a big time gambler who sucked at winning, he was a former biker gang member who had to "retire" when he could no longer ride. Being over 300 lbs. made riding a motorcycle a challenge. "If you can't ride with the gang, you're relegated to the sidelines or worse," he once told me. That suited Arch just fine, because it freed up more of his time for his two favorite activities, gambling and drinking.

I called Arch. I explained I needed to talk. He was always available to talk, when someone else was buying the drinks. He told me to meet him at 8 p.m. and to come thirsty, his way of saying we would be drinking all night, on my tab.

Before seeing Arch, I was scheduled to meet with Richard Brantley. I brought $5000 for his retainer fee. I dressed as professionally as I could, matching his professionalism. Making its debut appearance, my gray suit raised my level of respectability. I looked good. I felt good. I was ready.

Without my car, I had to take public transit. That brought me down, right to the ground floor of humility. Expensive suit, great shoes, original watch, and I was riding around on a bus. Not my idea of classy.

The offices of Goldstein, Bryant, and Dunn were located in the heart of Toronto. Situated on the twenty-third floor of a skyscraper, the décor of the lobby was ornately decorated, suggesting a large overhead leasing cost. An entire floor must be a small fortune. I wondered if the firm's monthly expense was more than mine.

SAVANNAH

Exiting the elevator and entering the waiting room, I caught an eye full of deep, rich wood and overstuffed leather furniture. The coffee table held the latest reading material that satisfied a wide range of interests from sports, to fashion, to investment strategies. The receptionist was a beautiful young woman, clearly hired for her typing skills. My suit didn't seem to impress her.

Richard Brantley came out to the front lobby after allowing me a few minutes to peruse the most recent issue of Sports Illustrated. His short, stubby frame featured a beginner's pot belly and stumpy arms. His swollen hand hid a firm handshake that demanded more respect than his appearance. His well trimmed silver beard covered pudgy cheeks. A receding hairline elongated his forehead.

He spoke quickly with me and thanked me for coming in on such short notice. I followed him as he waddled back into his office. I immediately noticed how well cut his suit was. His jacket had been tailored perfectly. His pants were the right length when he walked. Not too short, preventing exposure of his socks. Yet not too long, which would create wrinkles in the lower pant legs. He dressed well. At that moment, I knew Richard Brantley was very good at his job.

His office had the same feeling as a museum display. Extreme neatness. Obsessive order. Not a speck of dust anywhere. Behind his empty desk, which only housed a large laptop computer off on the right, he sat. He motioned for me to sit.

"Welcome Mr. Taylor. I see you have brought the documents I requested over the phone and assume that you wish to hire me as your attorney?" Richard Brantley said.

"Yes I would."

"Excellent. The reason I ask that is because as of right this moment, you can now speak as freely as you wish because I am bound by attorney-client privilege. Meaning, anything incriminating you tell me cannot be used against you in a court of law. Do you understand what I mean Mr. Taylor?"

"Yes I do. And please, call me Michael."

"Certainly Michael, call me Rich. I would like you to speak openly. Tell me everything about why you are here."

I told him. After ten minutes, he knew everything. Almost. I left out the Russians and the poker. Not relevant I figured. I stuck to the car wash, the missing tax years, and the CRA's investigation. I explained I was a professional poker player, then I handed him Agent Weisnewski's card. On his yellow legal pad, he took notes. I spoke. He wrote. His stare bounced between my stub and his legal pad of notes. He allowed me to finish, then he asked his questions.

"And that's the entire story? Nothing else you may have left out?" Richard said.

"Like what?"

"Mr. Taylor, I've been doing this a long time and I've represented all sorts of clients, from all walks of life. The more information I have, the better I'll be able to represent you."

"I don't really know what you mean Rich."

"Michael, c'mon. Don't waste my time. Level with me. I'm legally bound to take what we discuss with me to the grave. Remember, attorney-client privilege? What happened to your thumb? Should we call it a hazard of your profession?"

"Alright Rich. But I won't be answering any follow up questions."

"Fair enough. Let's hear it."

"I didn't lose my thumb in a home repair accident, as I told the police in their report. I was caught cheating at a game of poker and there were some gentlemen who weren't so thrilled about it. They cut my thumb off as a reminder of the seriousness of stealing from them. Every month, I owe them $10,000. It's a repayment and for the guaranteed safety of my loved ones. Funny enough, and just the way my luck has always gone, the reason I was even being watched, and was ultimately caught, was because the guy on the card I gave you, CRA Investigator Bradley Weisnewski, tailed me to the illegal poker room. Their security camera caught him taking pictures of me for his tax fraud investigation."

"Jeez, Michael. These guys sound like legit bad guys. Do I need to be concerned?"

"No. As long as I make the payments, everything should be smooth sailing."

"How long can you hold them off? I mean, frankly speaking, how much cash do you have set aside?"

"Not much. I had about two months left in cash. The car wash is worth $60,000, so that could buy me six months if I needed it to, right?"

"I'm sorry Michael, but unless you were able to find a buyer who was looking for a cash deal similar to yours, you probably won't be able to sell it. Most buyers aren't looking for trouble with the CRA. They would require legal paperwork. Frankly speaking, you don't have any."

"What are you saying? That I can't sell the car wash, if push comes to shove?"

"Honestly, no. If I were you I would use all the profits you can from it, as long as you can. As for your tax situation, I have some good news and a lot of bad news."

"Okay, I'm ready for this."

"The bad news is that it sounds as though Mr. Weisnewski has a slam dunk case. With Akbar Rahmin's confession of tax evasion, the cash payment for the car, and the three years of missing income tax, you're looking at trouble. If each of these things were separate, then I could probably plea down the case to a fine with no jail time. However, with all of these together, your case looks much more like a pattern of tax evasion and potential money laundering to any judge."

"What am I looking at here, worst case scenario?"

"Worst case? I would say a fine of about $10,000 and five years in prison. Depending on who is assigned to prosecute you, they might try to bundle your proceeding into one clean cut case or they could charge you with the three separate crimes. The most realistic course of action for the government to take would be to bundle your charges and plea you out to a large fine and some jail time. Best case scenario? I get the car and car wash purchase dropped and only deal with the three years of tax evasion."

"So, you're telling me there is a very real chance I will be going to jail?"

"Yes, Michael. It looks that way. But there is a lot to be worked out before then. I'm going to be representing you and that is a good thing. I also have a piece of news that my firm is keeping a very close eye on."

"Okay, let's hear it."

"The court officers of Ontario have been working without a collective agreement for the past few months. Their union has been working with the Province of Ontario to come to a fair deal, but all indications are that the court officers are unhappy with the province's offer."

"How does this help me? Are they going to strike?"

"No, they officially cannot strike in the traditional sense. The picket sign holding members standing on the side of the street simply wouldn't be allowed to happen. They'd be ordered back to work. However, rumor has it that the court officers have threatened to mimic the police officers' actions of some years ago where they planned an elaborate action nicknamed 'the blue flu.' That ring a bell at all?"

"No. Should it?"

"Not really. It wasn't publicized too much for fear of criminal behavior surging in the city. Police officers are not allowed to strike either. Their union came up with the strategy of large numbers of police officers calling in sick or taking vacation time. It acted as a passive aggressive strike."

"Interesting stuff, but how does this help me?"

"Well, if the court officers use the same strategy then all the court cases will be postponed. A few years ago in Spain, the court officers held a similar strike. More than 6000 trials were stopped, in one day alone. Everything from criminal trials to divorces to registering new born babies was stopped. It caused a major delay for the courts. That was one day and the ripple caused a two week backlog. If the court officers in Ontario performed something similar, the ripple would be more like a tidal wave. You might get a month or two extra before your case was even put before a judge."

"How realistic is this?"

"Tough to say, but the rumors are spreading that there could be a one day movement as soon as early next week."

I left Richard's office. Jail time was in my future, one way or another. The time extension from the strike was the silver lining. I needed more money before I went to jail. More time to make more money gave me hope. But I still needed some sort of high paying job.

CHAPTER 22

ARCH

Excerpt from Michael's Journal

Arch wanted to meet that evening at Racks. Showing up in a $1000 suit would have been a foolish move. Racks was a cross between a strip club and pool hall, with waitresses, if you want to call them that, who wore nothing more than a string bikini and a pair of shoes. It wasn't uncommon for the waitresses to go missing with a customer to the back room which housed secluded, private booths for personal dances. Racks didn't offer stages for dancers nor was nudity permitted. The owner didn't have to label his bar as a strip club with the government. Special permits were needed and surprise visits were common with strip clubs. However, pool halls generally had carte blanche.

Wearing my regular old clothes, from before Savannah upgrade, I walked into Racks expecting to sit with Arch at the bar like it was my last night before going to prison. To keep the illusion of a pool hall for the general public, and the local authorities, the outside of Racks had been decorated with a large neon sign of billiard balls arranged in an 8-ball triangle. For the common passerby, the twenty foot rack of balls on top of the roof made sense. Pool hall. Pool hall name. Makes sense. After entering the hall, the double meaning was evident.

Girls. Lots of girls. I paid my $10 cover charge and my eyes were met by excessively well endowed girls of every nationality. Each girl must have been handpicked by their breast size. The waitresses sported different colored bikinis and served drinks throughout the pool hall. The pool hall was surprisingly well lit. Two

133

lengthy bars on opposite sides offered seating. Instead of normally facing the bar and watching whatever the TV showed, the stools were all angled out toward the pool tables and the girls.

It was the kind of place where men whistled cat calls and the occasional slap on the butt was permitted, assuming you had just ordered a drink.

Arch was seated on a stool at the end the bar. Next to him sat an unoccupied stool, assumingly for me. He leaned his elbow on top of the stool back. Arch commanded both the stool he sat in and the one keeping his arm comfortable. No one would have the courage, or stupidity depending on how you look at it, to question Arch about the saved stool. Towering six feet and six inches and easily weighing in over 300 lbs., Arch filled his leather biker vest from top to bottom. The back of the vest was covered by a skull and crossbones and the words "Outlaws MC" above it, "Oshawa" below it.

The Outlaws were a motorcycle club that had a local charter in Oshawa. Their club was the epitome of the "one percenter" lifestyle. They called themselves a motorcycle club, but everyone knew they were a biker gang. Loyalty was the number one character trait required by the Outlaws MC. Members had been arrested and charged with a wide range of criminal conduct. Drug possession and trafficking, gun smuggling across international borders, and assault were common. Unlike other organized crime affiliates, the Outlaws weren't organized to make money. They made money to organize and fund their club.

I tapped Arch on his massive shoulder and tried to wrap my arms around his girth. He nearly crushed me with his embrace. Two shots of Jack Daniel's whiskey and two Budweiser's later, I slapped down my credit card and told the bartender to keep my tab open for the night. I needed Arch's help. Having a sympathetic ear that happened to be lubricated by alcohol couldn't hurt.

We slugged back more shots. I put out the fire in my throat by chasing with beer. It looked weak. I knew that, but there was nothing I could do. Arch, on the other hand, slapped my back and called me a light weight. After ordering another round of shots, I turned toward Arch and showed him my stub. He grabbed my wrist. He gazed at the spot where my thumb used to be. Then he eyed me with a pained, questioning look.

I explained my situation to Arch. He heard the exact same story I told Richard Brantley just a few hours before. I omitted Evgenii, the Russians, and the poker room, but Arch knew. He just knew. He was the one who had initially brought me to the poker room. That was only two months before. His word carried enough clout to bring a stranger. Members of the Outlaws apparently had some pull. Arch turned to me. His eyes were unfitting of a man wearing a leather vest.

I expected Arch, who had been a friend of mine since the garage poker games, to lend an ear. If I begged and pleaded hard enough for a job with the Outlaws, maybe I'd get lucky. Maybe Arch would pity me. I didn't have any leads. No future avenues of income to make my payments to Evgenii.

"I feel responsible for what happened to you. I should have never brought you there," Arch said.

I was surprised. I opened my mouth to speak; he beat me to the punch.

"Man Michael, this is some messed up shit. How much are you in for?"

"Ten G's," I said.

"Okay, that's not the end of the world. We can figure something out."

"Arch. Ten G's a *month*. Forever."

"Oh, fuck me, Michael! How the hell are you going to manage this?"

"I have no clue. I need some help Arch. And not a handout, I need some really honest to goodness cash. I'm begging you bro, I'll do anything."

Arch waved his massive right hand dismissively. "I'll take care of it. Don't worry about it anymore. Tonight, we're going to use the rest of the night to drink our worries away and enjoy the generous sights of the wait staff."

His attitude was reassuring. Ninety minutes later, I was well on my way to a serious hangover. I asked him what he had in mind as a solution for me. Turning instantly serious, Arch shook his head, rose off of his stool, and waved me to follow him toward the exit. Once outside in the parking lot, he motioned for me to get into his black Chrysler 300M. The car's width was generous enough to accommodate Arch's frame.

"Club business is never discussed in public. Never. Remember that," Arch said.

The gravity of his words hung in the air like helium filled birthday balloons. He was ultra serious as he explained the Outlaws code.

"Patched members never speak about club business with a non-patched member. Doing so would result in some rather gruesome consequences."

"Sorry man, I didn't know."

"You have to trust me. The president of the charter decides all business decisions. He'll be your contact."

"Arch, bro, I appreciate this. I really do. I didn't know where else to turn."

"Michael, you're a good friend of mine and I feel responsible for what happened to you, but I need you to be very clear about this. I am taking a huge risk. Even bringing you up for a job with the club is going to piss a lot of people off. Non-members are not welcome in our club. We never contract jobs out. It's just not how the club works. We handle our own business."

"Arch, I don't know what to say. I don't want you to catch any heat for me. But bro I'm desperate. I really need something, man. You know these animals I'm dealing with. They won't kill me, man; they'll go after Susie. You can trust me. I'll keep my mouth shut."

"I do trust you Michael. Because if something were to happen where you let the club down, not only would you be in their bad books, but so would the person who recommended you. Me. The Outlaws don't cut thumbs off. They don't demand monthly payments. They simply erase the mistake. Get what I mean?"

"Clear as daylight Arch. I won't let you down."

"Good. I'll call you in a day or so and let you know what the president says."

"Thanks Arch. You don't know how much this means to me."

With a glance toward my left hand, Arch nodded his head and started his car, indicating it was time for me to leave. Arch left the parking lot that night carrying my only hope.

CHAPTER 23

NEW CAR

Excerpt from Michael's Journal

Home was a blend of anxiety and nervousness. I waited for the phone to ring. Richard promised a call. Arch said he'd let me know either way. With each phone ring, I sprang to life. I muted the TV and checked the caller ID. Each time a long distance number that I didn't recognize came up, my heart sank like a stone.

The fourth time it rang, the caller ID had another number with a foreign area code. Believing it to be another telemarketer selling windows or doors, I abruptly answered the phone.

"Yeah."

"Michael?"

"Arch, that you?"

"Yeah, you got wheels?"

"No man, my car was, well, it's gone."

"I see. This actually is a good thing. You have some cash on you?"

"Some, but not too much, just a few thousand."

"Alright, I can front you some. Bring as much as you can and meet me in Racks' parking lot tonight at nine o'clock. I've got some good news."

"Okay, I'll be there."

I am not sure why, but I lied to Arch about how much money I had. I still had about $17,700. Something inside me told me to keep $10,000. A one month

137

insurance policy, in case Arch didn't come through. I gathered the remaining bills and buried them deep in my jeans.

I had four hours until my meeting with Arch. The anxiety wore a hole in my stomach. I paced the length of my living room floor, performed set after set of push -ups and sit ups, and still the nervousness lingered. Sitting hunched over, I tried to clear my thoughts. Calm your body Michael, I told myself over and over. My mind was in overdrive. Peace wasn't coming today.

My mind raced through possible jobs the Outlaws could offer me. Being choosey wasn't an option. Whatever it was, I needed to take it. I had to be prepared for anything. Naturally, I jumped to the seedier sides of motorcycle club business. Collection of debts owed? Assault? Murder?

I broke out in a sweat. The thought of having to hurt or kill crushed me. I wasn't a killer for hire or even a thug who could be called on to "deliver a message." I was a poker player who had been caught cheating and evading his taxes. How could I say no? Would Susie or Melanie, or both, die if I turned the Outlaws down? Could I find something else?

I wiped my brow and caught my breath. I planned possible excuses for declining the Outlaw's job offers.

As the sun began to set, I dressed and began walking the seven miles to Racks. I needed to get out, staying in was driving me mad. The walk eased the growing anxiety. Exercise, the ultimate stress reliever.

Glancing at my old Timex, I arrived earlier than expected. Arch told me to meet him in the parking lot, entering Racks seemed foolish. The parking lot was only half full. Arch's black Chrysler wasn't there. It was only 8:30 p.m. I found a dull gray guardrail that stretched along one end of the parking lot. I settled in for the wait.

As soon as I sat, a loud whistle, like the kind you make with four fingers and a creative tongue pierced the air. Two nights prior, when a good looking waitress walked by, Arch used the same whistle to let her know he liked what he saw. She blushed, slapped him on the ass and kept walking.

I walked toward the whistle. Arch sat in a small compact car. His large frame looked uncomfortable. He waved me toward the passenger seat. Reaching across, he unlocked the manual lock with his right hand. I sat down. The car was spotless. It may have been brand new if the new car smell hadn't diminished.

"I assume you can drive one handed Michael?" Arch said.

"Of course I can. Why, what's up?" I said.

"Just sit back and relax. We aren't going to talk here. In fact, I won't be the one talking with you today."

The drive to meet the two black SUVs lasted only a few minutes. The unusual silence between Arch and I was deafening. The subdued anxiety flared up greater than before.

138

SAVANNAH

The parking lot behind an abandoned factory offered the perfect location. Four sides of wide open viewing. No one could approach unseen. There was plenty of solitude to speak in secrecy.

The long forgotten parking lot, once paved and smooth, was now covered with potholes. Arch approached the other cars slowly. After parking the car, he told me to get out. His voice made me recall the childhood fear that once dominated me. My mouth filled with cotton balls. I stepped out of the Nissan Sentra and stood next to the opened door, without breathing.

Following Arch's exact instructions, I removed my shirt and threw it behind the car. Next, he commanded me to remove my pants, socks and shoes and to spin around. My arms were raised like a ballerina. I pirouetted in my green boxer briefs and waited for my next instruction.

"Alright, you can have a seat in the back of the SUV on the right," Arch said.

"Should I put my clothes back on first?"

"No. Just get in."

Walking the twenty feet over gravel stones of the neglected parking lot, my feet ached with every step. I tried to step gingerly. The surface was uneven. Small jagged stones shot pain through my soles.

I opened the door and saw an empty back seat. Arch was entering the opposite side of the Chevy Tahoe. The leather interior provided relief from the pavement. I hurried into the unknown. I slowly shut the door. Arch spoke.

Motioning toward the driver's seat Arch said, "Michael Taylor, this is Conrad Veech, the vice president of the Outlaws motorcycle club in Oshawa. You'll call him Veech."

"Nice to meet you, Veech."

Veech was younger than I thought a vice president would have been in a motorcycle club. His auburn hair hung behind his head in a short pony tail that barely had enough hair to keep it together. Wearing a dark blue T-shirt underneath his leather vest, he nodded as we were introduced.

Motioning toward the passenger's seat Arch said, "This is the president of the Oshawa charter. You'll call him Pinky."

"Nice to meet you."

Pinky was the stereotypical vision of what a motorcycle club's president should look like. His leathery face was creased with wrinkles from years of smoking and drinking. He smelled of after shave and cigarette smoke. He had dark brown hair cut close. His hair never needed to be styled and therefore was never messy. He shook my hand. His grip felt like my palm was in a vice. He locked his brown eyes on mine, asserting his dominance. Little doubt remained who was in control.

"You come highly recommended by Arch. You should know that he really

139

stuck his neck out for you. We don't normally contract out, but we do have an opportunity for you," Pinky said.

"Thank you. I do appreciate the risk Arch has taken for me."

"Let me start off by apologizing about the strip tease out there. It's not personal. We prefer to be extra careful when dealing with people who aren't patched over. The police have been trying to get information on our club for years. Through procedures like this, we have been lucky so far. That is also why we're meeting here. This parking lot is actually owned by a brother of the Oshawa charter. We use it to discuss such things as we'll discuss today."

"Alright. I understand."

Veech clearly playing the bad cop by speaking abruptly as if I was wasting his time. "Listen very closely to every detail because I won't repeat myself. The white Nissan Sentra is now yours. Arch has fronted the cost to purchase and revamp it. You owe him $12,000 as soon as you get it."

"Okay, what am I supposed to do with the car?"

"Don't interrupt me while I'm talking. The car has been outfitted with a trap. Are you familiar with traps?" Veech said.

"No, I'm not."

"A trap is a device that one of our mechanics has installed in the steering wheel of the car. The airbag has been removed and an air-tight hidden compartment has been inserted in its place. The trap can only be opened by completing a series of specific actions within the car. Once the actions are completed, the trap opens up for you to retrieve the contents."

"I understand so far."

"Good. Starting today, you are our mover."

CHAPTER 24

THE MOVER

Excerpt from Michael's Journal

Veech explained the job, leaving no question unanswered. It was clear; I wasn't to contact Arch directly anymore. I was to only deal with Veech. I was handed a disposable cell phone.

"Answer it when it rings. I'm the only one with the number. Don't make any calls on it. Understand? It rings, you answer it," Veech said.

"I got it."

Pinky and Veech drove away in the Tahoe, leaving me standing half naked in the parking lot.

I dressed quickly in the cool night air. Arch told me he had bought the Nissan Sentra the day before and taken it to the club's mechanic, who installed the trap.

"Air-tight traps can't be detected by drug dogs or any mechanical drug detecting device. As the seal begins to deteriorate, its effectiveness breaks down," Arch said.

"How long is it good for?" I said.

"Tough to say. I've been told that each seal is guaranteed for about fifty openings. After that, they break down. It'll have to be resealed."

Sitting in the driver's seat, Arch closed his door and told me to get in.

"The first thing you need to know is that all four doors and the trunk must be closed. From there, the first step is to lock all the doors using the automatic control on the driver's door panel. Got it so far?"

"Close the doors, hit the lock button. Got it."

"Good, number two is, and it has to be in this order, turn the key and start the car, then push the rear defroster button."

"Alright, close the doors, hit automatic lock button, turn on car, press defroster. I'm with you so far."

"Last one. With the car in neutral, depress the cigarette lighter."

He showed me the final command. The trap sprung open from the top down. Looking inside the cavity of the steering wheel, there was actually enough room to comfortably house a box of Kleenex. It became narrower toward the end. It was invisible to the naked eye when it was closed, undetectable as long as the seal remained intact, and required a series of complex rules to open it.

"Wow. That's incredible. Thank you Arch, I really appreciate what you've done for me."

"Yeah, well, don't mention it. And don't forget the order."

"I won't. Here, this is all the cash I had on hand. It's only $7700, but I will definitely get you the rest as soon as I can."

"No problem. Listen Michael, we can't talk or hang out anymore. That's part of the deal of working for the club. You're only to speak with Veech on the throw-away cell. Chain of command and all. Alright?"

"Alright, buddy. I get it."

"Michael, there's only three rules to remember. (Ticking them off on his swollen fingers). Don't ask any questions about what's in the packages. Don't EVER open a package. And don't be late. You'll be given two addresses, a time, and a date. The first is your pick up spot. You'll be given the packages there and you'll place them into the trap. The second address is the destination. The date and time is when the packages are expected to be delivered. Both addresses are manned by people friendly with the club and will be expecting you in this car. Never come with anybody else."

"I understand."

Arch opened the door ready to leave. "You'll be contacted sooner than you think, so go home and be ready to leave when you're contacted."

"Thank you again, Arch."

"Yeah, you're welcome. Just don't be late with your deliveries."

With a silent nod, conveying "Good luck," Arch walked off and drove away in the other Tahoe.

That was the last time I ever saw Lonnie Archibald.

~~~~~~~~~

The cell phone that Veech had given me vibrated in my front jeans pocket later that day. Fishing it out and fumbling it open, I answered the call.

"Hello?"

"Memorize what I'm about to say. Never write anything down," Veech said.

"Okay, I'm with you."

"Don't ever look for directions on your home computer. Shit can be traced back easily. Got it? Don't write shit down. Don't use your home computer."

"I got it."

He blurted out two addresses and a time and date. Without saying another word, Veech hung up.

The first delivery was ordered for the same day. I needed to drive to the location, pick up the packages from the people that would be waiting for me, then deliver them hidden in the trap by the set time. Piece of cake.

Pick up time was at 11:00 p.m. Both locations were just addresses. No home computer use to search directions. Throwing on my shoes and grabbing my new car keys, I headed to Starbucks. Free Internet, decent coffee. The public library was replaced. Poor hours.

I felt confident there. Many people used their Internet every day. Searching for the directions to both addresses felt safe. Being the public Internet, the police would have an impossible task proving I had used that specific computer to search for a specific address. Like I said: Safe.

I memorized the route to each location. The estimated drive time would be thirty-two minutes across town. This delivery was a test. Pass. I would gain Veech's trust. Fail. I couldn't think of that. It wasn't an option. I needed this.

~~~~~~~~

The first location was a home in the wealthy downtown Toronto community known as "the Beach." The high cost of housing, so close to Lake Ontario, weeded out the unwanted. Only the wealthy and the naïve could afford to live there.

The house was a small bungalow nestled between two larger homes. At the end of the driveway was a small, single car garage with a white painted door.

I killed the headlights and turned off the radio, not knowing what to do next. Arch had said that whoever was working this end of the delivery would be waiting for me. Without warning, the garage door slid open. An elderly man, standing at the back of the garage, waved me in. Hesitantly putting the car in gear, I inched forward. The wrinkled old man frantically waved his hands, urging me in further. When he suddenly stopped waving and held up both his palms in the air, I braked the car and eased down the window. The garage door closed behind my car. I killed the engine. Coming around the side of my car, the old man now carried a small revolver. A black snub nosed .38 appeared out of nowhere and into his right hand. He waved the barrel of the gun toward me.

SAVANNAH

"You're late," the old man said.

"I wasn't given a pick up time, only a drop off time."

"Yeah, figures. Well, here it is. Don't ask what it is because they don't tell me, so I can't tell you. All I know is to tell you not to fucking open it. And, don't be late."

"I understand."

"Don't turn your headlights on until you're a few houses down the street. I don't need any of my nosy neighbors asking questions about my business."

"Will do."

"See you next time friend. Good luck."

"Yeah, uh, thanks…friend."

The single package the old man had handed me sat on my lap until well after I had left. I chose to be cautious. I didn't want anyone knowing the trap's location or the sequence needed to open it. Sitting at a vacant four way intersection, I turned off the ignition and began the complex sequence. With all the doors and trunks closed, I depressed the automatic lock button on the driver's door. Then I restarted the car and pressed the rear window defrost button. After that, I put the gear shifter into neutral and pushed in the cigarette lighter. The front panel popped open, revealing the secret compartment. Eight seconds, not bad.

The package was small. It was smaller than a box of tissues, but shaped very similarly. The packaging was the same as the brown paper bags grocery stores sometimes offered. It was thoroughly covered with heavy packing tape. The edges were rounded, probably either heroin or cocaine. It might as well have been dead baby blood. I had no choice but to deliver.

One package. One single package. Now I was certain this was a test. It fit easily into the trap with room to spare.

I drove the speed limit to the final address given. The directions from Google maps estimated my driving time at thirty-two minutes from the first location, the old man's house. Draw as little attention to yourself as possible. Act casual, uninteresting.

Six minutes into the drive, a police car pulled alongside me. Two cops. One driving. One watching. The cop seated in the passenger seat glanced toward my car. Our eyes met. I saw a cop on a midnight shift, wired off too much coffee. His eyes probed me.

He saw a by-the-book driver who took safety very seriously. Both of my hands were firmly stationed at ten and two o'clock. I sat with my back erect. "Nothing to see here," I said in my head. "Get along with your shift."

I eased off the gas, changing lanes. I slid the car from the middle to the far right lane, as if I was expecting an approaching turn. The cop eyed me further. A moment later, he seemed uninterested. "Typical cop," I said aloud. "Probably just trying to assert his authoritative power. Well done Sparky, now go off and fight crime."

144

With only one turn left before arriving at my destination, I was well ahead of the delivery time. I debated in my head if I should slow down and try to time the arrival perfectly, or arrive early. *Would Veech appreciate that?*

I went with arriving early, to show my enthusiasm. "Professional and punctual," I thought. Delivering my first package early would prove that I could be trusted. It showed I was reliable.

My assumption was correct.

The delivery point was a sporting goods store which specialized in "lightly used" merchandise. My digital clock read 10:42 p.m. I was unsure where to go to make the drop off. I entered the strip plaza, slowly easing my car toward the front of the building. The store's sign read, "Oliver's Sports: We Buy Used Sporting Goods." A small, thin man, in his late forties, appeared at the front door. His slicked black hair made you think of grease and a black comb. "Slick," I mumbled. He stood with his hands in his pants pockets, as though he was waiting for his ride home. *A late shift at the sports store?* I pulled up next to the curb where he was standing and rolled down my passenger window.

I acted as though I was lost. "Hi, there. I'm looking for directions. Do you think you can help me?"

Slick walked up to my window and crouched forward into the opening. "We're expecting you Mr. Taylor. Drive your car around to the back of the building. I will meet you at the store's rear exit. Pull up to the door with the large red letter 'O' painted on it."

"I understand."

I drove the car around to the back of the plaza. Each store's rear exit was a carbon copy of the one next to it. Without the large crimson "O" painted on the sporting goods store's rear exit, the correct door would have been a mystery.

I parked the car and waited for Slick to come out. I left the engine running. I was nervous. This was the unknown portion. Up until now, everything had been made pretty clear how it was going to happen. Veech and Arch were very specific. The whole operation was planned out. This part had been left out. I wasn't sure who to trust, if anyone.

Slick came out of the darkened rear door. He stepped into the flickering street light that bathed the entire area. Its yellowish-orange color made his face look sickly. He approached my window, carrying a thinly padded envelope. In one hand, the envelope, in the other, a small darkened flashlight.

"I've been instructed to give this envelope to you for your services today, assuming the package is intact," Slick said.

"It sure is, give me one moment to retrieve it for you. Do you mind turning around and facing the door while I get it?"

"What? What kind of crap are you trying to pull?"

145

"Humor me. All I need is ten seconds of your patience."

"Make it fast."

Slick kept his back to me. I opened the trap and retrieved the package. Once finished, I whistled his way. He spun.

"Here you are. As promised," I held the brown package.

Slick grabbed the package roughly from my hand. "One second while I check the package's marking."

Slick flicked on his strange flashlight illuminating its black light glow. He scanned all around the package until he found what he was searching for. Hidden with invisible ink was the marking of the Outlaws MC. The skull, with crossbones made up of motorcycle engine head gaskets, flashed to life as Slick's black light beam crossed over it.

"Everything okay?"

"It is now. Here's your payment, minus the cash you owe Arch. It's not much this time, but you proved your reliability. Keep up the good work and you'll be assigned more lucrative deliveries."

"Thanks. Any idea when I can I expect another assignment?"

Slick started to walk back into the store now that our business was complete. "Who knows? Could be tomorrow. Could be two months from now. Just answer your phone when it rings."

CHAPTER 25
MORE PHONE CALLS

Excerpt from Michael's Journal

The envelope Slick gave me contained five $20 bills and a note. It stated that I still owed Arch more of my future earnings. The cash was to be used on gas. Nice. Pity money. I returned home to my bed and slept in a deep, dark sleep.

Waking up in the morning, I continued my routine of counting all the money I possessed. The first payment to Evgenii was rapidly approaching. Four days left. I had $10,000 set aside. Other than that, I had $55 to my name. Rags to riches, then riches to rags. Full circle.

I used $45 to gas up the Sentra for the next delivery that could have arrived at any moment. I had no idea how much I actually got paid for the previous night's delivery. The note stated that I still owed Arch. He had my $7,700. The Sentra cost $12,000. Before last night's delivery, I owed him $4,250. *How much do I get paid for these deliveries? How many deliveries do I have to make before I receive full pay?*

I was thankful to Arch for getting me the job. It gave me hope. I thought I might actually be able to pay Evgenii each month. I needed a steady flow of deliveries. Something Slick had said added to my hope. It began to burn brighter inside of me. He said, "The more trust you build with quality deliveries, the more lucrative the jobs will become." That word, "lucrative," sounded promising.

With hope alive inside of me, I called Melanie. I wanted to see how she was doing and to get together. I was really starting to like Melanie, a lot. When Evgenii spoke of harming or even killing her, I realized I was actually in love. The feelings were mutual between us. I could see it in the way she looked at me. Her eyes told me more than her words ever could have.

This feeling of being loved was both exciting and terrifying. I was excited because no one had ever loved me aside from my sister. I had plenty of girlfriends throughout the years, but never anyone who truly loved me for me. When she looked at me, for just a second longer than necessary, I knew. She had fallen madly in love with me.

Fear boiled in the pit of my stomach. It matched the excitement of being in love. If I ever failed to deliver to the Russians, Melanie would be the first to be killed. It terrified me. One part of me wanted to break up with her. It would spare her the fate that would always lurk around the corner. The other part of me wanted to keep her close and protect her. In the end, I knew there wasn't a guarantee. If we weren't together anymore, who's to say that psycho Evgenii still wouldn't have his men kill her? I needed to keep Melanie close, and make those payments.

After her shift, Melanie came over with her arms full of goodies. In a white plastic bag, she had a takeout container for us to share. In the other hand, she carried a yellow grocery bag with some food to put into the refrigerator. She wanted to care for me and pamper me a little bit because of my "accident with the saw."

I had to play along and soak up as much sympathy as she offered, of course. And with the added sympathy came the questions about my new car in the driveway.

Melanie didn't know about my money troubles, and I liked it that way. I no longer questioned whether she was into me because I had money. Those insecurities were a thing of the past.

"My car was stolen and the insurance company wrote me a check for a new one. That car is a temporary fix."

"Well, it's nice. Not as stylish as the old one, but I like it just the same," Melanie said.

"The deal was too good for me to pass on it. I'll hold onto it for a little while and then upgrade. You know, when the time is right."

With a nod, she accepted my story's plausibility. She opened the takeout container of triple chocolate cake. We shared a fork and ate bite after bite of the moist cake and rich frosting. As I was finishing the final bite, my cell phone rang. Veech's cell phone.

He blurted two addresses, a pickup and delivery time. There was a pickup time of next morning at 5 a.m. Delivery time of 2 p.m. that same day. I memorized the two addresses. The first address wasn't an issue. The old man's house. This time the delivery address was different.

148

SAVANNAH

The library was closed for the day. It didn't open until well after the pickup time. I assumed that there wasn't enough time for me to pick up the package, then get the directions to the delivery point. I had to get directions another way.

Melanie had a Blackberry Bold. She carried it with her all the time. It had a digital map and GPS navigation. She used it all the time.

"Hey babe, can I use your phone for a second?"

"Really? You want to check my phone? A little paranoid, are we Michael?"

"C'mon, don't make me beg. A friend of mine just called with a house he is interested in buying. He wants me to go with him tomorrow morning to check it out. I don't know how to get there."

With another shrug, she tossed me her phone on her way to use the bathroom. Lying was becoming too easy. I understood why I had to. Nonetheless, I didn't like myself when I lied. I didn't like who I was becoming.

I used Melanie's phone's navigation for my directions. She wasn't aware of what I was using it for and was more than happy to help me. Before she returned from the bathroom, I found the new location and memorized the exact directions needed to get to the drop-off the next day. I understood the length of time between the pickup and the drop off. I was going to be traveling a long distance and would need every minute Veech allotted. According to Melanie's Blackberry GPS, the driving time between the old man's house and the drop off spot was nine hours.

Thankfully, Melanie didn't stay over that night. We made love in my bed and then she slid out sometime while I slept. A sense of relief washed over me. I wouldn't have to come up with another excuse why she had to leave. I loved that about Melanie. It was like she knew what I needed. I was falling deeper in love with her every day.

~~~~~~~~

I met the old man the same way I had two days earlier. This time there were two packages. Same brown paper wrapping. Same packing tape. I opened the trap at the same deserted intersection, depositing both vessels. I looked for the invisible ink, but saw nothing. Without a black light flashlight, they looked generic. Was that Veech's master plan in case any of the packages were ever seized by the police? Would the police look for an invisible seal?

This delivery required a lengthy amount of time on highways, traveling north up to Sault St. Marie, Ontario. Melanie's GPS navigation app offered two directions. The first was the faster route. It required a much riskier approach. Toronto to Sault St. Marie, cutting directly through the state of Michigan. Thirty minutes faster. But with two border crossings into the U.S. and then back into Canada. Nosey customs agents. Drug sniffing dogs. Risk.

149

SAVANNAH

Option two allowed me to stay in Ontario the entire trip and avoid Canada's Border Services Agency, commonly known as Canadian Customs. It is a well known fact that crossing the border with mysterious packages, especially those potentially housing drugs, is a serious crime. I had crossed the border into the United States before and had witnessed another car being torn apart by the United States Customs Agents. These border guards tend to be a serious group of defenders that protect their countries borders with strict policies and suspicious eyes.

The second route was longer. Estimated driving time: nine hours and change. That distance required at least one stop. Nine hours and no bathroom stops equaled trouble. If I made one quick stop, driving slightly above the posted speed limit of 100km/h, I would make it in time.

~~~~~~~~~~

Maintaining 110km/h, controlled by the Sentra's cruise control, I arrived in the city of Sault St. Marie with twenty minutes to spare. The highway directions were simple enough to memorize. Once off, I forgot the distance for the final three roads. I knew their names and recalled the turns, but a dilemma pushed its way urgently forward.

Nature called. The delivery clock ticked down. A full bladder about to burst. Less than eighteen minutes to deliver.

I exited the highway. The first of the three roads was two lanes with a posted limit of 90km/h and gravel shoulders. The barrenness of the road enticed me. I stopped on the shoulder and relieved myself. The fear of leaving the packages unprotected kept me close.

Like a child looking before they crossed, I scanned the road in both directions as I went. And went. And went. I counted aloud, "One, two, three." As I finished, I snapped my eyes in the other direction, studying the horizon for oncoming traffic. One, two, three. Look. One, two, three. Look.

The roof rack of lights on the cruiser was unmistakable. Before I became visible to the officer inside, I pinched off the remaining urine and zipped my jeans. Urinating in public wasn't the offense I wanted to cause me to miss my deadline.

The police cruiser slowed as it came over the hill. It pulled alongside my car. Rolling down the passenger window, the lone officer glared at me.

"You alright sir."

His bark was more of a command, as if he had just been discharged from the armed forces. My heart rate tripled. My hands began to sweat.

I shouted much too loudly and grabbed my left thigh. "Leg cramp."

"Pardon me?"

150

SAVANNAH

"I'm fine officer. I got a bad leg cramp is all. Poor circulation."

"You sure? Not much traffic on these roads. If you need help, now's the time to ask."

"No, honestly, I'll be fine. Happens to me on long drives. Gotta walk it off."

"Try using the cruise control instead of holding the gas next time."

Nodding in appreciation, I waved as he continued his patrol. I had called attention to myself in a very amateur way. Peeing on the side of the road was the mistake. I needed to be more cautious. Less risk. More thinking. My new motto.

I arrived. It was a house, situated on a farm. The ranch style home was dwarfed in comparison to the massive barn behind the home. Pulling into the gravel driveway, a pair of heavily tattooed men met me. Their thin, white tank tops contrasted with their ink. Their arms, hands, and necks were completely covered in dark tattoos, as if they were embarrassed by the whiteness of their skin. Skulls and gasket head crossbones lined their forearms and shoulders. Flames from motorcycles, driven by skeletons, rode above the words, "Death before dishonor."

~~~~~~~~~

They waved me into the massive red barn as they slid the doors open, like Moses parting the Red Sea. They followed me into the barn. Both men used their muscular arms to close the doors once I was through, meeting them in the middle. I quickly opened the trap and retrieved both packages for their inspection. Using black light wands, similar to the flashlight that Slick had used two days earlier, both bikers smiled. They found their hidden logo.

The shorter biker handed his package over to the larger of the two men. He took both packages and walked to the back of the cluttered barn. Old farming equipment, mechanical engines, and even an old pickup truck filled much of the floor. Through the window, the smell of grease and manure wafted in. I cringed at the smell. Not my cup of tea.

The short tattooed biker reached behind him. His hand moved in slow motion toward the back of his waist. The perfect area for a concealed gun to rest. I saw the movement. I tensed, reflexively extending my hand toward the ignition. I wanted to leave. First, I needed to start the car.

The scenario played out in my head in a split second. He would need a second and a half to pull the gun and aim it. He was close range, so aiming was less of a fine art and more a thrusting movement. I needed only a fraction of a second to start the car. But how long would it be before the car would move? There was putting the car into gear that needed to be taken into account. What about the closed doors? Was my car strong enough to smash through the thick wooden barn doors?

My eyes never left the biker. My right hand fingered the keys. Right before I turned it over, an envelope became visible. It was thin. Same as last time. The same, except this time a message was delivered from Veech.

"Here, this is for you. Veech says that if you made this delivery on time that the rest of your debt was forgiven," the tattooed biker said.

"Okay," I said.

"He also told me to give you a couple hundred for gas and dinner on your way back. That's what's in the envelope. Two hundred dollars."

"Alright, thank you."

"We've got a lot of work to do in a short amount of time. So, if you don't mind closing the barn door on your way out, I would appreciate that."

"Sure. No problem."

"Good work on the delivery. We'll be seeing you soon."

I barely forced out enough words for something resembling a conversation. I wanted out of that barn. Fast. Old machinery. A broken down truck. Creepy.

I had no intention of making friends with the people I delivered to. They were wrapped up in something I didn't want to be involved in. Delivering an unknown package to an unknown receiver gave me a sense of detachment. I envisioned myself as a private courier service. No relationships. No friends. Just business.

The rules made me feel innocent. Never ask what is inside. Never open up a package. Be on time. I knew what was in the packages, but I convinced myself that I really didn't know what was in them and that, ultimately, allowed me to sleep at night.

My debt to Arch was forgiven. That was a huge relief. Every delivery, from then on, would be profitable. Cash in my pocket. I still had no idea when my next delivery would be, but whenever it was, I would be paid, in full.

Veech must have either been impressed with my ability to make such a long distance delivery or pitied me for not getting paid. Following the same route and driving the same speed, the return trip back to Toronto took longer. I gave myself a few more bathroom breaks and stopped inside a Subway for dinner.

As the daylight faded, my headlights fell onto the road ahead. I settled into a coma-like state of driving. I was aware, but only of the immediate road ahead. My phone vibrated to life from its perch on the front dashboard. Veech spoke roughly into the receiver in a rushed tone, as usual.

"I heard you made your delivery on time today," Veech said.

"I believe I even had a few minutes to spare."

"Good. I usually allot an additional hour for that delivery, but I wanted to test you Michael. You've proven you are reliable and can be trusted."

"Thank you."

"As you continue to make deliveries for us and reach the assigned addresses on time, you'll be rewarded with deliveries that pay more."

"That sounds good to me."

"With higher pay, the deliveries are either more rushed or riskier. The greater your risk, the larger the payment you'll receive. We have a need for deliveries that cross into the U.S. They pay very well and can really help you in your situation. Arch has explained it to me."

I was surprised at how well informed Veech had been about me. "Arch told you?"

"Yes."

"I see."

"Michael let's get one thing straight here. As much risk as you think you're taking, we took a greater risk trusting an outsider. Arch is the only reason you have this job. We insisted that he give us all the information about you that he knew, especially why you needed this job."

"If you don't trust outsiders to do club jobs, why me? I mean, I'm no one special."

"I don't trust outsiders. That's risky behavior. It's sloppy. Cops are always trying to bring down organizations like the Outlaws. But...Arch trusted you. In fact, he demanded a job for you. I trust Arch. I do. So, I trusted his judgment."

"I get it. Tell me about the U.S. jobs."

"The border crossing jobs are risky. There are a lot of outside factors to be considered. We've lost a couple of members to them in the past year. They weren't from the Oshawa charter, but nonetheless they're serving time because they got caught. Outsourcing those jobs is in the best interest for the club. And, in your best interest with your monthly payments. When you're ready to accept those jobs, let me know. I have plenty of good men from this charter who can make the deliveries within Ontario. I need you to make the riskier ones."

"Because I'm expendable, right?"

"Yes. And because you need the cash. It's win-win."

"Out of curiosity, how much do the border crossing jobs pay per delivery?"

"Depends on how many packages you deliver, but we are willing to pay $1000 per package you cross with."

"I can only fit two packages in the trap. It seems like a lot of risk for $2000."

"We can have an additional trap installed. A bigger one, which can hold ten more packages per delivery."

"How much does it cost to be installed? And how soon can it be ready?"

"If you're willing to make these deliveries, my guy can have your car ready to go by the end of the week. I'll even cover the cost."

"I'm in, on one condition. I don't want to be crossing the border too frequently."

"How does once a week sound, at a flat rate of $10,000 per delivery?"

153

"Sounds like we have a deal."

"I'll send you a text message with the address and time for you to bring your car to my guy. Like I said, there won't be a charge, but I need you to make a delivery the following day to the U.S. side of Niagara Falls. I'll call you. Be ready."

"I can do that."

~~~~~~~~~~

The next day I received a text message with an address, a time, and the mechanic's name.

The shop was a one bay garage with several cars lining the perimeter of the property. They all appeared ready for the junk yard. Missing engines. Rust. Axles on cinder blocks. The perfect setting for a scary movie.

I parked the car, entered through the front door, and waited to ask for the name from the text message. A scruffy looking man wearing greasy coveralls and a sewn on nametag that read "Fuzz," rounded the corner.

"Hey. Veech sent me."

He raised his hand and shook his head.

"Don't say another word," the mechanic said.

He waved for my keys.

"Come back the same time tomorrow to pick up your car."

CHAPTER 26

THE RAINBOW BRIDGE

Excerpt from Michael's Journal

The mechanic wasn't there for my pick up. I guess he was spooked and didn't want me seeing his face again. The work he had done was impressive. The second trap was undetectable, even when I was looking for it. When I walked in, the receptionist behind the desk eyed me from head to toe and back. With her glasses sitting low on her nose, she picked up a piece of yellow paper.

"Can I help you?" the receptionist said.

"Hi. I dropped off my car yesterday. I'm here to pick it up."

"You Michael?"

I nodded.

"Fuzz left this. I'm to read it to you."

I nodded again, uncertain.

"Everything went smoothly. Use the same sequence as the first one to activate both."

She made a face at the paper. She turned to me.

"Do you have any idea what this means? It's like Latin to me."

"Yeah. It's fine."

Fuzz worked in secrecy. I liked that. Less people knowing eased my tension. I grabbed the keys and politely left the garage.

I sat behind the wheel and searched for the second trap. I knew there was a trap there. I should have been able to locate it. After about five minutes of dissecting

155

every inch of the dashboard, front paneling, door paneling, center console, and glove box, I gave up. Frustrated, confused, and worried that Fuzz had screwed up, I drove to the car wash I still owned, for the time being. The back of the property offered privacy. I could run the sequence there.

Thick, lush leaves on the trees surrounded three sides of the rear. The building offered the fourth and final piece of privacy. I began the sequence. As I finally pushed in the cigarette lighter, I heard the steering wheel trap spring open. Something pushed against my back. The second trap.

I got out of the seat and angled my body back into the car. The entire back of the seat was hollowed out. A large plastic storage bin filled the inside. When I depressed the cigarette lighter, the middle cushion on the seat swung open like a door on hidden hinges, revealing Fuzz's second trap.

The brilliance of the trap was whenever anyone was seated in the driver's seat, it was hidden by the driver. I smiled. Big. Crossing the Canadian border into New York State, the border agent would be none the wiser. No way could they detect the second trap. I would be seated on it.

I waited for the next addresses and times. I gassed up on my way home. Ready and waiting. The call finally came.

Veech called. His voice was more relaxed and collegial than before.

"Hey Buddy. How is it going?"

Silence.

"Michael? You there?"

"Are you talking to me? I thought you must have dialed the wrong number. You called me *Buddy*."

"Hey man, c'mon. You've earned my trust. We're good now. Everything go okay with Fuzz?"

"Yeah, we're all set. I'm ready."

His friendliness disappeared after he gave the directions. He reminded me, again, that the Outlaws have friends everywhere. He alluded to the chance of getting caught. His exact words etched into my memory, "Remember Michael, snitches get what's coming to them. No matter where they are." His words still send chills down my back.

He hung up the phone. I needed to research my delivery. This shipment was different from the others. The risk factor was much greater. I had to clear American customs at the Rainbow Bridge in Niagara Falls. The Border Service Officers were going to ask questions. Why was I crossing into New York State?

I needed an excuse. Something believable. Something natural and common. The delivery wasn't set for the same day. Instead, I had been given the day to prepare. With every shipment before, I was given a limited driving time and no notice. Since I had proven myself trustworthy, I earned a little leeway. Higher risk

156

deliveries equal more respect. I got advanced notice of the delivery, as well as a time cushion between the pickup and drop off.

The Internet showed the drop off location to be only eight minutes past the border crossing at the Rainbow Bridge. The total drive time was one hour and forty minutes. The pickup location was a new address. Located in the west end of downtown Toronto, I used Google Earth to get a sneak peek at the address. The program zoomed in on the street level and showed a commercial complex. The kind where you might find tool and die shops and car mechanic garages. I angled Google Earth's camera around to the front of the building. The sign read *Oscar's Granite and Marble*. It was written in bold black letters on a plain white background. Simple. To the point. Not made to attract customers, rather to inform them.

I smiled and shook my head. *Arrogant*. On the top of the windowless door, a large red "O" had been painted. Same size and color as the one used by Oliver's sporting goods. The Outlaw's symbol. Clearly, that was their indication for drop off and pickup locations.

The pickup time was 7 a.m. from Oscar's the next morning. The delivery wasn't due until 1 p.m., which left me a large time cushion. The morning commute was sure to bring thick traffic onto Toronto's highways, but six hours was more than ample time to navigate my way to Niagara Falls before noon. Like my first delivery, I decided to drop off the packages early. It was appreciated the first time. I hoped it would be again.

Excitement and nervousness woke me before my alarm. I rehearsed the routine of the coming deliveries, just as I had when I was using Savannah. I detailed every aspect, including a bathroom break on the way to Niagara Falls. My main focus was the excuse. I heard stories from friends. With little more than suspicion, the Border Service Officers can rip apart your car and your life. I heard stories of "random searches" on cars passing through their lane. Friends of mine speculated that one in every ten or twenty cars is inspected and the passengers questioned. My experience was limited. My passport was valid and I had rarely crossed the border in the past couple years, so there wouldn't be any prior motive to pull my car over.

I chose the excuse of visiting the Seneca Niagara Casino as the reason for my visit. More specifically, I decided on craps as my specific reason. The devil is in the details.

In Ontario, casinos are not permitted to play craps, with the exception of two casinos far from Niagara Falls. Stemming from a fourteenth century English law prohibiting gambling involving dice, craps was outlawed. According to the Seneca Niagara Casino's website, craps was considered to be the most exciting casino game. I read a breakdown of the rules, how to bet, the odds, and layout of the table. Plenty of back-up detail.

As I left, I thought of the cash. $10,000 guaranteed. A one month reprieve. My giddiness was extinguished as I arrived at Oscar's Granite and Marble shop. The butterflies in my stomach fluttered fiercely.

SAVANNAH

I arrived five minutes early. A smiling man dressed in a cheap, wrinkled suit met me outside, as if he had been waiting. As I pulled up, he tossed the remainder of his half smoked cigarette into a paved corner.

A large garage door made up the entire rear of the building. It was easy access for trucks. They would angle their back end into the loading area and drop their contents. Quick. Easy. And private. The clearance on either side was barely enough to fit both of the Sentra's side mirrors through.

Wrinkled Suit waved me in. Once I had passed through the threshold he tapped the automated garage door button, shutting the door behind me. I didn't like that. Uneasiness settled in. It was the barn all over again. Wrinkled Suit's smile was gone. In its place was a stoic face. More butterflies gathered in my gut.

He walked to a cardboard box, labeled as *countertop caulk.* He pulled a short hunting knife from his pocket. He unfolded the four inch blade. Wrinkled Suit still hadn't looked at me. His eyes stayed on his work. My eyes never left his hands.

He sliced open the tape that sealed the cardboard lids closed. His hands moved fast with the blade. He refolded the knife and stuck it deep into his pocket. Wrinkled Suit reached in the box and pulled out two identical packages to the ones I had delivered in previous shipments.

I hadn't moved from my seat. My eyes stared at him, untrusting. He walked to me and slapped them into my hand. One at a time he put them through the opened car window. No words. No smiles. Just business.

He did this six more times, bringing twelve packages total. I moved each package onto the seat next to me. The entire area of the seat was covered.

After the last two, Wrinkled Suit walked over to the garage door button and pressed it. He stood there, waiting for me to leave. In. Out. Quick and dirty.

The twelve packages were exposed and needed to be placed into my traps. I searched for an abandoned parking lot. Something big enough, and full enough, to hide in plain sight. Among many cars, no one sees one person. Too few cars, one man stands out.

A nearby strip mall, housing a Buck or Two, a Popeye's Fried Chicken, and a Pizza Pizza had a large parking lot. Too large. A single car was parked at the far end. It looked as though it had been there many nights. I looped around the lot, away from the open exposure. *Not a great place to transfer the packages.*

A Wal-Mart was on the corner of the next strip mall. Perfect. Ample cover.

I drove to the opposite end of the lot, turned off the engine, and ran through the sequence. Once both traps opened, I got out of the car and loaded the bigger trap first. Stacking the packages neatly on top of one another, the compartment held ten packages. The steering wheel trap held the remaining two. I eased both doors shut, ensuring that the seal was properly closed. I continued my delivery plan.

158

SAVANNAH

Morning rush hour traffic in Toronto's downtown core sucked. *One giant parking lot. How do people put up with this crap every day?*

As I moved farther away from the city, the traffic thinned. Eventually it was clear enough to drive the speed limit. The Queen Elizabeth Way, or QEW, is a major highway that wraps itself around Lake Ontario. Connecting Toronto to Niagara Falls, the highway boasts some of the world's worst traffic. The oncoming side of the QEW held thousands of cars slowly making their way into Toronto's hub.

My first scheduled break was at a road stop station off of Casablanca Boulevard. It featured a newly renovated station with bathrooms and many restaurants, though at this hour of the morning, only the coffee shop was seeing any business. The spacious parking lot offered plenty of parking adjacent to the building. I allotted myself five minutes to be in and out of the station. Use the bathroom. Buy a coffee and a bagel. In. Out. Less risk. More thinking.

Being away from the car caused me a great deal of anxiety. *It'll be fine.* The fear of someone breaking into or stealing my car caused me to move faster than I planned. I didn't even wait for the coffee shop to toast my bagel. Explaining, three times, to the woman taking my order that, "I just want it as it is in a bag, PLEASE," nullified any seconds I may have saved. The coffee was hot and strong. It made up for the untoasted bagel.

I quickly walked back to where I parked the car. Walking on the tips of my toes, I spied the white roof sandwiched between two large SUVs. Once I saw it was still there, relief washed over me.

The remaining drive to Canada's half of Niagara Falls was easy. Sharing the Falls with their American neighbors, Canada had won the race. Their side was developed. Casinos, hotels, attractions, amusement parks, and a popular night life scene covered Canada's side. In contrast, the American side had one casino and poverty. The differences drew the tourists to Canada. It was cleaner. Nicer. And generally, friendlier.

I needed to cross the Rainbow Bridge, clear customs, and deliver my packages to the designated address. The hill leading down to the entrance bridge was high enough to see the traffic. It was thin. I watched for thirty seconds. Partly to see the traffic, partly to gather my nerve. I shook away the thought of Evgenii's $10,000 payment. I needed a clear head. I needed to appear much like I had when entering the poker room. Calm. Unthreatening. A "no one."

The Rainbow Bridge was named because of its design. The arch bridge spans the distance from Canada to the United States over the runoff from Niagara and Horseshoe Falls, which gush underneath. The arch is designed to represent a rainbow. It symbolized friendly relations between Canada and the United States. Its location is popular for tourists taking pictures of the panoramic view.

159

SAVANNAH

I idled the car across the bridge. By taking slow, deep breaths I calmed down. In through the nose, hold three seconds, slowly out through the mouth. Neck and shoulder tension manifested itself in a headache. I ran through my story again in my head. I snapped into character. Holding my passport, I chose the line with the least amount of cars and waited. I finally inched forward. *Go time.*

I handed the female Border Service Officer my passport and smiled. She nodded. She swiped my passport into her computer.

"What's your citizenship?"

"I'm Canadian."

"Where do you live?"

"Just outside of Toronto."

"Purpose of your visit?"

"Craps."

"Excuse me?"

"Sorry, I'm going to play craps."

"So, you're going to the casino?"

"Yes Ma'am, the Seneca Niagara Casino. It's the only casino anywhere near here that offers craps tables."

"Do you plan on any other stops in your visit?"

"No, just to the casino. Unless I get really hot and win enough money to go to Hawaii."

"What do you do for a living?"

"To be honest, mainly that. Gambling."

"Any legal trouble with Canada Revenue, Mr. Taylor?"

"Uh, um. I don't think so. I haven't been charged or anything like that."

Handing me back my passport. "Alright. It's just that, in my experience, professional gamblers sometimes tend to forget to pay taxes on their winnings. Make sure you pay the proper taxes on any horse race winnings over $600, any slot winnings of more than $1200, any keno winnings over $1500, and any other combined winnings of $5000 or more when you cross back into Canada."

"Alright, in that case, I hope I have something to report."

"Have a good day sir."

"Thank you, you too."

Driving through the booth, and into New York State, felt like a warm bath on a cold day. Excitement bubbled over inside me. The drop off remained. I figured that to be the easy part. If it was anything like the others, I would be on my way home with $10,000 in no time.

The dropoff was eerily similar to Fuzz's garage. It was a single bay garage that housed broken down cars in the parking lot. *What is with this biker gang and using places with broken down cars?*

160

SAVANNAH

I parked in one of the few spots that didn't house a total wreck. I waited. And waited. A couple of minutes turned into ten. Ten turned into twenty. No one came.

The digital clock on my dashboard indicated it had officially become the afternoon. I gathered what remaining courage I could find and entered the garage's office. Every other drop off had someone waiting for me. This nameless garage, with paint chips flaking off of the building, was abandoned. *Great, just what I need. More stress.* The headache pounded behind my eyes.

The sign on the door told me that I had arrived during the business's hours of operation. No one. No receptionist. No customers waiting. Nothing, except the high pitched whine of hydraulic tools. The cluttered front desk was surrounded by odds and ends and a fake silk plant. I smiled to myself. *This desk is probably operated by the same grease-ball that works on the cars.*

The grease stained keyboard in front of the computer confirmed my suspicion. It had one of those transparent plastic covers that was barely see-through. The sound came from the only bay. Someone was working. They hadn't stopped when I entered.

I called out. The noise coming from the garage stopped. I heard someone coming. Heavy boots pounded the concrete floor.

A tall black man, wearing blue coveralls with black smudges, came around the corner. Slowly, cautiously, he moved toward the front desk. He had a puzzled look on his face. His exceptionally manicured beard drew my eyes. Thin lines of hair met at perfect angles on the ends of his chin and upper lip. Tattoos crawled their way up to his jaw line in wide arching patterns. I dared a look at his nametag.

Sewn onto his chest, I read a name that I instantly recognized. I smiled. *Are you serious? You got to be joking me.* Stitched in black letters on a slightly greasy white background was the name, *Fuzz.*

Fuzz spoke in a deep southern drawl, "Can I help you?"

"Maybe. I'm Michael."

Turning unfriendly, possibly from the awkward smile smeared on my face. "Uh huh, and is that supposed to mean something to me?"

"I was hoping so. Veech sent me."

"You're that Michael? Damn, why didn't you say so? Man, y'all earlier than we was expecting."

"We?"

"Yeah, me and the boys."

"I don't see anyone else here."

"And that's the way we like it. Give me a second to lower that car off the hoist, so you can bring yours in."

"Okay. Yeah, sure. Say, out of curiosity, where are the other guys?"

"Oh man, Veech didn't tell you, did he?"

"Tell me what?"

"That fucking guy, he's hilarious. You'll see."

Fuzz, or whatever his real name was, walked back into the garage and lowered the hoist. The minivan eased down. His nametag was identical to that of the other mechanic who installed the second and probably the first trap in my car. I wondered what the odds were of two mechanics with the same name of Fuzz. *Too much of a coincidence. Two mechanics named Fuzz, both working with the Outlaws.*

The red "O" on both the sporting goods store and the granite and marble shop linked these places. The Outlaws secret marker. Hide in plain sight. Name the store something beginning with an "O", paint a red "O" on the door, and to the outside observer the "O" belongs. It made perfect sense. The store wanted to identify which door was theirs. As I saw different locations, all associated with the Outlaws, and well, it doesn't take a rocket scientist to make the connection. If I had, anyone could.

I felt uneasy about how Fuzz had said, "You'll see." I didn't trust Veech. I didn't trust anyone. *You made a high-value delivery. They won't want you dead. They want you delivering more.*

I needed this job much more than the job needed me. The butterflies came back, more powerful than ever. Vomit slowly rose up my throat. I convinced myself I needed to get out of there. *Flee. Run. Just go.* Fight or flight. I'm not much of a fighter. Clearly.

After reversing the minivan into a spot, Fuzz stood next to the garage door opening, waving me onto the garage hoist. I froze, staring at him. The vomit was nearly in my mouth. Moving would cause it to come all the way. Fuzz waved again, more frantically this time. He pointed to the hoist. Two ramps laid on the ground, waiting for all four tires to come to a rest on them. I sat there. Frozen.

"C'mon, bring it in. What are you waiting for?" Fuzz said.

I swallowed hard. My hands stayed on the wheel. *Flee. Run. Just go.* I thought back to Arch. He vouched for me. *If I just drove off, what would happen to him? Would he be killed? Would the Outlaws go after Susie or Melanie? Did they have a way to find them like Evgenii had?*

Fuzz waved his hands. He threw them in the air, exasperated. I didn't have a choice. Too many people depended on me. I had to risk it. *Less risk. More thinking.* I put my motto on hold and started the car.

"Yeah, alright," I said.

I drove the car onto the ramp. Fuzz closed the garage door behind me and began lifting my car off the ground. I sat there. The sunlight faded behind the solid metal door. *Is this the last time I'll ever see sunshine again?* Fear covered me like a blanket. My arms felt too heavy to move. Every heartbeat felt like my last. Sweat covered my brow.

A foot off the ground, Fuzz stopped the hoist and called out to me. He walked over to a metal shelf that was covered in oil containers, filters of different sizes, and various other car parts. He reached for a green plastic bin. He grabbed the black straps attached to both sides, swinging it while he walked. At first I couldn't place the bin. It didn't belong. It was clean. Brand new in fact, like it had recently been purchased at a grocery store, the kind shoppers use instead of plastic bags.

With each hand he held a strap. Fuzz began talking.

"Okay buddy, that's not too high. Put the packages into this bin and then I got something to show you."

I felt like a trapped animal about to be slaughtered. "Alright, just give me a minute here."

I felt protective of my car's secret. Inside me a debate was waged. *Don't show him. He'll know your only secret, your protection. What? You're going to risk Susie's life? What about Veech? And Melanie? You can't sit here all day.*

Future deliveries ran through my mind. Each one equaled one month to Evgenii. *Open it!*

I moved through the motions quickly, hoping Fuzz couldn't see the exact sequence needed. I figured the location of the traps wasn't as important as the sequence needed to open them.

I opened the traps. I placed both packages from the steering wheel into the green bin. Fuzz smiled. I wiggled onto the passenger seat and pulled open the bigger trap. I tossed the packages from the bigger trap into Fuzz's bin, through the window.

"Whoa, there friend. These packages ain't exactly cheap. Be careful with them."

"Oh, sorry Fuzz. It's just that the pick-up guy was tossing them around, so I figured that they were sturdy enough."

"Sturdy or not, personally, I wouldn't be tossing around $20,000 like that. One breaks, who's gonna pay for it?"

"What? These packages are how much?"

"Twenty G's…each."

"You mean I moved almost a quarter of a million dollars today?"

"Yeah, see why I would be more careful with them?"

"Holy crap. Yeah, I get it."

I finished the last package. I returned back behind the steering wheel. I peeked my head out the window.

Hoping that was the end of my stay in the garage I said, "There you go Fuzz. That's the last of them. Listen, I got to get going. I got a thing I gotta go do."

"I told ya already, there was something I had to show ya."

I slowly got out of the car. With my car on the hoist, I couldn't exactly make a run for it. *Breathe, Just breathe. You'll be fine, They need you.* I jumped the final foot onto the oil stained concrete. Fuzz raised the hoist to its peak.

"C'mon Michael. Follow me."

"Yeah, alright," I said choking back fear.

Fuzz led me to the other side of the garage. There was a staircase. The stairs were spotless, shiny in fact. He led the way, casually walking down. He talked about something or another, but I wasn't listening. All I could hear were the sounds of his heavy boots twanging on the metal stairs.

The oil changing pit lay below. It too, was exceptionally clean. The concrete was as white as the first day it had been poured. Something was wrong. Everything was wrong. It all seemed out of place. The green bin. The clean stairs. The oil-free concrete.

He reached the bottom, turning around and facing me.

"Hey, c'mon. What's wrong?"

The fear held me in place. *Go down there and you won't be coming back up.* Without hesitating, I blurted out.

"I, uh, well; I just am not sure where we're going, so, uh you know, I'm a little apprehensive. A little nervous."

"Y'all want yo money, right? Well, you better follow me."

I took a few steps down. He stopped next to a door. There, detailed with boastful pride, was the Outlaw MC logo. The same skull. The same crossing pistons. The same everything on Arch's patch. Holding his free hand out, Fuzz motioned for me to open the door and go in first.

I could feel my stomach in my throat, again. The sour taste of vomit approached. My mouth filled with saliva. I wasn't sure if I was going to be beaten or killed, tortured or maimed. The unknown lay beyond that door. The crazy look on Fuzz's face. It was all too much. My knees went limp.

I was delivering for a biker gang. Let's call it what it was, I was a drug trafficker. The kind that would make the national news if I was ever arrested. I couldn't show fear. Any respect would fly right out the window. I already made the mistake of blurting out that I was nervous. *Let's go! Get it together Michael. Swallow the puke. Straighten your back. Suck it up and stop being such a goddamn wimp. This is just a test.*

The plain wooden door was windowless and had a cheap brass doorknob. The unexpectedly cold touch of the knob caused me to unintentionally pull away. Fuzz had a crooked smile on his face. He enjoyed watching me squirm. He nodded his head to continue.

I gathered every speck of self respect and courage and turned the doorknob. It slid open. An underground tunnel, lit by a row of light bulbs in wire cages, greeted me. The walls were smooth concrete. The ceiling arched inches above my head. I

164

could see the end of the tunnel. About forty feet away was another unknown door, identical to the one I had just opened. It waited there. *You can do this.*

Fuzz followed me. After he was in the tunnel, he closed the door behind him, locking it from the inside. He held a button on a panel I had overlooked. A loud hiss came from outside of the closed door. The sound was unmistakable. The hoist was being lowered back to the garage floor. We were trapped. I was trapped. *Nothing you can do now.*

The musty, stale air stung my nostrils. The dampness in the hidden tunnel created small pools of moisture where the walls and floor met. Fuzz let go of the button, ending the hiss. He made direct eye contact with me. The light was dim in the tunnel, but I could still see the wicked look on his face. He held tightly onto the bin. Both hands clenched together.

"Keep walking to the next door, then open it up."

"What is this place?" I said.

"You'll see soon enough."

I took cautious, hesitant steps toward the door. *Left foot forward. Right foot. Left. Right.* I counted my steps until I laid my hand on another cold knob. Blazing light shone from the other side, causing me to turn my head away. My eyes adjusted. A large wooden table was centered in the room. The Outlaws' skull and gasket crossbones were carved deep into the table. Plush leather chairs surrounded it. Each one was filled by a member of the Niagara Falls chapter. *Holy crap. They're going to off me in some freak cult ritual.*

I walked a couple of steps. They all stared hard at me. I averted my eyes. These were hard men. They all had witnessed things I only ever saw in movies. They were criminals. I was just a delivery guy. A poker player with half a left thumb. I awkwardly looked back to Fuzz. He shut the door, the same as he had when I first entered the tunnel.

The man seated at the head of the table stood. His huge pot belly bulged out from underneath his leather vest. Underneath, a thin tank top covered his gut. It didn't reach the tattoos that covered his shoulders down to his wrists. His eyes turned toward Fuzz. His voice was deep and raspy. *Too many years of smoking.*

"Is this him?" the man at the head of the table said.

"Yes it is," Fuzz said.

"Was the delivery complete and on time?" the man at the head of the table said.

"Yes," Fuzz said.

"Good. Sit down Michael. We were expecting you, but not for another hour or so."

"I wasn't sure if you would appreciate me being early, or right on time, so I had to make a decision," I said.

165

"Don't be sorry son. Early is always better in your line of work; early and with a complete delivery," the man at the table said.

"That's what I was hoping you'd say," I said.

He waved Fuzz over to his end of the table. Fuzz approached. He began unloading the packages onto the table. He stacked them neatly in piles of twos. Pot Belly reached into his back pocket of his dark blue jeans and pulled out a small flashlight. A black light. Same as is in Sault St. Marie. He found each invisible Outlaw stamp.

"It seems you've done a thorough job. I like that. Veech tells me you can be trusted, which is why Fuzz has brought you down here."

"Yes sir. I can be."

"My name is Chris. I'm the president of the Outlaws here in Niagara Falls. I understand you've met my fellow brothers Pinky and Veech?"

"Do you mean Pinky Miller and Veech Pattern, the president and vice-president of the Oshawa charter? They are your brothers?"

"You're not an Outlaw Michael, so I'll forgive your ignorance. Every member of the Outlaws, no matter what charter, country, or skin color is a brother of mine. Fuzz here, even though he hasn't even carried his patch for six months, is as much a brother of mine as any other member you see here. It's about loyalty and brotherhood. It's about trust," Chris said.

"I understand, and yeah, I have met with Veech and Pinky. Although, I mainly deal with Veech," I said.

"He tells me you have been slowly earning his trust and have been quite professional in your services."

"I do what I can to make sure I meet the specifications of each shipment. That's what is required."

"Good, I like that because I've got a delivery that I'd like you to make on your way back."

I felt like I was riding a roller coaster without being strapped in. It started with the fear of being killed by Fuzz. Then I was made to walk a frightening underground tunnel to a secret meeting room.

Chris slid me a thick envelope. He assured me that with every delivery I brought him, he would make sure my trip home wasn't wasted. In addition to the $10,000 for the delivery to him, he promised me another $5,000 on my way home to Toronto.

Fifteen G's for every delivery. I sat behind the steering wheel and began crunching numbers. One delivery each week equaled $15,000. Four deliveries a month was $60,000. Two months would be 120 G's. One year's worth of payments for Evgenii.

I might just pull this off.

CHAPTER 27

THE NEXT THREE WEEKS

Excerpt from Michael's Journal

Veech called the next morning, friendlier than I had ever envisioned him able to be. He had spoken with the president of the Niagara Falls charter of the Outlaws MC. He expressed his gratitude and told me I was his most trusted "mover." His friendliness faded as he became more serious.

"Listen Michael, crossing at the border is no joke. These Border Service Officers have everything on you. They know the frequency you cross, your reason for entering the country, and which vehicle. By swiping your passport, they also know where you live, if you're married, and any criminal background," Veech said.

"I figured that Veech, which is why I think crossing once a week isn't a bad idea."

"Once a week is fine on my end. I don't want my best mover getting busted."

"I've already worked that out. When I first crossed, I used the casino as my destination. I explained that craps were only allowed in a couple casinos in the entire province of Ontario."

"Yeah, that's great Michael, but you're going to keep using craps as your excuse every week?"

"Let me finish. The way I see it is that I've already set a precedence of the casino and gambling as my reason for crossing. The casino's website told me that they offer daily poker tournaments that run Monday through Friday at 10 a.m. If you could arrange my pick-ups early enough in the morning and have my scheduled drop off between 9 a.m. and 10 a.m., then I think I've got a very plausible excuse."

"Not bad. I like it. Finally, I don't have to do all the thinking," Veech said rather impressed.

"I've also thought about contingency plans if I ever was asked to prove where I was going. Carrying a few hundred dollars would help. It shows I'm stocked for a trip to the casino. If I had a set day each week to cross, say Wednesdays for example, then that would look like it was my day off from work and I regularly played in the daily poker tournament. With each delivery, I'd set up a consistent pattern."

"Impressive Michael. I'll tell you what I'll do for you. I'll arrange to have your deliveries on the same day each week so your story will check out. How about this? How about, I have you pick up your packages the night before? You've proven you can be trusted. The morning traffic can hopefully be averted a bit."

"Thank you, Veech. That is much appreciated."

"Your next delivery is this Tuesday. Keep up the good work, and Michael, one last thing. If, something, anything, was to happen, I trust that you can keep your mouth shut."

"You can trust me, Veech."

"I hope so. For your sake."

Veech gave me the addresses with the expected drop off time before hanging up. The way he turned business-like ended our conversation on a sour note. I had been feeling more relaxed than ever with him during the conversation. When he got serious, the tinge of uneasiness crawled back into my gut. Glancing at the cash that I had stacked from my last shipment eased my tension and helped me relax. *You can do this. Less risk. More thinking.*

The next delivery wasn't for a few days. I needed to get my life in order. The car wash needing tending to. Melanie needed my attention. Most pressing on my list was that I wanted to speak with Richard. It had been nearly a week and I hadn't heard of any developments in my case.

I picked up the phone and dialed his direct number written on the back of his business card. His receptionist, Rhonda, a beautiful young woman with hair that always looked perfectly styled, answered the phone and transferred me to Richard.

He spoke rapidly, as though he had recently finished a pot of coffee. Caffeine energy. Very annoying. Richard's voice rang annoyingly in my ear, causing me to pull it away.

"Rich, it's Michael Taylor."

"Hey, Michael, I'm glad you called. I've been busy with another client, but was going to call you before I left today," Richard said.

"Alright. What's up?"

"Remember our previous conversation about the legal officers in the court system performing a quasi-strike? The one where they all call in sick on the same day?"

"Yeah, I remember."

"The rumors were true Michael. The reason I've been so busy is because yesterday they went through with it. You happen to read the paper or catch it on the news?"

"No, I was busy in Niagara Falls."

"I'll fill you in. Basically, as I explained last time, they took a page out of the police handbook on legal striking. They all came down with the legal officer's version of 'the Blue Flu.' Today has been a whirlwind of activity for the courts and my firm is trying to sort out rescheduling court appearances that were missed, the timetables for paperwork that was supposed to be approved, and things like that."

"Okay, Richard, but how does that all affect my case?"

"Well, it does and it doesn't. This whole thing is a mess. The good news I have is that this one day strike by the court officers has bought you some time. I plan on finding out more about what charges the CRA plans on bringing you up on and then the course of action we'll take."

"Alright, and I got a feeling you're going to give me some bad news too."

"No, not really. You already knew they were going to charge you eventually, so, this buys you some more freedom before you need to begin worrying."

"Okay, what have you found out so far?"

"I don't have tons of time to discuss it with you, but basically the agent that was investigating you, Agent Weisnewski, is trying to make a name for himself using your case as his stepping stone. He plans on bringing you up on every charge. So far, he isn't willing to negotiate a deal."

"What does that mean for me?"

"Basically, it means he plans on charging to the fullest extent of the law. He wants to go to trial Michael."

"How much time are we looking at until then Rich?"

"Tough to say right now because of the strike."

"Give a ballpark estimate."

"If the delays are as predicted, I'd say you have anywhere from three to five weeks until you're officially charged."

"What happens when they charge me?"

"It sounds a little scary, but I'll probably be notified before anything happens, assuming Agent Weisnewski has some professional courtesy. If not, a couple of police officers will come and arrest you. You'll be brought up on the charges, finger printed, booked, and then you'll have a bail court hearing. The judge will decide the amount of your bail."

"Jeez. But you'll give me some heads-up on all this?"

"Yes. The usual protocol is that the arresting agent contacts the suspect's attorney and gives a courtesy call. The attorney calls the client. The client turns themselves in voluntarily. It looks good to the judge. You know, cooperating and all, not resisting. Agent Weisnewski may or may not play ball that way, so I am advising you to get all your affairs in order in the next three weeks. Listen Michael, I got to go. We'll talk more soon."

"Before you go Rich, I need you to find out what the most probable jail sentence will be for me. I need to know that in order to get things settled."

"Yeah, okay. I'll see what I can find out. I'll call you in a few days."

I hung up the phone. The roller coaster, which is my life, reached its peak and started plummeting straight down. Three weeks. Five maximum. *I got to figure this out.* Depending on the length of my jail sentence, I needed to have a serious amount of cash saved up to keep Evgenii satisfied. And, someone to make the monthly payments.

CHAPTER 28
"IT" RETURNS

Excerpt from Michael's Journal

I couldn't wait another minute for Richard to call me back with my potential sentence length. I needed to know what I was looking at and start planning immediately. Seated on my couch, with my laptop open, I Googled every listing I could think of. I typed, "Canadian tax evasion cases" and the websites popped. Wikipedia explained all the technical terms I needed to refine my search. Using the search heading, "jail sentence for Canadian tax evasion," I found a website dedicated to tax crimes and potential sentences.

My anxiety flared once again as the roller coaster depicting my life banked hard to the left into a downward swirl. If I was convicted of tax evasion, like Richard said Agent Weisnewski was probably filing for, I was looking at a ninety-eight percent conviction rate in Ontario. The length of incarceration varied from one month to three years, depending on the severity of the case. Three years, at $10,000 a month, equaled $360,000.

I had three to five weeks to earn that money. And that was just the amount I needed to hold off Evgenii from killing Susie or Melanie or both, let alone anything else. *Oh God. What about my attorney fees? How much will those cost?*

I burned off the anxiety by pacing the length of my living room. When that wasn't enough, I flung myself onto the carpet and performed more push-ups than I had ever done in a row. Sixty-eight. I dialed Veech's phone number.

I needed more delivery jobs. A lot more. Our current arrangement wasn't enough. Not even close. I needed more. As Veech's phone rang, I took out a pad of paper and began scratching down numbers.

The only way I could ensure that there was complete trust between the Outlaws and I was to be open and honest with Veech. Jail time. *You're facing jail time. What is Veech going to think?*

Our relationship was built on trust. They needed to trust me to make their deliveries on time and keep my mouth closed about club business. I needed to trust that they would pay me, keep the future deliveries coming, and leave me unharmed. Breaking their trust was a very bad idea. My only hope was to throw myself on Veech's mercy.

"Hello?"

"Veech, its Michael Taylor."

"Yeah."

"Veech, listen, we need to talk."

"I'm listening."

"I need more deliveries. I know we agreed on one a week, but I need more."

"What the hell is going on here Michael? You need to start explaining yourself before you fall out of my good graces."

"Okay, let me explain. There's a CRA agent who is going to be charging me with tax evasion. There was a court worker's strike that happened and delayed all the paperwork before charges could be filed. My lawyer says that I have anywhere from three to five weeks before I'll be charged. After that, I will be arrested and a judge will decide how high to set my bail. If I am out on bail, I won't be able to cross the border."

"Jesus Christ Michael. How the fuck long did you know all of this?"

"Just five minutes ago, when I was talking with my attorney. What I am asking for is more deliveries, a lot more. As many as you can give me. I need to make as much cash as possible to set aside for my monthly payments."

"Listen to me right now. If any of this comes back onto the club, I swear, you're fucking dead. And not only you, but your entire family is dead too! And your bitch girlfriend too!"

"Veech, c'mon man, listen. No one knows about our arrangement. I've been extra careful about everything. There's no way anyone knows anything about my deliveries or anything like that. The club is safe. You're protected. This is an unrelated issue. I promise you, everything is still good. You can still trust me."

"Goddamn it Michael! I had big plans for you, and now you suddenly tell me you're going to prison."

"Veech, I'm sorry. I just found out. I wasn't holding anything back from you."

"What am I supposed to do now?"

"I know I don't deserve anything from you or the club, but I was hoping to make as many deliveries as possible. I'll do anything Veech."

172

"I need to check on some things. I'll call you back. Goddamn it."

"Thanks, Veech. I'm sorry about all of this."

I hung up the phone. I didn't know if Veech was going to put a hit out on me to tie up a loose end or give me more deliveries. Reading his reaction was difficult. Actually, impossible. He was temperamental on a good day. *I did it now. Is he going to kill me while I sleep?*

My mind raced. For the second time that day, I paced back and forth across my living room. More push-ups. Forty-two. More pacing. Less push-ups. Thirty-five. Repeat, until my chest and arms ached too much to continue. I prayed the phone would ring. *Anything, I'll take anything.*

The thought of prison didn't scare me yet. You can't be scared of something if you don't give it any thought. My only concern was the safety of Melanie and Susie. Susie or Melanie. Or both. *God, please, not both. What am I saying, not either.* With their lives on the line, I couldn't think of anything else. My mind flashed back to the night Evgenii cut my thumb off. It made my thumb ache. *First time in days I've felt anything.* The paralyzing fear of knowing I put them in harm's way left me unable to distract myself.

I stared at the phone. *Ring damn it, ring.* I checked it to see if the battery was charged enough. A minute later I made sure it was receiving a signal. I switched to crunches. Seventy-two. I paced. More crunches. Seventy-two again. I shouted at the phone to ring. "Why won't you ring for me!"

The minimum amount of time Richard told me I had before being arrested was three weeks. I had to set myself up for the worst case scenario. *Like I have a choice. My mind is hardwired to do that automatically. Thanks Dad!* Assuming I was in prison for thirty-six months, I needed to make around $400,000. Evgenii's payments. Legal bills.

I calculated the numbers on my laptop. One scenario. *Goddamn it.* I needed two deliveries a day.

Two deliveries.

Each day.

For the next three weeks.

I sat on the couch. Pacing, push-ups, and crunches weren't going to help this. I flicked on a sports show playing last night's highlights. SportsCentre. My right knee nervously bounced. I could feel the tension rippling through my body. I almost vomited twice. My head began to pound. The headache right behind my eyes was back. My hands were sweaty. I wiped them across my T-shirt. The third time, the vomit won. I ran to the bathroom, making it in time.

I sat there, next to the toilet and watched the vomit swirl away. *Is this my life? How the fuck did I get to this point?* I rubbed my temples. The phone rang.

"Hello?"

SAVANNAH

"Michael? It's Veech."

"Thank you for calling me back Veech. I assure you that, even though…"

"Shut up! Listen, don't say a word and listen, goddamn it. I spoke with Chris. Apparently you made an impression on him. He convinced me to give you more work. I was ready to cut you loose, but he wouldn't hear of it."

"Thank you, Veech. I won't disappoint you."

"Don't thank me. Thank Chris. I was ready to have you erased."

"Jesus Veech, tell me you're joking."

"Yeah. Joking. Right. Here's the deal. You can have as many deliveries as you can handle. We happen to have an abundance of packages that need shipping. There's, well, I'm not going tell you how many there are, but there's a lot. They would normally take months to be moved."

"I'll do it. Thank you."

"Chris also said he'll have some deliveries for you going back."

"Oh man, thank you Veech."

"Like I said before, don't thank me. Chris saved you, literally. It'll work like this; you can have a delivery as often as you want one. Your car can take twelve packages, so our deal of $10,000 per delivery stands. That's non-negotiable. Work out whatever deal you want with the Niagara Falls chapter. I'm not sure about their inventory."

"When can I start?"

"Not wasting any time, huh? Well, I guess we could go ahead tonight. Each pick up will be from the same location. We'll need to use middle of the night pick ups. Don't want to arouse any suspicion over the next few weeks. Each drop off will be to Chris's place, as before."

I felt something that I hadn't felt in a long time. Happiness. Hope. *I might be ok. It'll suck like hell for awhile, but I might actually pull this off.*

Then I felt *IT. IT.* The balloon of hope rose inside me. Hanging on the end of the string tied around it, *IT* rose too. It came back. Back from wherever it hides.

Not since the last night in the poker room had I felt it. I hadn't even thought of it. Its hunger for greed caused my hands to tingle. Excitement.

My left hand held the phone to my ear. Veech was still on the line. My right hand clicked the wireless mouse, figuring how much cash I could make. My arms tingled. It was back. Veech finished what he was saying. My legs tingled. *IT* had hooked its sharpened talons into me. *IT* took over the conversation.

"Veech, I'd like to make two deliveries a day. I'll pick up the entire shipment from you in the middle of the night, as you say, and then deliver the packages in two separate shipments to Niagara Falls."

"No. No. No way. That's too risky."

I was surprised at how confident I sounded even as I was saying it. "Veech, I

174

can do this. You can trust me. Your packages will get moved. You'll make a lot of money. I'll make enough to slide by. I need this."

"That's what the problem is. You need this too much. I've seen guys like you who need something too much. They always get caught or they trip up somewhere because their head's not in it."

"You've never seen someone making deliveries like me before, have you? I'm smart, prepared, and most of all, I'm not going to make a mistake and get caught. You trusted me before I told you about the goddamn CRA agent and these bogus tax evasion charges, so trust me now."

"I'll say this one time, Michael. The club will not be lenient on you because of your past relationship with Arch. Those days are gone. If you fail to meet our expectations, then we'll have a serious problem."

"This is on me. I know the consequences if I fail. And I assure you Veech, I can do this."

"You can make a pick up tonight. 2 a.m. Don't let me down."

I snapped the phone closed. *IT* slowly released me. It receded back down to wherever it lived. Deep inside me. I heard myself talking to Veech, not in conscious control of my words. I was impressive. Confident. Assured.

Once again, *IT* reared its ugly head. It demanded to be fed. Money was the only cure for its hunger.

Looking at the calculator plastered across the screen of my laptop, I saw the amount *IT* had figured for me to make; $630,000 in three weeks of work, two deliveries a day, starting right away. The agreement was done. Veech and I agreed. There was no turning back now. *You already have Evgenii and the Russians on your ass, you don't need the Outlaws too. You don't have a choice. You have to honor this agreement.*

I didn't have a plan. *What are you going to do with the extra twelve packages while you ship the first twelve across the border?*

You need to cross the border many more times. Surely that will attract attention.

I shook my head. It was too late to tell Veech I couldn't make the deliveries. I needed to come up with a plan. I needed a safe place to store the extra twelve packages while the first were being delivered. I needed an excuse to cross the border frequently. And I needed everything before tomorrow.

CHAPTER 29
TWO-A-DAYS

Excerpt from Michael's Journal

The next week was a blur. Constant driving. Frequent gas station fill-ups. And sporadic sleeping sessions. I woke up at 1:30 a.m. every day to pick up twenty-four packages. Twelve in the traps and twelve in my own green grocery store bin in the trunk. I then returned home to sleep a few more hours before heading to Niagara Falls.

I had used a mishmash of excuses to cross the border. I used every excuse from daily poker tournaments at the Seneca Niagara Casino to family health issues. If I threw it at the wall and it stuck, I ran with it. I quickly figured out the Border Service Officers were much more receptive to honest answers that were offered before the question was asked.

During my second crossing of the week, I decided to offer a lot of information. I lied that my father was being hospitalized at the Greater Niagara General Hospital after suffering from a heart attack. I knew, eventually, that some Border Service Officer would inquire about my frequent visitations. I did some good old fashioned research. I visited the GNGH to find names of cardiologists on staff.

The directory to the entire hospital staff was listed on the right hand wall of the main entrance, as well as each office number. The names were organized by the specialty of the doctors and surgeons. I found the cardiologists and chose the easiest to remember. I wrote the name of Dr. Andrew Choo on a piece of paper. I left, never to return. No need, I got what I came for.

There was a flaw to choosing the "family health" excuse. Once you ring that bell, it can't be undone. There would be tremendous suspicion if I used another reason for crossing. Going to visit my father in the hospital one day, and then going to the casino for a poker tournament the next? Bad idea. If it ain't broke, don't fix it.

The next question came to me in a caffeine heightened state of clarity. I needed to cross the border twice a day. Twice in. Twice out. My father's fake health issue was the foundation. I had to build off that. *If you're going to lie, do it with some thought. Less risk. More thinking.*

The question was sure to come. Why are you crossing back and forth so frequently? *Think more.* I needed answers to future questions. Better than the answers, I needed the questions. I compiled a list of potential questions. Then their answers. *Less risk if you know what the question is before it's asked.*

After deliberating long and hard, I settled on my plan. The question list was complete. The answers worked. There was detail. *More thinking.*

"It says here, you've been crossing rather frequently. What's the nature of your business here?" the border officer said.

"My Dad's pretty sick. He's in GNGH, intensive care. My company moved me down to Niagara Falls for a few weeks to train on some new equipment."

"What do you do for a living?"

"I work for Toronto Hydro."

"What do you do there?"

"I'm a linesman. My crew is being trained on heavy wires. Right now, we're being trained on working solo in the bucket truck on high-voltage lines."

"What's a bucket truck?"

"Those are the work trucks that have a lift on the back. We stand in the bucket and work on transformers, voltage regulators, ratio banks. You name it, we do it. Like I said, Toronto Hydro is training us in St. Catherines for a few weeks."

"You cross twice a day?"

"Our training day is broken up into two sessions. We get a two hour break in between. I take my Dad some lunch. He can't stomach the hospital crap they serve him."

"Alright. Go ahead."

Less risk. More thinking. During the garage poker days, I had a friend who had put himself through college and studied to become a high-voltage electrician. He went on and on about his new job. About how he worked on the power lines and went in after storms to repair blown transformers. He even went as far to wear the thick rubber gloves the linesman used. His talk annoyed me to no end. Same thing every night he was there. As Savannah snaked me all of his overtime earnings, I became less annoyed with his tales.

One particular night, he was especially excited about a training session he had just completed. He bragged about a huge pay raise. His company had paid for him to go to a three week training course in St. Catherines, Ontario. After finishing, he became certified to maneuver the bucket and work solo. I figured his co-workers loved his new found independence. Less of him talking, more working.

I used all the information he had annoyed me with.

The excuse worked every time. Whether it was my respected job or my father's hospital stay, crossing the border no longer was an issue. It developed into an annoyance. A momentary delay.

The other issue was the extra twelve packages. Picking up twenty-four packages at 2 a.m. became a tedious chore. Half went into the trap. The other twelve went in a grocery bin. Thanks to Fuzz's slip of the tongue, I now knew each package's value. *Not like you're going to do anything with them.* I made a mental note. *Become more careful with them.*

I stored them neatly at the bottom of the bin. Six fit evenly on the bottom. Two layers took about half the depth of the bin. A quarter of a million dollars, sitting right on the front seat next to me. Want to hide something? Put it in plain sight.

I packed the top with neatly folded laundry. I wanted to create the illusion of my grocery bin doubling as a laundry basket. *Not believable, think more.* One time with the laundry. Poor planning on my part. A twenty minute stop at Home Depot filled the top of the bin with heavy duty wire, electrical tape, various plugs, switches, and a thick pair of rubber gloves. *Better. At least it gels with your back story.*

What am I going to do with the bin while I cross the border? Can't take them with me. Less risk, remember? Where can I store a quarter of a million dollars?

I needed a place that was secure, safe, and easy to get in and out. The packages were sure to attract attention. I needed something private or very public. Either way, it didn't matter. Hide in solitude or hide in a crowd. Both worked. My initial thought was a locker at the bus station.

The Niagara Transportation Centre was an ideal location for me to drop off and pick-up. Quick. Easy. Plenty of people. My anxiety flared up. The lockers were narrow. Too narrow. *What if you catch the edge of the locker? Will the package tear? I should be careful.* In the bus station, people sat and waited. Some read newspapers. Some magazines. Others just watched everyone else. I knew I didn't want anyone watching my every move. I carried the bin in on my first, and only, visit. I swung around and headed back in the direction I came. *Cross that possibility off the list.*

The train station. Same problem, different place.

The first day, I left the extra twelve packages at home. I delivered the first twelve in the morning, then drove the two hours back to my house, retrieved the last twelve, and made the day's final delivery. Safe. Reliable. But utterly exhausting. I couldn't keep that pace up. Too many hours driving with too few sleeping. I needed something better, something less taxing.

The exhaustion was physically and mentally overwhelming.

A billboard off of the QEW displayed an advertisement for a storage locker company. Clean. Safe. Secure self storage units for rent. My jaw dropped. The smiling woman in the sign stood next to a unit with its door open. She pointed her hand toward the open space.

I didn't wait. I pulled in right away. The smallest locker they had available was a 5'x5' unit. It was more than enough. I paid the first two months rent, which they insisted on. For $59.99 a month, I rented privacy. I rented a sanctuary. I rented the solution to my problem.

The following day I brought boxes filled with general junk. The usual crap that houses accumulate, usually in the basement or garage. They were my decoys. I knew there was security for my protection not prosecution. *It's not like you can stroll in carrying mysterious packages.* The boxes were the perfect cover.

Most people who rent a storage unit are looking to clear out the crap from their homes. Stay at home wives who are sick of looking at their husband's mess, older couples who have downsized and lost storage space and young, single renters who don't have the needed space to store their valuables. The storage center was as deserted as the casino was busy. Few eyes and even fewer cameras. All I spotted was one on the entrance, and one on the exit. *Don't ask. Don't tell.*

I had a plausible excuse for crossing the border.

I had a safe storage area.

I had completed ten trips across the border in five days. It earned me $120,000. Chris wasn't as frequent with his return deliveries as Veech. I felt as though my chances were improving. *Sure the CRA is going to charge you with tax evasion any day now, but look on the bright side, three months ago that kind of cash would have put you on top of the world.*

I actually felt my body relax. I started to believe I was going to make it.

That was the last time I can recall feeling relaxed.

CHAPTER 30
CHARGED

Excerpt from Michael's Journal

For the sixth straight day, I woke up as a full-time mover. My alarm blared. One thirty in the morning was too early for any person. Especially the same person who had just done that five times before. I got out of bed. My eyes didn't focus for what felt like a minute. I rubbed them. I splashed water on them, finally they relented.

I picked up the half a million dollars in drug packages, or at least I assumed they were drug packages. No one ever discussed them. When I picked them up, they weren't spoken of. When I dropped them off, it was as though they never existed. Except, they did exist. They were crossing off my payment checklist. The more I delivered, the longer into my sentence Evgenii would get paid.

My only comfort at one thirty in the morning was I would be able to return to the warmth of my bed for a few more hours of sleep. Each day proved to be more challenging and less rewarding than the previous. The growing piles of cash, which lined my bedside table, comforted me initially. That fell away, as it always does with the realization that I didn't have enough money. I needed more. No matter how hard I tried, that fear of failing overtook my thoughts.

The second time on the sixth day that I woke up, my body ached. Exhaustion was setting in much quicker than I thought it would. I dragged myself across to the coffee maker. Caffeine. It was the driving force behind the first and last hour of each day. Without it, I was certain that I wouldn't be able to function. It got me to a high enough level to complete four border crossings each day. I filled my thermos. Coffee. Cream. Sugar. Then, more sugar. I drove toward my storage unit.

I placed the grocery bin, which appeared to be overflowing with tools and equipment for an electrician, in the front seat of my car. *Good cover. Safe. Effective.* In the backseat, I arranged cardboard boxes to act as my cover. Just carrying the same green bin with electrical equipment and tools may have appeared too peculiar. I was worried about nosey storage unit neighbors. I labeled the boxes with black marker. "Mason's stuff" was behind my driver's seat, "Kids clothes" next to it. Any leering eyes would be bored seeing run-of-the-mill cardboard boxes being stuffed into a small storage unit. *Nothing interesting here.* After I arrived, I transferred the entire bin of packages, which were to be shipped on the second run, into a box and stored them in the unit. Simple. Safe. Reliable. Just like they advertised.

The drive on the sixth day was normal. Fast. Slow. Stop. Traffic. Clear. Traffic. Same as every other day in the past and every other day to come. Halfway through a thermos of coffee, I made my usual bathroom stop. The sun peeked out. I took an extra minute to breathe in deep breaths of fresh air. The sun felt hot on my face. I closed my eyes and enjoyed the few seconds of peacefulness. *Enough rest, time to make a delivery.*

The storage unit was the same as any other storage unit. Row after row of hidden treasure lurked behind locked doors. The red doors set against white painted brick stood out. When a door was open, it stood out. The pattern of red, white, red, white was broken. Your eyes seemed to gravitate to the disruption. I drove around back to the far corner where my little haven resided. I had three large cardboard boxes, filled with stuffed newspaper, stacked on one another. A roll of packing tape rested on top of them. I carried the cardboard box labeled "Mason's clothes" in through the door. On top of it, I balanced my cell phone. In my pocket, Veech's throw-away phone sat, set on vibrate. *Answer when I call.* We hadn't spoken in days. I still kept the phone charged. It never left my sight.

I tossed "Mason's clothes" next to the other stack of boxes, in it, $240,000 waited for my return. I locked up. The simple pad lock cost under three dollars at Home Depot. The commercial still aired of a bullet being shot through its center and it still remained locked. *Funny how the TV commercial specialists never showed bolt cutters being used to shear right through the metal loop.*

I left without a second thought. *Stay here. I'll be right back.* I continued on my first delivery, leaving my cell phone still on top of "Mason's clothes." Locked away. Safe. Reliable. I always left my cell phone there for two reasons. First, carrying two cell phones seemed suspicious to me. *You're crossing the border with illegal goods. Don't draw unnecessary attention to yourself. Two cell phones is asking for trouble. Think more.*

SAVANNAH

Second, I was only away from it for a couple of hours. At most. Every time I returned from the first delivery, I checked the messages. *Right, like anyone is calling you.* Only once in five days had there been a missed call. It was from Melanie. She had wanted to talk on her break.

Twelve packages were safely packed away into my traps. I had my passport ready. I laid the directions to the GNGH in clear sight on the passenger seat. I was ready to cross the border. I drove the final few minutes to the Rainbow Bridge.

The traffic that day was light. Very light. The bridge had fewer than the usual number of cars on it. In my lane to cross into the U.S., I chose lane number six. There was only one car currently dealing with the Border Service Officer.

I wasn't superstitious. Never was. I always selected the lane with the least amount of cars. The late model green Honda sedan pulled away ahead of me. I inched forward. A fat, middle aged man slowly rolled his head in my direction. The thick goatee around his mouth was covered mainly in gray.

I handed him my passport. We made direct eye contact. I smiled. He took the passport to swipe it through the computer. I checked the clock.

"Good morning."

"Citizenship?"

"Canadian."

"Where are you headed?" He glanced at the passport and then at the computer comparing.

"My father is in the hospital, the Greater Niagara General Hospital, recovering from a heart attack. I'm going to visit him on my lunch break."

"Uh huh."

"I've been coming here the past week or so to see him, and he'll probably be in a couple more weeks, at least. The doctors say he's lucky to be alive."

The border officer looked back at me from the computer with a serious look on his face. "Are you Michael Taylor?"

"Yes."

"Your birthday is April 26, 1987?"

I hoped he was just diligently fact checking my passport's authenticity. "Yes sir, it is."

"Is your address 57 Broadview Avenue in Toronto, Ontario?"

Trying my damnedest to hold the fake smile plastered across my face. "Yes, that's my address."

The border officer quickly switched the passport from his right hand to his left and reached for his sidearm. "Sir, put the car in park. Turn off the engine. And put both hands on the steering wheel."

"Whoa. What's wrong?"

"NOW! Do it NOW!"

182

Raising my hands in the air. "Okay. Okay. Can you tell me what's going on?"

"There's a warrant out for your arrest. Do what I tell you to do! Turn off your car!"

The next few minutes felt like a dream. I was escorted out of my car. Two armed guards led me into a holding room. It was your typical windowless room with a stainless steel table and two hard plastic chairs. Little comfort for my aching body. The brick walls were painted a cream color. The smell of fresh paint hung in the air. The door was standard issue. Thick. Sturdy. Likely able to stand up to bullets or battering rams. The one foot by one foot window was lined with a meshed glass pane. The wire crisscrossed, preventing any broken glass from falling. The chair was cold. I shivered. *Jesus Christ. What the hell went wrong?*

I worried the Border Service Officers had found the drug packages. My thoughts shot to the storage unit. *Did they know about that too?* I worried that the pending tax evasion charges were the least of my worries. *Trafficking narcotics while crossing international borders.* I worried I was going to be federally charged. Years of jail time flew through my thoughts.

Susie.

Melanie.

Their images flashed in and out of my mind. *How could you have gotten yourself into this mess?* I held out hope that there had been a misunderstanding. A different Michael Taylor was being sought after. Not much hope. A speck of dust in the universe. Bad odds. No odds, really.

I prayed. I begged God. Begged. Richard told me that I had at least two weeks until the paperwork could be processed by the CRA. I would surely have received a call and been notified that the paperwork had been filed. Professional courtesy he called it. *Was I officially being charged?*

My cell phone, still balancing on the cardboard box in the storage locker, had been set on vibrate. I pictured the constant rumbling with each ring. Richard Brantley had probably called with the news. When I didn't answer, he surely would have left a voice mail in my inbox.

Then the fat, middle aged Border Service Officer entered the holding room. He sat down. I hated him. I hated his goatee. I hated his arrogance. I hated how he had me. I snapped to attention, forcing the fog to lift that had settled over me. He carried with him a manila file folder. He opened it. A single piece of paper was attached to the top.

The border officer pointed to the corner of the room toward the ceiling. "I am obligated to inform you that you are being recorded and monitored Mr. Taylor. Do you have any objections to that?"

I looked up at the object I failed to recognize before. "No. That's fine."

"Do you know why you're here Mr. Taylor?"

SavannaH
================================

"You told me that there was a Michael Taylor with an arrest warrant. I'm guessing you've made a mistake."

"No, I don't think I made a mistake. And now, I am telling you that Michael Taylor, who lives at 57 Broadview Avenue in Toronto, Ontario, is being charged with tax evasion and some lesser charges. Do you know anything about that?"

"To be honest, I do know about those charges. As of this morning, I hadn't been officially charged. My attorney said that there was going to be at least two more weeks until the paperwork came through."

"And you just thought you would skip the charges by entering the United States?"

"No sir. Honestly. I was going to visit my father. Like I already said at your booth, he recently had a heart attack and was staying at the GNGH. I have been visiting him for five days now, without a problem. Then suddenly there you were, reaching for your gun."

The border officer read the paperwork. "It says here, Mr. Taylor, that you are being charged with some very serious crimes. Attempting to cross international borders with a warrant out for your arrest doesn't look very good for you."

"I'm telling the truth. I drove here from my home this morning. As of then, the charges hadn't been filed."

"Here's what's going to happen Mr. Taylor. Your car is going to be impounded by the United States government. You'll be escorted back to Toronto when the Canadian Revenue Agency decides to come and get you. They'll decide whether to proceed with adding the charge of attempt to cross an international border with an arrest warrant issued to your already full load. For now, get comfortable, you'll probably be here for awhile."

I nodded my response. I felt low. The worst possible scenario. The words echoed in my head. *Maybe not. There's a silver lining here.* The Border Services never found the hidden packages. They're safe. *Pay the fine for the impounding. Get the car, get the packages. No harm. No foul.*

I slammed my forehead down into my crossed arms. The fat officer exited the room, carrying the manila folder. I buried my forehead in my arms. A subtle smile crossed my concealed face. The fear of the police tearing apart my house, car, and storage locker faded. I clutched to the hope of getting bailed out. *Get the car. Get the packages. No harm. No foul.*

The longer I sat and waited in the cold room, the more I worried about the Outlaw's reaction to my arrest and missing my delivery. Not the Outlaws. They, as a whole group, didn't scare me. Just Veech. He seemed like a psycho. Like someone who would make rash decisions. He knew the time was coming when I would be charged. But that was two weeks away.

I worried. He threatened me about keeping my mouth shut. I would, but he

184

didn't know that. I feared he would assume I would talk. That I would give up the Outlaws, make a deal. Get some leniency. I knew things about their operation. The locations. The members involved. The underground tunnel and secret room in Niagara Falls.

Would some unknown prison assassin, hired by the motorcycle club, silence me permanently?

My sly smile faded. Fast. My heart rate peaked. The anxiety built up inside my gut again. This time, more than ever.

As soon as I was transferred I needed to get Richard to contact Veech. He needed to know that I had every intention of honoring our agreement. Being my attorney, I knew that having Richard deliver the message was completely within my rights as a client. *Would Richard catch some of Veech's wrath as the messenger?*

Having half a million dollars in undelivered, impounded packages was a good enough incentive to guarantee Richard's safe return.

I hoped.

CHAPTER 31

BAIL

Excerpt from Michael's Journal

The next day and a half was filled with nothing but disappointment. One after the next. Not only was the CRA extremely late, but I was denied access to the bathroom until my escorts arrived. I almost relieved myself in the corner of the interview room out of shear panic. Five hours I sat there. Luckily, the CRA escorts arrived just in time. They found me already standing. I had convinced myself there was no choice. In my pants or in the corner. *Easy decision.* I unbuttoned my jeans. I unzipped my fly. They walked in, saving me that humiliation. That was the last time I can honestly say I had any form of good luck.

The escorts were two men teetered on the realm of sleep walking. Neither of them spoke. Neither showed any emotion. For three hours I was in their custody and nothing happened. A deep grunt was the most elaborate response either of them gave.

Both were well built. They definitely had starred on their high school football team, that, or were ex-military. They had the look. The only things larger than their monstrous shoulders were their enormous hands. As I was re-handcuffed, after using the toilet, those massive hands gripped my wrists. Theirs were easily twice the size of mine. It felt as though they could crush me like a pop can.

With one behemoth leading me from either side, we exited the building. They walked me toward their black passenger van. It was as if I was a child again with an adult guiding me toward my car seat. I was handcuffed. My feet were shackled. *Overkill. Two grizzly bears against me.*

186

SAVANNAH

Sitting in the van, with a crooked smile on his face, was Bradley Weisnewski. He had accompanied the men. He sat and waited for me in the middle row of the van. I hadn't noticed any one was in the van until the door was opened for me. The windows were deeply tinted, almost black. The van's middle door was opened. I was pushed toward it. I made direct eye contact with him. For the second, but not last, time we stared at each other. He silently gloated.

My shackles were removed. My head was pushed down as they shoved me into the van. Bradley slid over, making room. The shackles were looped through a stainless steel O-ring attached to the floor and clasped around my ankles again. *Overkill. Two grizzlies and a snake against me.*

I sat. My handcuffs were released. *Thank you. My ankles are shackled, isn't that enough?* The larger of the two escorts looped the freed handcuff through the steel hook that was buried between the seat cushion and reattached it. *C'mon guys.*

I was silent. My hands were locked behind my back. My feet were fastened to the floor. Bradley began talking. He was quieter than I remembered, as if the escort guards weren't privy to our discussion.

"You weren't making a run for it, were you Mr. Taylor?"

"No. I wasn't."

"May I ask why you were trying to cross into the United States when you had an arrest warrant?"

I faced the CRA agent. "I already told you I wasn't making a run for it. I did not know there was a warrant out for my arrest. I found out when the Border Officer informed me with his gun drawn."

"Standard procedure, I'm sure. Your lawyer didn't contact you this morning?"

"I didn't have my cell on me. So, he may have. I am not sure."

"Either way, Mr. Taylor, it doesn't matter. I filed the charges and gave a professional heads-up phone call to your lawyer. You have been officially charged with tax evasion and money laundering through your phony car wash business."

"Phony car wash?"

"Yes, Mr. Taylor, I plan on proving to the court that you committed tax evasion through the purchase of your car wash and then planned on laundering money through the car wash's profits. Not to mention the illegal means in which you make money and refuse to file proper income tax statements."

Something flashed across his eyes, like he was fishing. *He doesn't know. He doesn't know anything. One giant fishing trip, isn't it Brad?*

I shook my head. "No. You got this all wrong. I'm not laundering money through my car wash. I bought it straight up from that guy. Sure I paid in cash, but I'm not laundering money or intending to launder any money through it. That charge won't stick. You can't prove that."

"I don't want to hear your excuses Mr. Taylor. You and your attorney can

187

work that out with the court. I'm only here to make sure you understand what you're being charged with and where we are going from here."

"Yeah? And where's that?"

"The Oshawa Holding Center, until you have a preliminary hearing in front of a judge. Most likely tomorrow."

I sat there. Stunned. I felt sorry for myself. *So this is rock bottom?* I didn't make eye contact with the other three passengers. The radio was on. It was low. I couldn't make out whether it was an AM or FM station or whether it played music or discussed news events. Agent Weisnewski sat with a smug smirk on his face. He read a folded newspaper, proud of himself.

Scenario after scenario ran through my head. What was I going to do once my bail was posted? How would I pay for it? Who should I call to post it? Melanie? Susie? Did I dare call Arch? *No. Don't even mess around. You can still smooth this all over with Veech.*

I had some fancy footwork to do in order to make things right with Veech. I needed to retrieve my car from the impound lot and also make one final stop at my storage locker. My days of being a "mover" were seemingly over. I couldn't cross any international or provincial borders out on bail. Veech would insist on me returning his undelivered packages. *Best case scenario: he would sever all contact. Clean and dry. Nothing personal. With me whole.*

Returning $500,000 in undelivered packages was hopefully proof enough that Veech could trust me to keep my silence. On the other hand, I had made a deal to deliver these packages and I knew the Outlaw's weren't a store where you could return your purchase and get your money back. Not fulfilling my end of the deal would surely irritate Veech.

The other thought that bounced in and out of my troubled mind was Evgenii and his ridiculous monthly payment I owed. *Ten G's; every month.* I had enough, not for the maximum sentence that Agent Weisnewski was going for, but enough for a good portion of that. I needed to know what length of prison sentence the CRA, and Bradley Weisnewski, intended to pursue.

"I know you don't owe me anything, but can I ask you a favor?"

"What's that?"

"Can you tell me what's going to happen after we get to the Oshawa Holding Center?"

"No. Your attorney can do that once he arrives."

"C'mon Brad. I'm asking you for a favor because I'm in a tough spot. I don't know what is going to happen. You know, so just fill me in with the protocol. I'm not asking for any special treatment, just a conversation about the legal proceedings."

"Fine. When we get to the Oshawa Holding Center you'll be processed by the

188

officers. They will take your photo, fingerprints, and any possessions you have on you. You'll be assigned an inmate jumpsuit and slip-on shoes. Nothing pretty, I assure you. You'll be put in another holding cell. Depending on how many other people are there, you may or may not have your own cell. Because it is so late in the day, you'll spend the night there. In the morning, you and your attorney will be able to discuss your case and then be put in front of a judge. I'm not a prosecutor, but I do advise them on how firm our case is against the charged individual. I also advise the prosecutors what deal the CRA would accept."

"What deal would you accept with my case?"

"Cases vary in strength anywhere from time served with probation and a fine, all the way up to no deal because those cases are so strong against the accused."

"Where does my case fall?"

"Your case is a slam dunk. No deals will be accepted. I'll advise the prosecutor to tell your attorney for you to plead guilty and hope that the judge gives you a lighter sentence than the maximum that we're seeking. Nothing personal, of course."

I closed my eyes in defeat. "Oh my God. What am I going to do?"

"I advise you to speak with your attorney and hope that he can persuade the judge to go easy on you because you're cooperating. However, trying to cross an international border into the United States right after the charges against you were filed, looks really bad. That could play a factor in the judge's sentencing."

"I know you don't owe me anything, but can I ask you one more question?"

"Go ahead. I'm listening."

"In cases such as mine, how much is the bail usually set at?"

"Bail? You got to be joking. Mr. Taylor, I would be very surprised if the judge allows any bail at all. At best, you're looking at turning in your passport and something in the half million to one million dollar range. I bet your bail will be set at $500,000 with passport turned in, only because you don't have any prior convictions."

"Oh my God. You can't be serious."

"No, I take that back. I actually think you will have your bail denied and you will spend the time waiting for your trial in jail."

Deafening silence filled the van for the entire ride home. None of the four people in the van so much as parted their lips. Three sets of eyes stared straight ahead. The other set buried in a newspaper. The road passed by quickly. The traffic was light, making the trip unusually quick. I wanted traffic. I prayed for it. I had driven that stretch of the QEW, what seemed like, countless times over the past week. Each time I cursed the eventual traffic. *Fourth worst city in North America for traffic.*

This time, I wanted the drive to last forever. The sooner it ended, the sooner I was in jail. No such luck. Clear sailing the entire drive.

The van pulled into the Oshawa Holding Center loading area. Both guards

189

exited the van. Bradley Weisnewski remained seated next to me. They came around and opened my door. The larger of two men unlocked my ankle shackles, unlooping them around the grounded O-ring. He reattached them to my ankles before I could even make a move. *Well, running is out of the question.*

He did the same with my handcuffs. He took much more care as if worried I may use one of my hands to strike him. He never broke his grip from my freed hand. Corded steel underneath human skin. He was swift. He had done this before. I was handcuffed again. *There goes fighting my way out of this jam.*

The guard stepped back. He waved for me to come out. I shook my head. He waved again, this time the shorter guard perked up. I shook my head again. *When all else fails, act childish.*

"Agent Dumbass over here said I basically have no hope in hell of receiving bail. I think I'm done cooperating today," I said shaking my head.

Both guards looked at one another. The corner of their mouths curled up. *Crap, what have I done?* I was dragged out of my seat and dropped on the concrete ground. My shoulder took the brunt of the fall. Pain seared through my body. I was grabbed again. *Again with the meaty hands under my arms?* They whisked me from the van to a door. They pushed a button. It buzzed. As if synchronized, they both lifted their heads toward a security camera. They waited and stared. Three seconds later, the door popped open. The noise startled me. Both guards shook their heads.

Two correctional officers greeted me with a smile. I was handed over to them. More like, thrown to them. They grabbed and pulled me. I was tossed around. My photograph was taken. I was fingerprinted. Then, I was made to strip. I had to redress in a jumpsuit. The orange one-piece smelled of musty body odor. Its fabric was scratchy, making me instantly itchy all over. It irritated me more than anything else about the holding center. Finally, I was thrown in a jail cell. My own sixty-four square feet of solitude. Except for the animal in the corner.

I tasted his odor before I saw him. His blazing orange jumpsuit somehow turned brown. His beard hadn't been trimmed in months. When he wickedly smiled at my entrance, I noticed the few teeth he had remaining in his mouth. Rotten isn't a strong enough word. I gagged. The smell oozed. I made no attempt at hiding my disgust for my roommate's lack of hygiene.

It was the longest night of my life.

The stink emanating from the other bunk made my stomach turn somersaults all night long. The wretchedness in the air scurried down my nasal passage and set up camp on my tongue. Every few minutes my mouth filled with bile from the coming vomit. I fought it. The thought of Melanie and how much I loved her saved me more than once. I thought back to Susie and how close we once were.

The smell bypassed reality and entered my memories. When the lights came on for breakfast, I couldn't have been more relieved to see the next day.

SAVANNAH

My attorney showed up first thing to discuss my case with me. Richard Brantley was a name that had some pull around the Oshawa Holding Center. The guards seemed to give him more leniencies than the other inmate's attorneys received. We were able to sit next to one another and talk in loud whispers. He explained that he tried to call my cell phone, but there was no answer. I nodded. He also told me that the CRA agent had given him a professional heads-up phone call, but did not hold off on issuing the arrest warrant to allow me the commonly received twenty-four hours to voluntarily turn myself in. I nodded again, biting my tongue.

Richard detailed the procedures of the coming events. We agreed our only option was to plead "not guilty" and take my case to trial. He explained that the judge had a reputation for being lenient on first time offenders when it came to bail.

I waited for an eternity to have my name called. I appeared before the judge. Richard instructed me to only say the words "not guilty" and remain as quiet as possible. This was only a brief appearance before the judge where the prosecution would have to make their case to the judge proving they had enough evidence to go to trial. Once that was done, the judge would set the accused's bail and move onto the next case.

My appearance in front of the judge was over in a flash. The prosecution had enough evidence to go to trial. *Clearly.* They displayed only a limited portion of the charges. The prosecution moved for remand, sending me back to the cell with the nauseating smell. They brought up the fact I attempted to cross the border into New York State with an arrest warrant in my name and that I was apprehended through the process. They claimed I had access to liquid cash and illegal connections. *That didn't sound good.*

Richard tried to ease the Judge's apprehensiveness by telling him my fictional father was in the hospital across the border after suffering a major heart attack. He weaved the tale better than I could have ever done. He nearly shouted that I didn't know the warrant had been issued. He offered that I would turn my passport over to the court. He pleaded for the judge to set the bail limit at $100,000. *Whoa, wait a minute. One hundred G's?*

The judge shook her head once, denying my bail. I was sent back in the cell to await my court hearing.

CHAPTER 32

ROCK BOTTOM

Excerpt from Michael's Journal

The initial $5000 retainer evaporated. Gone, in a matter of days. Richard was getting rich, I was getting nowhere. He warned me that if we went to trial he would need additional money.

I had one option. One single chance. A last hope. I put all my eggs into Richard's basket.

I needed to have faith and trust.

The faith was the easy part. He was extremely professional in the courtroom. The air of confidence he carried soothed my strained nerves. He got respect in the courtroom when no one else did. He was esteemed. *If I had him on my side, then who did they have?*

The trust came slower. He continually needed money. He wasn't willing to work on I.O.U.s. Lawyers like to be paid and make sure that they are paid first, before services are performed. "Money up front," the lawyer's credo.

I sat in my cell, long since separated from the human waste of the first night, only able to think of one solution. Richard had told me he needed money, and fast. He wasn't willing to continue next week if he didn't receive a $10,000 payment. First Evgenii, now Richard. One illegal, one in accordance with the law. Both leeches. The cash was in my house. I trusted no one to get it. I hadn't contacted Susie out of embarrassment. Involving Melanie was the last thing I wanted her to deal with. It dawned on me I had to give him permission to get it. I had to trust him.

My dilemma was complex. The more money I spent on Richard's defense, the less would be able to go to Evgenii. Every $10,000 that Richard charged was one month less for Melanie and Susie. Every dime I spent on my defense was going to lead to a lesser sentence, hopefully. I needed either a not guilty verdict, which seemed increasingly unlikely or to convince the judge to lessen my sentence. Three years was too long. The math didn't add up.

Richard told me he needed more money, again. He threatened to walk. I finally told him where I kept the hide-a-key. I explained where to find my neatly stacked piles of cash. I asked him to take every dollar. I instructed him to hold onto my money while the trial was ongoing. He agreed. He explained that the funds were within the attorney–client relationship.

I had him make two additional stops for me; to the poker room, for a $10,000 payment to Evgenii, and to speak with Veech regarding his packages. I outlined, in painstaking detail, each stop. He reluctantly agreed.

The next day came. It will forever be known as my personal rock bottom. The day when I knew. I just knew.

Richard met me, as scheduled, at 10 a.m. for our pretrial meeting. He scheduled to break it all down. His attention to detail was thorough, to say the least. He was supposed to tell me what to do. Everything from when to stand and address the judge, to how I was to sit in my chair, to how I should be taking notes on a pad of paper.

He entered the holding center's meeting room. *Crap.* Something was wrong. His face was grim. He avoided eye contact with me.

"Give it to me straight Rich, I can see it on your face. What is it?"

"Look, Michael, I like you, so I'll be honest. I went to your place like you said. There was no cash. Your place is trashed, like somebody was looking for something."

"What? What are you talking about?"

"Michael, I'm telling you that your house was ripped apart and there was no money there."

"Nothing?"

"Nothing. I'm sorry to have to tell you this Michael. Really, I am."

"Oh my God. What the hell?"

"I don't like this either Michael. I don't deal with criminal cases. I represent clients that have tax issues."

"Hang on a second here Richard, I can pay. I have money. Don't go getting cold feet on me now."

"Well, between the look of your house and the amount left of your initial retainer, yeah, I'm nervous about your case."

"Okay, slow down Rich. I can pay, but first things first. I need you to make a drive to a storage locker in Niagara Falls that I rent out. There's cash there. I promise. No one knows about this locker. There's also a cardboard box that I need you to return to an associate of mine."

"In Niagara Falls? C'mon Michael, I'm not a transport service."

"Listen, Rich, I know I'm asking a lot, but I got the money there for you and a payment I need to have taken care of before today is over. Please Rich, I wouldn't ask if there was anyone else."

"Look, Michael, I'd like to help, but…"

"Rich, there are lives depending on this payment being made today. Do you understand me? This is a matter of life and death!"

"Jesus Christ, Michael. What do you have me mixed up in here?"

"I wouldn't ask if there was another way, Rich. I am begging you here."

"I'll go, but if there isn't money there, our relationship is terminated. Am I being clear?"

"Yes, crystal clear. Your money will be there, along with a cardboard box that needs to be returned to its rightful owner."

"After this, I'm finished with the delivery service. One time only gig, got it? One time, that's it."

"Okay, I got it. I'll figure it out. I just need that money delivered today and the box returned to Veech."

I gave Richard the directions and combination for the lock.

I hated having to put him in that spot, but Melanie and Susie's lives were at stake. Evgenii's payment was due. I knew that if Richard was late getting the money to the poker room, then the fate of the girls was bleak.

I gave very specific directions where to take the money and how to deliver it. I also instructed him how to contact Veech to return the cardboard box containing half of my last shipment. I hoped the gesture of good faith was enough to buy me some time with the Outlaws before they came looking for their other twelve packages still hidden in my car's trap. I considered it my security blanket from the Outlaw's ending my life. I still had a quarter of a million dollars in product. They couldn't kill me if they wanted it back. They would have to trust me not to talk to the police about my deliveries. With them in my possession, I was worth more alive than dead. If they had them, I was just a former mover who had been arrested, who wasn't needed any longer.

I didn't like the idea of the Outlaws not needing me. It made me feel like I was a dead man waiting for my executioner.

~~~~~~~~~

The next morning Richard showed up on time. The look on his face said

194

everything. He had made the payment and returned my delivery. Fear splashed across his face. Only a demented Russian mobster and a drug dealing biker gang can do that to a man's face. The worst part, for me, was that I knew it would never be wiped off. *You can't un-see things.*

"Never again, you understand me? Never!"

"I'm sorry. Thank you Richard, you have no idea what you did for me or what it means."

"I want to hear it. All of it, right now."

"What? What do you mean?"

"A man named Evgenii came out and met me, insisting I join him in his office. It's hard to refuse when two of the angriest men I ever saw nudged me through the door with their guns stuck in my back. I didn't say a word. You understand me? I didn't say a thing and the sick son of bitch told me my name, my wife's name, where my children went to school, even the breed of my family dog. For Christ sake, he had a print out like some report or something. He knew all about your situation and insisted that I tell him everything about your case."

"What did you tell him?"

"I tried to hold my ground. I managed to say something about you being my client and I wasn't going to say anything. That bastard! You know what he did? Goddamn it Michael, he pulled out a photo of my wife shopping at the grocery store, with both of my kids. I talked. Of course I talked! I'm not ashamed about it. I'm a tax attorney, not a criminal lawyer. I have a family. I told him that you're probably going to serve some time and that we were working toward reducing that time as much as possible."

"What did he say?"

"He didn't say much. He reached across the desk in a flash and yanked my tie. Before I could react he had my head pinned to the desktop with a knife at my throat. He whispered in my ear that I would be the one bringing him the $10,000 every month, in your place."

"Oh God, what have I done?"

"I have a family Michael! This freak knows what they look like, where I live, for crying out loud, even where my wife grocery shops. You know what he did before he let me up from the desk? The asshole used the knife to cut my tie off. He pinned it to the wall and called it 'his reminder' of who would be bringing him your money."

"Richard, I'm so sorry. How did it end?"

"I assured him he would receive his money. God forgive me. He officially threatened my family. He told me that in his home land that they don't kill the person who disrespects them, they kill their family. Evgenii told me that if you miss a payment, then I was the one who would need to cover you and make sure the $10,000 was paid."

195

"Oh my God. Richard, I'm so sorry. Honestly, I didn't think this was going to happen."

"You didn't think this was going to happen? What did you envision happening?"

"A simple drop off. In. Out. Less than a minute."

"That's not all. There were the Outlaws as well. What was in the box Michael? The one I delivered to the bikers?"

"Packages; twelve of them. Why? What happened?"

"Your biker friends were not too happy that there were only twelve of them. They said something about half of them being unaccounted for. One very large biker told me to tell you that they want their packages back. Soon. Or else. What does that even mean Michael?"

"Richard, I'm so sorry. Honestly, I never thought that this would happen."

"What did you think was going to happen? Let me guess. That Evgenii, the insane lunatic, would let someone besides you come in and simply drop off your payment? That the bikers would thank me for giving them only half of what they expected to find? You moron."

"Honestly, I didn't think that…"

"No, you didn't think. That's the problem with you Michael. You don't think! Now my family is at risk because of you. And what am I supposed to do with this cash? $30,000 was all that was in the storage locker. Ten of it went to psycho-Russian-Evgenii, leaving only twenty for my payment and Evgenii's future payments. Where's the rest Michael?"

"The rest was in my house. I had over $100,000 there. Obviously either the bikers or Evgenii's men broke in and took it. I've thought about it and my guess is the bikers did it. When I didn't make my delivery on time, I bet they came looking for me. They found my cash instead. They probably took it as collateral for their missing packages."

"I'm taking $10,000 for my next retainer. That leaves you one month to figure everything out. You hear me? You have one payment to Evgenii left. You better call someone because this isn't on me. You can be damn sure my family will not be harmed."

CHAPTER 33

TRIAL

Excerpt from Michael's Journal

My trial. *Those words still don't sound right. I'm not the kind of guy who has a trial. I'm a card player. A nice guy. A lover, not a fighter.*

Each day started to blur into the day before it. One big inkblot nightmare. There was no happiness, no excitement, and no relief. Constant anxiety brewed inside my gut. When the trial finally arrived, I was so numb from the monotony of jail that the drive to the courthouse seemed thrilling.

I met with Richard briefly before the trial started. He went over our game plan one more time. He reinforced that I wasn't to show any emotion. Walking behind him into the courtroom, I felt as though my life, and that of Melanie and Susie, was literally in his hands. If he performed a miracle, then we would all be saved from Evgenii and Veech. I could go back to being the Outlaw's mover and making money and payments.

If he failed, I would be sentenced to a long jail term. God help us all. I hadn't thought about what I would do if the judge sentenced me to the maximum sentence. Like that mattered anymore. I needed an acquittal. A get out of jail free card.

I focused on the trial.

The courtroom we entered was different than the pretrial courtroom. The hustle and bustle of the previous courtroom was replaced by empty seats and squeaky clean granite floors. The seating for the audience resembled that of church pews, in off hours. The thick scent of freshly spread lacquer hung in the air, bringing back

197

childhood memories of a long forgotten church. Only one person sat in the front row. His drab gray suit screamed of a department store bargain rack. His cold eyes locked onto me as if he was stalking me.

Bradley Weisnewski.

He wasn't going to miss a second of my trial. In fact, if the judge would have allowed him, he would have put himself through law school, passed the bar exam, and prosecuted me himself. I walked past him. We made eye contact. For the last time, I looked into his heartless brown eyes. I saw the predator inside, yearning to feast on the weak prey.

I broke eye contact and never looked in his direction again. His gaze was too intense. It reminded me how badly he wanted me behind bars. He was someone who wanted something so badly, that just by looking into his eyes, I felt defeated. I felt imprisoned. I felt like a dead man.

In courtroom dramas and movies about trials, the attorneys always seem to have extended amounts of time and trials seem to always last days, if not weeks. The length of the trial was never spoken of, so I assumed it would take multiple days.

The judge was the same woman as in the pretrial hearing. Her short auburn hair was styled close to her scalp. Dressed in flowing black fabric, she quickly asserted her dominance over the courtroom with short bursts of orders. She wasn't willing to waste her time on unimportant matters. *Me.*

As Richard instructed, I sat at the table, upright and attentive. He gave me a yellow legal pad and told me to take notes. He wanted to show the judge that I wasn't a hardened criminal, rather a normal guy who never received any proper guidance growing up.

A moment before the trial started, Richard stared directly in my eyes, not more than a foot from my face. His warm breath reeked of coffee. He whispered just loud enough for me to hear.

"Convince the Judge that you're not a criminal. This case is no longer about you going to jail. It is about how long you're going to jail."

"What's changed? Richard, my only hope is getting an acquittal."

"Sorry kid, but this case was never about your innocence. The CRA has more than enough evidence against you to put you away for the maximum. My job is now to get you as short a prison sentence as possible. I do that by proving you're just another misguided young adult who never intended to hurt anyone."

"No. No. Wait. Richard, you don't understand. I only have enough money left to pay Evgenii once. I need an acquittal!"

"Sorry, it's not going to happen."

"Jesus, Richard! Why the hell didn't you tell me all this before?"

"Because Michael, you would have never paid me. Now just let me try to get you a good deal."

My trial was over before it started.

Everyone in the courtroom knew it, except me. Even my own lawyer was resigned to the fact that I was going to prison.

The prosecution wasted little time brandishing their big guns. They laid out for the judge just how much evidence the CRA, by way of Agent Bradley Weisnewski, had gathered on my numerous tax related crimes. They spun the offenses against me to look as though I was a criminal mastermind who had given seminars on tax evasion. The preposterousness of their claims seemed like they were overreaching the limits of their evidence.

When it was Richard's turn in front of the judge, he did his best. Sad and pathetic childhood. Couldn't find a steady job. A hard-luck boy turned adult. Couldn't correct his off-course ship. He made no attempt to refute any of the prosecution's charges against me. Instead, he focused on my lack of positive role models.

The trial ended abruptly.

The judge waved her hands. She exclaimed that she had heard enough from both sides. She stated that since the defense wasn't refuting any of the charges the whole trial was a massive waste of tax payer dollars. The judge questioned the two sides to why there hadn't been a deal and why hadn't the defendant pleaded guilty. Richard explained that the prosecution was out for blood against his client and that no offer was ever extended to him. She scolded the prosecution for not offering a fair deal and wasting her time and court space for a "real trial."

Before my stomach even felt the pain of lunch approaching, the judge swung her gavel down onto her desk.

Kingston Penitentiary.

Three years less a day because of the weight of my crimes.

I was escorted out of the courtroom by the bailiff. Before the shock had even set in, I was handcuffed to the van that had brought me to the courtroom. I sat there dumbfounded. *How could this have happened?*

Tears began to stain the front of my clothes. I let them fall. Silently. I was still wearing the suit that Richard had picked up for me from my house. The gray silk darkened around my chest.

A minute later, my upper body began to heave in convulsions. Emotion and the realization of my fate collided with thoughts of Melanie and Susie. My life was over, I knew that now.

I had no way to return the twelve packages back to Veech. *He'll kill me for that. Safer for him that way.*

I didn't have enough cash left to satisfy the deal I had made with Evgenii. *One month more to offer him. Never could he accept that deal.*

One of them would surely end my life, one way or another. This much, I knew. I accepted it.

What I didn't know was the fate of Melanie and Susie. Evgenii's threats against Richard were clear enough that they wouldn't go unnoticed. I never spoke with Richard again. His last words to me were about him worrying about me never paying him.

I don't resent him for that. I hope that he and his family truly know just how sorry I am to ever have involved them in my troubles. I never meant to put them in harm's way.

As for Susie and Melanie's safety, it took me a couple of days to see that they still needed my help. I had $10,000 to pay off Evgenii and buy a month of safety.

What good is a month?

I needed some way to make sure that once I was incarcerated in KP that they would be able to go on.

CHAPTER 34

KINGSTON PENITENTIARY

Excerpt from Michael's Journal

My trial was the opposite of television's portrayal. Prison was not. TV shows and movies nailed it, right down to the food. Watch shows like Oz and Prison Break, or movies like The Fugitive. The portrayal of prison life isn't far from that reality.

What TV doesn't convey is time, and how it messes with you. Time doesn't move. Outside of prison, time flies when you're having fun. There is no fun in jail. It often stands still, barely moving along at all.

I arrived at KP with a plan. An actual plan. I needed to get word out to Susie and Melanie as soon as possible. They needed to be warned about the dangers coming. But I couldn't just tell them to watch out. They deserved an explanation. I had to tell them everything.

Evgenii didn't deserve to get away with what he did to me. Or what he promised to do once he didn't receive a payment. He deserved justice. He deserved the cell next to me.

Veech's secret package delivery service didn't deserve a free pass either. He hid behind his motorcycle club to traffic huge quantities of illegal drugs. *Or so I think, to this day, I'm still not 100% sure what I moved.*

The least I could do, seeing as I messed up their lives, was to make, what I could, right. I came to the glaring realization that eventually, I would be killed. Whether it was when the money ran out and Evgenii finally wanted me dead or when a sudden bad mood struck Veech. Either way, I was certainly a goner. But I wasn't a lame duck. I could do things. Knowledge is power, and I had secrets that could end these guys. I could expose Evgenii and the poker room. I could divulge the Outlaw's illegal smuggling business.

And maybe, somehow, I could give Melanie and Susie a fighting chance. A prior warning that people were coming for them.

My plan was to write as much as I could in the time I had. I wanted what I wrote to be enough of an explanation so they would understand. I wanted them to know that I never intended to hurt either of them and that I deeply love both of them. There was no way a phone call, a letter, or an email could do all that.

In my first hour in prison that plan came to a sudden and abrupt halt. I didn't think. *Isn't that what Richard said? That I don't think enough?* I focused solely on the plan. I assumed that prison would be the same as the Oshawa Holding Center, just on a larger scale. It wasn't. Far from it. There was no preparing myself for what it was like.

Two guards escorted me to my cell, barefoot. Both of my hands were full. I carried the typical things you see inmates on TV carry. One towel. An alternate jumpsuit. A wash cloth. And my pair of shoes, which rested on top of the pile.

"Your cell mate's name is Stinger. I suggest you make nice with him."

I stared straight ahead. We entered Unit B. I focused on the never-ending rows of cells. Just concrete and steel. One after another.

We walked. No one shouted. No whistles. Nothing. Just silence. No one spoke at all, at first.

Then someone called me "precious." He told me I was theirs for the taking. I tried to swallow. My mouth was dry. My tongue wouldn't move. Each step became increasingly laborious. I made one foot move. Then the other. I tried to blink. When I finally managed to close each eyelid, I paused. Both tasks overloaded my nervous system.

The brief pause fanned the other inmate's flames. They whistled and shouted. It horrified me. One inmate told me he was going to use me as a puppet. That he was going to stick his hand up my ass and make me dance.

The prison was old. It was in disrepair. Paint flaked off the wall and was scattered along the edges of the floor. I centered all my attention on the flakes. It almost allowed me to block out the awful images that played through my mind. *The first walk was the worst.*

My cell was no different from the twenty-six others along the walk, except it was occupied by only one inmate. He laid on his bunk with his legs crossed. His hands were behind his head. I recognized the tattoos. They covered every inch of the visible parts of his body. My memory flashed back. I looked at my nub, where my thumb used to be, before it was taken. Images of Russian tattoos appeared. Stars. Serpents. Spiders. Crosses. The artistry of his tattoos told me everything. *I was cellmates with a connected Russian.*

The cell bars slammed violently behind me. It startled me from my semi-conscious state, snapping me to reality. The protection it offered on my first walk ended. I looked at Stinger's eyes. He knew I was coming that day. He wore a blazing orange jump suit tied at his waste. His upper torso was exposed to the stale air. From the waist up, Stinger was nothing more than tattoos and bones. Even his knuckles were covered by part of the Russian alphabet.

He smiled. I smiled back. He was intimidating. *Don't let him see you're scared.* The size of this body reassured me. *He is no more than a 130 pound skeleton.* I didn't fear him. I should have. He began talking. He knew who I was.

"So, you finally arrived," he said in a less thick accent than Evgenii, but still quite pronounced.

"Yeah, I'm here," speaking with as much courage as I could muster.

"Well, put your stuff down and let us talk."

"What do we need to talk about?"

"We have much to talk about Michael, so please, don't argue."

"How do you know my name?"

"Did you think that I became your cellmate by some random selection? No, Michael, someone was paid to put you in here. Evgenii wants me to offer you a deal that you need to strongly consider."

"You work for Evgenii? What's the deal?"

"Please sit," he said motioning towards the edge of his bed where his feet were lying.

I took a hesitant seat on the edge of the bottom bunk bed. He taped photos to the wall next to where his head rested. He sat up. His body was skinnier than I had originally thought. His muscles in his arms and chest flexed as he sat. The skin over his torso was stretched tight. No fat. Just skin, tattoo, and muscle. Scrawny muscle. His abdominal muscles seemed to continuously pop through his taut skin.

"Alright, so, what do I call you?"

"Stinger."

"How did you get that name?"

"I'll be doing the talking now and that's not important. What is important is Evgenii's command. You see, Michael, Evgenii is extremely well connected and you are indebted to a powerful man. Even in KP his reach is strong. He has requested that I take care of you while you're in here. This way you can continue to make your monthly payments. I assume that you've arranged someone other than that moron lawyer of yours to continue delivering your payments?"

"I have. You can let Evgenii know that he doesn't need to worry. The money will be delivered as promised."

"Excellent. He'll be relieved to hear such news."

"What did you mean that you're going to 'take care' of me?"

"My apologies Michael. I suppose I should have said that he requested that I care for you in here. Kingston Penitentiary is a dangerous prison with many, many inmates who are not as friendly as I am. Vicious men who do terrible things to one another. Without protection, inmates are gobbled up by stronger, more connected groups that make them do unsavory things."

"And I am just supposed to believe that the man who took my thumb cares about my well being?"

"No, Michael, Evgenii does not care about your well being. He cares about his payments. You owe him $10,000 each month. If you are unprotected, who knows what might happen. A dead man doesn't make payments. That's where I come in. I'll be your personal security guard for the duration of your stay."

I smiled.

"I'm supposed to believe that Evgenii has assigned you to be my body guard in prison? You have got to be joking."

"Yes. But you must know, we Russian's rarely joke. Evgenii expects his payments to be made."

"No offense Stinger, but how is someone your size going to protect me? I saw guys three times your size just on the walk to this cell."

"When you have our protection, you have all of our protection. You will eat with us. You will stand with us in the yard. When you are out of this cell, you will always be with one, or more, of us."

"Who is 'us' that you're referring to?"

"You'll see. You have about 5 minutes until lights out. Lucky for you Evgenii wants to continue receiving his payments. Otherwise your first night wouldn't have been so easy."

Stinger turned his attention to a book hidden under his pillow, signifying our conversation was over. I stood up. The few belongings I had were laid out across my bed. Three items. Towel. Wash cloth. Toothbrush.

Jumping up to the top bunk wasn't difficult. I gazed out through my cell bars for the first time. The adjacent cells were all occupied. Some men, like Stinger, were reading books. Most stood with their hands hanging between the bars. Their eyes bore holes deep into other cells. One man, with his feet perched on the middle row of the horizontal bars, performed push-ups. One after another. Up. Down. Up. Down. Until he couldn't lift his body one more time. *I know that feeling.* The lights suddenly died. Darkness rushed in. Shouting accompanied it. Terrible screams filled the air.

I heard them. I heard them calling out to me. Obviously unaware that I had Russian protection, they shouted at me.

One inmate chanted in a deep raspy voice. "Fresh meat. Fresh meat. Fastest one there gets the fresh meat."

Another inmate further away shouted. "See you in the morning newbie."

One particularly loud mouth kept calling me "skinny boy." He told me he liked the way I walked. He shouted. "I can taste your fear. And it smells good."

I laid on my top bunk in the absolute darkness. *Jesus, I'm actually thankful for Evgenii.* The irony of the situation hit me. I silently laughed to myself.

No matter how well prepared anyone thinks they are coming into prison, they can never prepare enough for the first morning. Stinger told me what to do. Where to go. How to do it.

I would have stuck out like a lost lamb. Breakfast trays. Powdered eggs, scrambled. One slice of white bread. One milk carton. The unappealing meal left my stomach feeling nauseous.

Stinger pointed. I sat. Head down. Shoulders slumped. *Not all that different from my poker room days.* The table was predominately filled with men that looked similar to Stinger. Each man sat in near silence, eating without as much as a comment. I followed their lead. I slowly ate my slop. It wasn't until after he finished eating that Stinger looked at me. He spoke his first words to me in front of the men.

"What did you do to make it into KP?"

I looked up. Many sets of eyes leered in my direction.

"Tax evasion, mainly."

"And how did you come to lose your thumb?"

"I got a feeling you already know the answer to that. Let me ask you something, how did you get the name *Stinger*?"

"Unlike you, Michael, I was convicted of a serious crime. Weapons smuggling."

"I don't get it. How does gun running earn you that name?"

"My specialties were surface to air missiles called 'stingers.' They were highly profitable and favored by rebel forces around the world that don't have an air force."

"Let me get this straight. You were arrested for selling Stinger Missiles in Canada? Who would buy something like that here?"

"No. I didn't say that. I was arrested for gun smuggling here and sentenced to 7 years in KP. I have four and half to go before I am free."

"Who did you sell the guns to?"

"Anyone who would pay. But, mainly, the guns were transported into the United States where there was more of a demand for automatic rifles. It was easier to transport the initial shipment into Canada and then cross the border by car or truck to their destination."

"I see."

"I bet you do Michael. I understand you know a little bit about crossing international borders."

"How do you know that?"

"Evgenii likes to keep a very close eye on things Michael. He has filled me in on everything about you. He knows about your storage locker, your arrest at the Niagara Falls border, and, of course, your ongoing relationship with the Outlaws."

I was unprepared for that conversation. I had underestimated Evgenii. He knew more about me than I ever thought he would. He left very little up to chance. Stinger's knowledge made me nervous. Very nervous. *Shit. If he knows this much, does he know how many months worth of payments I have saved up?*

I had to know if he knew more about my money situation. I waited until we returned to our cell to speak. A private conversation seemed more appropriate rather than discussing it in front of a table of tattooed thugs. I followed him into our cell.

"So, what else do you know about me?"

"Everything Michael. Like I said, Evgenii takes very little risks and demands to know everything about people he does business with."

"You know about my family?"

"Yes, we know about Susie, your sister. We also know you don't speak with your parents. You are, what they call, estranged from them. No?"

"And you know about my friends?"

"We know you have a girlfriend, whom you love. Her name is Melanie Cooper. She works at a jewelry store."

"Anything else you know about how I intend to pay Evgenii each month while I'm locked up in here?"

"I have been told you have been the Outlaws *mover* for the past little while. We know they pay that position well and that you've been very busy before you were arrested."

"That's all?"

"Is that not enough?"

"No, I just wondered if there was anything else. You seem to know everything."

The nervous energy, which coursed through my veins, dissipated. I returned to my bunk. Stinger didn't know about my money situation. Either that or he did a good job at concealing the truth of how much he knew.

Since Stinger seemed to be bragging about how much he knew, Evgenii's men must not have been the ones who broke into my house and stole my cash. I suspected the Outlaws the entire time. Their products hadn't returned. They had a motive. *Bastard Veech. He knew I needed that money.*

It didn't change the fact that I still faced a timer that was running out. It sped it up. The clock showed one month left. I wasn't going to find a solution from inside my new concrete home.

CHAPTER 35

THREE PROBLEMS

Excerpt from Michael's Journal

I was assigned a job that mirrored Stinger's. Convenient. Safe. We washed bathrooms and cleaned the toilets. *Not my first choice*. Every day for five hours, we scrubbed, mopped, and sanitized the toilet stalls, showers, and sinks. The work was awful. The smell permeated everything. I tried sticking balled pieces of toilet paper in each nostril. The smell seemed to enter through my mouth. As the first few days passed, it got better. I became desensitized. Unclogging toilets, wiping dirty sinks, and scrubbing shower tiles became, somehow, normal.

Janitorial duty had one benefit. Time. A lot of time. Too much time. All to think. The best medicine is hard work. For me, the best time to think was when I was working with my hands or what was left of them. It also gave me one-on-one time with Stinger. Like most prison inmates, he wasn't as rough around the edges as he came across. In fact, he spoke lovingly about his wife and children. He knew the exact number of days until he could reunite with them in Syracuse, New York. I figured a man who spoke so tenderly about his family couldn't be too vicious. Then again, I wasn't going to test his humanity versus one of Evgenii's commands.

The solution came to me as I was washing the bathroom door handle with a rag and bottle of sanitizer. I spied another inmate passing by pushing a library cart full of books. He slowly strolled, thumbing the pages of a thick novel. *Light bulb moment*. My brain suddenly flicked to the "on" position. The plan fell together. Missing puzzle pieces aligned themselves.

SAVANNAH

I planned on writing everything down, but details are details and in classic Michael Taylor fashion, I felt them out. Finally, things came together. *Write your own book*. Four words. So simple, yet not.

Three problems stood glaring me in the face. The first was the continual ticking down of my life. I knew from the second the judge ordered me to the maximum sentence my life was over. I fought the feeling for as long as I could and clung to any speck of hope that lingered. Ultimately, there is no hope. I understand that now. I have come to grips with it. Time to move on.

I had some time, albeit a very short amount, to get my story on paper. The more I thought about it, the more I believed it was Susie's and Melanie's only chance of survival. *Write it all down. Everything. Get it to them. Give them a chance. All before the clock reaches zero.*

The second obstacle was Stinger. He goes everywhere I go, and vice versa. He was everywhere and nowhere. As part of my protection, I am never alone. If he isn't with me, then a trusted comrade of his steps in. Stinger and I work the same job detail, sleep in the same cell, eat our meals together, and spend our time together in the yard, lifting weights. Writing a book in front of him, detailing his boss' business, wasn't a good idea. This problem worried me most of all. *I'll need time. Lots of it.*

The least troublesome of the three was acquiring something to actually write with and on. Pens and pencils aren't permitted in KP. They are too sharp. They can be used as weapons. Safety for the prison guards we are told. Pads of paper, notebooks, and such are scarce. No need for a journal if there isn't anything to write into the journal with.

The best piece of advice Stinger gave to me that first morning was to keep my mouth shut and eyes open. He mainly meant that as my first line of defense against any potential attackers. Most inmates need an excuse to fight, keeping my mouth shut and eyes averted helped. Unfortunately, our prison block was fully stocked with the other kind of inmate. The crazy maniacs who needed no reason. *Protection is a good thing to have.*

I kept my eyes open. The more I paid attention, the more I saw. The prison guards continually look away, like a synchronized change of the guard, as inmates smuggled in particular items. Cell phones, drugs, pills, and food were the main items. Prison business. Very profitable. It kept the prison guards pocket's lined with extra cash.

I needed something to write in. Getting a notebook or a pad of paper couldn't be that difficult. It wasn't banned. I noticed them here and there. They didn't seem difficult to obtain.

I needed something to write with. A pencil. Not a pen. Ink runs out. Pens fail. If a pencil fails, it need only be sharpened. I spoke with Stinger about getting each item. He had contacts.

He came the next day. A month's worth of desserts for a pencil. Unsharpened. Brand new.

I quickly agreed.

I sat on my bunk. The pencil was thrown, end over end, into our cell. It looked exactly like the kind used in schools. The pink eraser on top was a perfectly unused cylinder. The yellow paint was undisturbed. Black lettering ran down the side identifying the company and signifying it as a number 2 pencil.

The rough concrete walls lining each jail cell easily wore away the even end. Sharpening the pencil was much easier than I expected. Not perfect. Not even sharp, but enough to begin.

Getting the paper was the next obstacle I needed to clear. After scrubbing some toilets, I snuck into the prison's library. The librarian was a massive black man with arms that appeared to have coconuts under stretched skin. His shoulders hid cantaloupe halves. Whole watermelons on his chest. His smell was a mixture of prison food and body odor. Clearly he hadn't showered that day or the previous day for that matter. Weight lifting trumped personal hygiene on his priority list. I blinked back tears. The smell nauseated me. I stood in front of the giant.

"Do you have any pads of paper or blank books or anything I can write in?"

He didn't answer. Instead he grunted through nostrils big enough to be blow holes. A desk separated us. I waited. I stared at his eyes. *Turn and walk away.*

I waited longer, holding my ground. The giant finally blinked. He moved slowly.

"It ain't free white boy. What you got for it that I want?" the Giant said.

"I don't have any money. I don't have anything for that matter, but I can offer you food each day."

"The shit they serve us in here ain't food. It's trash they force us to eat or die. I don't want more of it."

"I don't have anything else to offer."

He rose from his chair. He eyed me from head to toe, and back again. He rubbed his chin with a massive hand.

"Your milk."

"What?"

"Your milk for three months."

"Two weeks and I get the paper now."

"Listen to you little white boy, negotiating with me like you have a leg to stand on."

"Take it or leave it. Two weeks is a lot of milk to give up for a pad of paper."

"I like you. I don't know why, but I do. We got something you might be interested in. It was mistakenly shipped to KP."

"What is it?"

"Oh hell no whitey. This is a negotiation, remember?"

"C'mon man. What do you want from me?"

"The price has gone up. I like you, but I like milk more. Four months."

"I don't even know what it is and you want me to pay four months of milk for it?"

"Remember just a minute ago when you were acting all hard and tough? Remember that? I believe you said, 'take it or leave it.' Now it's my turn. Take it or leave it."

You're an idiot. What was the exact game plan here? Piss off the angry giant even further?

I took the deal. *Sucker. I'll be dead before you get your full payment.*

He handed me a thin paperback book. I thumbed the pages. Blank pages flung across my eyes. No words. Nothing. Just pages. Probably a printing error, but it was in good condition. Before leaving, I checked out the biggest book the library housed.

The fresh air, however "fresh" the air in prison can be is debatable, never smelled so good. I sucked in mouthfuls of it. I tucked my small blank paperback book deep into the pages of the large novel. It almost looked closed, but not quite. I tucked it under my arm.

The novel was a test. I wasn't sure how much attention Stinger would pay to what I was doing. He stayed on the bottom bunk all the time. The old little book inside the big book trick. In elementary school, I hid comic books inside the pages of textbooks. When the teacher looked up from her desk, she only saw the cover of my history book. I hoped that a similar trick could be performed on Stinger.

Game time. I tucked my paperback under my pillow. The first part of my test was to see just how much Stinger would pay attention to me reading a book. I opened the novel. I began reading. His bunk squeaked. He stood. Before I had finished the first page, his eyes were on me. He stood, eye level with my bunk, and watched my every move. I lowered the book. I turned toward his gaze.

"Can I help you?"

"Where did you get that?" Stinger said.

"The prison's library. Why?"

"What are you doing with it?"

"I'm reading it. What's the problem?"

"Oh. No reason."

"Seriously, man. What's the deal?"

"I was never taught to read."

"You're being serious with me?"

"Yeah, want to make fun of me about it?"

"No. Stinger, c'mon man. I wasn't making fun of you. I just couldn't tell if you were telling the truth or not."

"What are you going to do with that pencil you got?"

"Well, to be honest, I got this book that I traded the librarian for. I planned on writing some things."

"What sort of things?"

"Like poetry or short stories. I don't know, just something to pass the time."

"Would you read me some of it when you finish? I'd like to hear some of your stories."

"Sure."

Holy crap, did I actually catch a break?

Problem number two just resolved itself. Since Stinger couldn't read, that meant that he wouldn't be able to understand what I was writing about. Make up a story that I supposedly had written and the pencils would keep coming. All the while, he would be none the wiser that I was writing about him and his boss.

CHAPTER 36
CALL TO MELANIE

Excerpt from Michael's Journal

Three problems. Three solutions.

I started writing.

Everything had come together. I wasted only the time needed to create a dull tip on the pencil. I spent every free second I had writing. I obsessed over it. It consumed me. I was engrossed in nothing else. I needed to complete my last goal in life.

The process of writing my book was easy compared to thinking about the completion itself. The more I completed, the closer the end became. The end of everything. Me. Life. *This isn't about you; it's about giving Melanie and Susie a chance. A chance to live, a chance to understand--and hopefully--a chance for them to forgive me.*

The month was coming to an end. Stinger reminded me, constantly. I had one stash left that wasn't raided by the bikers in the storage unit. I planned to contact Melanie. I had to ask her to drive to Niagara Falls, retrieve the cash, and deliver it to Evgenii. *There's no one else. You have to call her. Somehow.*

A letter would take too long. The prison phones were monitored. Using Evgenii's name was a bad idea. Stating the poker room's address would be a breach of our agreement. Not pretty consequences. My options were limited.

Prison business happened everywhere. All the time. Watch long enough, you will see it. Drugs. Food. Anything. Even cell phones. I witnessed a transaction at the breakfast table. Stinger slid it across the table top to another man. A cell phone. An older model flip phone, similar to Veech's disposable cell. It was out, across the table, and hidden again before any guard could make out what they saw.

I approached Stinger.

"I need to use that cell phone you had at breakfast today. The call is regarding the delivery of Evgenii's payment."

"When? And to whom are you calling?" Stinger said.

"I don't care if you listen in. It'll take me less than five minutes."

Once Melanie claimed the last of the cash, the storage locker would be useless. If Stinger was to tell Evgenii about it, nothing of importance would be lost. All that would remain would be boxes of junk, used to hide the Outlaw's packages.

The next day, Stinger shoved me into a bathroom stall. He palmed the cell into my hand while we were on our janitorial duty. He explained that I had two minutes to make and end the call before the prepaid minutes expired. The silver Motorola RAZR felt cold and heavy in my hand. It was an older cell phone, heavier than modern versions. I flipped it open and turned it on. I quickly dialed Melanie's cell phone number. I held the phone to my ear.

I silently prayed that she would answer. *Unknown number* would come across her cell phone's caller identification. *Answer Melanie, please*. Being so early in the day, I was confident she hadn't left for work yet. *C'mon, Mel, answer*. The dial ended. I heard her raspy, soft voice.

"Hello?"

"Melanie?"

"Michael?"

"Yeah, it's me."

"Where are you? I haven't heard from you in almost six weeks."

"I know. And I'm sorry. I was embarrassed."

"Embarrassed about what?"

"I was arrested, Mel."

"For what?"

"Tax evasion. I was sentenced to three years in Kingston Penitentiary."

"And you just thought you wouldn't call me to let me know what happened to you?"

"I couldn't. Melanie, I'm truly sorry."

"You're sorry? I went over to your house and found it turned upside down like a tornado hit it. I thought the worst Michael. I thought you were dead."

"Yeah Melanie, I am sorry. So sorry. I just thought it would be easier on you if I never contacted you again. I thought I would make the decision for you to end our relationship."

"That wasn't your decision to make for me. We were in love."

213

"I know. I'm sorry. I'm truly, one hundred percent sorry for doing that to you."

"I love you Michael."

"God, I feel awful. I'm so sorry. I hate myself for what I have to do."

"What? What now?"

"Mel, I need a favor. You have every reason to say no to me."

"A favor?"

"Look, you can say no, but I wouldn't ask unless it was very important."

"What is it?"

"I owe a guy some cash. A lot. I don't need to borrow it or anything. All I need you to do is go get it and drop it off for me. The only problem is that the cash is in a storage facility in Niagara Falls. The drop off is all the way back in Scarborough."

"Jeez, Michael."

"I know. I know. I wouldn't ask you if there was someone else who I could trust to do it, and I promise this is the only time I'll need you to do me a favor."

"Michael, this sounds scary. I don't know if I can do this."

"Look Mel, it's a simple drop off of a bag of cash and then you turn and walk away. You don't even need to say one word. Get a paper bag, write my name on it, and drop it off with one of his employees."

"What is the money for?"

"A poker debt. And I'm not going to lie to you; it's quite a bit of money."

"How much is it?"

"$10,000. But like I said, this is the only time I'll ever ask you to do this."

"WHAT? Ten thousand dollars?"

"Mel, this is more important than you think. I can't get into details. I only have a moment longer."

"I'll do it Michael, but on one condition."

"What's that?"

"That I can come and visit you."

"Mel, I don't want you to see me this way."

"Then find someone else to be your delivery bitch."

"Okay, okay. But you have to give me some time before you come and see me in here. Come in a month. Exactly one month, from tomorrow."

"It's a deal. Give me the details."

I told her everything. She wrote it down, repeating it to me. I said my thanks and ended the call.

I wasn't lying when I told her it was the only time I needed her to make a delivery for me. There's no more money. After this $10,000 was delivered, I was officially tapped out. Nada. Zip. Zilch.

One month and one day. That's when Melanie was coming to visit. I had bought myself thirty one more days to finish my story. If she came sooner, I couldn't be sure it would be finished.

The writing was slow. *Thirty one days*. It sounds like a long time. It wasn't. I felt more of a crunch than I expected. My obsession morphed into a compulsion.

I dedicated every second I had to writing. I needed to increase my productivity. I needed more time. I quickly calculated the current pace I was writing and how much I had left. They didn't equal thirty one days. I had to find more time.

Writing outside of my cell was too high of a risk. Too many eyes. Sensitive material. Even though many of the inmates in KP appeared to be Neanderthal cavemen, I suspected the vast majority of them could read. If even one inmate saw the name *Evgenii* or *Outlaws,* word might get out. Bad idea.

Inside my cell, I had an illiterate cellmate. The risk of him understanding my writing was extremely low. All I had to do to please Stinger was pretend I was reading from my writing, making up fictional stories as I went. After a few times, I began creating less and less interesting material. He began to lose interest. After the fifth one, he told me he no longer wanted to hear my stories. I played hurt.

Not enough time. *Find more.* I began sacrificing sleep in order to write after lights out. The darkness was cut by the reddish, taunting glow of the exit sign. *I used to hate you exit sign, now I'm thankful for you.* It was stationed at the top of the ceiling, some thirteen feet off the floor. The daily ritual of trying to swat it to the ground was a favorite exercise of many inmates.

The light coming from the sign was barely enough to read what I wrote on the paper. My eyes strained each night. They adjusted. I found the extra hours I needed.

CHAPTER 37
LAST ENTRY

Excerpt from Michael's Journal

Melanie is coming tomorrow. I was permitted to have an open meeting because of good behavior. I haven't seen the meeting room. Stinger told me that the room is made of concrete and stainless steel. He said there are metal picnic tables around the room for visitors and inmates to sit together. Meetings are a maximum of thirty minutes. No physical contact is allowed.

Inmates and visitors are not permitted to exchange any property in the meetings, which poses my final obstacle. The book is a standard paperback novel. I can conceal it easily in my waistband. Transferring it is the difficult part. I don't know the details of the meeting room. Where do the guards stand? How alert are they?

I have one shot at this. I need to get it right. I plan on dropping it into her purse while it is resting on the floor or slip it into her bag when we hug goodbye. I don't care if that isn't permitted. I'm doing it. I'll never see her again.

I completed my writing in the early hours of the morning. I haven't felt this sense of satisfaction since I first developed Savannah. It's ironic how I still view Savannah with love and tenderness, like a father would toward a child. The actual fact is that Savannah brought me here. Without Savannah being so profitable, I wouldn't have ever spent a day in KP or had to write my life story. Savannah isn't to blame, I realize that. I am. Me. I always have been. It just took me a long time to understand that. I've been in control of my own destiny.

SAVANNAH

Yesterday I took the time to write two letters. I mailed them immediately. They are the first letters I had ever written. And the last. I wrote the first to Susie. The mistakes I made hit me hard while I was writing to her. Tears poured down my face and soaked the bottom half of the paper. I waited for it to dry before sealing it in the envelope. It is still difficult to deal with the fact that my actions will land in Susie's lap. My actions. Her consequences. Seems unfair. The more I wrote to her, the harder reality slammed that home.

My letter to Melanie was similar, except I had already gone through the range of emotions with Susie's. A little easier the second time around. Finding the words was incredibly difficult. I had to tell each of them what I had done, what was coming, and what they need to do. It was the hardest thing I've ever done. I'm so sorry.

Both will receive their letters tomorrow, assuming the mail is delivered on time and they check their mail daily. That will give both of them three days to get themselves to safety, whatever that means. However. Where ever. I wanted to write them earlier, but I couldn't. Logically, I needed Melanie to visit me, to get my story. Had she known, she might have not come. Same with Susie. Another part of me, a darker part, a selfish part, couldn't mail the letters earlier. I knew all along I needed to eventually write and send those letters. The longer I waited, the less real it was. I only hope three days is enough time.

I wish I could offer them some advice on what to do, but all I can really say is how truly sorry I am for getting both of them involved in such a mess.

I am all but certain that either Stinger, or another of Evgenii's men, will kill me the day after my payment isn't received. When both girls can't be found, they'll know I got ahead of them. The more I witnessed how these men do business, the more certain I am Evgenii will cut ties with me. *Such a nice way to say "I'll be killed."* I have come to accept my fate. I realize that I am the one who chose my path. I chose to use Savannah at the poker room. I allowed *IT* to control me, as much as I don't like to think about it, I controlled *IT* more than *IT* controlled me. Greed was my downfall. Greed and a lack of self control.

I could blame my parents, or *IT*, or Evgenii for my troubles. For my approaching death. But as I sit here, I know it was me who made the choices.

In her letter, I have asked Melanie to read my book. Then pass it onto my sister. I wrote it so you both have a fighting chance against Evgenii and the Outlaws or both. *That's the logical part of me talking. The selfishness inside me wrote it so they can understand how deeply I regret everything I've done.*

I love you both. I am so sorry.

For everything.

Michael Taylor

CHAPTER 38

NICOTINE AND CAFFEINE

Outside Melanie's Motel

"Yeah, it's her alright," whispered the man into his cell phone. He slumped low in the driver's seat. His eyes followed Melanie. He spoke again, "I know, it sounds crazy, but it's true. I was driving along the road and this crazy hot broad almost jumped out in front of my car. I slammed on the brakes, looked at her, and realized it's one of the girls from the pictures you showed me."

After recognizing her, his anger died down. He slowly drove off, watching her in his rearview mirror. Once she safely crossed the street, he snapped the wheel to the side, suddenly whipping his car around into the adjacent parking lot. He parked and waited. She hadn't seen anything. His tires hadn't squealed. The speed of the turn was perfect. Fast enough to be cunning yet slow enough to be silent. He had to be sure before he called. He waited.

His shaven head slumped below the height of his headrest. His black Mercedes sat among a smattering of other cars, waiting for their owners to return. Through the heavily tinted windshield, he watched for her, sure that he wouldn't be seen. He dialed a number he knew by heart.

"She's crossing the street right now," he said, pausing to listen to the speaker. "Okay, yeah, I'll follow her." He paused again. "Don't worry, I won't alert her. I'll call you back in a few minutes with the details."

~~~~~~~~~~

Melanie needed a coffee. Her head hurt from caffeine withdrawal. Usually, she drank two or three cups a day. But now, in her scummy little motel room, she had nothing. Not even the awful tasting crap they tried to pass off as coffee to the guests. She would have accepted that. At least it would have been something. Three days without a coffee or a cigarette fried her nerves. She was on edge. She hated how her hands shook.

After Emmett had left the day before, she had slept like the dead. He had pulled the curtains tight and lowered the air conditioning. Under her covers, she allowed herself to rest, finally. Sleep came to her, hard and fast and long. It wasn't until the sun had been up for hours her body let her wake. She checked the prepaid cell Emmett had bought her. No missed calls. She was amazed it was already 1:48 p.m. Nearly thirteen hours of sleep. She felt rested, but ached for a smoke and a coffee.

Melanie broke the seal Emmett had made with the curtains. She peered out. Sunlight blared in. She squinted, shielding her eyes from the sudden brightness. Across the street, not more than a few hundred feet away, sat a gas station. One of those newly built versions that offered its customers every convenience they could think of. Drinks, snacks, a bank machine, freshly made sandwiches, fresh brewed coffee, cigarettes, lottery tickets, candy, gum, and most importantly, gas. One-stop-shopping at its best.

She could almost taste the delicious combination of coffee and the first glorious pull of a lit cigarette. It would be heaven for her if she could only have this one little treat. *I deserve it, don't I? I'll be fast. In and out. And Emmett said this place was safe, so a quick jog over there wouldn't be a big deal.*

She convinced herself. Shoes, wind breaker, jeans. *This is pretty inconspicuous. I'll be okay, it'll be fine.*

Melanie opened the door and made the plan. She would move quickly, though not quick enough to draw attention. A woman sprinting from a motel room was sure to get noticed. But a woman who walked with purpose was just another pedestrian. No one special. Nothing interesting to see.

Down the stairs. Cross the parking lot. Dart quickly over the street. In, out, back in five minutes.

She left. No one was around. Midday on a Tuesday isn't the busiest time for pay-by-the-hour motels. Sure, there's always someone looking for something, but the evening hours are different. The type of person that rents this quality of room usually prefers the cover of darkness. The motel office rarely got a renter anytime before 7 p.m.

Halfway through the parking lot, the light changed at the intersection up the street. The four cars that waited there were given a green light. All four moved toward her intended path. Emmett's words played in her head, *Just sit tight, I'll be back tomorrow with some groceries.*

Melanie panicked. Sweat beaded her palms. Her heart raced. Halfway was a bad spot to stop. She was out in the middle of the parking lot, exposed. The cars accelerated toward her. The lead car was a shiny black Mercedes, like the ones in the commercials she'd liked. Deep tinted windows. Shiny chrome hubcaps. Polished ebony paint. Even the bored headlights sparkled.

She had a split second to make a decision. Proceed forward or turn back. Instinct told her to turn back. Stay safe. The draw of nicotine and caffeine was too strong. She wanted them, bad. Needed them. As much as her heart raced and her hands sweated, her head hurt worse. Caffeine withdrawal can be torture. Nicotine withdrawal was worse.

She decided to sprint ahead in front of the coming cars. She could beat them, no problem. She was in good shape. She ran. She considered five kilometer runs easy. It wasn't until she approached eight or ten kilometers did the run become a challenge.

Hard and fast she covered ground through the parking lot toward the approaching sidewalk. Panic gripped her. The Mercedes kept coming, faster and faster, still accelerating.

Survival instinct took over. Her legs seized at the last moment. They wouldn't allow her to risk a head on collision with a moving vehicle. Her whole body stopped on the curb. In plain sight. No cover at all. *Shit, that was a stupid idea!*

The car braked hard, nearly stopping in the middle of the road. The driver turned to look toward her. Melanie raised her hand as if to say, "Sorry, my mistake." She couldn't tell if it was a man or woman. All she could make out was a silhouette. The Mercedes kept on going. After the fourth vehicle, an old green pickup truck, Melanie finally crossed the road. Victory was hers. Her reward would be sweet.

After paying for her dark Colombian roast and pack of cheap generic cigarettes, Melanie stopped before opening the gas station door. She didn't want a repeat scenario. She checked the traffic light up ahead. A red light. She was clear. She pushed the door open and lit the cigarette.

From behind, the gas station attendant wasn't impressed. *What kind of idiot lights her cigarette near a gas station? At least wait until you're at the sidewalk, moron.*

Gas station safety protocol wasn't a concern at that point. She had a cigarette in her mouth and a pack of matches open, ready to strike. She could barely wait. Her mouth salivated. The tiny tube of tobacco hung from her barely parted lips. She lit it and moved back across the street. She deeply inhaled. It was sweet and delicious, just as she knew it would be. Just as she needed it to be. She could feel her body relax, her ragged nerves soothed.

She scanned her immediate area. Again, no one was around. Without the coming traffic, the street was dead. Nothing moved. Not even the wind blew. After crossing the road, Melanie paused a moment, feeling the sunshine on her shoulders. The warmth felt great. Her room was cold, a great sleeping temperature, but cold nonetheless. She let the sun beat down on her.

After a brief moment, she climbed the flight of concrete stairs that brought her up to her room. She butted the smoke on the walkway before reentering her room. Melanie was a thoughtful woman, she didn't litter. She hated people who were too lazy to throw their trash away. Her extinguished cigarette rested between her thumb and fore finger, ready to be thrown in the toilet and flushed. The proper, polite way.

She entered her room, closing the door behind her.

~~~~~~~~~~

"Room 209," the man said after his phone call was picked up on the first ring. "She's in room 209, I'm sure of it."

He had slouched in secrecy not more than fifty feet from where she paused. He was sure she had somehow spotted him, that his hidden presence was somehow detected. He froze, waiting to see what she was going to do.

She kept walking back to her room. Tailing her had been an incredible stroke of good luck for him. The $10,000 bounty on her or the other girl would surely come in handy. *Ten G's is ten G's. Who wouldn't turn in their own Grandmother for that amount?*

"Okay. I got it. Alright, I said I got it. I'll wait here and keep an eye out," he said, then paused again, listening. "Yes of course I'll call right away if she leaves the room." Annoyance filled his tone. He quickly corrected himself. Had he forgotten to whom he was speaking with? No, certainly not. "I mean, yes, of course I'll stay in contact. I'll call every hour with an update."

CHAPTER 39

BURNT FLESH

Emmett's Basement Apartment

Susie slept the best sleep since the night before she had stood on her front porch and opened the letter from her brother. She had finished copying the entire book. Satisfaction of completing such a large task calmed her. Weariness set in her bones. She planned on sleeping only a few hours, just enough to reenergize her mind.

Sleep came instantly and didn't relinquish its hold until Emmett opened the basement door. His heavy footsteps aroused her dreamless sleep. She sat up in bed. She rubbed her eyes, wondering how long she had slept. Darkness surrounded the small basement window. She had slept through the day and into the evening, longer than expected.

"I'm sorry Susie. I didn't know you were sleeping. I would have been much quieter than that," said Emmett in a gentle voice reserved for someone he had just woken up. The computer screen, still shooting stars at him via its screen saver, caught his attention. He made a particular effort to shut down his computer and turn off the power strip to the wireless Internet router whenever the computer wasn't in use. He wiggled the mouse, bringing the screen to life. He stared. Word after word of Michael's writing looked back at him.

Susie commented to Emmett, "I've been busy." She made her way out of bed and took a seat in the computer chair. She began reading his words. She felt the talons of rage clutch her, again. Never before had Susie felt such urgency. Her stomach burned. Her skin felt hot. She craved justice.

Emmett watched her slip into the chair and begin reading. His left hand came to rest on her shoulder. Firmly. He gently squeezed, showing support. She flinched. His hand wasn't expected, yet it wasn't unwanted. She looked at him. He spoke. "I understand what you're doing Susie. I want to help, don't hesitate to ask."

"Thank you Emmett. I need to do this. It proves Michael was killed. He highlights who the potential killers were. In his last entry, he wrote that the Russian guy, Evgenii, was probably going to have him killed. That's where I plan to start," said Susie without even blinking an eye.

Her right cheek twitched as she spoke, indicating she was serious. Dead serious. Emmett saw the change. Her eyes held anger. Her shoulder was tense, like a wound spring. He hadn't seen that before. He only witnessed sorrow. He lifted his hand from her shoulder. "What do you plan on doing Susie?"

Turning back to face the computer screen, she muttered, "I plan to burn them all---Evgenii, the Outlaws, anyone and everyone who wronged Michael--they are all going to be brought to justice."

"Let's think this through. How do you plan on doing that?" asked Emmett. Realizing how poorly thought out his question was, he quickly followed up with, "Don't get me wrong, I support you one hundred percent. We should get in touch with Mason and see what he thinks from a police perspective."

"Then that's where it starts. Michael's book is good solid evidence. He should look at it." Susie paused, realizing she was coming on too strong for someone who just received support for her cause. She took a deep breath. "I don't care how it's done Emmett, but these people who are responsible for Michael's murder will be brought to justice. I'll do whatever needs to be done."

Emmett stood behind her, silently nodding his head. Her passion rose up inside him. He had become a private investigator because he wanted to help people, without the red tape and restrictions of the police department. Private investigators can bend the rules. They are governed under the same laws as everyone else, working solely for themselves. Political ambitions never interfere with their investigations. Emmett liked his line of work for that reason, he was the boss. He chose what was right and just and which path to follow. His ambitions were the only ones that mattered.

He felt something he hadn't felt before. Taking photographs of cheating husbands wasn't what he had wanted when he first became a P.I. He wanted to do something honorable. Something noble. Finally, his "right path" presented itself.

"You're right. I'll let you get to work. I want to go check on Melanie and make sure she's alright for the time being. I will be back in a few hours," informed Emmett. He bounded up the basement stairs. He felt motivated.

Before leaving, Emmett tried calling the prepaid cell phone he had given Melanie. The battery was fully charged when he had given it to her. He knew that. The phone didn't even ring once. An electronic recording told him that the phone number he had dialed was not in service. Fear crept in, edging toward panic. He rushed to his SUV.

Fear crawled deeper into his thoughts. Emmett wondered if it would be his last drive to see Melanie. His mind swam with questions. Had whoever tortured and killed Susie's roommate somehow found Melanie? Was it his fault? Or had she run off? Did she merely drop and break the cell phone?

He parked his Ford Escape in the spot closest to the motel office. From the center console he pulled out his SIG Sauer pistol. He shoved a full magazine into its end. No cocking required to insert a bullet into the chamber. It did it automatically. A handy feature of the Swiss made pistol. Seventeen 9mm bullets. One already chambered. After making sure the safety was securely on, Emmett tucked the pistol into his rear waistband. He walked toward Melanie's room.

Windshields collected dew. Emmett scanned each car parked. All had plenty of condensation. A good sign. If a car had been recently driven, the windshield would be cleared. Unless the car was used by some bad guys who had been there awhile.

The cool air heightened Emmett's sense of urgency. His palms began to sweat as he hustled toward Melanie's door. His right hand pulled the butt end of the buried SIG Sauer free. The thick smell of a foreign cuisine unknown to him made his eyes water. Too much garlic. Or was it onion? He blinked back the subtle tears.

The door to Melanie's room was slightly ajar. Small amounts of dim light crept out onto the concrete walkway in front of her door. He paused a moment. *Here we go. Focus. Don't squeeze the trigger prematurely.*

He placed his left hand gently on the door. Emmett leveled the SIG Sauer P250 into the opening of the door. He crouched down, one foot in front, one behind, into the prone position. *Make a small target. Stay low.* He began gently pushing against the weight of the sturdy door. It silently crept open.

Inside the room, the TV played a car commercial. Four young adults drove their new car on a beach road. Their smiles were wide and broad, all perfect teeth and fun. Emmett swept the room. It was empty. He crossed through the threshold. He waved his pistol, scanning back and forth. Ready. Alert. His finger was off of the trigger. Too many movies showed actors with their fingers firmly holding the trigger. Emmett hated that. Just once he wanted Hollywood to get it right. *Gun handling 101 –Don't touch the trigger unless you want the gun to fire.*

The smell hit him. Hard. It was unforgettable. He had smelled it once before. The scent of burnt flesh. The memory came back of a childhood camping experience. His friend had accidentally tripped into a smoldering fire pit. One elbow. Half a second. More than enough time for third degree burns to blacken the boy's skin. The sight bothered him, but the smell made him want to throw up that first time. Emmett was only eleven years old then. Now he was older. And a professional. It didn't matter. He tightened his throat against the upheaval.

224

Against everything his nose was telling him, he shut the door. Onlookers would have seen him waving a gun around. No doubt a call to the police would follow. The door swung nearly closed. Same as it was before he had entered. His feet made little noise. The well soiled carpet had a generous under padding. He stayed alert. The smell pained him. He slowly made his way toward the hidden area between the bed and wall. Someone could be hiding there, waiting. Aside from the TV noise, the room's silence frightened him. Deathly quiet.

Moving quickly along the silent carpet, Emmett dropped the level of his SIG. The muzzle pointed into the potential hiding place. A comforter had been thrown there, but nothing else waited for him. The bathroom. The last place to check.

The bathroom door was open, just a crack. Emmett centered himself. The smell was thick. He could taste the burning. His nasal cavity scolded him for staying within range of the smell. He maneuvered into kicking position. *Front kick. Level the SIG. Don't shoot Melanie, assuming she's alive.*

A mirror hung on the exterior of the door. Long ago it had received a blow from a fist. Maybe a foot. Maybe a head or a knee. Spider web cracks grew from the impact. Emmett planned on kicking the exact same spot.

Emmett snapped forward his right foot. The door, lighter than the entry door, flung on its hinges. It slammed into the tiny door stop. He leveled his 9mm pistol and found the source of the smell.

There, in a crumpled heap in the bathtub was Melanie's dead, naked body. Her hands were tied behind her back. Four inch burns crisscrossed her chest and stomach. Large black and white X's branded her. Her skin oozed. A curling iron lay on the outside of the tub, singeing a bath towel. Emmett placed two fingers on Melanie's neck, looking for a pulse. No luck.

His worst fear realized. He removed the wet washcloth from her mouth. She had been gagged to suppress her screams. He tried to close her eyes. Another Hollywood falsity, eyelids didn't close easily.

He voiced his apology. "I'm sorry for what happened to you. It's not your fault. It's mine. I really thought you'd be safe here. I'm so sorry. Please forgive me."

Guilt set in. Hard. And deep. She had been tortured.

Emmett didn't wait for the police to show up. Hanging around the scene of a murder wasn't a good idea. He made an anonymous call from the pay phone near the outside corner of the motel's office. The motel clerk that checked him into that room would be questioned. He would cooperate. Motel clerks always cooperated. They couldn't afford the police hanging around. Bad for business. He would give a detailed description to the detectives.

His fingerprints were scattered throughout the room's interior. He had been careful not to touch anything, aside from the washcloth. Can't get fingerprints from fabrics. At least he hoped not. But the first time he hadn't been so aware. He touched things. His mind raced back. A chair. The table. Lots of people surely had touched it. The cleaning staff wouldn't wipe everything. Not at this type of motel.

Crime technicians would be called. Fingerprints taken and cataloged. Eventually, his prints would get their turn through the police databases. His file from his private investigator's license would pop up. Detectives would come knocking on his front door. With questions, if not handcuffs.

Emmett felt his professionalism leave him. Like Susie, something else replaced it. Something that hadn't been there before. The sensation started in his fingertips after the phone call. It stretched into his chest as he sat in his SUV. By the time he had returned home, it engulfed him.

His drive home contained many unnecessary turns to ensure no one was following him. Emmett studied the art form of tailing someone, as well as evading a potential tail. The key to evading a tail was identifying the tail as soon as possible. Blow their cover. He made a series of turns. Random, often circling back.

Halfway home, a small compact car slid in behind him. He turned left. So did the car. Emmett came to a stop sign. Without signaling he quickly gunned the SUV right into a housing development. The car turned right, though not as fast. Emmett turned right again. So did the car. He turned right again, this time taking the SIG out of the console and laying it on his lap. He slowed his car after making the turn. His thumb flicked the safety off. He brought the gun up, just below the window. Emmett watched through his mirror. The car turned left, away from Emmett. No tail. *Engage the safety. Now breathe.*

Susie sat at the computer, as though she hadn't moved since he had left. Sensing something was wrong, she spun with a puzzled look on her face. Her eye brows scrunched together. She asked, "Emmett, what's wrong?"

He lowered his head and closed his eyes. "It's Melanie. She's dead." He put his left hand over his eyes. His thumb and index finger squeezed the bridge of his nose, relieving stress.

She stood and walked over to Emmett. She took his right hand into hers and gently pulled him to the couch. "Emmett, I'm so sorry," she said. Her arms wrapped around his large frame. His body began to rhythmically shake. Tears of sorrow fell from his eyes. He kept his left hand over his eyes to prevent Susie from seeing the shame built up from Melanie's death.

"I got her killed, didn't I?" he asked, more to himself than to Susie. "I did this. I'm the one who moved her to that motel and now she's dead because of me. She was probably safer at the first motel. I should have never moved her."

Susie mixed sympathy and sternness in her voice. "Listen to me Emmett. You aren't the one who killed Melanie. You were trying to help her. The same monsters

226

that killed Michael killed Melanie. And I won't let you blame yourself for that. You did everything you could."

She waited for a reply. None came. Anger grew inside her. It became evident through the tone in her voice. Susie snapped, "Get a hold of yourself. Those scumbags that killed my roommate, Michael, and now Melanie, need to pay. Together, we're going to make it happen. Got it?"

Emmett used the back of his hand to wipe away the tears that smeared his face. He liked this new version of Susie. He didn't mind being told to "get a grip." He connected with her anger and her passion for payback. Once his eyes were cleared, in a tone that no longer held any hint that he had just been crying, Emmett asked, "What did you have in mind?"

"While you were out, I thought for a long while. I see two options for us. The first is help from the police," said Susie who stood up from the couch while she spoke. She took a few steps back toward the computer and turned to face Emmett, "You need to contact Mason and see if Michael's book is enough evidence for the police to reopen the investigation into his murder. I have to believe that there is enough circumstantial evidence in there for them to at least take a look into Evgenii or the Outlaws."

"Okay. I can get behind that plan. Mason is a pretty straight up guy. He always has been," remarked Emmett. He continued, "You said there were two options? What's the second option?"

Susie's face twisted into a wicked grin Emmett had never seen before. Not ever, except in movies. Such a grin only happened when a character planned on taking revenge. At least Hollywood got something right.

She said to Emmett, "Assuming the police won't help us, we kill them all. We kill them for what they've done. We kill them for who they did it to. I can't live with myself if these animals stay free. I'll kill them all by myself if I have to."

CHAPTER 40

MEETING WITH MASON

Emmett printed out every page of Michael's book, binding them with a heavy fastener. He had a meeting with Mason. That afternoon he would wait in the same coffee shop parking lot where he met Susie the first time right after she received Michael's letter. Mason would help. He had to. Emmett had convinced Susie of that much. He believed, deep down, Mason wasn't the kind of guy to let his friends down. As he drove to meet him, he felt strange. Nervous. Anxious. Tension. They both had a lot riding on this meeting. Emmett had seen enough death at the motel to last a lifetime. Going along with Susie's second plan was dangerous. Mason's help could prevent that.

Parking in the corner spot, Emmett waited. He made a habit of arriving earlier than the agreed upon time. It gave him the advantage. Scope the scene out. Get a feel for the best positioning. Emmett angled his SUV into the best vantage point.

Paranoia was setting in. The Russians and Outlaws. They could be anywhere or everywhere. Every decision Emmett made was based around risk. Was he being tailed? Would Susie's location be compromised? A three minute drive to the coffee shop became a ten minute gallivant around town. The extra seven minutes assured him no one was there. At least no one he could make out. Now parked in the corner lot, Emmett's heart raced. How sure was he that there hadn't been a tail? He scanned for anything out of the ordinary. A coffee drinker lingered at his car longer than normal and glanced in his Ford Escape's direction. For the second time in two days, Emmett's right hand wrapped around his loaded P250.

The lingerer drove off. Emmett eased toward calmness.

A black pick-up truck, with deep tinted windows, sped too fast into the parking lot. The tires squealed as the driver parked. A small, stocky man jumped out of the truck. He was moving much quicker than any of the other customers had.

Emmett's hand darted again. It came to an uncomfortable rest on the Sig, only to have the threat dissipate. The man must have been in a rush. He ran to the coffee shop. Moments later, carrying two large coffees in a carrying tray, he ran back to his truck. Emmett shook his head as the driver sped off out of the lot. "You almost got yourself shot idiot. Slow down."

Mason arrived minutes later. Finally. Emmett concealed the pistol in the center console of the car. Brandishing a pistol, in front of a police officer, no matter how friendly you are with them, wasn't a good idea. Mason parked his car next to Emmett's and sat in the passenger seat. He shook hands with Mason and said, "Thanks for coming. I need you on this one."

Smelling of stale coffee and bad breath, Mason resembled a cop who had been on a stakeout for the past twelve hours. Unshaven. Tired. Mason replied, "What do we got?"

"Listen Mason, you know me. You know I'm not some nut job. I don't get carried away on crazy ideas about people out to get me. But this one is real. I trust you as a friend and as a damn good police officer."

"Alright, tell me about it," remarked Mason.

Rubbing the back of the bound, printed pages, Emmett replied, "This is the book Michael Taylor wrote."

"The same guy who was killed in Kingston's prison that you asked me to check out?" asked Mason puzzled.

"Yeah, him. His sister has hired me. She wanted me to look into his death. We found evidence. It's way above my pay scale. Look, Mason, I know I'm asking a lot here, but do me a favor and read this. He wrote this entire thing about his life and how everything went wrong. It has some stuff in there that you will definitely want to read."

"C'mon man. Look at the size of that thing. I don't have time to read the whole thing. What's in here that's so interesting?" asked Mason skeptically.

"How about organized crime? Or illegal gambling? Or biker drug trafficking? They are all in it. Trust me Mason, this won't waste your time. Just read it over and give me a call when you're finished. Once you have read it, we'll need to talk," explained Emmett.

Mason carried the bundled paper to his car. The interested look on his face told Emmett that, as tired as he was, he would read every page. Organized crime. Illegal gambling. Drug trafficking. Mason was ambitious. He was one big bust away from a giant promotion.

Emmett started the SUV and pulled out. He glanced through his window.

Mason sat, in his driver's seat, already starting to read. He smiled to himself. He had accomplished the first step. Get Mason involved. Maybe he could investigate Michael's death further.

Emmett found Susie sitting at his garage desk, waiting for him to return. Her purse sat on her lap. Clearly, she intended to go somewhere. "Hey. What's going on?" asked Emmett as he closed his door.

Susie stood. She wrapped the strap of her purse around her right shoulder. Susie walked the length of the loft, speaking in a matter of fact tone. "Come on Emmett. We've got work to do." She walked right past where he stood. She opened the passenger side door. Emmett stood dumbfounded. "Are you coming or what?"

Since Michael's death, Susie hadn't left his house. Shock settled on Emmett's face. He opened the car door half way. He stuck his head in. "Do you think this is a good idea? I mean, there is a bounty on your head right now."

"Come on. I'll explain everything as we're driving. We have a long day in front of us," answered Susie as she riffled through her purse. She retrieved a yellow Post-It with scribbling on it. Emmett reversed his SUV out of the garage. She stuck the paper to the dashboard near the steering wheel. "That is the address where we are picking up Michael's death certificate," explained Susie.

"Don't those things usually take some time to process?"

"Yeah. They do. That's why I called yesterday morning to have it arranged for today. You see, we're also going to the Niagara Falls Border Crossing impound lot. Michael's car should still be impounded there. I called and inquired about retrieving it. With an official death certificate, I can pay for its release."

"You can? Not to sound skeptical, but are you sure?"

"Since I am a direct family member, who will have his death certificate, I'll be permitted."

Emmett's face showed that he was impressed. Initiative. He liked that. A lot. He remembered why he had been so intrigued by her that first time at the party. She was smart. And sexy. And beautiful. Something still bothered him. "Susie, I completely support you on this one. But, does it make the most sense to get the car now? Can't we wait on this awhile?"

She smiled. He cared about her, and she could tell. She turned toward him and placed her left hand on his elbow. "Thanks Emmett for your concern. I know there is risk, but the plan calls for us to get the car. It doesn't matter if we wait a couple of days or go today. We still need the packages that are stored inside Michael's trap, along with the cash he was paid for his deliveries. There are twelve packages in there he hadn't delivered."

"I remember. What about them? What do we want them for?" Emmett was skeptical. He didn't have the foresight Susie had.

"The packages and cash are going to be our bait. I did a lot of thinking after I finished Michael's book. I read it twice. From how he described them, I feel like I have a pretty good understanding of who Evgenii and Veech are. They aren't just going to expose themselves to kill me. They'll send someone else to do it. I asked myself, "What would be a big enough reason for them to risk meeting with me?" said Susie.

Scrunching his eye brows together, Emmett thought. A moment later he asked, "I don't know. Michael's book?"

Susie cocked her head slightly to the side and gently nodded "Well, yeah hopefully. That's the first plan. But I am assuming that the police aren't going to really be able to do much. Call me a cynic, but I don't think they are going to come through for us."

"What makes you think that Susie? Mason's a good cop, and…" started Emmett who was abruptly cut off by Susie waving her hands.

Susie raised her voice over the level of Emmett's. "Emmett. Stop. Before you take my words personally, let me explain. Nothing against Mason, but he has a boss to answer to and get permission from before he reopens Michael's case. His boss needs proof. The written word of a dead convict isn't the most reliable piece of evidence. If someone doesn't know Michael, they'll probably chalk it up to another convict claiming they're innocent. You and I both know this is real. People are being murdered, not to mention tortured. I just can't foresee the police having enough evidence to proceed."

Emmett bit his lower lip and was quiet for a moment. He thought about what Susie had said. He always wanted to believe that good prevails over evil. That right always beats wrong. However, after hearing Susie's rationale, he saw it too. They were on their own. Neither one of them spoke. The tension blew out through the lowered windows. Emmett broke the silence. "I can see what you're saying. It actually makes a lot of sense. We need a good back up plan. Let me hear the rest of what you got."

Susie spun in her seat toward Emmett. She took out another Post-It with much more scribbling than the first. "Okay. Assuming we're alone in this, we need to give Evgenii and Veech a good reason to personally come and meet with me. Michael's book probably isn't enough of a reason. They don't know it exists. And frankly, these guys aren't idiots. That book has a lot of dangerous material in it that could ruin them. Getting the book isn't enough of an assurance that we didn't make copies. They would stop at nothing if they knew we had it. I think Michael's book should be our insurance policy against that."

Emmett nodded. Susie was more than a little bit ahead of him. She was three giant steps further.

She continued, "But, the Outlaws' twelve packages probably are enough to draw them in. He wrote that the street value of them is around $250,000. That's

231

probably a good enough reason for Veech to make an appearance. He won't come alone, but he'll be there. And, this is just a sense I get, but I don't think the Outlaws' want me dead. Nothing in Michael's book indicated that they threatened anyone but him."

"What about Evgenii and the Russians?"

Susie smiled at Emmett's question. "Everything that Michael has written about suggests that Evgenii is driven by two things: respect and money. If he feels disrespected, he's much more likely to handle the situation himself. Flaunting Michael's money that was owed to him is likely to do the trick."

"How would we do that?" asked Emmett.

"Remember Michael sent Melanie to the storage locker to get the last payment? Well, he also said he left his cell phone in there and that was why he never received his lawyer's phone call. If we can get that phone, Veech's phone number will be in it. As for Evgenii, we'll picture text me holding the money that is buried within the trap. The both of them will be chomping at the bit to get what's theirs. All we need to do is figure a way to get out of that meeting alive."

CHAPTER 41

WHAT'S THE PLAN

Returning well after dark, Emmett pulled his SUV into the left side of his garage. Susie followed him into the right, driving Michael's white Sentra. He clicked both buttons again. Both doors closed them in. Retrieving Michael's car was surprisingly easy. Once Susie produced a death certificate and flashed the cash, Michael's car was released from the impound lot. They agreed to wait for the safety of the garage to open the trap.

The visit to the storage unit's main office was more difficult. Tenants used their own lock, a detail Michael never explained. The death certificate was no use to the manager on duty. He shook his head and muttered something or another about the company's privacy protocol. Emmett pulled Susie aside. "The storage company just wants guaranteed money. Tell him you want to cancel your brother's lease, but renew up front for twelve months. That should get some cooperation." The manager quickly agreed. Susie signed the general contract and had the man use his bolt cutters to remove Michael's pad lock. It was clear, the manager was only worried about one thing: profit.

"How did you know that was going to work?" asked Susie.

"In the past I've rented storage units for clients. One client had it as our secret meeting place where I filled her in on the dirt her husband was up to. Occasionally, I needed something. Locks removed. Confidential access to other's units. Money made it happen. It's the universal language. A hundred dollars goes a long way to getting what you need at a place like that." Emmett smiled at her. "And your good looks might have helped a little too."

SAVANNAH

Susie blushed. She hadn't expected the compliment. Emmett had been professional, almost robotic, so far. She didn't mind it though, a little innocent attention made her feel good.

The cell phone was right where Michael had left it. The battery was dead. Emmett flipped the phone onto its side and examined the connection area. "My phone charger might fit this one. We'll try at home. Otherwise, I'll have to take it to Radio Shack and buy some fancy universal charger." The remainder of the boxes contained nothing of value. They decided to leave them, only taking the cell phone.

Since Susie had taken up residence in his basement, Emmett had taken extreme measures to ensure privacy throughout his home. In the garage, small windows that once let in the sun had been covered by window film. The film was designed to allow the light to still come through, but prevented anyone from peering through the windows. They gave a frosted view. Emmett got an added sense of security.

After closing both garage doors, Susie and Emmett tried to recall the necessary steps to open the trap. Unsure of the exact order, Susie retrieved Michael's book. She found the section where he wrote about the trap being installed for the first time. She read the steps in order. "Depress the automatic lock button on the driver's door. Start the car. Press the rear window defrost button. Put the car into neutral. Last one, push the cigarette lighter." The front panel popped open.

They gazed into the hollowed out steering wheel. Two brown paper packages stared back at them. Situated behind them, two tightly rolled cylinders of cash sat in secrecy. Emmett spun around. The driver's seat cushion opened. Ten more packages and two more rolls.

Emmett grabbed a plastic shopping bag with the local grocery store's name in big black letters across the middle. He laughed.

Susie asked, "What is it? What's so funny?"

"I just always thought if I ever had a quarter of a million dollars worth of anything that I wouldn't be using a five cent bag to carry it in."

Susie tossed the twelve packages to Emmett. The weight of the load stretched the bag handles. Emmett hesitated. He placed his free hand on the bottom to ease some of the tension. Susie clutched the four rolls of cash with her hands, and then closed each trap. They carried the items to the basement. Susie counted the cash. Emmett laid out the twelve packages.

Emmett went to the upper levels of the house as Susie counted the money for a second time. When he returned, Susie said, "Twenty thousand dollars. Each roll had exactly fifty one hundreds. This was all Michael had left to his name. It would have bought him another two months. Why hadn't he used it?"

Emmett held a small lamp in his left hand. In his right, a cell phone charger. He shoved the charger into the wall socket. The connection was a proper fit. Nothing happened.

234

He looked up toward Susie. Disappointment covered his face. "I didn't know your brother. But from what he wrote, he wasn't a dumb guy. He seemed bright. He must have seen the writing on the wall. Eventually time was going to run out. What's another two months, when you know the third isn't coming?"

The phone's small light lit up. It was receiving a charge. He placed it aside and held up the lamp he had carried down stairs. "I bet this will work."

Susie thought about her brother in silence. Emmett left her with her thoughts. She was still grieving his death. He worried he had overstepped his boundaries. She responded, "You're probably right. And anyways, I think he probably knew I would retrieve this and get the cash. Maybe in a way, it was his way of making sure I had something."

Emmett plugged the cord into the wall, next to the charger. He flicked the lamp on. Inside a black bulb glowed, displaying purple light. "I had this in a closet upstairs from years ago. I think we might be able to see the invisible ink stamp the Outlaws used."

Susie rose from the leather couch and turned off the basement lights. Instantly, the black bulb showed the logos. Skulls and crossing gasket heads. Emmett said to Susie, "Flip over the ones that don't have a skull showing and see if we can find it on the other side."

Susie adjusted the packages. All twelve Outlaw stamps lined up. She reached for the lamp Emmett still held and said, "This is good. I'll hold the lamp. You take a picture with your cell phone. Make sure the flash is off so it shows the logos on the packages."

Emmett snapped a picture using his phone's camera and saved the image.

"Did it appear okay in the photo?" asked Susie.

"Yeah, it's dark, but you can see everything," replied Emmett excitedly.

Susie sat down on the carpet next to where her brother's phone charged. She cradled it in her hands as if it were her brother's body. The connection between her and the phone ran further than a piece of abandoned electronics. She felt Michael's presence. She flipped the phone open and depressed the power button. Life shot back into it. It ran through its start-up process. Susie found the phone's telephone number. She looked at Emmett. "Send the photograph you took to Michael's phone in a picture text message." He did.

Susie rummaged through the phone's received calls. Only one number appeared. She said, "I bet this number is Veech's. When we're ready, we'll send Veech the picture you took. That'll ensure he'll attend the meeting. There's no way he would risk his twelve packages turning up as evidence for the police."

Emmett smiled at Susie, nodding. His eyes leered toward the cash. He asked, "And the money? Are we going to do the same thing to lure Evgenii to the meeting as well?"

"I can't find any contact in here regarding Evgenii or the Russians. I think getting a cell number for him might prove difficult. We should print a picture of the cash and include a note explaining whose money it is. We'll get somebody to drop it off at the door to the poker room."

"I like that. I would love to see the look on his face. But something still bothers me. How can we guarantee that we walk away from this meeting unharmed?" asked Emmett. "I mean, this meeting is going to be with some of the biggest scumbags walking the face of the Earth. There's no telling how insane they are."

"I don't know. That's the part I haven't come up with yet," said Susie. She was disappointed with herself. She should have had an answer. "Let's see what Mason comes up with first."

~~~~~~~~~

Late the next morning, Emmett's cell phone vibrated. His caller ID read: Mason --cell. He answered the phone in a chipper, excited voice, "Hey Mason. Tell me something good."

Mason's voice was anything but excited. "Meet me at the same parking lot as a couple days ago in twenty minutes. We got to talk." He hung up.

Emmett left the house without telling Susie where he was going. He didn't want her worrying. The tone in Mason's voice told him everything. This wasn't going to go smoothly. Leaving her waiting and hoping wasn't in her best interest. He wanted to protect her as much as he could, if only for another hour.

Parking exactly as he had two days prior, Emmett watched Mason pull into the parking lot. His body language told Emmett everything he needed to know. Sunken shoulders. A bowed head. A contentious look. They were clearer than any words.

Mason sank into the passenger side of the Escape. It looked as though he had been defeated in battle. "I'm sorry, Emmett. I tried, honestly I did."

Emmett spun in his seat and faced Mason square on. He shook his head. "Mason, I know I've asked a lot of you and am grateful for all the help you have given me along the way, but this one is different." Emmett began waving his finger in the air. "This isn't just some case. I'm involved in this and I can confidently say, without being dramatic, that this is a matter of life and death."

Puzzled, Mason asked, "What does that mean?"

"Do you remember the girl in the townhouse that was tortured a week or so ago, Lisa Cappolla?" asked Emmett.

"Yeah. You asked about any leads involving her. What about it?" asked Mason.

"Remember the dead woman in the motel in Scarborough? The one with burnt X's on her torso in the bathtub?" Emmett continued his line of questioning.

236

"Yeah," nodded Mason, still yet to put the puzzle pieces together.

"Mason, that dead woman was Melanie Cooper. She's the same girl from Michael's book. She was killed eerily similarly to Lisa Cappolla, wouldn't you say?" asked Emmett in a rhetorical manner. He continued, "These aren't coincidences. The killers Michael wrote about in his book are eliminating everyone connected to Michael. Lisa Cappolla was the roommate of Susie Taylor, Michael's sister. Melanie Cooper, the body from the motel, was Michael's girlfriend."

Mason's face glazed over. He was tired. He was used to his brain firing quickly. Having the puzzle pieces forced together for him was something he wasn't used to. His mind scanned Emmett's statements, looking for a hole in the logic. He settled on the fact that he wasn't going to find one. He asked, "And Susie? Where's she?"

"As I told you before, she's a client of mine. I assure you she's safe. What did the higher-ups say about investigating all of this?"

"Nothing that you want to hear. My boss spoke with the prosecutor's office and they said that an inmate's journal would be viewed as very suspect evidence. Because Michael is dead, that hurts the case's chances even further because he wouldn't be able to testify even if the police could corroborate his story. The prosecutor's office said that they would have a really tough time getting any judge to sign off on a search warrant based on the only piece of evidence being a dead convict's journal. The only way they are willing to pursue this in the least bit is if they have a firm agreement with Susie that she would be willing to testify on her brother's behalf."

"Are you kidding me? They want Susie to openly expose herself to the freaks that did that to Michael, Lisa, and Melanie?" Emmett shook his head. "No way. I won't allow it. That's straight reckless decision making. I won't compromise my client's safety. Thanks for nothing Mason," barked Emmett. The rage he felt burn inside him, after finding Melanie's body, finally boiled to the surface. His finger depressed the unlock button, showing that he wanted Mason to leave.

"Hang on a second Emmett," said Mason. He responded to Emmett's gesture by pressing the lock button on his door. He hadn't finished yet. He continued, "I said that's what the higher-ups said. I never said that's what I'm going to do. Before I sat here, nothing connected for me. I can see there is truthfulness in Michael's book. I want to help you, and Susie. More specifically, I want to make detective. Showing a little initiative on a potentially huge bust can't hurt my chances. I can't bring the entire police force, but I'm in. What's the plan?"

CHAPTER 42
I'D KILL THEM ALL TOO

"First things first Emmett. If we're going to be successful, we need to be smarter and more prepared than the Outlaws and Evgenii. We need a meeting place. It can't be any old place, it has to have a clean line to the exit," said Mason. Emmett filled him in on everything Susie had put together so far. Their plan. Their suspicions. Their approach.

He sat in Emmett's Escape. On his fingers he ticked off the objectives for a successful mission. "Fingerprints on the twelve packages are good pieces of evidence. There have got to be some. Bikers aren't the brightest candles. Someone would have left a usable print. But it won't be enough. They will probably skate on any charges that they're brought up on. This isn't exactly a police investigation we're doing. Unless, we get a recorded confession out of Veech. That's the kind of evidence that sticks. Whoever goes into this meeting is going to have to wear a wire."

"Susie's not going," insisted Emmett. The seriousness in his voice was enough to convince Mason. "We'll use her to get them to the meeting place, but I'll be the one going in. Agreed?"

"Sure. Fine by me. I'm much more comfortable with that scenario. Does she know that?"

"Not yet. I'll be the one to tell her. She's not going to like being put on the sidelines, but it is just too risky having her exposed. Those guys are psychos. Evgenii could pull a gun and kill her on sight," commented Emmett as he turned his attention back toward driving his SUV home.

Bringing Mason to meet Susie was the first giant step toward getting their mission accomplished. He had experience. He had access to police hardware. Wire taps. Bullet proof vests. And --maybe the most important--immediate back up. Calling in the cavalry could surely prove useful. Emmett called Susie. He informed her that she would be meeting Mason and what role the rest of the police force would be taking.

When he ended the call, Mason continued, "As for the Russians and this Evgenii character," he moved onto his next finger, "gathering evidence on him should be easier. Michael documented where the poker room is located. I can pay that place a visit tomorrow night and see their operation. A few photos and a well timed call to dispatch and they will be in serious hot water."

Emmett wobbled his head side to side.

"I know what you're thinking. If I was a gambler, I would bet the poker room is no longer in the same location too. We think alike. From what I know about those places, they don't stay in one spot very long," commented Mason.

"What does that mean for Evgenii? Assuming the poker room isn't up and running there anymore," asked Emmett.

"Not ideal, but just like with the Outlaws, we'll need a confession from Evgenii. Something on the record that he either was involved with Michael's death or that he runs an illegal gambling operation," answered Mason.

Emmett opened his garage door. He pulled inside. Again, Susie sat at Mason's loft desk waiting for his arrival. A pencil rested in her hand. She stood to greet the stranger arriving with Emmett. Before putting the Escape into park, Emmett pressed the remote opener and closed the door behind them. Full privacy. Emmett held up a finger for Mason to wait. Once the door was completely closed, he gave a thumbs up, indicating it was safe to exit.

Mason exited the clutches of the seatbelt and shut the door behind him gently. He looked up toward the loft. He raised a right hand and gave a subtle wave. "Hi Susie. I'm Mason. I'm Emmett's friend from years back. I'm sorry to have heard about your brother." He had had plenty of experience with grief stricken family members from his years on the force. He found it was always best to come out with it and be open.

"Hi Mason. Emmett has told me about your help. Thank you," she replied as they walked up the stairs to the top of the loft. She turned toward Emmett. "How much have you filled him in on?"

Emmett placed a hand on Mason's shoulder and nodded. "He's fully caught up, and he has some good ideas to add to our plan."

Smiling at the compliment, Mason felt compelled to say, "Listen Susie, I'm not here to take over your plans, just to help. Technically speaking, I'm not actually here in an official police capacity. What I mean is that, I'm off duty."

"So, the police aren't going to investigate Michael's death any further or look into what he has written in his book?" Susie asked.

"I'm sorry, but no. The prosecutor's office said that getting a judge to sign off on a search warrant based on a written journal of a dead inmate isn't solid enough evidence. I know this is hard to hear, but I'm here to help and I've got some friends who owe me some favors."

She shook her head. Susie's tone hardened, "See Emmett. I knew this was going to happen. When you need someone, the only person you can trust is yourself. That's why I've been writing more ideas down for the second option. I had a feeling that was how this was going to have to play out."

Mason tried to calm her down. "Like I said, I'm sorry about the police not helping. Will you fill me in on what more you've come up with?"

The three of them followed Susie to the desk. A yellow legal pad of paper sat atop the empty desk. The entire sheet of paper was full of notes. She sat and spun the pad toward the curious eyes of the two men. "Remember a guy named Arch in Michael's writing? He was the ex-biker who introduced Michael to Veech. He claimed they met up at a bar called Racks. That's where we should have the meeting," she said.

"Jesus Christ. I didn't put it together the first time I read it, but I've actually been to that place," commented Mason. "The lay out would be pretty good for the meeting." Again, he started ticking fingers off. "Lots of easy lines to the exit. It's fairly spacious inside. Easy access off a major intersection. I like it. The only problem is that it is dark and loud inside. That means we would need more sophisticated microphones. The usual run of the mill kind won't work."

"Is that going to be a problem?" Emmett asked turning his head toward Mason.

"No. I should be able to get us whatever we need. I got a guy who owes me. Big time. He runs the audio hardware office. Shouldn't be a problem," responded Mason.

"That's good, because I also thought more about the question you asked me yesterday Emmett. *How do we ensure that we leave the meeting unharmed?* The Russians are sure to be armed to the teeth. The Outlaws aren't coming there empty handed either. With only me in there, the numbers won't be pretty. I need some guarantee to walk out," commented Susie.

Emmett and Mason exchanged a concerned look. Neither man said anything. They each knew what the other was thinking. *She's not the one going in.*

Unaware of their exchanged glance, Susie continued, "Ever hear the saying, 'You don't bring a knife to a gun fight'?"

"Yeah, of course," responded both men.

"They will all be strapped with guns, right? Well, what should I bring to a gun fight if I want an advantage?" Susie asked as though she was teaching a classroom full of children.

Mason wrinkled his eye brows, unsure of the question. Emmett's face sprung to life. He blurted out, "A bomb. You bring a bomb to a gun fight."

"Exactly," said Susie slapping her hands together.

"Wait a second here," said Mason. "What are we talking about? A freaking bomb? C'mon be serious. How the hell are we going to get a bomb?"

"I don't need a bomb. We need the illusion of a bomb. Look at this sketch." Susie flipped the page on the legal pad. A rough drawing of wispy lines formed together what looked like a vest with a long cylinder along the front. She continued, "If I am wearing something strapped to my chest that looks like a real bomb, they won't shoot me. I'll show the bomb and some hand-held detonator taped to my hand. I'll shout, 'Shoot me and we all die. This is rigged to my heart beat. If it stops, the bomb blows.'" Susie smiled. "That's how I guarantee I walk out of there alive."

"That's crazy Susie. I don't mean to toss your idea into the garbage, but a fake bomb strapped to your chest is a bit far-fetched. What if they don't believe you? They'll kill you on the spot. Too risky if you ask me," said Mason looking toward Emmett for support.

Emmett seemed to be weighing the options. He kept from making direct eye contact with Mason or Susie. He finally succumbed to the pressure of their combined stare. He said, "Susie's plan does seem radical. But I have to admit, I don't have a better idea. It's one of the craziest risks I've ever heard of. The only way it works is if the bomb looks very believable. Very real."

"I knew I could count on your support," said Susie.

Mason took a deep breath. He slowly exhaled through his mouth. He closed his eyes and nodded, "Okay. Alright. This is crazy. I'll go along with it. But for the record, I don't think this is a good idea. And I have another question that I have to ask. I don't want to come across the wrong way by asking, but Susie, are you sure you want to go through with this? This could very well get you killed. Are you willing to risk everything?"

Susie's gaze could have turned Mason to stone. Her eyes burned with fire deep inside. The faint smell of smoke seemed to come from her ears. "Do you have kids Mason?" she asked.

"No."

"Are you married?" Susie asked him again.

"Yes. I've been married for four years to Beth," answered Mason curtly.

"Imagine these monsters killed Beth the same way they killed Michael or Melanie or Lisa. Now ask yourself, 'what would you do'?" Susie's words were cold enough to freeze water on the spot.

"I get it," responded Mason. His head hung low, eyeing his shoes. He raised his gaze. "I'd kill them all too."

"I want them all to pay for what they did to Michael. I want vengeance, retribution, whatever you want to call it. I want justice. I don't really care how it comes. I just want it for Michael. He didn't deserve what he got. He made mistakes. I get that. And he cheated in a poker game. That isn't reason to kill a man like an animal. I'll get justice one way or another. If that means they go to jail, then they go. If that means they die, then they die. Either way, they aren't going to be walking out of that bar as free men."

CHAPTER 43

ROAD FLARES

Each of the trio had a specific job to accomplish in order to carry out the plan the next evening. Mason needed to acquire a wire, with its accompanying receiver, which was going to be used in the meeting. He knew the exact model that wouldn't transmit background noise, usually heard on the lesser technological models. To go along with the wire, a recorder was needed to make sure the conversation was documented. These together came as a package. Put the request in for one, you get them all. Very standard.

Mason arrived at the police station. He made a direct path to the surveillance department. He was calling in a favor he had been sitting on for a while. Without making direct eye contact with anyone on duty, he arrived at the department's window. He tapped on the protective glass. "Murph. Hey. How's it going?"

Officer Greg McMurphy, "Murph" to everyone who ever knew him, was seven months from retirement and wasn't ashamed of it. He had worked the streets for years. His patience had worn thin. He knew why he had been stuck behind some desk cataloging equipment. And yet, he still wasn't ashamed. He had put his time in.

Aside from putting his time in, Murph had learned how to tell when someone needed something. He usually wouldn't hesitate to tell them to buzz off or worse. He didn't like to be bothered. He considered his work important. If a piece of his equipment was required, an appropriate request form needed to be filled out. The old days of walking up to a window and getting an item were long gone.

He heard Mason's question. His face brightened. He rose from his chair, which happened less and less these days. He extended his hand. "Mason, my friend. It's good to see you."

"Hey buddy, listen, I need you on this one. I got to call in that favor. You know the one I'm talking about, don't you?" asked Mason rhetorically. Smiling his best million dollar smile, Mason shook Murph's sweaty hand. "If I remember correctly, you owe me."

Years back, Murph's oldest daughter was being stalked. It was your run of the mill stalking. The police department saw them all the time. A guy would become infatuated with a certain young woman and cling on too tightly. Usually they were harmless. *Usually.* Cops hated that word, especially when their own family was involved. Mason was the kind of guy who the other cops could call on to handle certain issues. Mason fixed things around the department. Things people wanted to go away.

After receiving the details, Mason handled it. He stalked the stalker. Mason wasn't discreet about it. When the stalker waited outside the department store in the mall where Murph's daughter worked, Mason would show up. He just stood there. Arms crossed. Chest out. Head high. When the stalker moved, Mason moved. When the stalker started to head for the exit, as they always do, Mason met him in the parking lot. He stood right behind his car, not allowing him to reverse out of the spot. He took out a pad of paper. He wrote down his license plate. The stalker exited his car, furious. Mason brandished his gun. Once. Just once. That was all that was needed. Murph's daughter was never bothered again. That was four years ago.

"C'mon Mason. You don't need to come at me like that. After what you did to help my family, I'm indebted to you. Anything you need, I got you. So, tell me. What can I do for you?" smiled the old man, retaking his seat on the stool.

Murph sat behind his window. *His window.* It looked as though it came from an old style teller's window found in a bank. The lacquered wooden counter was polished. It gleamed all the way up its wooden sides. Murph took particular care in the appearance of his window, and his department. He was the only officer assigned to the surveillance department, making it easier for him to keep its appearance to his standards. He was sure of only one thing after his retirement. A significant drop off. No cop cared for anything the way Murph cared for his window.

Resting his elbows on the smooth counter, Mason inched closer to Murph. "I need to unofficially borrow some stuff. And I need the good stuff. The Infinity package."

"Whoa, Mason, that's a tall order buddy. The Infinity package is brand new. That's some heavy duty hardware you are asking for. Everything alright?" muttered Murph. He wiped his brow. He had been caught off guard.

"This could be big Murph. Something that gets me a promotion pronto. But listen buddy, don't ask any questions. I don't want to have to lie to you. I respect you too much. Trust me, you don't want to know either," answered Mason.

SAVANNAH

Murph didn't hesitate for more than a second or two. He couldn't turn down Mason, not after the stalker thing went away. He disappeared into the back. A moment later, he walked out with a black backpack. The bag appeared empty. He shoved it under the window. His window.

Mason carried it over his right shoulder, out to the parking lot. It felt as though he wasn't carrying anything inside it. He knew better. Murph would take care of him. Inside the bag was the most technologically advanced surveillance devices the department owned. Twenty-five thousand tax payer dollars.

Mason promised to have everything back in working condition within forty-eight hours. After that, Murph would have to mark them as stolen.

~~~~~~~~~~

Susie and Emmett were busy with their tasks. They had to lure Evgenii and Veech into the meeting. Veech was a breeze. Michael's cell phone housed his personal phone number. Emmett forwarded the photo from his phone to Michael's. Then he sent it to Veech. Twelve undelivered packages and a message: *Racks. Tomorrow night. 8 p.m. You, Veech, need to personally attend. I promise no cops. Otherwise, the packages get flushed down the toilet. Susie Taylor*.

The message left no choice for Veech. Twelve packages. Two hundred and fifty thousand dollars. He couldn't risk that being flushed down the toilet, or worse. He had to show up to the meeting.

Getting a message to Evgenii proved more challenging. Michael's phone didn't have any other contacts. Not one. Mailing the photo of the twenty grand in cash would take too long. There was only thirty six hours until the meeting.

Emmett used his laser printer to create an 8 ½ x 11 photo of Susie holding the cash. Along the bottom he typed the message. It read: *Racks. Tomorrow night. 8 p.m. You, Evgenii, need to personally attend. Michael's monthly payments will be continued if you assure me that your men will leave me alone and stop hunting me. Susie Taylor.*

Emmett drove to the carpet distributor during the normal business hours. Showing up at the poker room during playing hours seemed foolish to Emmett. It made him nervous. He used the cover of a normal customer looking to match a piece of carpet. He exited his SUV and retrieved a tightly rolled piece of beige Berber. He tucked it under his arm. Inside the roll was the photo for Evgenii.

He strolled through the front doors, expecting to find an active business. Instead, he found an empty warehouse. Nothing. Only a few giant rolls of carpet remained. They had been pushed up against the edge of the abandoned building. Not even the forklift, which was parked next to the rolls, occupied a driver. Emmett stood at the entrance of the warehouse. *What do I do now?*

245

Emmett marched forward, through the empty warehouse, back toward where Michael explained the poker room was once housed. He acted as though he was a lost customer, looking to make a purchase. No one was there. He wondered who he was acting for.

The back of the warehouse was as deserted as the front. The door that led to the poker room was closed. A sign hung from a thumbtack. *CLOSED*. Emmett paused for a moment at the door. He looked over both shoulders, wondering what he should do. No one was in the immediate area. The faint clanging of metal on metal came through the door. Finally someone.

Growing up, Emmett rarely did anything other than what was expected of him. He didn't act out in school. He never disobeyed his parents. Lying was difficult. Misleading someone left him with a stomach ache. He hated that feeling.

Emmett needed to deliver the envelope. There wasn't any way to contact Evgenii other than through the poker room. He shook his head. He gritted his teeth. *Time to perform*. He was finally ready to lie. The plan required it.

The door gave a squeak as Emmett turned the knob and opened the door. He used his other hand to heavily knock three times, alerting anyone to his presence. He stuck his head through the half opened door. He raised his voice and shouted, "Hello? Is anyone in here?"

He felt his cheeks flush. Lying always had that effect on him. He steadied his voice and repeated himself even louder.

"We're closed for business," said a voice on the other side of the room. The voice was rough. It implied intruding any further was an unwanted annoyance.

Emmett opened the door all the way. He found the owner of the rough voice. A short, tanned man was stacking padded chairs. The high columns towered in the corner of the vacant poker room. Most of the poker tables were turned on their side. A few still stayed upright. Their colorful felt tops caught Emmett's attention. The cashier's area was easily identifiable. It was the only section of the room that was closed off. A sign must have hung there, recently removed. A dust outline of a large rectangle still remained above the barred windows.

He raised his free hand and waved hello. Emmett felt ridiculous. He used his softest voice which he reserved to talk with young children and the elderly. "Oh, hi there. I was wondering if you guys happened to have any stock left over that might match my carpet sample."

The man behind the voice wasn't impressed. Initially the voice sounded clear. However, an accent, that Emmett hadn't heard, crept through the man's voice. "The carpet distributor has moved their business to a new location." Thick Russian. Emmett smiled. *I know who you are.*

"Oh okay. Do you know if there are any products that haven't moved yet?"

"I'm not a worker for the carpet company," said the rough looking man,

246

turning his attention back to the stacked chairs. He didn't want to converse any further with Emmett. He wanted to be left to his work.

Emmett understood. The message was quite clear. He knew when someone was trying to brush him off. His gentle voice had gotten him the information he needed. Russian accent. Didn't work for the carpet company. The distributor had closed. The man clearly worked for Evgenii, in some capacity or another.

He flipped his voice from gentle to tough. "Good. You can do me a favor then," said Emmett. He walked toward the man. When he was close enough, he continued, "I need this envelope delivered to Evgenii. Immediately. He'll want to see it right away. You do know Evgenii, don't you?"

The man was stunned. Emmett's change had caught him completely off guard. He set a chair down in front of him, creating a barrier between him and the advancing man. He opened his mouth, unsure how to respond. He lost the words in his throat. He stumbled, "Uh. Yeah, I know Evgenii."

It was all he could respond. It was all he was sure he should say. Offering too much information was bad. He knew that. Evgenii wouldn't like it. The small man erred on the side of caution. He caught the words before saying anything further.

"Good. Then give him this now. Do you understand? You and I both know that Evgenii wants what's his. He'll need this envelope. Don't be the guy who caused him to miss out on the money that he's owed. Are we clear?"

Emmett was more stern and forceful than before. Using the fear of Evgenii against the small man worked. The man reached for the envelope even before it was offered to him.

Emmett walked out of the abandoned poker room, back into the carpet warehouse. He tossed aside the roll of carpet and quickly walked toward the exit. He peered over his shoulder. Nothing there. He broke into a jog about halfway. His anxiety moved faster than his feet. *Get out of the building.*

In the parking lot, he found everything as it had been before. He fumbled for his keys. A car sped past him, out of the parking lot. Emmett looked up. He saw the small man quickly driving away. Apparently, Evgenii's wrath carried some weight. It motivated him to deliver the envelope quicker than Emmett had anticipated.

~~~~~~~~~~

One last loose end needed to be addressed. The bomb decoy. Emmett returned home. In the garage, Susie had spread out newspaper pages on the floor. A can of red spray paint shook in her hand. The ball bearing rattled, loosening the pressurized paint. An emergency kit Emmett had stored there for years was open. Across the newspaper, Susie had laid six road flares. Each flare was covered in a red wrapper with thick black lettering running from top to bottom. The companies name and the word *FLARE* were visible. Susie started painting.

Emmett found a vest, from a suit he hadn't worn in over three years, laid out on his basement floor. Behind him, Susie strode down the stairs carrying electrical wire and thick black tape.

"I hope you don't mind that I used that vest. It's perfect for this. I have six flares painted. They'll need another coat or maybe two depending on how realistic they look. We can put three on each side of the buttons and line them with these wires. This tape should hold it all together. I was going to run a separate wire from the vest through a sleeve. See, I'm going to sew the vest directly to a long sleeve shirt that I'll wear. The detonator button can be fixed at the end of the sleeve. I found a vague picture off of Google of what a suicide vest bomb looks like. I think we should use a simple wire and attach Michael's cell phone to represent our detonator," said Susie confidently.

She had given the vest plenty of thought. Clearly. Her attention to the small details impressed Emmett. His voice cracked when he spoke. "Susie. Wow. Holy crap. This is great work. It's going to work. I know it."

His voice surprised her. She had expected resistance. Instead, he had supported her. She turned and hugged him. He hugged her back. His strong arms helped ease her fear. She allowed herself to relax, if only for a moment. When he finally relinquished his hold, she looked up at him. Her eyes filled with tears. "Thank you Emmett. I needed that. I know this is going to work too."

He wanted to kiss her. *No. You can't. You're a professional.*

They turned back to their preparations. Over the next hour, they assembled the vest. They worked in near silence. Susie fought her growing concerns about tomorrow's meeting. Emmett resisted his growing love.

When they finally finished taping the wires and flares into place, Susie slipped the oversized vest onto her body. She held the wired phone in her hand. "It feels good," she exclaimed.

"Do you mind if I give it a try, just to see how it feels?" asked Emmett. He knew he wasn't going to allow Susie to risk her life. He would never allow her to walk into that meeting. He needed the vest to fit him properly. He felt the weight of the flares through the vest. Not much, but enough to feel them. Come tomorrow night, he would take control and make everything right. For Susie and for Michael.

SAVANNAH

CHAPTER 44
TIME TO GO

That evening they sat in Emmett's living room, with the decoy vest, with the sewn in long sleeve T-shirt, laid out on the carpeted floor. The three of them barely moved. Mason had added the wireless transmitter tap to the vest's front pocket. He explained how the rest of the equipment worked. Very simple and straight forward. The two identical backpacks, one for Evgenii, one for Veech, were next to the vest.

The three partners sat silent, staring at the items. The only sound came from the blowing wind outside. The heaviness in the air was finally lifted when Susie rose to use the bathroom. She climbed the stairs with nervous energy propelling her two at a time. After she was out of ear shot, Mason turned to Emmett. He asked, "Does she still think she's going to be the one wearing the vest?"

Emmett nodded his head. He bit his lower lip. "I need your help with this. We'll put the vest in the trunk of the Escape. I'll put it on in the parking lot when we get to Racks. She plans on using a zip-up sweatshirt from my closet to wear over top. At least the size will fit me." Emmett wiped his face with both of his hands. He continued, "Mason, when we get there, you may need to restrain her. I'm going to need time to put on the vest and sweatshirt and walk into the bar. She's not going to be happy about this. Once I'm in there, she won't risk the entire operation's success."

"Alright man, I'll do it. It's for the best. We should park in the front of the lot, facing the road, in case we need to get out of there quick," responded Mason.

The toilet upstairs flushed. They both heard it. Emmett put an index finger over his lips, indicating for Mason to end their conversation. Susie came down the stairs.

249

When she was back in the living room, Emmett said, "We were just talking about where we'll park. Mason figures the front of the lot will be best for us. Far away from the entrance, closer to the road."

Susie nodded her head silently. The tension from the coming meeting was more than she could handle. She flew up the stairs, back up to the bathroom. The contents of her stomach came up. She looked at herself in the mirror. Rinsing her mouth with water, she spit the acidic taste off of her tongue. She swallowed the next mouthful to ease the burning from the back of her throat. She cupped her hands together. Full handfuls of water splashed her face. Cold water. Refreshing water. She held her wet hands over her eyes, letting the water run through her loose fingers, down the drain. She sucked in the air between her palms. When her chest filled, she released the stress through a deep breath. *You can do this. For Michael.*

A quick rap on the bathroom door startled her out of her stress induced trance. "Susie? Sorry to bother you, but it's time to go," whispered Emmett. He was using his soft, soothing voice. She dried her face and hands on the lush green bathroom towel. Susie stared into the mirror again. Fury rose inside her like rising flood waters. *You will do this. For Michael. And Melanie. And Lisa.*

~~~~~~~~~~

Racks was exactly as Michael had described in his journal. The horseshoe shaped parking lot offered more than enough parking for the cars that evening. Too much. The place looked empty. Emmett, Susie, and Mason slowly passed by the lot. They were early, just as Emmett had insisted they be. They all peered into the parking lot, looking for any sign of Evgenii or Veech. Susie shouted out in disgust. She pointed her finger toward the rear corner of the parking lot. "You have got to be fucking kidding. Look. There. See it? That scumbag Evgenii, I can't believe he did that."

Puzzled, Mason asked, "What is it? I don't see anything."

"In the corner of the parking lot, see the orange Dodge Charger? That's Michael's. He wrote about it in his book. He loved that car. He bought that with his first big payday Savannah had given him, remember?" screamed Susie, hysterically. She added, "Michael wrote that Evgenii took the car when he was caught. I bet that bastard drove it here to mock us. Motherfucker is going to pay for that."

On the slow pass-by, the perfect parking space showed itself. No other cars around it. Perfect sight line to the door. Easy exit to the street, if need be.

Mason sat in the back. He videotaped everything. "Documentation," he said. Mason alerted Emmett of the spot. "Right there, on the edge of the parking lot, that's the one. Pull us in so I can film everything right out of the rear window," instructed Mason.

250

Emmett guided the Escape in. The lot's emptiness exposed the mid-sized SUV. From what Mason could see, there weren't any men hanging around the orange Charger. He said, "It looks like Evgenii and his men are already inside. No one is near Michael's old car. Susie, what did Michael write that Veech drove again? I don't see any motorcycles parked out front," asked Mason.

"When he first met them, Veech and Pinky Miller, the president of the Outlaws, both drove black SUVs. They were big and had heavily tinted windows. There," pointed Susie.

At the opposite end of the parking lot, two identical black Chevy Tahoes sat. Both vehicles had been reversed into their spots, facing outward, toward the bar. Their darkened windows covered the interior.

None of the three could see if anyone was seated inside either SUV. They studied both vehicles for a minute. Susie spoke first. "Those two black SUVs have to be with Veech, that's too much of a coincidence."

Emmett removed the keys from the ignition, placing them on the dashboard. He spun in his seat toward Mason. "Can you hand me the vest and sweatshirt?"

Susie began removing her windbreaker. The cool evening called for something more than a T-shirt. The air was damp. She prepared as though she was about to wear the vest, then walk onto the battlefield.

Mason handed the vest to Emmett. He laid it across his lap. The wires and flares looked as real as any pictures they could find. Painted a deep red, the flares had wires taped to the top of them. Each rested in the vest's pocket, which also held the wireless Infinity microphone. Mason had made sure it was secure.

"Emmett, turn the radio on as loud as it will go. Then have a quiet conversation with Susie. I want to make sure everything is set in the back here," instructed Mason. He flung himself into the cargo hold of the SUV. The open space offered plenty of room to set up the camcorder's tripod. Mason crossed his legs and placed oversized headphones over his ears. He gave a thumbs up to Emmett, signifying he was ready for the test. Emmett turned the volume up.

Emmett turned in his seat and faced Susie. She had been watching Mason's every movement. Sweat gathered across her brow. It had grown from a glisten to large drops falling onto her eye brows. Both of her hands were shaking. She was nervous and excited. She felt like she was going to vomit again.

With the vest still lying across his lap, Emmett took both of Susie's hands into his. He looked her squarely in the face and whispered, "There's no way I'm going to let you go in there." He squeezed her hands tighter before continuing, "Evgenii is a psycho. He'd kill you on the spot just to keep his reputation. There's no telling what the Outlaws will do."

Susie tried to yank her hands free. Emmett wouldn't let her. He squeezed even tighter. "My best guess is that neither the Russians nor the Outlaws know that the other is in there. Both will be looking for you. That's when you'll lose the advantage."

Anger and frustration shot across Susie's face. The rage that hid within her body over the past week spilled out. She pulled her hands again. Emmett's grasp held once more. She glared at him, "No. This is my fight. I want this. I need this."

She struggled to free herself from Emmett's oppressive hold. His grip was firm and unrelenting. He now held her wrists. From behind, she saw Mason coming to her aid. She turned to him. "Get him off of me Mason. This is my fight."

A shiny object flashed across her eyes. Before she recognized the handcuffs outline, Mason reached down and grabbed hold of her right wrist. His grip was well developed from years on the police force. No breaking that hold. Mason latched the first cuff around her wrist. The cold metal on her wrist felt like prison. She flailed around in the passenger seat. Emmett held her left wrist. He tried calming her, but she heard nothing. The vomit rose quicker in her throat. This time, not from being nervous, but from not accomplishing her mission. Revenge.

She wanted to look Evgenii in the eyes and see the fear the bomb would bring to them. More than anything, she wanted that. She was being restrained. Both men easily held her hands behind her head. The second cuff landed around her wrist.

She tried to pull her hands back down to her lap and release herself from her confinement. She screamed aloud at Emmett, then to Mason, "No. No! This is my fight. My brother was killed. You can't do this!"

Her hands were prevented from dropping back down to her lap. They were caught. She thrashed her body around to see what held her hands. The handcuff had been looped through the seat's headrest. She screamed at the top of her lungs.

She knew they had won. Resisting handcuffs was futile. Her rage turned to pity. Her words were barely above a whisper. "Emmett, wait. Don't do this. I'm begging you. Don't. I need to go in there."

Emmett looked at her. God she was beautiful. Even now, handcuffed to his passenger seat headrest, he saw how beautiful she was. His eyes were soft. The softest she had ever seen. Love emanated from his irises, catching her by complete surprise. She saw it, and knew.

He rested his warm hand on her knee, trying to get her to understand. "I, one hundred percent, believe if you go in there, you won't come out. At least, I have a chance of leaving there. No one in there has ever seen my face. They're not expecting me. I'm going to do this."

"Emmett you don't have to do this. Let me. Michael was my brother. This burden isn't on you. It's too much of a risk for you," implored Susie. "You can't do this Emmett."

"I have to. Mason and I have talked about it. It's the only way there is a chance of this ever working out. I love you Susie. I know I've never told you before, but

252

I've fallen in love with you. I can't let you do this and risk losing you to those freaks in there," Emmett slipped the vest on. He averted his eyes from Susie's gaze. He felt her staring at him. He wrapped the hooded sweatshirt over the vest.

Emmett's words shocked Susie. Her mouth hung open. Never before had someone told her that they loved her. Michael had, of course, but he was her brother. She was stunned. Her words became stuck in her throat. She tried to choke them out. Twice, three times she tried. Each time his words echoed in her ears causing her to fail. *I love you.* Before she was able to respond, Emmett left his seat and quickly shut the door. He walked around to the side door and retrieved the two backpacks. One for Evgenii. One for Veech. He slung them over his right shoulder, looked at Mason, and nodded. "Thanks for everything. I can never repay you for this."

Mason stuck out his hand, shaking Emmett's hand. It was a long, endearing handshake indicative of soldiers entering battle. Emmett released Mason's hand. He leaned further into the Escape and kissed Susie's cuffed hands.

"I'll see you soon. I'll make this right for Michael," he said. He shut the door and walked toward the entrance. She watched how easily he strode toward the door as if he knew all along this was his destiny.

SAVANNAH

CHAPTER 45
CONDITIONS

The backpacks were slung over Emmett's shoulder. For whatever reason they didn't garner too much attention from the patrolling security guards. Maybe the lighting was too dark, allowing the bags to blend into the background like camouflage. Maybe bringing a backpack into a bar like Racks wasn't all that out of the ordinary. Maybe no one cared. His irregularly shaped mid-section, caused by his fake bomb, didn't even register on their radar. The hooded sweatshirt nearly hid it perfectly.

In the Escape, Mason released Susie from the handcuff's possession. As he fiddled with the release key, he said, "I'm sorry I had to do that to you. Emmett insisted. And I have to admit, I agree with his reasoning. He persuaded me that he was better off in there than you. Stay in the vehicle. There's a very good chance that there are eyes on us from somewhere in the parking lot."

Susie said nothing. Once she was free, she spun in her seat. She jumped into the backseat and listened in on the recording coming from Emmett's vest pocket.

The inside of Racks was dark. The bright sun setting outside magnified the dimness. The only real light in the bar came from the pool tables. They were to the right of where Emmett entered. Their bright lights shone down on them, permitting the patrons to actually see the billiard balls. One lone sleaze ball stood holding a pool cue. He regarded the table as though he was trying to impress someone with his skill, though no one was around. *My kind of guy*, Emmett sarcastically thought.

The bar was loud. Too loud. Raunchy music blared over huge speakers that were stacked on both ends of the stage. A dancer stood on one high-heeled foot,

254

while she held the other nearly vertical. Her mouth was close enough to kiss her knee. She spun. Once. Twice. After the third time, her hand flung out and caught the pole that was centered on the stage. She locked her tanned muscular legs around its top. Again she spun. Once. Twice. Her hair whipped around. She seemed to be able to defy gravity's hold.

Pretty talented. Emmett's attention didn't linger on her. He knew he needed to identify the two parties. They had already entered the building. He could feel their gazes. Everyone seemed to stare at everyone else. Emmett glanced at his watch. Twenty minutes to eight. He was early, as planned. *Just not early enough.* In the darkened room, his eyes struggled to adjust.

Racks was only half full compared to the amount of customers on the weekends. Being a weekday, the crowd was steady enough. Money could be made. Strippers always make money. The bar stretched far across the length of one end of the room, opposite the pool tables. Most of the patrons sat in the bar stools. Their attention was glued to the stage. Jaws dropped. Tongues licked lips.

The corner near the door offered a table with four chairs. He situated himself in the chair directly in the corner. He looked out upon the room. The bar stools that lined the bar held most of the customers. He looked for two groups of men. A group of well dressed Russians. A group of bikers wearing a patch reading "Outlaws." A waitress approached him. She was bigger than the stripper. Maybe ten years older too. She may have been that stripper many years ago. Now she had been relegated to fetching beers.

"What can I get you honey?"

Emmett looked in her direction. Her top only covered the upper portion of her bulging belly, revealing a scar from a caesarian section delivery. He quickly looked away. "I'll have a bottle of Budweiser."

His words sent her away, allowing him to continue his search. His eyes slowly adjusted. Situated in the opposite far corner, Emmett spied a few well dressed men seated at a table. They sat close to each other. Too close. Their table was clear. No drinks. *Hello Evgenii. Now I know where you are. Where are the other idiots?*

Spotting Veech was more difficult. The crowd in Racks predominately dressed as though they were bikers. Nearly every customer had on jeans and a shirt emblazoned with a motorcycle company or biker gang. Many of the T-shirts worn by the customers seated at the bar read, "1%ers" somewhere on their shirt. Emmett struggled. Identifying a biker gang in a biker bar was impossible. The waitress returned carrying Emmett's beer.

"Here you go honey. You want me to start a tab?" she asked.

"No, that's okay. I'll pay now," said Emmett laying down a $100 bill. He kept his index finger on the bill, pinning it to the tabletop. "I need a couple of favors. You can keep the rest of this as a tip. There's a group of well dressed men in suits in the opposite corner without any drinks. I'd like to buy them a round of beers." He slid the money toward the waitress.

"Okay honey, but I already asked them what they wanted to drink. They said they were waiting to meet someone and didn't want to be bothered. Friendly bunch."

"All the same, bring all three of them a Budweiser. And one last thing, I was wondering if you know a man named Veech? I'm supposed to meet him here," said Emmett.

Her face sunk. Excitement of a big tip turned to nervousness when Emmett mentioned the name Veech. She pointed toward the far end of the bar with one hand while the other reached for the money. Not her first time exchanging money for information.

"Yeah, I know Veech. He's over there."

Emmett's finger still pinned the hundred in place. "Excellent. Send him a Budweiser as well. Tell him it's from me," Emmett said boldly. He made a show of finally releasing the hundred. "Thank you for your help. I won't need anything else tonight."

His words carried an eerie sort of vibe that left the waitress feeling uncertain. She knew that feeling. Trouble. Working in Racks had always been a juggling act of steering clear of any actual danger and flirting with ugly, rough bikers. After delivering the bottles of beer to their intended destinations, she planned on taking an extended smoke break.

Emmett's eyes followed the waitress. He watched her quickly retrieve four bottles of the domestic beer and carry them on her circular tray. She darted and dodged through a small crowd toward the table with the three men. The three Russians. Emmett watched her place the beers onto the table. She seemed to offer an explanation of where they came from. She spun and pointed in his direction, just as he suspected she would. The three men immediately stood. They buttoned their suit jackets. They began their slow walk across the bar.

Emmett's attention was halved between the lazily approaching men and the waitress who had positioned the final bottle of beer in front of Veech. She pointed, again, in Emmett's direction, presumably answering Veech's question. He stood from his bar stool. Four other men jumped off their stools. They were seated much closer than the Russians. Their path to Emmett was much shorter.

Emmett placed the black backpacks on the floor next to his left foot. He rested both of his hands around his bottle of Bud. Both parties arrived simultaneously around the small table, Veech on Emmett's left, Evgenii on his right. Neither man averted their eyes from Emmett's hands.

Emmett smiled. He was in control.

Standing behind Evgenii, the two men unbuttoned their jackets, revealing a pair of guns fastened in their shoulder holsters. Though dark, the black pistols were visible in the bar's dim light. Their fingers slowly unclasped the holster's strap. Only gravity held the guns in place.

His eyes shot back to the four men flanking Veech. They were unlike the Russians. They wore T-shirts and jeans and leather Outlaw gang patches. They hadn't shaven since puberty. They opened their vests and pulled up their shirts. Each man had a firearm hidden in his front waistband.

Veech placed both of his hands on the table, wobbling it from his weight and displacing its balance. The rough features of his face inched closer as he lowered his head toward Emmett's.

"Gentlemen, now that we're all here, please have a seat," announced Emmett. He had totally transformed his personality. He was in charge. Inside, he felt like a scared child who wanted to leave the bar and run away. On the outside, he owned his confidence. His voice was calm and clear. His arms opened wide, inviting the two men to sit and join him.

No one moved. Emmett felt the confidence being challenged. He grinned at the show.

Evgenii waited for the seated man to speak first. He would not show any weakness by doing what he was told. He was Evgenii. No one told Evgenii what to do. He declared, "I am not sitting with you. I don't even know you. Who are you and what is this all about? Answer quickly or my men, here, will kill you. Do you understand?"

His impatience and accent informed Emmett that he was, indeed, Evgenii. The man on Evgenii's immediate left made a move for his gun, ready to obey his leader's command. He rested his hand on the pistol's grip, leaving it tucked into the holster.

"I understand your confusion, but you don't want to do that. Sit down Evgenii!" Emmett demanded. He motioned, again, to an empty seat. He turned his attention to Veech. The gesture was defiant. Emmett was in charge. Evgenii's challenge was tossed aside. Emmett repeated himself, "Please Veech, sit. We need to talk."

Veech eyed Evgenii. Then he turned his gaze at the seated man. He was stunned. His attention shot back to the man's hands, which had left the bottle of beer and were now palm up on the table. He cautiously reached for the back of the chair. He spun the flimsy chair one hundred eighty degrees. He inserted it between his legs, easing his body down.

Evgenii watched Veech slowly sit in the chair. He did not like being so easily dismissed. He produced a pistol from behind him. He slammed it onto the table with much more force than was needed. He angled it directly at Emmett.

Both groups of men reached for their guns en masse. Evgenii's men reached both of their hands under their jackets and pulled out fistfuls of pistol. Black. Dull. Each pistol looked huge in their small hands.

Veech's men reached into their waistbands. They pulled their own firearms. Each man only had one, as compared to the Russian's pair. But there were four bikers with one gun each. Four guns. Two Russian men with two pistols. Four guns. Stalemate.

Everyone aimed at everyone else. Russians at Emmett. Outlaws at Emmett. Russian at Outlaw. Outlaw at Russian. Veech and Evgenii didn't react. They sat still. Tense, ready to uncoil.

Emmett slowly raised both hands, motioning for everyone to lower their weapons.

He looked squarely into Evgenii's eyes. He slowly unzipped his sweatshirt, revealing his suicide vest to the group. He parted the opening and shrugged the sweatshirt off. His right hand came through the cuff where the cell phone had been hiding. He wrapped his fingers around Michael's cell phone, the wires in place. Emmett calmly laid it on the table. He said, "You know what this is, don't you Evgenii?"

No one spoke. Veech blinked rapidly, trying to clear his eyes. Evgenii stood motionless in his spot. To acknowledge the vest would be a form of weakness. He raised his chin and pursed his lips.

"This vest has two ways of detonating. The first is if my heart stops. You kill me and it explodes. The other is through this cell phone. I press the send button and boom." Emmett's voice was clear. He impressed himself. He was really in charge.

The crowd of men that swarmed the table instinctively took a step back. Their eyes grew large. Their feet carried them away from the table. One step. Then two.

Emmett looked at Evgenii again. "So please, Evgenii, sit down so we can talk."

Nervously, Evgenii lowered his body into the chair, placing his right hand on top of the gun that was on the table.

"Thank you," commented Emmett. He sat back in his chair to show he was comfortable and at ease. He crossed one hand over the other. He explained, "I am here on behalf of Susie Taylor, who is the sister of Michael Taylor, whom you both know. First off, this vest is my insurance policy. I do not intend to kill us all, but like I said, it's my insurance policy so I can walk out of here alive."

Evgenii interrupted Emmett's speech. "Where is my money?"

Glancing toward his left knee, Emmett said, "I have both your bags Susie has given to me. Your money is in one Evgenii and your twelve packages are in the other Veech. I have no quarrels with either of you and am willing to give you each your property on two conditions."

Looking under the table, Veech noticed the two bags he had earlier missed when he took his seat. He was nervous. This situation left him feeling exposed and unprepared. "What are the two conditions?" His words came out too quickly. He closed his eyes in embarrassment.

Hearing the fear in Veech's voice, Evgenii sneered at him and exclaimed, "I am not here for some game. I want my money and then I am leaving. Give it to me. Now!"

Emmett smiled at the Russian's demand. His need for dominance and power over every situation was amusing. "Miss Taylor thought you might say something like that and has instructed me not to give you a thing until the two conditions are met. Once they are, you're free to walk out of here with your rightful property."

Emmett flipped open the cell phone and began thumbing the buttons. He was in charge. The crowd stepped further back. He turned toward Veech. "The first condition is for whoever has ordered the hit on her life, to cancel it. She just wants to live a normal life, free from fear. Obviously she is willing to give you what you want." He toggled his gaze between both Evgenii and Veech and asked, "So, who put the hit out on her life?"

Veech shook his head. The seriousness of his face told Emmett he hadn't ordered the execution of Susie Taylor. Emmett saw sincerity.

Emmett turned his head toward Evgenii. He cautiously asked, "Evgenii, can we agree that the hit on Susie is called off if she gives you what is rightfully yours in exchange?"

Evgenii hated feeling as though he didn't have any options. Walking out of the bar without his money would be a sign of weakness. Being forced to agree to conditions that were laid out in front of him was a sign of weakness. His mind raced. He needed to show strength. His men were watching his every move and surely they would speak of his actions.

Evgenii rubbed his chin stubble, nodding in agreement to the first condition. He waved his left free hand in the air to move onto the last of the conditions. "What else?" he muttered as if speaking to a dog.

Emmett sat back again, easing into the second condition's explanation. "Very well, then it is agreed that the hit on Miss Taylor will cease today, permanently. The other condition is for Miss Taylor's peace of mind. She loved her brother very much, but they had grown apart from each other over the past few years. She has questions about him. Obviously we don't have enough time to ask all of her questions, so she has the same question for each of you. When you answer it, I'll hand you your bag and you can leave. Simple as that."

Acting impatient and needing to be in control of the situation, Evgenii asked in a nasty tone, "What is the question?"

Emmett glanced back and forth between the two men.

"Did you have someone kill Michael Taylor?"

259

CHAPTER 46
SCOTTISH KISS

Susie and Mason listened through headphones in the back of Emmett's SUV. It was brilliant. Emmett controlled the conversation's direction. Sharing an ear piece each, they angled their heads together, conjuring up images of teenage girls listening to the latest pop sensation. They both donned prideful, hopeful smiles. Through the dull background music of some exotic dancer's routine on the pole, they heard the change in Emmett's voice.

Just minutes before, Emmett had professed his love for Susie, only to quickly walk away before she had a chance to respond. She hadn't ever looked at Emmett that way before. Not all those months ago at their first meeting at that lame party, and not since. She was too focused on the task at hand. Too focused on following the vengeance inside her heart. Too focused on the hurt from Michael's death. But now. Now was different. This man was risking his life for her, literally. She heard the control in his voice. She pictured him in her head. In control. Macho. Dictating to hardened criminals. She allowed her mind to wander. She allowed herself to envision a future with Emmett. She liked it. But first he had to get out of the bar alive.

They hadn't rehearsed what Susie was going to say when the plan still included her entering the bar. Susie realized Emmett was winging it. And it was convincing. She didn't hear the fear in his voice, which he repressed deep down. She nudged Mason with her elbow. He gave her a thumbs up. Neither said anything. Neither wanted to miss a word.

The video camera rolled footage of Racks' entrance. No one had come in since

Emmett entered. No one had left. Mason called his sergeant. He explained he was outside a strip club and a high ranking Russian crime boss was inside the bar brandishing a pistol. With him were five Outlaw bikers, one of which was probably a leader. Mason requested backup. His sergeant hesitated. Mason demanded backup. Susie heard Mason screamed into the phone, "Get me the goddamn Emergency Response Team to this location now!" Mason ended the call. He nodded to Susie, "They're coming. Trust me."

~~~~~~~~~~

The look on Veech's face confirmed for Emmett everything he already suspected. Veech hadn't killed Michael. For the vice president of a feared biker gang, Veech was a push over. A push over compared only to Evgenii. Veech didn't try to hide his emotions like Evgenii did. Whether the threat of the vest or being seated next to a lunatic Russian, it didn't matter, Veech didn't have a very good poker face. He blurted out as fast as he could manage. "No way man. Not us. The Outlaws loved Michael. He was our best mover. We didn't kill him."

Emmett felt like a detective in the interrogation room. He shot back at Veech. "You want me to believe that a mover of yours, who had over a quarter of a million dollars in product, wasn't on your club's hit list? Bullshit Veech."

"You got to believe me. We had no intentions of killing Michael. We tossed his house looking for the missing packages, but that was it. He was our mover. I trusted that guy. He moved shipments across the border for us and we paid him well. Our relationship was always professional and respectful. The club and I liked Michael. And we knew his predicament with the Russians. The payments. The $10,000 a month. Honestly man, we just wanted our packages back."

"And the cash that was in Michael's house? I understand he had a significant amount saved up that was taken when his house was rearranged," asked Emmett.

"Listen man, the Outlaws have a business to run, you can appreciate that. We lost an investment of ours that was worth quite a large sum. When we found the cash, we called it even with Michael. No harm, no foul. A day or two later we heard he was arrested and in jail. As far as I was concerned, our business was settled and he was debt free from the Outlaws. That's not to say we don't want our packages back, but we did not, at any time, have or want Michael killed. I was upset when I learned that Michael was killed. He was a good worker for the club," explained Veech. Sincerity was evident in his voice.

Emmett shook his head at Veech. "No harm, no foul? You knew about Michael's deal with the Russians and that he needed that money. Taking it from him essentially killed him. I believe you didn't put the hit out to kill him, but what you did dramatically shortened his life. You're not innocent here."

Emmett turned his gaze towards Evgenii. He squared his whole body towards the Russian. Evgenii sat, resting against the wooden chair's back. He crossed his arms in front of his chest and held his chin high. His nose twitched. The mobster showed no emotion or concern, as if this was just another meeting. Through his thick Russian accent he spoke, "What do you want me to say? Do you want me to say that I didn't kill Michael?"

"You must have killed Michael. Process of elimination. Did you have that skinny bitch cellmate of his, Stinger, kill him?" snarled Emmett at Evgenii. He was confident he was the killer. After hearing Veech's side of the story, he had no doubt in his mind. Anger fueled his confidence. Rage controlled his words. He spoke down to the powerful crime boss as though he was a toddler who had misbehaved.

The disrespect caused Evgenii's face to redden instantly. His front lip curled. "I don't need to discuss my business with you. Who are you? You are no one. I am Evgenii."

"That's fine. Walk away. Show your men you are weak and feeble. Leave without the cash and you'll be laughed at behind your back."

"You think you can provoke me? I kill pieces of shit like you every day."

"That's irrelevant. If you want the money Michael owes you, then you'll answer the question. Did Stinger kill Michael or was it someone else on your orders?"

"If someone comes into your home and steals from you, are you going to just allow them to do that? No. I think not. Nor am I. Michael came into my business and stole from me. He offered me an agreement where he would pay me a monthly amount, which he did not follow up on. He deserved what he got."

Emmett flew into a rage. He stood and slammed his open palms down onto the table, nearly breaking the surface from the pedestal. The slap of his skin on the polished wooden surface gained the attention of the entire bar. Heads turned. The dancer on the stage stopped. She quickly gathered her discarded articles of clothing and hopped off stage. She had seen this before. Time to leave.

Evgenii's men stepped forward. They raised the barrels of their pistols to Emmett's eye level. He stared down the length of two pistols. His eyes never wavered from Evgenii's.

Veech shot out of his chair after the loud slap. He took a couple of steps back. Both hands raised in surrender. His two closest men grabbed him, pulling him behind the safety of their massive bodies.

Spit flew from Emmett's mouth. He barked, "He got what he deserved? He didn't deserve to die over a missed payment you fucking psycho. He was a good man and you killed him."

Evgenii stood. He rose to Emmett's level. He spoke barely more than a whisper, "You think a little bomb scares me? You don't get it. I am Evgenii, I don't die. The hit on Susie Taylor stays. No matter what happens, the bounty remains on her head. My people will never stop looking for her. Never," he paused, inhaling sharply. "And, yes, Michael got what he deserved. I would kill him again, if I could."

His words came out, taunting Emmett. He was sent into a wild animal madness. He reached out and grabbed Evgenii by the lapels of his $3000 suit. He took a firm hold of the silk around his collar. Both hands jerked Evgenii towards him, as hard as he could manage. Emmett pulled hard. Faster than he imagined he could. Stronger than he ever remembered being. Emmett lowered his forehead into Evgenii's oncoming face. The coppery smell of blood filled Emmett's nostrils as Evgenii's nose exploded on impact with his forehead. A Scottish kiss.

Blood splattered in every direction. A faucet of blood poured onto the table. Evgenii's mouth filled with the crimson fluid. He cried out in pain. His men stood in momentary shock.

Woozy from the violent collision, Emmett stumbled back until the back of his knees hit his chair. He fell into a seated position. He instinctively wiped away blood off of his face. He touched his forehead searching for an open gash.

Emmett wiped two palms full of blood off his face. Evgenii's bottom teeth must have cut his eye brow. A gash, the length of his fingernail, leaked blood. Touching the wound sent white hot shocks of pain throughout Emmett's body. He looked at his hands. Blood. Lots of it. The cell phone wasn't in his hand anymore.

Emmett had dropped the cell out of his hand when he had grabbed Evgenii. The thin red wire, which was attached to the phone, had disconnected.

His eyes frantically searched the tabletop. Then the floor below the table. The light was dim. Really dim. Almost dark. A reflection from the phone's screen shone like a beacon. He stretched an arm down to recover the phone. His fingers grazed the phone. Then his body spun.

Emmett felt a burning sting in his right shoulder. The flash of pain was far worse than the gash. Twice as worse. Three times. Emmett stumbled to remain in his chair. Something spun him back the other way. This time, against the wall. He finally heard it. A boom, as if cannon fire exploded in his ear canal.

The man on Evgenii's left squeezed the trigger only feet from Emmett's shoulder. His GSh-18 hand gun was originally designed for the KGB's use in Russia. Armed with armor penetrating ammunition, the bullet ripped through Emmett's skin, exiting his shoulder through a larger hole than it entered. The 19mm bullet had stopping power. It slammed Emmett against the wall, temporarily pinning him in place.

The other Russian man reached under both of Evgenii's arms and escorted him away from the table to safety. Evgenii held his nose. He caught the blood as if that would prevent any further damage. When he was on his feet a few steps from where Emmett was in a crumpled heap, he shouted to the gunman, "Kill him! Kill that fucking dog!"

The gunman turned to face his boss. Unsure if Evgenii fully understood the ramifications of shooting Emmett to death, he questioned him, "Sir, the vest. If I kill him it'll explode and kill us all."

Evgenii straightened up. He yelled, "I don't care. No one strikes me and lives. Kill him or I'll kill you." His high-pitched scream echoed throughout the entire bar.

Veech's men steadily retreated. The more the violence escalated, the further they got away. This wasn't their fight. When the four Outlaws heard Evgenii's command to kill, they joined the other customers in the bar and ran towards the exit.

A mob of thirty five people scampered towards the exit. A bottle-neck jam slowed the Outlaw's exit from the bar. Strippers. Waitresses. Drunks. No one was special in a mob. Everyone moved as a mass, an entity. Only one rule: Don't fall down.

"Wait," yelled Veech, but his voice was tossed to the side by the repeated booms that came from the Russian's pistol. Five more rounds struck Emmett in the chest. The bullets plunged into his chest, ripping apart his back. The vest was shredded. No explosion. One of the bullets skimmed a flare, revealing the paint underneath.

The assault instantly ended Emmett's life.

SavannaH

Chapter 47

Black Van

Waiting outside of Racks was the Emergency Response Team. Guns drawn, barrels pointing at the exit. Each member carried a C7 assault rifle tethered around their shoulders. The scary black weapons weighed less than nine pounds fully loaded. The stocky shoulders of the team easily held them level. Loose PlastiCuffs hung from belt bands, ready to restrain anyone or everyone. The one time use handcuffs were easier to use than the traditional steel bracelets. Each officer carried a dozen.

Gun fire erupted in the bar. The ERT officers fidgeted with their rifles. Three made sure the clips within their rifles were secure. Five others realigned themselves behind the rifle's sights. The officer in charge yelled commands. Everyone readied themselves. They had trained for this. Long, hard hours had been logged. Muscle memory would take over.

Patrons spilled out of the bar. They fumbled for their footing. The bottle neck squeezed people out in single bursts, sometimes double. They stepped through and all went wide eyed as fifteen muzzles stared them in the face. Shouts of, "Get down!" and, "Put your hands on your head!" went unnoticed. Each person searched for a direction to run. Fight or flight. Easy decision for most.

ERT members tackled, PlastiCuffed, and pulled the patrons to safety behind numerous police cars. Near nude dancers and drunken patrons alike were corralled as they ran from the violence exploding inside Racks. Most were quiet. Some whispered to others, asking confused questions. The blank look of helplessness was smeared on every face, with no exceptions.

Advancing into the front door of the building was impossible, too much of a stampede. People felt they were running for their lives.

Veech and the other Outlaws finally ran out. The waiting arms of several ERT officers greeted them. Veech thankfully screamed. His face was shoved into the gravel parking lot. "It was a fake. The bomb was a fake the whole time." A wide grin crossed his face. The kind a man gets when a near death experience is survived.

The ERT unit finished PlastiCuffing the bikers. They readied themselves for a frontal assault into the bar. Massive gunfire had erupted no more than twenty seconds earlier. The front members carried ballistic shields. Full protection from below the knee to above the head. The model they carried was bullet proof against most ammunition, highly explosive incendiary rounds excluded. The sound within Racks was easily identifiable. Common handgun rounds. The explosive *pop* alerted the ERT officers. Worst case scenario, hollow point rounds. Most served extensive time in the military. All of them knew guns and ammunition. The shields would offer above average protection.

The team of twelve ERT officers formed together in a tight bunch. Dynamic entry grouping. They stacked up. Two officers up front, shouldering the shields. Two rows. Six men each. One officer right behind the other. No wasted space. Right hand on shoulder in front of you, left on your rifle. Laser pointers. LED flashlights. Everything you need, nothing you don't.

Red beams were flicked on. Blaring white LED lights highlighted their path. The team plunged through the front entrance. They shouted, "Police officers! Lower your weapons! Get on the ground!"

The front men quickly identified the three threats. They squared their shields. They repeated their command. "Police officers! Lower your weapons! Get on the ground!"

CHAPTER 48

BUNDLES

Evgenii's wooziness passed as the gunfire from his men echoed in the bar. His men had killed Emmett. Eighteen bullets, nine from each man, made sure. He shook his head. He smiled. "Fucking liar. Think you can kill Evgenii that easy, do you?"

Emmett had lied about his vest bomb detonating if his heart stopped. Evgenii reached inside his jacket and pulled his firearm. Both his men held their two guns, ready to die for their boss. Evgenii walked to the black backpacks. He placed both of them on the table top. Unzipping the first one, he pulled out heavy brown paper packages. He tossed them to the ground, quickly discarding the entire backpack.

Evgenii opened the second. He reached his hand inside the bag. Bundled wads, tightly bound by rubber bands. He smiled. He laid his gun on the table. Both hands reached deep into the bag, extracting as large a handful as he could. He said, "This is what we came for. This is what we leave with. My money! Evgenii's money!"

Light from the police officer's beams lit the bundles in Evgenii's hands. Red dots scampered across his chest. Under the bright LED light, he saw his money for what it really was, nothing more than tightly wadded strips of newspaper. Rubber bands and newspaper, wrapped in a single $1 bill.

The police shouted for the other Russians to lower their weapons. Rage boiled inside him. His temper exploded. Evgenii threw down the worthless bundles and grabbed his pistol. He pointed it at the approaching ERT officers. Their bright lights and shields and guns didn't scare him. He was the mighty and ruthless Evgenii. He shouted to his men, "Kill them all."

CHAPTER 49

GET AWAY

The crackling explosion from automatic weapons simultaneously fired, snatched everyone's attention outside the building. Their eyes darted toward the lightning flashes coming from the open doorway. Inside Racks, the ERT officers opened fire. Mason and Susie both exited the Escape. Susie opened the rear passenger door and held it for Mason. Hurdling the backseat, he charged out. He grabbed Susie by both of her shoulders and looked her squarely in the face. She could feel both of his damp palms on her sunken shoulders. "It's going to be alright. I'm going to help out. Stay here!"

Mason ran toward the rest of the police officers, who frantically began pulling and aiming their weapons at the front door. They took cover behind vehicles and opened doors. Mason ran to a police cruiser, which protected two officers, and waved his badge to them. He shouted, "I'm the officer who called this in. My guy is in there." He pointed his Glock 17 toward the door.

Susie stood shocked. The last minute's events horrified her. Her mouth hung open, making breathing a chore. She tried to blink. Everything moved in incredible slow motion. The squeal of halting tires from behind her snapped her out of her daze. She spun, curious. She was too slow.

A black conversion van with tinted windows suddenly stopped on the street, right behind where Susie stood. Three men, wearing black ski masks, rushed out of the van. They were big and moving fast. Their hands were covered in black leather gloves. One hand held a white cloth.

Susie instinctively began to back away. She tried to turn and run. Her legs didn't respond as expected. At first they moved slow and heavy, like walking through thick tar. The marauders were faster. She began to run toward Mason. She was moving fast now. Adrenaline fueled her muscles. She passed the back of the Escape toward the open parking lot.

She was tackled from behind. A black hood was slipped over her head. Her hands were, once again, handcuffed. The assailants used a lot less care than Mason had just moments earlier. They were rough with her. She was pinned to the ground, her head pressed hard against the rough gravel. Multiple hands worked together in silence. The noise Susie heard was the breathing coming from the invisible assailant on her back.

A cupped hand wrapped itself around her mouth and nose. The black hood stuck to her face. The air smelled toxic.

Susie faded.

Two powerful hands wrapped themselves around her ankles.

Further toward the darkness.

Another set of more powerful arms encircled her waist and began carrying her. She floated off the ground.

Susie was out. Her neck went limp. Her whole body sagged. The hand over her face pulled the cloth away.

Susie didn't thrash against her captors as they laid her into the waiting van. She couldn't. She was unconscious. Her body was tossed into a padded, cushioned seat. The men laid her across a row of seating. The tuned V8 engine roared away. The van lurched forward.

A deep voice from the back of the van asked, "Are we clear? Did anyone see us?"

"We're clear. There aren't any cars following us. Everyone was focused on the door," shouted a different, softer voice from the passenger seat.

CHAPTER 50

WHITE HAIRED WOMAN

Seated in an overstuffed leather chair, Susie felt her body's weariness from the past day. Her shoulders ached. Her back was stiff. More than anything, her head throbbed. The hood still remained over her head. She had lost all concept of time inside her sensory deprivation chamber. Panic had long since left her. As it faded, numbness took over, then apathy. She knew, deep down, she was being taken to her grave.

She cried for Emmett. Then for Michael. And finally for herself. Her brother had been killed by the same people who had killed the man who loved her. Now they were going to kill her. She didn't want to die.

When the rhythmic rocking of the van finally stopped, she was placed into a chair. It was big and cushy. Under the hood her eye brows frowned. It didn't make sense to her. *Why are my killers going to the effort to treat me to a nice chair? Are they just raising my hope, only to have it crash down on me? I wish they would just get it over with.*

The light crept through the hood. Not much, but it leaked in. Someone removed her hood. Gently. Almost softly.

Bright sunshine blasted through the windows, stinging her eyes. *How long were we driving for? What was it that they put over my mouth?* Susie's mind raced, trying to recall details. Her mind was blank. The last firm memory she had was Mason grabbing her by the shoulders before he ran off to take position. She searched back further. *What happened after that? Where am I?*

The same strong hands that had removed her hood unlocked her handcuffs.

And they were noticeably gentle. Another pair of weaker hands touched her wrists. They began washing them with a warm wet washcloth. Someone wiped the sweat over her brow that formed from the suffocating hood. Her eyes still stung from the light.

Susie rubbed her eyes. The tender treatment puzzled her. *What is going on here?*

She had assumed Evgenii's men had finally captured her and were taking her to her death. Some remote forest, like Michael had written about. She shook her head, loosening the cobwebs. Her vision slowly came into focus. She blinked several times. She squeezed her eyes shut, then opened them.

Someone cleared their throat before speaking. "It's okay dear, you're safe. No one is going to hurt you. Give your eyes time. I know you have lots of questions. You'll get your answers," said a soft female voice. Susie was sure it came from an elderly woman.

She blinked again, finally making out the room she was in and the people that surrounded her. The soft voice spoke again, "Your safe Susie. You have nothing to be afraid of."

Susie finally narrowed in on the voice. She saw a white haired woman seated in a wingback leather chair, identical to the one she was sitting in. The woman held a cup of steaming tea with both hands over her lap. One hand held the fine china's handle, the other held the saucer.

Standing next to the woman were two large men dressed all in black. Susie recognized them immediately. *The men from the van.* She coiled her body. The shine of their boots indicated they were former military. Soldiers of some capacity. Dark circles under their eyes, they had been up all night, driving. Their hands were crossed in front of them, like soldiers at ease.

Susie couldn't understand why the kind old woman was with two men who had just abducted her. She rubbed her eyes one last time and asked, "What's going on here? Who are you people? How do you know my name?"

The old woman smiled and extended her hands toward Susie, offering the cup of tea. "Here child, take this. It'll warm you."

At that moment, Susie was safe and the woman was being kind to her. *No need to test the limits of her kindness. Accept the cup. Be patient.*

She reached and accepted the mug of hot tea. She rested it on her lap, as the elderly woman had done. As she sat back, the woman spoke again, "Susie, we're friends of Emmett Irvin. I know you have a lot of questions, so let me start from the beginning. First, let me apologize for the manner in which you were transported here. There are certain security measures we take to ensure that no one knows where you are. Not even Mason would know."

Susie frowned and asked, "How do you know Mason?"

271

"It'll all make sense to you in a moment. But just know, not even Mason knows you're here. Emmett told us of his involvement. That's part of your safety," she said, pausing to clear her throat and sip her tea. She continued, "I'd like to explain who I am and what I represent if that's okay."

Susie said nothing. She nodded.

"My name is Martha Richardson, at least that's the name I go by now. I am part of an organization that is here to protect you. I'm not sure what Emmett told you about us, so I'll try my best to explain everything. We're a secret organization that is something similar to the witness relocation program the government uses."

Susie's jaw came unhinged, slowly parting. Her head tilted forward.

Martha continued, "Our group accepts people, mainly battered women, and gives them a new identity and a new life. We aim to help. Because we're secret, our organization is quite expensive. I, too, one day sat in the chair you're now sitting in, so I know you're reluctant to believe me. Most of us in the organization have been there," a reluctant smile crossed Martha's face. "Let me reassure you my dear, you're safer than you have been in a while."

As she listened to the old woman speak, Susie felt her body relax. The tension lifted like the steam from her tea. The white haired woman's voice was so calm, so soothing.

Susie looked further around the room. It was elegant. A quaint sitting room covered in expensive Oriental carpeting. Susie hadn't noticed until then, but her shoes had been removed. Only her socks she wore the day before covered her feet.

The old woman continued, "I can see you've been crying. I was told of Emmett's death and am very sad to hear of it. My condolences. He was a good man who worked with us for a few years. We will miss him dearly."

Susie's eyes dropped to the ground.

"Did you know that he is responsible for saving four different women, some with children, in the last few years? You're number five." Again, Martha smiled, a little firmer this time. "You see Susie, Emmett arranged for you to be taken away to safety. The men who sought to have you killed would never stop. He knew that no matter the outcome of yesterday, they were never going to quit until you were killed."

Finally finding her voice, Susie asked, "Emmett set this all up? How?" Her voice cracked. The words were all she could muster. Tears came to her eyes. They ran down her face.

"I know dear, I know. Your heart needs time to mend. Emmett explained everything to me on the phone. About your brother and how everything spiraled out of control. Emmett used the last of your brother's money for your safety with our group. He never intended on handing Michael's money over to the men who killed him, not when he couldn't guarantee your future safety," answered the woman. "Emmett was a good man, and we'll all miss him dearly."

She rose from her seat. Both men offered a hand to the rising woman who waved their assistance away. Before she left the room to go up the stairs, she pointed up to the second floor of the house and mentioned, "Your room is the first on the left. All of your belongings from Emmett's house have already been laid out for you."

Exhausted, Susie allowed herself to relax in bed. The view out of the window stunned her. Tree covered mountains extended forever. Northern Quebec in the summer. She loved it. Instantly. Deeply.

The air coming from her window helped to ease her sorrow. First the loss of her brother, and now Emmett. She slid under the covers. The house was silent. Finally, she let herself sleep.

~~~~~~~~~

She woke from a long and restful sleep. The kind only fresh mountain air can bring you. It was the morning. She saw the sun barely crest over a mountain. Again she smiled. Then the tears came again with the memory of the past week's events. Long hard sobs heaved her body as she cried. No one came to comfort her. No one she loved was alive anymore. Everyone was dead.

For the next two days she cried. She only left her modest bedroom to use the bathroom, then returned to the safety of her bed. The bed where she cried uncontrollably. And slept. And awoke. And cried again. Finally the third morning came. She rose from the bed, forcing herself to break the routine of the past few days.

In the corner of her room was a desk with a computer. It wasn't new. She hadn't noticed it the previous day, but next to it someone had placed her brother's picture from Emmett's basement apartment. In between the buttons of the keyboard it was wedged vertically. Next to it was a smiling picture of Emmett. Side by side. Together, just as they were in her heart.

The photo of Emmett seemed to be from a few years before. His hair was longer and he was wrapping his arm around the old woman. Susie picked up the photo and curiously flipped it over, looking for a date. There, on the back of the photo written in loopy black letters, were the words "I thought you might like to keep this. Now it's time for you to write this story."

SAVANNAH

EPILOGUE

Weeks Later

She walked down the gravel driveway toward the mailbox, her Ruger nestled between her waistband and the small of her back. Susie looked over her shoulder. Fear tugged at her. The outside world scared her. She wasn't more than a hundred yards from her sanctuary and the anxiety inside her spiked.

You can do this. She inhaled hard, forcing herself to calm down. She held her breath before exhaling it through her nostrils. *Calm down. The Russians don't have a clue where to find you. You're safe.* She had read the articles online about the Russian crime boss who died in a firefight with the ERT. The location and date were the same, although his name wasn't released. Nor was a photograph. But Susie knew. Evgenii was dead.

She made it safely to the rusted mailbox fixed atop its weathered wooden post. She opened the hatch and placed the thick package inside. Her tell-all book. It told all about the Russians and Outlaws. Susie named the key players and highlighted each group's underground activity. She knew it was only a book; most people would blow it off as fiction. But to Susie it was more. It was a way to honor Michael and Emmett's death.

Accepted for publication under the pen name Michael Irvin, a combination of her brother's first name and Emmett's last, the book was set to be released nationally. The return address was a P.O. Box outside of Montreal, signed in under an alias. The city was hours away. She felt safe. She took precautions. The

274

Russians weren't going to find her through her book. But she knew her book would find the Russians and the Outlaws, hopefully in a heap of trouble.

She heard a twig snap in the distance. It came from the woods on the other side of the road. She spun on her heel, pulling the Ruger and leveling it with the sound. She dropped to a knee, resting her left elbow atop it, scanning for the target. She waited. Nothing moved. Neither did she.

Time didn't matter. She wasn't risking it. She would wait until she felt completely certain any threat was clear.

Susie crouched, waiting. For what, she wasn't sure. The gravel began to dig into her skin through her jeans. Her knee began to throb. Still she waited, eyes scanning for movement. The muzzle of the Ruger held steady. It moved along with her eyes, just as she had been trained to do.

Since her abduction, Susie worked every day with a personal safety specialist. Her PSS, for short. He was a former CSOR member. The T-shirt he wore every training session always read the same thing, Canadian Special Operations Regiment. Retired, yet not.

He donned a tan beret on his head every session, along with a wicked, sinister smile. The kind only a man who is about to torture someone can have. No one ever said he was kind. Or polite. Or caring. But he was good. Very good. He took training seriously. All three facets were equally important. Strength training. Weapons training. And something he called tactical training, which Susie had no idea what that meant exactly, but she liked it.

As Susie continued to kneel on the gravel, Hammer's continual reminder played over and over in her head. *Don't allow your mind to wander. It'll be the only thing between you and death.*

After a particularly tough session, she asked him, "Why does everyone call you Hammer? How did you get that name?"

He snorted at her question, seeming annoyed.

"No seriously, I'm curious," she dared ask again. Her legs felt like Jell-O after the strength training workout he had just put her through, but her eye contact remained locked on him.

He looked back at her, not backing down from her gaze. He shook his head. "You really want to know, huh?"

"Yeah, I do."

"Alright, I'll tell you, but on one condition Roxanne, it doesn't leave this conversation." Roxanne. She hated the name. Why wouldn't she, it stood for everything that was wrong in her life. It was the name Emmett had given her. She remembered it from the black lettering on the file folder he carried into his basement weeks ago.

She nodded at Hammer. He continued, "You don't just get a nickname in the

CSOR, you earn it." He turned and walked toward the firing range, where he was training her with small arms weapons.

She smiled at the coincidence. He had earned his name. She had been assigned hers. She asked, "How did you earn it?"

"Did you ever see a particularly good carpenter work with a hammer? Ever see them hit a nail with one?" he asked softly, almost gently. Something she was completely unused to.

"No, not really. Why?"

He spread his hands, turning his palms upward. His right hand became a thick, muscular fist. "A good, experienced carpenter doesn't hit a nail multiple times to drive it in. It only takes one time. One hit." He exploded his fist into his opened hand. He smiled a toothy grin. "You understand?"

The slap and thud resonated with Susie. She nodded, choosing to say nothing.

"Good, cause now you need to learn how to fire this Ruger properly. I'm getting tired of you spraying your shots all over the target. Quit the chatter and let's go," he barked at her, transforming himself back into the insensitive bastard everyone knew he was.

~~~~~~~~~~

An hour passed. Susie remained in the same position. Nothing had moved, but that didn't mean a thing to her. *Just because you think you're paranoid, doesn't mean someone's not out there. Trust your instincts.*

Her eyes remained focused down the sight line of the Ruger. Its molded grip was easy to hold, almost inviting. Eyes focused. Scanning. Ears listening. She waited.

Her mind, though, was different. It never could stay on point too long. Too much hurt, too much recent pain. First the loss of her brother, then the loss of Emmett. For weeks she had stayed within the house's four walls, never daring to step outside. She had cried and mourned and asked God why. All the typical things she had seen other people do when they grieved, but never her. Until now.

Days passed. Things got easier, though the sting of it all still remained. She often wondered about that. Had the sting become less painful? Or had she become less sensitive to it?

The training helped. Exhaustive exercise has a way of helping the brain cope, as if giving it a break from emotional pain. Susie liked it, often requesting Hammer push her harder than the others he trained.

She knew the threat loomed. Hammer's voice again, echoed in her head. *Your training will one day save your life. The Russians will never let up, never stop searching for you. In return, you must learn to never drop your guard and never let your training fall off.*

276

SAVANNAH

Darkness fell on Susie. Dusk had given way to darkness, which gave way to complete blindness. She rose, silently from her crouching position. Her knee ached. Her shoulders burned with pain. None of that bothered her. She was alive. And silently, moving quickly.

The gravel was noisy. She hated noisy. Noisy was fine for the predator, not the prey. She leapt onto the grass gracefully. She landed and listened. Nothing.

She took a few steps on the lawn. All she could hear was the sound of the crunchy grass protesting beneath her shoes. Early Quebec frosts had hardened the blades, making them louder than Susie liked.

She dropped her left hand off of the Ruger's grip. Her right still held tightly on it, but darkness had closed in on her fast. She needed a free hand in case she stumbled. Something to catch herself. Something to brace against a fall.

A hundred yards is a long way in the dark. She felt confident enough to move. If she couldn't see them, they couldn't see her. Good, solid reasoning. She hoped.

She knew about night vision goggles. *Damn. Were the Russians that technologically advanced?*

She shook the thought from her head. No use worrying about that. It didn't matter. She needed to move.

The crunchy grass became slick with dew. Susie moved in a giant Z-pattern. Another thing Hammer taught her. *Tougher to hit a zigzagging target than one that moves in a straight line.*

The house was surrounded by a typical white picket fence. A little cliché she thought, when she first saw it. She moved through the open gate and past the front porch, toward the back. She angled her body against the corner of the house, finally reaching some level of safety. She breathed hard from the run. The cold, damp air from the mid October night filled her lungs, stinging them as she inhaled. She dared a peek around the corner into the darkness.

Nothing.

She entered the house feeling a little embarrassed. Had she imagined the whole threat? Susie returned to her room. Tomorrow her novel about Michael and Emmett's life would be shipped to the publisher, ready for print. That gave her satisfaction. She smiled.

Slowly, it faded as the recent events crept back into her forethought. Was this going to be the rest of her life? Was she going to have to live in constant fear, constant paranoia of the Russians finding her?

She sat on the edge of her bed. Her elbows rested on her knees, her head between her palms. She sat like that for a long time.

And cried. Everything was gone. Michael. Emmett. Her freedom. Tears soaked her jeans above her knee. She was scared and tired and pissed off.

There was a threat out there. It would always be there. The Russian hit Evgenii put on her wasn't going away. Especially now that they also held her responsible for what happened at Racks. She gritted her teeth. Anger slowly replaced her fear.

She rose from the bed, wiping her eyes with the sleeve of her clean sweatshirt. She looked down at the Ruger sitting on the end of her bed. She hated being pinned in the corner. She said to herself, "The hit will always be there. I'll never be free."

She picked up the revolver. "I'll always be scared. Always." She shook her head. "Unless…" she trailed off, opening the Ruger's cylinder and eyeing the six chambered .357 rounds.

Susie tilted her head slightly off center as if realizing something for the first time. She raised an eyebrow. She flung the cylinder back into the frame of the Ruger. A sinister, wicked smile darkened her face.

She repeated herself, "Unless," she paused. Her smile turned into a snarl. The rage from her childhood, from Michael's death, still lived inside her. It would never fade away. It would always be there, pushing her, fueling her. "Unless I take them all down."